Sarah Barrie is the author of ten novels including her bestselling print debut *Secrets of Whitewater Creek*, the Hunters Ridge and Calico Mountain trilogies, and a crime series starring Constable Lexi Winter. In a past life, while gaining degrees in arts, science and education, Sarah worked as a teacher, a vet nurse, a horse trainer and a magazine editor, before deciding she wanted to write novels. About the only thing that has remained constant is her love of all things crime.

Her favourite place in the world is the family property, where she writes her stories overlooking mountains crisscrossed with farmland, bordered by the beauty of the Australian bush, and where, at the end of the day, she can spend time with family, friends, a good Irish whiskey and a copy of her next favourite book.

Also by Sarah Barrie

Secrets of Whitewater Creek

The Hunters Ridge Trilogy
Legacy of Hunters Ridge
Shadows of Hunters Ridge
Promise of Hunters Ridge

The Calico Mountain Trilogy
Bloodtree River
Devil's Lair
Deadman's Track

The Lexi Winter Series
Unforgiven
Retribution

VENDETTA

SARAH
BARRIE

FICTION
HQ

First Published 2023
First Australian Paperback Edition 2023
ISBN 9781867274544

Published by
HQ Fiction
An imprint of Harlequin Enterprises (Australia) Pty Limited (ABN 47 001 180 918),
a subsidiary of HarperCollins Publishers Australia Pty Limited (ABN 36 009 913 517)
Level 19, 201 Elizabeth St
SYDNEY NSW 2000
AUSTRALIA

A catalogue record for this book is available from the National Library of Australia
www.librariesaustralia.nla.gov.au

Printed and bound in Australia by McPherson's Printing Group

FSC www.fsc.org
MIX
Paper | Supporting responsible forestry
FSC® C001695

To my brilliant brother, Peter
(who'll never let me forget I called him that),
without whom Lexi would be no better
on a computer than I am.

PROLOGUE

Ten years ago

Laura clenched her jaw tight in an attempt to stop the desperate sob escaping her throat. Her body hurt. Her head ached. She needed to be sick. To fall apart. The constant beep, beep, beep in her ears wouldn't leave her alone.

Her son sat on her lap, playing cars on the table. He wore his cartoon pyjamas adorably askew, the buttons out of place. Mikey insisted on doing them himself. They're allowed to be cute at three, aren't they? Like the time he wore his undies over his shorts for a week because he'd made the mistake once at daycare and the kids had picked on him, so his teacher had told everyone he was a trend-setter. None of the kids had had any idea what that meant, but her praise had given him some serious cred in the pony room. Made him feel good about himself, rather than silly. Mrs Mayes was a lovely teacher.

She breathed in the sweet scent of his Minions shampoo as he twisted around to snuggle that beautiful baby face into her neck, still clutching his red and yellow Matchbox cars in his tiny hands.

He was tired, needed a nap. But he never slept well without Goatee, his favourite stuffed brown goat. And Goatee wasn't here. She swallowed another sob, bit down hard on her lip. It wasn't fair, this wasn't his fault.

'Mummy, why are those men meanies?'

She struggled to find her voice, make it normal. 'They're mad, baby.'

'You had tears.' He drew a line down her cheek with his finger. 'If I was big I would protect you. Like Superman.'

Her soul shattered. She was big and she couldn't protect him. 'They didn't hurt me. Not really.'

'They're mad at Daddy.'

'Yeah, at Daddy.'

'I'm hungry. I miss Daddy.'

Her own stomach churned, but not with hunger. 'If you could have anything in the world, what would it be?'

'Ice cream!'

She pressed her lips to the top of his head and cuddled him close, ignoring the pain every movement his small body caused her broken one. 'Double scoop?'

'Yeah!' he said and bounced on her lap. 'Ice cream forever! Can we have some soon?'

Her eyes welled again. This time there was no stopping the tears from sliding down her cheeks. 'I hope so, baby. I hope we can have ice cream. All the ice cream ever.'

'It's hot, Mummy.' He shifted on her lap and tried to get more comfortable, his forehead dotted with sweat. 'Do you think we can go soon?'

The hope in his voice was too much. Just too much.

'Yes, we'll go. Soon.' Her voice choked and her arms trembled around him as she watched the bomb's timer.

5 … 4 … 3 …

Oh, God. No. *No.* 'I love you so much, baby.'

His eyes beamed back at her out of his flushed little face and his arms snaked around her neck. 'Love you too, Mu—'

CHAPTER ONE

Monday, March 21

I flatten the accelerator to get around a P-plater in a beaten-up work ute and my tired little Civic revs hard. I swerve into the next lane, have to brake quickly to avoid rear-ending a Lexus before the gap increases. I pass two more cars before diving back across. I have a vague recollection of some weird dream about a car accident last night, have to hope it's not prophetic. I take a chance anyway and put my foot down again, slide into a rudely tight gap and earn a beep from the car I cut off. Whatever. The M1 motorway is slow with peak-hour traffic and I need to get through.

I see a sign for the Morisset exit and swing back into the left lane to take it, following three other cars onto the offramp. In the fast-dying light, the horizon stretches into a sea of dense bushland forming shadowed, rolling mountains. I turn right onto a single-lane road. Where is all this traffic going? Am I still on the Central Coast? I'm pretty sure I won't be by the end of this. I spot some light industrial buildings, signs to suburbs I've heard of. Shops. There's life out here. The knowledge is reassuring as the phone message plays over and over in my head. 'Lexi dear, it's Dawny. I'm afraid Desmond and I have gotten ourselves into a rather urgent little pickle. Now, try not to worry too much, but I'd appreciate it if I could meet with you. Just you, please. Now would be good. So no one dies. I'll text you the address. Ta-ta.'

My fingers catch painfully in my hair as I sweep some stray black wisps from my line of vision. *Urgent little pickle.* I can only guess what that could possibly mean. Coming from Catherine Dawn Delaney, the sweet old pie-making, dodgy-kneed lady who once helped me stash a body in a freezer, I'm guessing it's nothing minor. I haven't seen her for more than a year, and as her plan was to stay gone with that gangster-style husband of hers, I'm intrigued. I'm also very nervous and hoping the 'so no one dies' part includes me.

I glance at my phone to see I'm still seven minutes out. More, probably, because the old twat in the funny hat in front of me doesn't seem to be able to do over fifty in the eighty zone. I'm trying not to sit on his arse. There's got to be somewhere I can overtake. I hope Dawny doesn't have a gun to her head or something.

My phone rings and I hit the button. 'Yeah?'

'You didn't take the apartment keys,' Finn tells me. Finn Carson, friend and temporary landlord, is subletting me his apartment and I'm moving in tomorrow.

'Oh, right. I'll … get them later.'

'When you tell me what's really going on?'

I'd been last to leave his housewarming party, sitting on his back veranda trying to pry information on a current case out of him when Dawny's message had come through. I'd gotten up as casually as I could and made what I thought had been a reasonable excuse to take off. But being that he's a detective sergeant—and a pretty good one—I'm not surprised he saw through me.

'Can't believe I forgot those keys. I'm looking forward to moving in. You said the cleaners would be out before two? I'm sure that's when my furniture is supposed to arrive.'

'It was Dawny on the phone, wasn't it? I heard her voice.'

'I mean, Tom's great and I thought a night or two staying in a room at his pub while waiting to get into the apartment might be fun. But no. No, it's not. Way too noisy!' An overtaking lane opens up—yes!—and I jump into it, put my foot down.

'You know the dead giveaway here is the small talk, right? You don't do that. Ever.'

Smartarse. 'I'm evolving.'

'Do you really think you should be rushing off on some Dawny-style mission? You're not fully recovered from our last case.'

He was right. The thumb that had been sliced to the bone is still bandaged, I have a chest full of not-quite-healed ribs and my face looks like a slowly fading war zone. But what can I do? I was the one stupid enough to join the police force. 'You've got to be shitting me!'

'Why would I be—'

'Not you! Turbo here!'

'Sorry?'

'The old snail in front of me who suddenly got a rocket up his arse when the overtaking lane began. For fuck's sake!' I lean on the accelerator and end up having to do twenty over just to edge ahead before the lane closes. I glare as I pass but the gaze of the dick straining to see over the steering wheel never shifts from the road ahead. 'You know, I'm a police officer. There should be some way to arrest people for that shit.'

'Yeah, like we do with people who drink and drive.'

Drink and— What had I had to drink? A Champagne, a JD, another couple of sips of Champagne. Shouldn't be over the limit, should I? Maybe. A headline flashes in front of my eyes. LOCAL PROBATIONARY CONSTABLE FIRED FOR DRINK DRIVING ON HER WAY TO AID AND ABET A FORMER FELON AND HER WANTED HUSBAND.

Damn it, Dawny. 'I'm not over. I barely drank any of that second Champagne.' Even though I've eased up on the speed, Turbo's rapidly losing ground, trapping the cars still behind him as the lanes merge back into one. Poor bastards.

'*Where* are you *going*?'

'I told you.'

'You told me you were going home. Home was a half-hour ago. You're still driving.'

'You're using your fancy detective skills on me now?'

'You get a phone call with a mysterious message then all but sprint to your car with the lamest excuse I've ever heard and tear out of my street at light speed. It doesn't take much in the way of detective skills. Nor does knowing that, whatever this is, you shouldn't be doing it.'

'Don't be dramatic.'

'I'm being anything but dramatic. You know how this goes. You get into trouble, then I nearly die stopping you from dying.'

I want to argue, but it's a valid point. 'Can't you just be grateful I'm not dragging you into it then?'

'No, because I'm bound to be dragged into it. It's only a matter of when.'

'I could say the same about you and Rachael not telling me everything you know about Vaughn's next move,' I say of the murdering arsehole I've been hunting for more than a year.

'Can we deal with one thing at a time, please?'

I see the road I'm looking for and make the turn. It's a quiet enough street lined with narrow, small-acreage blocks stretching back to what looks like a lake. Pretty. There's a large brick fence hiding the number I'm looking for and I pull up in front of it. 'I've got to go.'

'Lexi—'

'I'll call you as soon as I know what's going on. Bye!' I want to push out of the car, hurry to reach Dawny, but I force myself to wait. Look around. Listen. There's no traffic on the street. Lights are on in homes and someone in the house over the road has a monster TV with the nightly news showing. I hear a kid squeal, another shout and laugh. Otherwise, all is quiet. Seems safe enough.

I get out of my car and lock it. Then on another thought, I type Dawny's address into a message to Finn. Anything goes wrong, I just have to hit the send button. I open the gate and am faced with a very ordinary eighties brick home with a serious security system: one of those military-grade screen doors, cameras, warnings of a potential guard dog on duty. Shit. Really? Where?

I step around two Harley Davidsons parked by the front step. One's an old shitbox, the other is a seriously nice bike. I bang on the door, hope for the best.

'Dawny?'

Nothing. I bang again. 'Hello!'

A curtain moves and I get the fleeting impression of a round, hairy face in the window before I hear a snapped, 'What?'

'I'm looking for Dawny?'

'Why?'

'Because she asked me to come.'

'Who are you?'

'My name's Lexi.'

'Lexi who?'

I growl impatiently. I didn't bolt over here to play knock-knock with some random arsehole. 'Winter! Is Dawny there or not?'

'Strip down.'

'Ask me that again. I dare you.'

'I need to know you're not armed!'

Oh, for fuck's sake, who are these people? I pull off my jacket, do a spin. 'Happy?'

A dog barks and I freeze in fear before deciding it's behind next door's fence. My nerves are returning. What's taking so long? Maybe I should call Finn.

Maybe I should toughen the fuck up. 'Look, I'm not leaving until I've seen Dawny.'

'You'll do what you're fuckin' told, bitch, or else.'

'Or else *what*? I kick this door off its hinges, smack you over the head with it and use it for your fucking headstone? Where's Dawny!'

'Lexi! Better late than never. You can let her in,' I hear Dawny call out.

'I'll do more than let the bitch in!'

I hear three locks click over; the door opens an inch. A shotgun barrel emerges, pointed straight at my head. Before I can process more than an initial flash of *Oh shit!*, I'm shoved sideways and a large figure barges past into the house, pointing the gun barrel skyward and sending its hulk of an owner back several steps into the room. The door slams back against the wall with a crack.

'Don't move!' Finn demands, now in possession of the gun and pointing the barrel at the hulk.

For a moment, I'm as stunned as the hulk. Then, 'You *followed* me?' I ask stupidly.

'What's going on?' Finn says, ignoring me.

'Oh, Lexi, dear! How lovely to see you … eventually.'

I spot Dawny and another arsehole, younger and weedier, in the doorway to the kitchen. Dawny hasn't changed much, she's still dressed like a street kid, but her Clairol brown hair now sports a purple streak. Other than looking a little dishevelled, she seems unharmed. 'And you brought that big, bad boyfriend of yours. How's business, Finn? I hear the body count's going up? No need to be taking anyone out tonight though, please. How about we all sit down, eh? Have a nice calm chat.'

I take my eyes off Dawny and flick a nervous glance around. Black leather lounge, old carpet, smart TV, coffee table. The stink of cigarette smoke and old beer courtesy of an overloaded ashtray and half-a-dozen empty beer bottles. Beyond is a hallway with an older-style kitchen to the left. More mess.

'Great idea,' Finn says, then, 'Sit,' he orders, waving the gun towards the lounge.

The hulk is probably fifty-something, dressed in ripped jeans and a stained tee with a patched leather bikie vest, big boots and a chilly expression. He does as he's told.

'You too,' Finn tells the tattooed and multi-pierced weed standing next to Dawny.

Dawny hobbles in behind the weed on the knee that's been dodgy as long as I've known her. My gaze returns to the hulk's vest, the patches. The ones I'm most interested in tell me he goes by Woolly and belongs to the Chaos Reigns Motorcycle Club. He's a full member. I check the weed. Just a prospect. I'm not familiar with this MC, but they're both displaying one-percenter patches.

'Dawny,' Finn says. 'Are you hurt?'

'Oh, no need for all that drama, dear,' she says with a casual wave of her hand. 'I'm perfectly fine.'

Finn shoots me a glare and I aim my own at Dawny.

'You're perfectly fine?' I say, before placing my hand to my head. 'That message you left on my phone suggested you were about to die!'

Dawny's eyes crinkle with amusement. 'If I ever am, I'll call someone who drives a bit faster.'

'Okay,' I say, because honestly what's the point? 'You said, "urgent little pickle".'

'Well, it is rather,' Dawny says, taking a seat in an armchair across from the lounge. 'I need you to sort something out for me. Nothing major, I'm sure you'll be fine.'

I'm not fooled by the conversational, all-the-time-in-the-world speech. Nothing fazes this woman. Nothing. Armageddon could be imminent.

Her gaze moves over my bruised face and she grimaces. 'Although from the looks of you, I might have overestimated things slightly.'

'Can we get to the point?' Finn prompts.

'Ah, yes. Desmond's depending on us, so we'll push on.'

'Fine,' I say. 'Let's get out of here and you can tell me about it.'

'She's not going anywhere till we got proof!' Woolly snaps, folding his arms and glaring at Dawny.

'You're not exactly in any position to call the shots,' Finn reminds him.

'Oh, he is, dear,' Dawny says. 'At least, as long as I want to see Desmond alive again.'

My stomach sinks. 'Desmond's in trouble?' I ask. 'What do they want proof of?'

Dawny sighs dramatically. 'A very desperate young fellow bailed up a few of the members last night at gunpoint.'

'Where is Desmond?' Finn asks.

'Not here, unfortunately.'

'Is he injured?'

'Oh, please, dear. Desmond just gave this young fellow a bit of a bop on the head and that was that. Turns out the young fellow wasn't supposed to be where he was and it all got a bit out of hand and … these things happen. Anyway, someone needs to see this young fellow and we need you to get him for us.'

I shift my weight onto my foot closest to the door, as though by backing up I can lessen the impact of the drama I know I'm about to be hit with. 'Why call me?' I ask suspiciously. 'You don't know where he is?'

Dawny pulls a face. 'Well, that's the problem, dear. We do.'

'So … he doesn't want to come in?' I ask.

'Oh, I don't think it would bother him too much to be honest.'

'Dawny.' I hear the exasperation in my tone, but seriously. 'What's the problem then?'

'Ah, well, Desmond didn't realise the boss would need to see this fellow and he'd already … removed the evidence.'

'Evidence?' I stare at her for two seconds. Three. Then it hits me. 'How hard was that bop on the head?'

'And where is this young fellow?' Finn demands.

'Oh, just off Patonga Wharf. It's not deep.'

'He took him all the way out to Patonga?' Is that even really the question I should be asking? 'Why?'

'Supposed to be lots of sharks.'

If Finn clenches his jaw any harder he's going to break teeth. My gaze shifts to Woolly just to make absolutely sure no one is taking the piss. He certainly seems serious enough.

'We need to know he's dead,' Woolly tells me. 'Make sure Desmond hasn't jumped ship. Changed sides.'

'Sides of what?' I ask, but the look on his face tells me I don't need details.

'I can't believe this,' Finn mutters to the ceiling. Then to Dawny, he says, 'You called Lexi here to dive into shark-infested waters to recover a murder victim to prove Desmond is loyal to a motorcycle gang.'

'You need to relax, dear,' Dawny soothes, 'you'll give yourself a migraine.' Then to me, she says, 'And yes, please. It's a bit past me, I'm afraid. In the dark would be best. Shouldn't take you long.'

Like fuck. 'Dawny, I am absolutely not—'

'I know it's not a glam job,' Dawny hurries on, 'but I'll make sure you get your normal fee. And you don't even have to kill anyone! It's your lucky day, I'd say.'

Normal fee? Kill anyone? I'm trying to keep up but I've got nothing.

'Right, that's enough,' Finn says, and I can see he's done with whatever game this is. Fuck. I need to manage this. 'You're both—'

'Okay! Fine!' I cut in loudly. I'd rather he didn't tell these guys we're cops. 'But only because we owe you a *serious* favour,' I add to remind Finn that Dawny and Desmond once helped save his daughter's life. 'We'll get your proof, but nothing better happen to Desmond in the meantime,' I say with a glare at Woolly. 'What do you need?'

Finn takes his eyes off Woolly long enough to give me the sort of *what the fuck?* look I've become accustomed to. I pretend not to see it.

'Photos. Video. Whatever. Just some general proof. Once we know he's dead, they're both off the hook,' Woolly tells me.

'Oh, we have until tomorrow night,' Dawny adds.

'Then what?'

'Then we stop being nice,' Woolly says with a mean smile.

'Dawny, you're coming with us,' Finn orders.

'Oh, no, dear—'

'That's non-negotiable,' Finn tells Woolly. 'You've got Desmond, we get Dawny. That's the deal.'

'Fine! Take the old bat. She's as annoying as fuck anyway.' Then to me, he says, 'You send the proof to this number I'm gonna give ya. You don't come through, Desy's getting some dentistry, a solid meal and a long cruise.'

The prospect sniggers like he's sharing some private joke. Half-wit. Still, the idea Desmond might have his teeth removed and concrete poured down his throat before being dumped far enough off the coast to never be found is not a nice one.

'Won't be a problem, dear,' Dawny promises. 'These two are very dependable. What's the number?'

Woolly reads it out and I store it in my phone. 'Got it.'

'Right. Go,' Finn tells me. 'Get Dawny out of here.'

'Give me my damn gun back!' Woolly demands as Finn follows us out.

'Not going to happen.'

'There'll be hell to pay!' Woolly growls.

'You're right on that,' Finn mutters. But I'm pretty sure he's talking to me.

CHAPTER TWO

'You followed me!' Lexi hissed as they reached her car. 'I can't believe you were talking to me on the phone while you were behind me the whole time!'

Finn barely took his eyes off the house as they went through the gate. All quiet. 'I think the words you're looking for are "Thanks, Finn".' He paused when they reached Lexi's car. His was right behind it. 'Get in. I'll follow you back to the pub with Dawny so you can leave your car there. I'll call Rachael, let her know what's happening, then you can come with me for whatever we do after that.'

Both women looked set to argue, so he added, 'Or I do this the traditional way, call it in right now and bring those two with us for questioning.'

Lexi pressed her lips together over whatever she wanted to say and exchanged looks with Dawny. He noted the slightest shake of Lexi's head before she silently opened her door and slipped into her car. He watched her pull out onto the road before going to his.

'You may as well know now,' Dawny said when they were on the road, 'I won't be setting foot inside one of those police stations tonight, dear. I want to get Desmond out of this alive and that's not the way to go about it.'

'Desmond murdered a man, Dawny. And if you had anything to do with it, you're an accessory.'

Dawny barked out a laugh. 'Desmond didn't kill the poor fellow. Where'd you get that idea?'

'You said he bopped the guy on the head and dumped him at Patonga.'

'Ah, well, he did, but he didn't kill him.'

'Just … hold on.'

'What are you doing?'

'Calling Rachael.'

'Rachael? You mean that inspector lady?'

'That's the one.' He hit Rachael's number, had to wonder if his aunt and the leader of his homicide team had even made it home to Sydney from his housewarming yet.

'Hi, we just got in,' Rachael said, answering his question. 'Everything okay?'

'Not exactly. What's the chance you could get divers out to Patonga Wharf within the next twenty-four hours to recover a body?'

A pause, then, 'I'll find out.'

'Thanks.'

'I'll call you back after it's sorted and you can fill me in.'

'Will do.' He hit the end button.

'Finn, dear,' Dawny said. 'No disrespect intended of course, but if you get the police all tangled up with this—'

'The police are already tangled up in this,' he said. 'Lexi and I are police. You called Lexi for help.'

'What?' she squawked as her face went blank with shock. 'Lexi joined you coppers? When did that happen?'

'You've been gone a while.'

There was some unintelligible muttering out the window before she said, 'I *knew* she had too much fun catching that Spider pervert.'

'I wouldn't have called the Spider case fun.'

'I thought she had more sense,' Dawny complained. 'I'm guessing this police business is why she looks like she's gone ten rounds with Mundine. I thought more of you, Finn.'

He glanced at Dawny in disbelief. 'I'm not the reason she looks like that!'

'No, of course not. I'm sure you had nothing to do with it.'

'That's right. Thank y—'

'Even though you should have had something to do with it. Something that involved keeping her safe. I never pegged you as inadequate. I hope you can live with yourself.'

'I—' He bit back his reply and answered his phone. Rachael.

'We'll have a team in the water at first light. Cass and Linc will head out there to oversee the recovery.'

'Oh, that's wonderful news!' Dawny gushed in a sudden and complete change of tone. 'He's just off the front of the wharf. We'll need some photos of the unfortunate fellow, please.'

'Dawny?' Rachael asked in surprise. 'Is that you?'

'Oh, it's Dawny all right,' Finn answered.

'He's a bit cross,' Dawny told Rachael. 'Think I might have hit a nerve when I asked him why he let Lexi cop all those terrible bruises. Do you think the police divers can go in without too much fanfare? I'm a little bit worried they'll be spotted and things won't end well.'

'Do the divers have anything to worry about?' Rachael asked sharply.

'Oh, no, dear. Of course not. But it'd be much better for Desmond if no one knows the police are looking for that body.'

'Would someone care to fill me in?' Rachael said weakly.

'Desmond's being held by two men belonging to a motorcycle club called Chaos Reigns,' Finn said. 'They want proof of death on that body. Dawny called Lexi earlier to get it, not realising she was now working for the police and it's just gotten more … interesting from there. We need to check ownership of the house at an address Lexi will be able to give you and I have a gun belonging to the more senior member of the club called Woolly that we should be able to get some prints off for a more accurate identification.'

'You didn't arrest them?'

'I did say it got more interesting. Dawny's given us alter egos and it seemed important for Desmond's longevity to keep them.' He glanced at Dawny almost threateningly. 'Temporarily, at least.'

'So who did they think—actually, never mind,' Rachael said. 'Bring Dawny down to headquarters. You can fill me in and Dawny can give us a statement.'

'No offence, dear, but you can sit me in that place all night. Until you find that body, I've got nothing to say.'

'That'd be a first,' Finn muttered.

'Let's aim for a cup of tea and a chat tomorrow,' Dawny said, ignoring him. 'Once you've found that young fellow and we clear Desmond. Okay then?' Dawny said. 'Ta-ta.' She reached forward and pressed the end button on the screen.

'Dawny!' Finn snapped.

'Oh, weren't you finished? There's another call coming through.'

From Lexi, he saw, and pressed the button. 'Yeah?'

'I have questions.'

'Don't we all.'

'Like why don't we need to kill anyone and what's our regular fee?'

Dawny chuckled. 'The young fellow's already dead, isn't he? And your regular fee is for cleaning up. I have no idea what cleaners charge these days.'

Lexi gave a huff and said, 'I get cleaner, Finn gets hitman?'

'You're right, dear. No one who saw your house would believe that. I meant one that takes care of sensitive messes. The kind we don't want police nosing in on. No offence,' she said for the umpteenth time as she shot Finn a look. 'And I told you to come alone. Remember? I had to come up with something spur of the moment. Thought the hitman tag looked good on Finn. Might hold some sway. And what better partnership? Finn kills 'em, you clean up the evidence. Very clever, actually, when you think about it.'

'And you just assumed we'd go along with it?' Finn asked.

'Not everyone could pull off a successful hitman. Those big, broad shoulders of yours are still looking pretty good,' Dawny said. 'I'll make you a pie, just as soon as Desmond's released.'

'What do you mean "still"? And as I'm so *inadequate*, are you sure you want us getting Desmond out of this?'

'Inadequate?' Lexi cut in.

'Well, anything's possible,' Dawny rolled on. 'The fact you didn't mention you were with the coppers is miraculous in itself. Desmond would be dead for sure if you'd given that away. They'd be after us, too. I'd never be able to show my face again!'

'Who's the victim?' Lexi asked.

'I suppose it depends on your point of view. Desmond was only trying to help and—'

'The dead guy, Dawny. The one in the water. What's his name?'

'Oh, I wouldn't know.'

'And those men?'

'You already know the big one goes by Woolly. The skinny one with the funny haircut is Skink. Skink told me all the noms are given terrible nicknames.'

'Noms?' Finn asked.

'A club prospect, dear. Nice enough kid, actually. Had a bit of a bad time of it growing up. Had a lovely chat. Much nicer than Woolly. Did you see the size of Woolly's ears? Kept wanting to call him Dumbo. It was bound to have slipped out if you'd taken much longer. I—'

'Is Desmond in the MC?' Lexi cut in.

'Oh, no, dear. He just does odd jobs for whoever needs them done. Jobs that aren't advertised on regular channels. Because he's good at minding his own business, you know. Which is why this is all so ridiculous.'

'What job was he doing?' Finn asked.

'He picked up some work doing deliveries from the Newcastle docks, oh, probably going on six months now. Never had any trouble until yesterday. That young fellow has turned out to be quite the headache.'

'Yes, poor Desmond,' Finn muttered sarcastically. 'Rachael's calling back, I have to go,' he told Lexi.

He ended Lexi's call and answered Rachael's. 'Yep.'

'This MC is flagged on the system with the Organised Crime Squad. I messaged Chad McCabe. He's asked for an early meeting before proceeding. That's at seven. Dawny, I'm going to assume for this evening that you're an innocent party in all this, but I need you on standby to come in as soon as the victim is located. If you don't show I'll put a warrant out for your arrest as a possible accessory after the fact to murder. That's jail time. Are we clear?'

'That's very understanding of you. People give coppers a bad rap, don't they? But you don't *all* deserve it, that's what I say. I'll be in for that evidence when you find it. Don't you worry about that.'

'Then I'll see you both tomorrow.'

'Do you need me to stop anywhere to pick up some things?' Finn asked Dawny after ending the call. 'Where have you been staying?'

'Here and there, and never mind that. I'm sure I'll survive a night. Lexi will put me up.'

He doubted it would be just one, but they could sort that out later.

'She's staying at her friend's pub in Gosford. Her house was destroyed during our last case.'

Dawny's mouth fell open, her eyes wide. 'She's been beaten up *and* had her house destroyed? And you lot put her in a *pub*?'

'She's been in a great apartment under protection—'

'Well that obviously worked.'

'—which she hated and because she's moving into my place—'

'She's moving in with you? Maybe get her a German shepherd. Something that can actually protect her.'

'Not *with* me, I have a new place …' Why was he bothering to explain? 'You know what? How about we focus on this latest disaster. Are you sure there's nothing else you can tell me?'

Dawny stared out the window as he took the onramp to the motorway. 'That's the problem with the police these days. Always looking for someone else to do their job for them.'

He bit back the retort and concentrated on merging. He might owe this woman, but he had a feeling by the end of this that favour would be well and truly repaid.

CHAPTER THREE

From the outside, the building looked like any other residential garage in a typical Sydney street: a grey Colorbond shed separated from a red-brick eighties build by a narrow path. Tonight a light shone brightly from under the roller door and the high, narrow window that faced the house. Though the house was quiet, busy noise came from the garage, where a radio played the latest hits.

Arthur Cronin had been there before, many, many years ago, so he'd known when he'd entered last night that inside was a workshop containing the usual assortment of benches, pallet racks, hanging tools and storage containers, along with miscellaneous junk stored on the tops of shelves because it could come in handy 'one day'. He'd remembered dusty cobwebs that had found space in cracks and crevices; the resident house spider they'd nicknamed Jerry that had nestled in the corner of the back cornice above a whirring fridge; that the concrete floor had been oil-stained, evidence a car had once lived there. And he'd remembered, very clearly remembered, the sights and sounds of practised hands building, moulding … creating to destroy.

Most importantly, he'd known that the back wall was not, in fact, the back wall. He'd known that behind that fridge was a doorway to a space just wide enough to store a row of caged and locked shelves. On those shelves had sat containers of motor oil, RDX, polyisobutylene and dioctyl sebacate, alongside a portable stove, solvents, agitators, distillation and filtering equipment, and on the shelves above those, detonators, blasting caps and the equipment to make more.

So when he'd visited again, last night, when he'd carefully broken into their house, retrieved the keys to the two large locks that guarded that ordinary-looking garage and let himself in, he'd known that nothing much had changed. And that had suited him perfectly.

'You don't have to do this,' she whispered from beside him, a sad tone of admonishment creeping in to her generally smooth, musical voice.

He kept his gaze on the house, the garage, as crickets chirped and a baby cried in a nearby home, his face falling into a frown. 'We've talked about this. It's necessary.'

'It's not.'

'I need to know!' He looked at her then, the golden hair, the dark eyes, that lovely glow to her still youthful features, and his voice softened. 'I've waited a long time to know.'

She placed a loving hand on his shoulder. 'You can't change anything.'

'That's where you're wrong. I can change plenty.' His gaze returned to the garage while his fingers played with the small clay heart in his pocket. The one the paint had mostly worn off. The one that said *Daddy*.

He knew they were inside, Victor and Seth, those two he'd once called friends. Brothers. He left her and walked up the driveway, around to where a grassed yard stretched out from a back deck to a tall paling fence. He snatched a chair from a wooden outdoor setting and set it against the side of the garage, stepped up and risked a quick glimpse through the window. It was open a few inches to ventilate an otherwise airless space. He saw that work was well underway and much of the equipment he'd noted last night was on or close to the main workbench, where Seth mixed RDX with water and Vic fiddled with detonator wires.

They had no clue he'd been in there. No idea what he'd left so carefully hidden in plain sight. They had a job on, an urgent one by the speed at which they were working. They weren't expecting surprises.

He stepped off the chair and turned his attention to the side door, where padlocks dangled loosely. He quietly locked them into place. The main garage door wouldn't open. He'd already made sure of that.

Though his body surged with the thrill of imminent revenge, he couldn't help but feel disappointment that he couldn't draw this out. That there'd be no opportunity for a satisfying discussion about their life choices. But at sixty, he already felt like a much older man, capable of pulling the odd young punk into line in Supermax, sure, but his time of physically taking on two military-trained soldiers was over. He would settle for this. It was better than doing nothing. Doing nothing was unthinkable.

There were just one or two things he needed to know first, questions that had to be answered, so he went back to the window, stepped up onto the patio chair. A voice on the radio announced they'd be starting their top fifty tunes of the nineties after the ad break. Cronin wondered if they'd live long enough to hear the first song.

'Gentlemen.'

'Fuck!' the one named Vic cursed, dropping his pliers. The other, Seth, stopped stirring and slowly put down the spoon. Vic and Seth had done too many patrols during the Gulf War to enjoy surprises. Seth snatched a shotgun from under the bench and aimed.

'Uh-uh!' he told them, shaking a mobile phone at them. They'd been in the game long enough to know he wasn't threatening to make a phone call.

'Cronin?' Seth said. 'What the fuck!'

'It's been a long time.'

The men looked at each other, at the door and backed up. 'You're supposed to be in jail.'

'That was never going to protect you forever.'

'Look, that shit wasn't our fault!' Vic said, reaching behind him for the door as he got close enough.

'Is that how you want to go out, *brother*—' Cronin spat the word, '—as a coward and a liar?'

'We didn't know!' Seth said. 'It was just another job!'

Vic tried the handle, shook the door furiously when it didn't open. 'You knew. Who hired you?'

'You let us out, we'll tell you,' Seth said. 'We'll pay him back. Help you get him.'

'How is your lovely wife these days, your twin girls? One has a baby, yes? I know where they live. And Vic, my old friend, your son—'

'It was Blake,' Vic blurted. 'He organised it.'

'Ah, of course. I'll need more explosives. Where are they?'

'Storage unit in Percy Street.'

'Keys?'

'On the hook at the front door. Please, man, we're sorry.'

'Yes, I'm sure you are. So, I'll be the bigger man here.' He saw cautious relief in their faces before adding, 'I'll let your families live.'

He stepped down and walked away, heard the smash of feet against the door, the shattering glass of the window they were too large to slide through.

He gave himself a moment to enjoy their panic before sliding into the car.

'Arthur … please,' she said.

'It's done. Now I find Blake.' He turned on the car and crawled down the street. Only when he was far enough away did he detonate the square of C4 he'd left sitting on a high shelf.

CHAPTER FOUR

Tuesday, March 22

Following the GPS directions, Finn took a right and turned into a residential Auburn street lined with parked cars glistening in the early morning sun from a heavy overnight dew.

'I can't believe she told a motorcycle club you were a hitman.' Rachael laughed.

He'd been appalled. Yesterday. But Rachael seemed to think it was entirely too funny for his ego to accept. 'Why exactly could I not pull off hitman?' he demanded. 'Even Dawny was with me on that one.'

Rachael made a very poor attempt at pulling back her grin. 'I never said you couldn't. I'm sure you'd make a fabulous hitman.'

'Thank you.'

But her laugh burbled back up. 'The only thing funnier than that is that she made out Lexi would clean up after you.'

'The only thing funnier than *that* is that I played along.'

Rachael sobered. 'A hostage's life depended on it. You did the right thing at the time.'

'So it turns out. But it was a close one. Weren't we supposed to be meeting with McCabe at seven?'

'I called him. He's happy to meet with us after this.'

'Because the Bomb Squad need us to see an accidental explosion.'

'Jake thought I'd like to take a look,' she said. 'One of McCabe's officers from organised crime is coming out, too. Seems everyone wants a piece of these victims.'

'Can you fill me in on why we do?'

'Homicide has dealt with a few murders over the years due to C4 explosives, but we've never managed to make an arrest.'

'And?'

'And these could be the two that carried out the recent attack on Lexi's house.'

That made things more interesting. 'Really?'

'It's a pretty narrow field of expertise.'

'And they blew themselves up. Shame.' Finn slowed as a tradie jogged out onto the road ahead to meet a waiting car. There was a smile, a greeting as the guy climbed into the passenger seat. 'Let's just hope this thing with Dawny turns out to be as straightforward and easy.'

Rachael's lips twitched. 'We can't blow people up, Finn. It's against the law.'

'Yeah, there's that … I'm guessing we'll find that body belongs to a rival MC member.'

'You're probably right. Dawny really didn't know?'

'Didn't *seem* to, no. But I still can't decide whether Dawny's an eccentric old lady who enjoys a drama or a criminal mastermind.'

'Why not both?' Rachael asked.

Finn's brow lifted. 'You'd want to hope not. You left her to her own devices last night.'

'Whatever she is or isn't, she came through when we needed her last time. And let's face it, it's better we keep her onside while we untangle this unless our hand is forced.'

He clicked on the indicator, turned into the next street. 'Here we are. Obviously.'

The house and several either side of it were obscured from view by a large number of police, emergency and forensic vehicles.

Behind those, a long line of barrier fence and a white canvas tent kept the prying eyes of neighbours and media off the scene. Finn found a spot to pull up and they walked the short distance back and signed themselves in, ignoring the curious gazes of the public and the shouted questions of two nearby reporters.

'Detectives!'

Finn spotted Jake Preston, a Bomb Squad team leader, picking his way through the debris towards them.

'Hey,' Finn said.

'Hi,' Rachael echoed. 'What can you tell us?'

'It's a hell of a mess,' Jake said, gesturing around the ruined remains of the garage. Part of the house was also damaged and the neighbour's fence hadn't fared much better where it bordered the property.

'Blast went off at approximately half-past ten last night.' He walked them over to where spare forensic clothing sat neatly on a table. 'No witnesses to anything in the lead-up. Plenty of people heard the blast, a few neighbours and drivers on the nearby main road spotted it. One apparently has dashcam of it over the roofs of a couple of houses.'

'I'd like to see it,' Rachael said as they slipped on shoe covers and gloves.

'You found bodies?' Finn asked.

Jake's grin was wry. 'We've found parts. Not sure how many victims yet. At least two.'

'It must have been a large explosion.'

Jake nodded. 'C4 makes for one hell of a blast.'

'I saw the results of an IED once,' Finn said, taking another look around, 'but it had nothing on this.'

'That would be because the C4 plastic explosives fall into the high explosive category,' Jake said. 'They have much higher detonation velocities than low explosives.'

'I didn't know there was a difference,' Finn said.

'High explosives work through the use of a primary and secondary explosive. The primary detonates when it's exposed to heat or shock, then the secondary detonates from the primary. The shock front it creates passes through material at supersonic speed.

Detonation velocities can reach up to around nine kilometres per second, which basically means C4 is designed to shatter and obliterate, not leave behind evidence.'

'Wasn't C4 used in the Bali bombings?' Rachael asked.

'Yeah. Bodies don't stand a chance, I'm afraid. You know about the other detective inside?'

'No,' Rachael said, already walking in that direction.

'Someone … Brighton, I think. She's found some evidence you might be interested in.'

'Thanks.'

They stepped into a small living room and went through to a dining room with a large table in the centre. On it were several documents, passports and driver's licences. A blonde woman in a grey skirt suit sat sipping coffee from a Styrofoam cup as she looked them over. Early thirties, athletic build, pretty face and, when she looked up, sharp green eyes.

'Good morning,' Rachael said. 'Detective Inspector Rachael Langley and Detective Sergeant Finn Carson, homicide.'

'Detective Senior Constable Olivia Brighton, organised crime,' the woman said in return.

'You're McCabe's newest recruit?' Rachael asked.

'That's right. From Perth. I've only been here a couple of weeks.'

'I think very highly of your mother. It's good to have you on board.'

'Thank you. Jake was telling me you might have come across some of our victims' work?'

Rachael picked up a driver's licence and studied it. 'It's possible. Homicide has dealt with three separate C4 attacks in ten years, with the same MOs and no apparent links between victims. A recent fourth attack carried out on behalf of a Sydney crime family has led us to believe our POIs were contract killers.' She dropped the IDs back on the table. 'Are any of these identities real?'

'All counterfeits. We can't confirm yet, but I believe the victims will be identified as Victor Thomas and Seth Roberts,' Brighton said. 'Both ex-military ammunition specialists with ties to organised crime. They were employed by a Sydney-based demolition company but were making their real money through the sale of fake IDs and the odd contract kill. If you wouldn't mind sharing anything homicide has on previous cases that could be linked to these two, I'd appreciate it.'

'Of course,' Rachael said.

'Tying up loose ends?' Finn asked. 'Or are they linked to another case?'

'Option two. We're building a case against a man called Evan Blake. McCabe believes he's a major underworld middleman responsible for dozens of murders, though we've yet to prove it.'

'Middleman?' Finn asked.

'An agent, if you like. Blake's clients contact him through word of mouth or via his dark-web site. They hand over details and large sums of money or crypto and Blake hires the right men for whatever job needs to be taken care of. We intercepted details that these two were preparing to do another hit for him just prior to the explosion. If McCabe's correct, these two were far from the only killers on Blake's books, but we need evidence of their dealings as far back as we can go to build our case.'

'If these two were pros, the neighbours are probably lucky the damage from the explosion wasn't more extensive,' Rachael said.

'I'd guess they wouldn't have kept much stock on hand,' Jake said. 'Too dangerous. It'd be safe to assume they'd store most of their wares offsite.'

'So you're sure this was an accident?' Finn asked.

'No evidence to the contrary at this stage,' Brighton said. 'Neighbours didn't see or hear anything suspicious, the pair had a workshop full of explosives, both men were inside and the place went up from the inside out. I'd just about guarantee they were building bombs for this next hit. If forensics come across any reason to believe it could be a homicide, we'll be in touch right away.'

Rachael's phone rang. 'Excuse me.' She stepped into the next room.

'I should collect this evidence and get going,' Brighton said. 'It was nice to meet you, Detective Carson.'

'Finn, please, and likewise.'

A smile erupted on her face and he noticed the dimple, the way her features softened. She was a striking woman. 'Olivia.'

'Finn?' Rachael interrupted. 'That was Cass. They've found a body at Patonga.'

'Then we'll need to move too.' He sent Brighton a return smile. 'I'm sure I'll see you around.'

'Lovely to meet you,' Rachael added for Brighton. 'I'll get copies of those files. McCabe is meeting with us on another matter later this morning so I'll pass them on then. Let us know if we can be of any further assistance.'

'Thanks. I will.'

'She seems nice,' Finn said as they got back into the car.

'Hmm,' Rachael said, as though privy to something he wasn't. 'We'll see.'

CHAPTER FIVE

Patonga, located in a small bay close to the mouth of the Hawkesbury River, hosted a pretty seaside village that marked the southern end of the Central Coast. Its beach was a long, golden stretch of surf-free serenity glistening under the growing warmth of a perfect Autumn morning. Such an idyllic location, but even this place couldn't escape murder.

Detective Sergeant Lisa Cassidy took her eyes from the police operation going on just beyond the end of the wharf to watch a couple of paddle boarders sliding their boards smoothly across the water towards them. The pair noticed Cass watching and changed direction, back the other way. Good. She didn't feel like yelling at anyone this morning. The tranquillity had already been broken by the police and forensic vehicles, the boat, the divers and a car belonging to a local TV station with two men inside, patiently waiting for a story. They'd taken some footage, had bailed up her partner Detective Jack Lincoln for a story and received the usual response of following up on some information. Nothing more at this stage for their trouble.

Footsteps behind Cass alerted her to Linc's approach and a moment later a large skim flat white was handed over.

'Thanks.' She barely ever drank hot coffee; it inevitably got cold before she remembered it. But she hugged the cup in her hands, breathed it in.

'And a ...' He held out a bag, shook it at her. 'Danish lattice.'

'I don't eat junk,' she said. At thirty-five she was having more trouble than she used to keeping her figure in line. Having a sweet tooth, a four-year-old child and a divine cook for a partner didn't help stop the inches from settling where they shouldn't.

'It's not junk. It's a crafted-to-perfection work of culinary art.'

'Yeah, yeah,' she said, but grinned, peeked at the luscious, glistening pastry and thought, *Oh, what the hell?*

Linc smirked as she bit in and groaned happily. 'They haven't got him out yet?'

She swallowed and shook her head. 'He's in a bag weighed down with concrete. It's causing them some grief. They're going to tow him in while the divers guide him up as safely as they can. They're just getting set up.'

'I wonder who it is.'

'Lexi and Dawny are involved. Whoever it is, I'm betting this is the start of some new and cataclysmic disaster.'

Linc pulled a face at her. 'You know, you're going to have to stop with the personal vendetta one day.'

'Am I?' Cass had never made any secret of the fact she believed Lexi shouldn't be on the team. The prostitute turned vigilante turned cop was barely even a police officer, yet she spent more time with the top homicide team in the country than she did writing up traffic violations. 'I'm sure she wraps herself up in these things just to get out of going back to general duties.'

'Can you blame her?'

Blame her? No. She didn't blame Lexi. But that didn't mean having the woman in her face so much of the time didn't bring back memories she'd rather stay gone. That her extended presence didn't keep that gnawing worry in the pit of Cass's stomach that Lexi might remember, might at some stage put together a past Cass needed to stay buried, forgotten.

'Morning!' A middle-aged man jogged down the beach towards them from the café.

'Good morning,' Linc replied. 'Can we help you?'

'What's going on?'

'Police operation, sir. I'm afraid we can't comment.'

'Got it. Sorry.' He made to turn around, hesitated. 'It's just that, if whatever you're looking for was put in the water on Tuesday night, I might have seen something, that's all.'

'Oh? What did you see?' Linc asked.

'I manage the restaurant over there,' he said, pointing to the building where patrons were enjoying breakfast. 'We had a function that ran late, so I was up half the night with some of the staff, cleaning. Around two, George—one of the staff—said I should have a look at this old bloke. We watched a man wheeling a wheelbarrow right along the path there. It had a massive fishing bag in it, one of those flash ones with all the pockets and zippers. He spotted us and nodded politely enough, said his back wouldn't let him lug his fishing gear around any other way these days. Asked us if the fish were biting.

'I commented that he certainly had plenty of stuff; he told me it saved him going back and forth from his car if he took it all up at once. He went out onto the wharf. Couldn't see what he was doing out there. Too dark.'

'What makes you think something was amiss?'

'We'd only been back at it ten minutes when we saw the bloke again, walking back with nothing in the wheelbarrow.'

'Are you absolutely sure?'

'Positive, the streetlights shine right down on that bit of path.'

'Are you sure he wasn't just coming back for something he'd forgotten?'

Man shook his head. 'He put the wheelbarrow in the back of his car—one of those big troop carriers—quite easily for someone with a dodgy back, dropped something in the Cleanaway then drove away.'

'How big would you say that fishing bag was, sir?'

'Oh, I don't know. It overflowed the wheelbarrow a bit.'

'Would you mind if I took your details?' Linc asked. 'If we need any more information, we'll be in touch.'

'Of course.'

Cass walked down to the water's edge as the boat slowly puttered towards shore. More officers waded into the water to help the two attempting to drag the large bag from the water.

'Looks like our witness was on to something,' Linc said, joining her. 'That matches the description he just gave me of the fishing bag. Unless there really is fishing gear in it.'

One of the police divers heard the comment and looked over his shoulder, puffing. 'Mate, we wouldn't have dragged this thing out for fishing gear.'

Cass pulled on some gloves then stepped forward and unzipped the bag. A solid block of concrete—no wonder it had been so heavy—then she made out the shape of a body curled in the foetal position. One side of a face and shoulder, hip and knee poking out of its encasement.

'Van Zettan's going to find this one fun to autopsy,' Linc said, peering over her shoulder.

'Yeah, well, you don't get to be our top forensic pathologist without taking on the odd challenge. Let's get him to the lab.'

Headquarters was a mess. The changes associated with the building's upgrade in line with a cleaner, greener future had begun. Cass was almost taken out at the lift by a large cardboard box carried by a technician wearing overalls advertising Coolglobe Air Conditioning. 'How long is this going to go on for?' she complained, quickly ducking sideways to avoid it.

'As long as it takes, I suppose,' Linc said, stepping over more packaging. 'At least the air-con might work properly and be a whole lot quieter after this.'

They rode to the eighth floor, where Cass ducked and weaved her way through more chaos to the meeting room and found Rachael and Finn already seated, sipping coffees. Linc followed her in and shut the door on the noise. 'I hope that doesn't take too long,' she told the room.

'Couldn't agree more,' Rachael said. 'How did you go with the victim?'

'Body is encased in concrete,' Cass said, taking a seat. 'It took a while to recover. The whole thing is on its way to Van Zettan. I think it could be a while before we get any real answers.'

'We have a witness though,' Linc said. 'A local restaurant owner saw and talked to the guy who dumped the body. He wheeled the bag containing our victim out in a wheelbarrow, on the excuse he had a bad back and couldn't carry his fishing gear. Forensics found some empty concrete bags in a nearby bin, so it looks like he's put the bagged body in the wheelbarrow, then added dry concrete mix. No way he would have lifted the whole lot out of the car and into the wheelbarrow otherwise.'

'Wait. Can concrete set underwater?' Rachael asked.

'Funny you should ask,' Linc said, flashing a grin. 'I googled that very same question. The answer is, even better, apparently, than it does in air. Something about chemical reactions and particle hydration and a whole lot of that straight-over-the-head stuff that had me not finishing the article.'

Cass shook her head in amusement. She wasn't sure why Linc liked to downplay his intelligence; she knew how his mind worked and when it wasn't focused on eligible females—which, due to dark good looks and cute boyish charm, was a little too often—that mind was capable of great things.

'So while we're waiting on the body,' she said, returning her attention to Rachael, 'we should be able to follow up on our POI. I'm sure there's CCTV at one or more of those shops. We know what type of vehicle he was driving.'

'You should certainly do that for evidentiary purposes,' Rachael agreed. 'But we already know who dumped the body.'

'I'm sorry, what?' Cass asked in surprise.

Rachael took a deep breath, sighed. 'I didn't fill you in fully last night. I'm still waiting to talk with Dawny in order to get a better picture myself, but the person responsible for our victim ending up at Patonga is Desmond Harris.'

As Rachael filled them in, Cass carefully kept her expression neutral. She'd had more than one run-in with Finn and Rachael over Lexi. It might look as though Lexi and her ex-con friend were dragging them into a shady drama but Cass kept what she wanted to say in her head and instead asked, 'So what have we got to work with?'

'We're testing a weapon Finn confiscated for fingerprints, hoping to find out the identities of the men who were holding Dawny. We also need to find out who the house they visited belongs to. I have the address here.'

'I'll take care of it,' Linc said. 'But what about bringing them in on kidnapping charges?'

'I doubt that would come to anything,' Rachael said. 'I can't see Dawny or Desmond wanting to press charges, testify or in any way cooperate with us against these people.'

They were interrupted by a knock on the door and Cass immediately recognised the solidly built man with the tidy brown hair, a shirt that hugged muscled arms and the open, friendly smile.

Rachael waved him in. 'McCabe, thanks for coming.'

'Rachael, hi,' he said, stepping through the door and closing it behind him. 'Hi, all.'

'Does everyone know each other?' Rachael asked.

There was a round of nods and greetings, then McCabe spun a chair around and straddled it, leaning his arms on its back. 'I hear you've got a murder linked to one of my MCs.'

'We do,' Rachael said.

'Catch us up,' Cass said. 'Who is this motorcycle gang?'

'Chaos Reigns MC,' Rachael said. 'McCabe?'

'Relatively new kids on the block. The club formed about ten years ago with sixteen founding members from a former club called Combat Crew, who were disbanded after their president was arrested on drugs charges and put away.'

Cass's breath caught as her throat constricted. Lexi had gotten them involved with Combat Crew? The club may have changed names, but with all those old members, it wouldn't have changed culture. They were bound to still consider themselves one percenters. She'd learnt during her first case as a detective that, back in the sixties, the president of the American Motorcycle Association had made some speech about ninety-nine per cent of bikers being law-abiding citizens, so the term 'one percenter' had been adopted by those gangs who like to think they're above the law. The ones that like to cause trouble in all the usual places: drugs; theft; prostitution; organised crime rings. Combat Crew hadn't been any different. That case had destroyed a part of Cass she'd never get back.

As her mind drifted to the little clay heart she kept among her most treasured possessions, she shoved the memory away. Told herself to focus on what Chad McCabe was saying.

'The club owns a motorcycle repair shop with a side business of rebuilding and restoring vintage bikes. They import parts and bikes from all over the world. They've been at it since the club was still Combat Crew and they've earned themselves quite a reputation. Some of their bikes sell for big money.'

'So why are you investigating them?' Finn asked.

'We're not so much investigating them as keeping tabs on them. They're dealing with a South American shipping company called Oxacot. Oxacot vessels regularly come in and out of Australian borders carrying thousands of shipping containers from all over the world. They have business interests in South America, Asia, Africa and parts of Europe as well as Australia. The company has been linked several times to international smuggling operations. The Australian Federal Police, FBI and the UK's National Crime Agency have been trying to pin these guys down on charges for more than a decade without success. When Arthur Cronin, the president of the former Combat Crew MC, was put away for importing crack cocaine, the million-dollar haul was found to have been stored in small packages bearing the same stamp as a shipment that was intercepted coming off an Oxacot vessel in the UK. The re-established club has recently resumed dealing with the company and seem to have come into a lot of unexplained money. We find that suspicious, so every now and again we flag their containers, go over them with a fine-tooth comb. We haven't caught them out yet but I think they're back into it. Call it a hunch.'

'Then maybe we can help each other out,' Rachael said.

'I hope so. Tell me more about Dawny and Desmond.'

'Yes, of course,' Rachael said. 'Catherine Dawn Delaney is a battered wife turned solicitor who represented abused women in court. She did time in the eighties for attempting to dispose of the body of a monster who'd murdered his girlfriend and child after the courts had let him off on assault charges. Police were unable to prove she'd murdered him and at least one other nasty piece of work who'd killed another of her clients, but she did time for accessory after the fact and has since stayed out of trouble. She even assisted us in tracking down Damon Vaughn during the Spider case. Desmond Harris is Catherine Delaney's husband.'

'You said she was an abused wife,' Linc said. 'So … he's violent?'

'No, Desmond's Dawny's second husband.'

'What happened to the first one?'

'He … disappeared,' Rachael said. 'Desmond Harris has several warrants out for his arrest dating back decades. Nothing major. Reads a bit like a modern-day Robin Hood. A problem solver, standover man, thief. Generally for a cause. He's been off the radar completely since 2008 up until he also briefly turned up during the Spider case.'

Cass fought the temptation to roll her eyes. They're Lexi's friends, so of course Rachael makes even these criminals sound like saints. 'And what cause, exactly,' she couldn't help but ask, 'was behind dumping a murder victim off Patonga Wharf?'

Rachael picked up her phone. 'Let's get Lexi and Dawny up here. Let Dawny explain.'

CHAPTER SIX

Dawny and I have parked ourselves at a little café close to headquarters, because what else can we do until Rachael and Finn call us up? Due to Dawny's refusal to talk until a body is found, we don't have any timeframe to work from and if they don't find him, well … wasted trip.

The street is busy and the wind occasionally sweeps through with a bite, but the tables inside were all taken and I'd rather listen to traffic than Dawny's whining. Besides, feeding her is the only thing keeping her from bolting on me. She's tucking into a big breakfast like she hasn't eaten in days while I pick at a blueberry muffin, more interested in my extra-large flat white. After a marathon effort to convince her to get in the car for the drive down to police headquarters in Parramatta, I need all the caffeine I can get. Now that it's kicking in, I'm curious enough to ask, 'So, Dawny, what are these deliveries Desmond's been running for the MC?'

Dawny shrugs, her eyes not leaving her food. 'The sort where he picks up goods from one place and drives them to another.'

'What are these goods?'

'He doesn't ask. It's better that way.'

'I see. But—'

'You, on the other hand, ask a lot more questions these days. I suppose the police force will do that to you. I've been meaning to ask, what on earth possessed you to join?'

I take another sip of my flat white. 'All the Spider stuff. And desperation. I had no clients left. I had to do something.'

'Rather drastic career shift though, wasn't it? Don't even look yourself in all that fancy get-up.'

As opposed to Dawny's black tights and Midnight Oil tee, my 'fancy get-up' was a very ordinary pair of black work pants and a blue silk shirt with low-heeled ankle boots. A flatteringly cut but hardly fancy outfit I bought for working with the Homicide Squad. I much prefer it to the standard uniform, though. The sooner I can get out of general duties and make detective, the better.

'And are you enjoying yourself?'

'Well.' I watch a twig of a woman wrestle a Rottweiler away from a traffic pole. 'I've been in the force less than a year and I've almost quit already. Twice.'

'And why's that, dear? Did you wake up one day and find your common sense had returned?'

'It's the working-with-other-humans part. It's important. I know it's important. I'm just no good at it.' I frown at my muffin and pick out a blueberry. 'And the rules. There are so many damn rules.'

'Are they the ones that are supposed to stop you getting hurt? You're black and blue.'

'I had a run-in with a nasty crime family. There was a situation or two I probably could have handled differently.'

Dawny screws up her face. 'Bad judgement?'

I frown at her, offended. 'There's nothing wrong with my judgement.'

'I have to question that, since you brought Finn along yesterday. He doesn't really fit in, does he? And he did seem awfully put out by it all.'

'He was put out because I *didn't* bring him along. I was with him when I got your message and I made up an excuse to leave. He didn't buy it and he followed me. At least, I think that's why he's put out. It could also be the situation he ended up in last night. Or a bit of both.'

'Well, thank goodness he didn't pull the cop card on Woolly, that's all I can say. I am a bit worried about the police divers, though. I do hope the club doesn't have spies out.'

'It was the only way to get that body back, Dawny. I've been in the water with a dead body recently and never again.'

'Now that sounds like an interesting story.'

I grimace as the unpleasant memory resurfaces. 'Not while we're eating, okay?'

'I'm just about finished,' she says, dusting off her hands and looking down at her plate sadly. 'Lovely breakfast and all, but I can't see why we couldn't run through this at your place.'

'We've talked about this,' I say not quite grating my teeth. *And talked, and talked …* 'Rachael needs to know the full story so she can put the best people on it. She's homicide, not organised crime, kidnapping or whatever else you two have gotten into. You need to make an official statement so the right teams can move on getting Desmond back.'

'Hmph. If I'd wanted all the hoo-ha I'd've called the cops myself. How's that muffin? I could go for something sweet.'

Whatever nerves Dawny's feeling about Desmond's predicament don't seem to have affected her appetite. I dump the untouched half of muffin onto her plate and breathe in the remnants of my coffee, consider getting another one.

Because Dawny's quiet for a moment I have time to wonder what crime scene Finn and Rachael had to attend and where. I get that crime scenes take precedence and that it's my own fault I didn't get the keys for the apartment off Finn, but I don't want my delivery truck left stranded on the kerb. I consider calling them for an update, but a phone message pings, putting me out of my misery.

'Okay, we're on.'

'They found the body?'

'I guess so. Let's go.' I get up and push in my chair then find myself standing in the way of pedestrians while Dawny relishes the last few bites of the muffin, drains her tea and carefully folds and taps a serviette to her mouth.

'By all means, take your time,' I mutter. 'I have furniture being delivered this afternoon, remember?'

'If I have to be here, you should too. It's only fair.' She gets up, stretches. 'Where exactly is this place? I can't walk far on this knee, you know.'

'Look across the road,' I tell her, already moving to the crossing. 'It's one building that way.' And impossible to miss. The police headquarters is two impressive towers linked by a central atrium. A large bright artwork decorates the lower facade in a DNA pattern, shading a pretty fern-laden water feature. As we get closer, I notice it's more chaotic than usual outside, with workmen's vans and bins blocking off much of the outer parking area. Men in blue overalls and joggers, some with hard hats, are going in and out of the building with boxes and equipment.

We've barely stepped into the foyer when I spot Finn.

'Hey,' he says. 'Glad you made it.'

'You found him?' Dawny asks.

'Yes, we did. This way,' he says, and guides Dawny towards the lifts. We step around more construction work, avoid cables dangling from the roof and travel up the lift.

'What's with all the chaos?' I ask.

'Air conditioner upgrade. Among other things.'

'Exciting.'

'Lots of changes going on. The commissioner is copping some flak for a few bad decisions he's made lately so he's looking for some good press. We're in the meeting room.'

Rachael stands up as we walk in. I spot Linc and Cass—the whole team is here—before my gaze lands on an unfamiliar face.

'Good morning,' Rachael says. 'This is Inspector Chad McCabe, organised crime. McCabe, this is Constable Lexi Winter and Catherine Delaney.'

'Call me Dawny, dear,' Dawny tells McCabe warmly. 'Looks like you keep fit, eh?' She very deliberately looks at Finn then back to McCabe. 'Maybe you should be the one looking after Lexi.'

Ouch. She's harsh. I make a mental note to bombard Dawny with stories of Finn coming to my rescue.

A moment of surprised silence is broken by McCabe's big laugh. 'It's nice to meet you, Dawny. And you, Lexi. If you ever need looking after, let me know.'

'You might live to regret that,' Finn mutters, stepping around us, but he sends me a cheeky smile. My eyes narrow in on his before returning it.

'Dawny, it's lovely to finally meet you in person,' Rachael says. 'Please take a seat. Can we get you a tea?'

'Oh, thank you, dear, I'd appreciate it. I got rushed away from my last one and all that walking's left me a bit parched.'

'I've got it,' Finn says.

'Well, everyone's good for something, that's what I say,' Dawny says, settling her ample weight into a slim-backed chair. Finn halts at the door to send her a look of disbelief and she takes the opportunity to elaborate on her order. 'Don't forget the sugar. Two, please. Stirred in well. Not too much milk, just a dribble. And not that full cream stuff. Gives me indigestion. Do you have any nice biscuits, dear?'

'I'll see what I can do,' he replies with mock pleasantness.

'So the divers got the young fellow?' Dawny asks Rachael.

'That's right,' Rachael says. 'The body was heavily weighed down, so it was exactly where you thought it would be. We'd appreciate it if you could run us through everything you know about the murder.'

'All I want is to get Desmond out of trouble and the longer I'm hanging around you people telling you things—no offence—the less likely that is to happen.'

'We're not going to do anything to endanger Desmond further,' Rachael promises. 'And we will certainly share evidence with those holding Desmond in order to secure his release. We simply need a small amount of cooperation from you to make that happen.'

'All you need is a couple of photos of a dead body to make that happen.'

'Dawny,' I threaten.

Finn reappears and puts a tea and a twin pack of biscuits in front of Dawny, then takes a seat at the table and folds his arms. 'Okay, Dawny. From the beginning.'

'It's like I said, dear. Desmond was doing a delivery to the clubhouse. He and two of the prospects—they're probationary club members—were unloading out the back when they noticed a young fellow sneaking around with a phone in his hand. There was a bit of a confrontation and then the guns came out. Desmond stepped in—was just trying to stop the young fellow getting shot—but in the scuffle he got a bang on the head and stunned himself. The sergeant took him inside while Desmond and the prospects got the rest of the stock unloaded. When they were done, the prospects were supposed to chain the young fellow out the back, but he was unfortunately deceased. Desmond felt awful because he figured the young fellow must have slipped in when he opened the gates to bring the truck through, so he told the prospects to let the sergeant know he'd do them a solid and take care of the body. Actually, it was more because he thought he'd cop it for not being careful, so Desmond was playing it safe, you see. Getting in first with a nice gesture.'

'So what went wrong?' McCabe asks.

'The sergeant didn't seem to realise he'd killed the poor fellow. Then they got suspicious. Wondered if Desmond had let this fellow in on purpose, played along when he'd been caught out, then helped him escape under the guise of dumping the body.'

'Why would he do that?'

'That's what he said! But they're on high alert. Worried about something. The sergeant's got it in his head that the young fellow was spying for whoever they're worried about, and that being the case, Desmond could be in with them, too.'

'But he's not,' Finn clarifies.

'Oh, no, not at all. He's just a delivery man.'

'So where is this clubhouse?' Rachael asks. 'And do we have names for any of these members other than Skink and Woolly?'

'Let's just get Desmond out first, please. I'm sure he'll help you with any details he knows once his life is out of danger. I really can't tell you any more. I don't ask questions, you see. Tend to live longer that way.'

Rachael's phone rings. 'It's Van Zettan.' She puts it on speaker. 'How are you going?'

'He's just arrived. Rather solid young man.'

'So I heard.'

'It's likely going to take a while before I can tell you much. We'll take some X-rays and CT scans before we begin chiselling the body free. A few days, perhaps. I'll keep you in the loop.'

'Thanks, Steven.'

'We need proof,' Dawny reminds them before Rachael can end the call.

'Steven, could you send me a couple of shots of the victim?'

'Just a moment.'

I hear a ping as the first picture comes through, then another. Rachael checks them then shows them to McCabe. I catch a glimpse of a body in the foetal position partially encased in concrete, short brown hair poking out in bits.

'Are there any fingertips sticking out of the concrete?'

'No, but I'll expose the hands as early on in the process as I can. See if we can get you an ID.'

'Appreciate it. Thanks.'

'Yes, thank you very much!' Dawny says. Then to Rachael, she says, 'We should call Woolly and show him the evidence. I'm sure Desmond will be keen to get out of his situation. Lexi, dear, you have the number?'

Poor guy, I think. I'd been prepared to see a lot of hair and tatts, but this was no bikie, at least, not an obvious one. I know what gangs do to each other, but when they do it to someone else, it's somehow worse. Because when you live in that world, on the fringe of society, you expect it. The violence, the lack of respect for life, the terrible things people do to each other for the stupidest reasons. When you don't—

'Lexi!' Dawny says again. 'Wake up, dear, we need Woolly's number.'

'Sorry. Yep. I have it.' I pull my phone out of my pocket, find the number and slide the phone to Rachael.

'What's the plan?' Finn asks.

'I think from both our perspectives, getting Desmond safely away from the club and into custody is key,' McCabe says. 'We can't make arrests based on hearsay. You need a first-hand account of what happened to our victim and if possible, some proof. I'd also like to speak to him about what he was unloading from that truck.'

'Agreed,' Rachael says with a nod. 'Okay, Dawny, we need a pick-up point for Desmond. You need to tell Woolly we'll do a swap.'

'Oh, Desmond doesn't need to go anywhere. We just show them the photo, they'll tell him he's all good and everything will go back to normal. He does some good work for them. He'll be fine. You'll see. This is just a precaution.'

'I think you're missing the point,' Rachael says. 'We're willing to trade this proof for Desmond. We believe he has valuable information he can share with us. Make no mistake. No Desmond, no proof.'

Dawny's look goes sour. 'What on earth makes you think I can tell these people what to do?'

'I'll give it a go.' I take the phone back, key in the number and wait.

The line rings once, twice, is answered with a grunted, 'Yeah?'

'Yeah, it's Lexi. We've got the proof on that job. We want Desmond.'

'Send the proof. Desmond's free to go.'

'You think I'm sending this shit over the phone? I'll show you in person when I pick up Desmond.'

The phone is suddenly muffled and I hear murmuring in the background. Then he's back. 'Come back to the house. Nine pm.'

The line goes dead.

'Okay,' Rachael says. 'Let's work out the logistics. Cass, would you mind taking Dawny to another room and making sure she's comfortable for a few minutes?'

'Yes, of course,' Cass says, getting to her feet.

'Lovely working with you coppers,' Dawny says. 'Looking forward to having my Desmond back. I'm sure you won't stuff it up.' She sends Finn a look as she leaves.

'So how is this going to work?' Finn says when the door closes behind Dawny and Cass. 'Get our hands on Desmond then crash the place?'

'Or,' McCabe says, 'we let things play out until we've questioned Desmond for more information.'

'You want to continue the charade?' Rachael asks.

McCabe shrugs. 'Dawny's story and the fact they want proof of death isn't going to stand up in a murder trial. We need Desmond's first-hand account. If we arrest these guys and Desmond needs convincing to talk, we may run out of time to hold them. Once they know we're onto them, they're in the wind.'

Rachael considers that. 'Sending Lexi and Finn back in alone is a lot more dangerous.'

'They've already got cover and a reason to be there,' McCabe argues. 'And any intel they can provide into the club and its members could be valuable.'

'So we go in, pretend we're still hitman and cleaner,' Finn says with the slightest smirk at me. 'I'll wear a wire, initiate some conversation. See what we can get.'

My pulse takes off like a rocket. 'Nope! No way.' I'm already nervous enough about going back in, I'm not doing anything suicidal. 'If you wear a wire they'll find it and they'll kill you. They might anyway. And you don't ask questions. Ever. You're a hitman, remember? No one that lasts in that game gets curious.'

'You seem quite well versed on this,' Rachael says with a narrowed gaze.

'I know a bit about club culture. You want to get Desmond, fine. We go in, show them the pics and cross our fingers they let us walk out. That's the best we can hope for.'

'Sounds like a wasted opportunity to me,' Finn says.

'But I have to admit she makes a good point,' McCabe says. 'As useful as this could be for both our investigations, you're risking your lives to go in and rescue a wanted felon with multiple arrest warrants to his name who was recently involved in the cover-up of a murder. Do you think he'd do the same for you?'

'He turned over evidence in the cover-up of another murder to save my daughter's life,' Finn tells him.

'Okay, so you feel like you owe him. But even if you get him out, we're going to need to speak to him, after which he'll be charged and going to prison. Not sure how grateful he's going to be that we didn't just send them the proof and let him walk. He may not even willingly leave with you.'

'Which is why we need the wire,' Finn presses. 'If this all blows up, we need you to know to provide backup.'

I shake my head. I want to get Desmond back safely too, but this is a bad idea. 'If you don't want to go in there without one, I'll go in by myself,' I tell him. I'm way less than keen, but I figure I'm also less likely to die, on this occasion, without him.

The resounding 'No' from everyone pisses me off enough to throw my hands up in defeat. 'Then stuff it. We get Desmond, flood the place with cops and hope we end up with enough to charge them.'

Finn stares at my set face for several seconds before asking Rachael and McCabe, 'Do we have a cop anywhere in HQ that looks enough like Lexi to fool Woolly and come in with me?'

'Oh my God, you're gonna die,' I mutter with my hand on my forehead.

'Who the hell could pull off being Lexi?' Linc asks in disbelief.

Finn sighs. 'Then I'll go in alone.'

I try not to be offended when no one shouts that one down. And fuck, fuck, fuck! I'm not letting him do that.

'Okay!' I snap, scouring my mind for another solution. 'We can rig a phone as a listening device. We're bound to have them taken off us but they shouldn't be too far away to hear the commotion if all hell breaks loose. Hopefully.'

'Not bad,' McCabe says.

'And we need to tone down the whole,' I wave my hands around, encompassing all of Finn, '"cop billboard", okay? Dig out the oldest jeans you've got, find a t-shirt—be careful what, if anything, is printed on it, leather jacket—got one? Some decent boots, but only if you've got some worn in. You need to look like you live in these clothes. And … scruff the hair a bit.'

'I need to look like a bikie?'

'No, but it wouldn't hurt to try to fit in—' I can't help the grimace, '—which you might if you don't say too much.'

'Anything else?' Finn asks dryly.

'Yeah. Walk slower, sloppier. Practise doing a bored look in the mirror and lose the human CCTV gaze. Oh, and we need to give that gun back.'

'We're not returning the gun,' Finn says firmly.

'It's a goodwill gesture.'

'I'm not handing an illegal firearm to a—'

'For fuck's sake!' I snap. 'If you want me to go along with this, then damn well listen to me! It's my life on the line, too!'

I can't miss the exchange of glances around the table and I know they think I'm overreacting. I wish I was. I don't want to go in, I don't want to deal, I don't want to remember. I don't want to get involved in that fucked-up life again.

CHAPTER SEVEN

I open the door to my new apartment ten minutes before the furniture truck is due and step inside, Dawny on my heels.

'If you would just tell me the plan, dear, I'm sure I could offer some advice.'

'No and no thanks,' I tell her. 'I'm good with this one.'

'I can't help but worry they've got you in the wrong headspace. These paramilitary organisations do tend to stifle one's creativity. We did risk quite a bit for you just a couple of years back. Not that I'd ever expect you to repay that. I'd just like to help.'

'I know that,' I say. Because I can't say she's not helpful when she chooses to be. 'But I have to do things differently now.'

Dawny wanders around the apartment, sticking her head in each of the rooms. 'I've gone along with all this police business because you said it's the right way to go. I decided I'd better trust you on that. So that being the case, can't you trust me? It's called mutual respect, you know.'

'Save it, Dawny,' Rachael says, coming in behind us. 'She's not allowed and she won't.'

'Someone's got to look out for her,' Dawny huffs as Finn comes in behind Rachael.

'Cleaners did a good job,' Finn comments, ignoring the jibe.

I look around the empty space, the strong smell of disinfectant bothering my nose. We're standing in a small kitchen with shiny white cupboard doors and a black marble benchtop. Beyond is a lounge and dining area overlooking the tops of fig trees and beyond, to glimpses of Brisbane Water. To my left is a bedroom, a bathroom and another bedroom. A small balcony hugs the side of the apartment off the lounge area. It's a big enough space and will do fine. At least for now.

'Let's get some air in here,' Rachael suggests and opens the balcony doors. She steps outside and looks down the street. 'We just made it. Here's your furniture.'

It doesn't take very long for the removalists to get it all inside. I don't have much. A new table and chairs, lounge, bed and a desk, some appliances and the few boxes of my things that Rachael saved during the last case before my house was destroyed.

'It's a start,' Rachael says, looking around when we'd finished unpacking and assembling.

'Oh, this is lovely,' Dawny says, making herself at home on my new three-seater lounge.

Another knock has me getting up and going to the door.

'Lexi Winter?' Two men are at the door holding a large box.

'Yes … What is that?'

'Housewarming present from Finn and I,' Rachael says, showing the men where to put it.

I get a look at the side of the box as they carefully set it down. My eyes bulge. 'You bought me a television?'

'You needed one,' Finn says, stepping in to start unpacking.

'That's a … big television.'

'Same as mine,' he says. 'The brackets will fit into the wall where the old ones were and I already know how to set it up. I'll get it on the wall for you now.'

'Thanks,' I say, slightly stunned. I don't even want to think about what it cost.

'Welcome,' Rachael replies. They don't seem to think it's a big deal. I do.

'I hope you've got another bed coming,' Dawny says, emerging from my bedroom. 'I'd rather not spend another night in that noisy pub.'

'You take the bed, I'll crash on the lounge.' I'm busy helping Finn wrestle the huge television from its box and can't be bothered arguing.

'I appreciate that. I hope the mattress is firm enough. I might end up with it forever if you don't come back tonight. I'm sure I could help you come up with a better plan.'

She's nothing if not repetitive.

'What are you going to do if Breen decides not to let you go?' she presses.

My gaze is still on the TV, but I'm no longer seeing it, my consciousness rapidly shrinking to a pinprick on the memory of a face that was round and harshly grooved, of small, mean eyes, a nasty, nasty temper.

'What did you say?' I manage, my voice not quite even.

'I said I'd help you come up with a better plan,' Dawny repeats.

'Not that part. The other—the ... who?'

'Oh, Woolly said the boss wants to meet you, remember? The club's boss—president's—name is Breen. I know that because Desmond mentioned him in passing a few times. Called him as mad as a cut snake and twice as ugly.'

Finn takes the weight of the television and I step out of the way as he leans it on the floor. *Fuck.* The shock of hearing that name again, of knowing who I'm up against, sabotages my ability to mask with my regular calm. 'Did Desmond mention any other names?'

'Don't know. Don't think so.'

'You hadn't arrived at HQ when we were discussing this,' Rachael says. 'All we really know is Chaos Reigns was founded by some members of a club called Combat Crew after it disbanded.'

'Oh.' I'm fucked. I'm so fucked.

'What's wrong?' Rachael asks.

'She needs a cuppa,' Dawny says. 'Been a big day. Make us all one, would you, Lexi, dear?'

'Sure,' I mutter, needing a moment to gather my thoughts. I turn my back on them and go to the kitchen, then open the box containing my new kettle. I'd rather sit by myself with my JD while I process the enormous pile of shit heading right at me, but that won't be happening. I'm supposed to be going in there. Tonight. To 'meet' Breen.

I take a few deep breaths as I unwrap the kettle. Will he recognise me? I was just a teen. There's been a lot of years and no doubt plenty of drugs between then and now. What other Combat Crew members am I likely to run into? Who of that old gang would tolerate Breen as their president after what happened?

Because the instructions fell out as I opened the box, I glance at them. They tell me to boil a full jug of water, toss the water then go again. I fill the kettle and set it to boil.

If anyone does recognise me, they're probably going to say things. Things Finn will hear that I haven't told them. Bad things. What do I do about that?

Mugs. Shit. Do I have any?

I should tell them now, just in case?

I press my palms onto the benchtop and lean into it, stare at the tiny specks of gold glinting out of its shining black surface as I contemplate how that will go.

There's no good scenario. Is it too late to pull out?

I scan the rest of the kitchen boxes for coffee mugs that I'm pretty sure I didn't buy. Dawny has plonked herself back on my lounge and is trying to make the TV work while Finn struggles with cables, but in my peripheral vision I can see Rachael's watching me. She has a bat-like radar for this shit. She knows something's up.

'Ah … I don't have any coffee mugs,' I say and laugh at myself. It sounds hollow. 'I don't have any tea or coffee or milk … and yet I'm boiling the kettle.' Then louder, 'Sorry, Dawny, I don't have tea.'

'Can't you do one of those fancy food delivery services? I'll do you a favour and wait at the bottom of the lift. Bring it up. You know how I like my tea. See if they've got anything nice to eat too, please. It's been a long day.'

I shoot Finn a helpless look. 'What was that local café we used during the Spider investigation?'

He pulls out his phone and scrolls through his contacts. 'I'll take care of it.'

'Thanks.' I shove the kettle packaging back into its box and put it with the rest of the rubbish in the spare room until I figure out what to do with it all.

Rachael and Finn step apart as I reappear.

'Okay, Dawny,' Finn says, 'it's on its way. Let's go wait for it.'

'Do you think they'll be long?' I hear Dawny ask as the door closes. 'I'm starving.'

'So ...' Rachael prompts.

What and how much do I tell her? All of it? None of it? I stare longingly at my JD and consider having just one glass. How do I tell her one part and not the other? Do I just blurt it all out and hope for the best? It was another lifetime ago. Not a good one. Does it even matter?

Of course it does. It could affect—probably end—my career. I'm still debating if I really want to do the cop thing, but I'd like the choice to remain mine. I've known I was going to have to broach this one day, but always at some stage in the future. Not on the spur of the moment. Not without planning, without thought. I need time to figure it out. I glance at my watch and realise I've got four hours until we're meeting at the station before going to see Breen. That's not a lot of time.

Rachael's waiting for an answer so I shrug, hope it comes off as casual. 'Just a whole lot of past-life crap with bikies and brothels.' I look up and manage a tight smile. 'Honestly, I wouldn't even know where to start.'

'How about with why the mention of Breen has you so freaked out?' she asks.

Okay, I'm not getting out of this so easy. 'When I worked at Madame Suzie's, she used to send girls out to Combat Crew's clubhouse to dance and shit. I came across him a few times. He was a nasty piece of work, fucked in the head from Afghanistan or whatever desert he fought in. Caused some trouble.'

'Are you worried he'll recognise you?'

'I guess there's a chance he might.'

'Will that be a problem?'

'I can't see why.'

Rachael stares hard at me for several more seconds. 'I don't want you going in if there's anything in your past that's going to put you in any increased risk of danger.'

'There's not. And we've already established Finn's going with or without me, so I'm doing this. Assuming I'm still on the homicide team and not expected back on general duties.'

'I've sorted that.'

I wait out one more long stare then Rachael checks the time. 'We'll have these coffees then I'm sending Finn home to get ready.'

'I should unpack some clothes. Find something to wear.'

I'm at the doorway to the bedroom before Rachael pulls me up.

'Are you sure about this?'

'I'll be fine.'

I go into my new bedroom, close the door and wonder if there's any real chance that's true.

CHAPTER EIGHT

'Are you ready?' Finn asked Lexi. They were parked a hundred metres down the road from the house, waiting for the last few minutes to tick over until nine pm. Lexi had worn tight, ripped jeans with a thick black belt and a red leather something that laced up at the back. He hadn't seen all her hair out in ages and, along with the just too heavy make-up she'd applied, the overall image packed a punch.

'Yep.'

She looked the part and was playing it cool but he could feel—almost see—the tension radiating off her. He was still trying to get his head around the fact she had any sort of history with this motorcycle gang. He hadn't missed her reaction when Breen's name had been mentioned earlier and Rachael had warned him Lexi knew more than she was willing to divulge. It wasn't reassuring. He'd tried to pry more information out of her on the way out here but she hadn't given him anything other than a grunt of approval over his jeans and tee, borrowed jacket and scuffed work boots.

'Should you set the phone up?'

'Already on, listening and recording. They can hear us.'

'Okay,' he said with a deep breath, 'here we go.' He started the car and pointed it onto the road. They drove past a few houses, lights blazing, until he found the one he was looking for and pulled up on the kerb. Two men wearing full gang colours were drinking by the gate and approached the car cautiously.

'We're here to see Breen,' Finn said through the window.

'Are you just,' the bigger one with a bald tattooed head said.

Finn felt a hand on his thigh as Lexi leant across him to smile up at the pair. Her perfume was sinful. 'Hi. I'm Lexi. This is Finn.'

The guy rested an arm on the roof of the car and poked his head down. 'Hi there, darlin'. You here about Desmond?'

'Yep. Got that proof Breen's after. Oh—and we brought Woolly's shottie back. It's in the boot.'

The other one went around the back of the car. When he heard the tap on the boot, Finn popped the release. A moment later the boot shut and the guy returned, checking the gun over before dropping the barrel to the ground.

The bald one took another long look at Finn before shooting Lexi a wink. 'Everyone's down the back. Follow the driveway. You're good to go.'

Lexi's smile was wide. 'Thanks, handsome.'

Finn managed not to roll his eyes and turned the car into the driveway. The garage opened front and back and guarded a long drive.

'Didn't know this was here,' Lexi said.

'I think that's the point.' He bounced the car along the rutted driveway then turned around before pulling up outside a shed that was large enough to be a second home. If they needed to get out fast, the car should at least be facing the right direction. He noted motorcycles parked in a long line, a beige LandCruiser Troopcarrier, a white Mercedes and a significant amount of noise coming from inside. Some sort of spirited argument perhaps.

Lexi hadn't moved.

'Good to go?' he asked.

She chewed her lip. He knew that face. She was pretending not to be worried.

'Yeah. Okay.' She put a hand on the car door, then sank back. 'Just … wait, wait, wait.'

'Yeah?' he asked.

Woolly appeared with his ear to a phone and eyed them nastily.

'I wasn't expecting this,' Lexi said. 'We should run through some protocols because it looks and sounds like there's a few in there.'

'Protocols?'

'They're not gonna expect you to know everything because you're not a member but you do need to know enough basics to get us in and out in one piece.'

'Okay, but make it quick, Woolly's waiting.'

'So let him wait. This is important. You walk in there, you're respectful. To everyone, from the president to the prospect. Someone talks to you, you take the time to talk back. You're gonna be friendly but not too friendly. Especially if there's any women in there. Don't initiate small talk with them; you never know how who will take what and you have such a pretty face someone's bound to want an excuse to mess it up.'

'Great. Anything else?'

'Plenty. No extended eye contact, no cop stares. Own your space, but don't push in on anyone else's. If for any reason we're asked to hang around, someone might speak to you. Don't overdo the talking, don't call anyone "bro". Don't try to be funny, don't get too familiar, don't ask about patches, insignia or any other inner club questions. Never touch a woman.'

'Why would I—'

'There'll be cameras. Always. Whatever you do in there, whatever you spend too long looking at, they're gonna be watching, they're gonna see it. Stick to the plan. If they've got a bar set up in there and they invite you to it, you buy drinks. Do not refuse. Also, let me handle me. If they insult me, shut up. They touch me inappropriately, shut up. Let me deal. Do not play the tough guy. It's all about fitting in and getting Desmond out. Got it?'

'You know, when we get back, you're going to explain to me exactly how you know so much about all this stuff.'

'And promise me you're not wearing a wire.'

'I'm *not*!' he said, feeling his own nerves build as her rules whirled through his head. 'Can we go now?'

'I guess so.'

She stepped out and he followed suit. Woolly stuck his head in the door then returned to his post, folded his arms and blocked the door until Skink came out.

'Carrying?' Woolly asked in way of greeting.

'Nup,' Lexi said.

Finn shook his head and allowed himself to be patted down.

'Give him your phones,' he said with a head toss to Skink. 'You'll get 'em when you leave.'

Lexi gave Woolly a sulky look before stepping in close to Skink and sliding hers slowly into his pocket. She simpered up at him as her hand lingered a little longer than necessary at his crotch. What the hell was she playing at? 'Take good care of it for me,' she purred.

Skink seemed to grow a full foot taller and his return smile was all appreciation. 'I will, darlin'. You can count on it.' Then with a much nastier face for Finn, he said, 'Yours?'

He held his hand out and Finn gave the phone to him.

Woolly pulled a small handheld device from his pocket and ran it over them. Lexi had been right about the wire. When he was satisfied, he opened the door. 'In you go.'

With no idea what they were walking into, Finn stepped in tight behind Lexi to a cloud of cigarette and cannabis smoke. Woolly and Skink followed. A dozen big guys in denim and leather crowded around a television on lounges and stools, and the spirited debate seemed to revolve around an ugly-looking cage fight. They eyed him and Lexi with brief interest before returning to the game.

'This way,' Woolly grunted.

He opened another door. In this room sat a table and chairs, plenty of beer and a poker game. Three men sat around the table and an empty chair with cards laid face down suggested Woolly might have been playing before their arrival had interrupted him. Two of the three got to their feet. One wore a sergeant-at-arms patch: this was their prime suspect in the murder of their unidentified victim. Another patch revealed the sergeant went by 'Rocco'. He stood at least two inches above Finn's six-foot-two and had possibly the largest arms Finn had ever seen. Woolly's patch, Finn noted, read 'Enforcer'. Both looked like they'd stepped straight out of a prison workout yard and neither of them were pretty, but the meanest face award had to go to the guy still seated and obviously in charge. Breen, he gathered.

They were waved into two extra chairs against the wall by the door with a 'Sit'. Finn stalled and stared just long enough to suggest he was no pushover before sitting impatiently next to Lexi as Breen looked him over, sizing him up. Breen's gaze moved to Lexi, spent some time there. Almost too long. Finally he spoke.

'You have the evidence?'

'On my phone,' Finn said.

'Woolly, get it.'

Woolly left the room, returned with two phones and handed Finn's back. Finn pulled up the pics, handed it over.

Breen took a look then handed the phone to the sergeant. 'Rocco, that our man?'

Rocco took a good look, nodded. 'Yeah, same fuckwit.'

Breen looked relieved. 'Excellent! Desy came through. I have to say, I'm happy to hear it. He's a handy guy to have around.'

'So we're square,' Lexi said. 'Where is he?'

Breen's eyes narrowed. 'Not quite.' He sat forward, elbows on knees. 'This is where I'd like to invite you to join us for a beer and a friendly chat. But … unfortunately … I'm not sure you two are who you say you are. Desmond didn't seem to be able to tell us much and I've never heard of either of you.'

'Well, fuck, I should hope not,' Lexi said, crossing her legs and flopping back in her chair.

'And yet I've seen you somewhere before, haven't I?' Again those mean little eyes raked over her.

Finn held his breath. Backup was one minute out. Would that be enough if this fell apart?

Lexi raised an interested eyebrow and appreciation glowed in her face. 'You remember?'

'That's quite the face you've got on you. Remind me.'

She leant forward, mimicking his pose. 'I hung around Combat Crew for a while. One of Suzie's girls.'

Breen sat up and slapped his thigh. 'Of course! You would have been so young. I couldn't quite place you. You've moved up in the world, I see.'

She shrugged. 'Surviving. And Breen, we had a deal. Where's Desmond?'

Breen's smile turned back to suspicion. 'Why do you want him so badly?'

'Dawny's a friend. She's worried.'

'He's fine.'

'I haven't even laid eyes on him. How do I know he's *fine*?'

Finn hoped Lexi knew what she was doing.

'Well, I'm going to be honest with you, Lexi,' Breen said, expression darkening.

The other guys suddenly sat straighter and glanced at Breen as though waiting for an instruction. Finn tried not to visibly tense, wondered if he had any chance against all of them. He only had a chair to work with. If he got in a couple of good swings and managed to stop anyone else from coming through the door, they might last the required minute or two until help arrived. But he wasn't confident.

'You bargained for Desmond like cops would over a hostage. And not knowing you, I gathered some of my boys together here tonight and decided I'd kill you both just to be safe.'

Finn's fingers closed over the sides of the chair as he put some extra weight in the balls of his feet.

'But now I discover we have a bit of a shared history. The good sort, right? So maybe you are legit and I find myself reconsidering.' He stared into space and took a long drink of his beer before his gaze snapped back. 'How about this. I've got a job I need doing. From what Dawny told us, you two should be perfect for it. You do it, I'll give Dawny back her Desmond. Then we're square.'

Finn's grip relaxed on the chair.

'You want us to work for you for free?' Lexi asked in disgust.

'And I won't kill you. For old times' sake. That's fair, isn't it?'

She considered him with a pissed-off scowl. 'I'll let you know when I know what the job is.'

Breen laughed, shook his head. 'Evan Blake. Heard of him?'

'Nup,' Lexi said.

Yeah, Finn thought. *Just this morning. Interesting.*

Breen caught the gleam of recognition on Finn's face and said, 'You have.'

'Disgraced councillor, right?' he asked. 'The guy misappropriated a couple of mill in government funds, took bribes to push through illegal business deals.'

Breen's forehead creased as he shook his head at Finn. 'Big words. Big, cop-type words. See, this one I can believe,' he said, nodding at Lexi. 'You, I just …' He shook his head again.

Finn realised his mistake and changed tack. 'Because I use big words? Because I sound smart? Being dumb tends to get you killed.'

'He thinks you're dumb?' Breen asked Lexi, who was staring, mouth agape.

'He'll pay for that later,' she promised, sounding a bit too genuinely angry. 'Look, does he scream "hired killer" to you?'

'No, that's my point.'

'And mine. We don't get caught. Where are we going to find Evan?'

Breen kept his eyes on Finn's for several more seconds before answering. 'He owns a trendy little wine bar and boutique accommodation in Erina. Tends to spend a lot of his time there. He likes women.' Another long look at Lexi, a smirk. 'A lot. There's a safe somewhere in his office suite. Don't leave without whatever files are in it.'

Finn opened his mouth to agree but Lexi cut in over him.

'That's a hell of an ask for "square",' she told Breen, 'so once it's done, you throw some more work our way. We're not cheap, but we're better than everyone else.'

Breen nodded thoughtfully. 'Perhaps. Sooner you get this done, the better. Tomorrow night is cheap drinks night. Cheap drinks, cheap chicks. He'll be there.' He got to his feet and gestured for Woolly to let them out. 'This could be the start of some very mutually beneficial business. Prove me right.'

CHAPTER NINE

Wednesday, March 23

Cass sat in the meeting room surrounded by the homicide and organised crime teams, listening to the next instalment of the *Brought to you by Lexi* drama.

Brighton was seated across from Finn, and it hadn't escaped her notice that the woman had been shooting him covert looks on and off since she'd come in. It was annoying. It hadn't escaped Lexi's attention either, but if the slight tilt of her mouth was anything to go by, she seemed to find it amusing. Finn, as far as Cass could tell, was oblivious.

'Why would Breen want Blake dead?' Rachael asked the room.

'And what's in that safe?' McCabe added.

'We should have tried to squeeze him for more details,' Finn said.

'Oh, save me from that!' Lexi muttered, suddenly a lot less amused.

'Sorry?'

'So you should be! *Disgraced councillor. Misappropriated government funds* ...' Lexi's voice imitated Finn's. 'Oh yes, how did you guess? I'm a cop!'

'How would you like me to speak? We can't all fit in with deadbeats with the ease you can.'

Cass bit hard on her lips against the grin as Lexi's eyebrows hit her hairline at the insult.

'Maybe it's better you don't speak at all. And just try calling me stupid again.'

He sighed. 'It was *dumb*, and I didn't—'

'Oh, so much better.'

Linc's snorting laugh made them both turn to him with a unified, 'What?'

Linc's face immediately straightened and he threw his hands up in peace.

'So,' Rachael said, regarding them like a mother would squabbling children, 'well done both of you on how you handled that. Breen was never going to turn Desmond over and there was nothing more that could have been done on that front, but, Lexi, it was smart to suggest you're open to working with him again. That could prove useful depending on how the investigation progresses. First we need to deal with Evan Blake. McCabe?'

'Yep.' He drummed his fingers on the table. 'Right. Let me catch you up. Blake owns several legitimate businesses but we believe he makes his real money as, yes, a middleman for organised crime. He puts clients in touch with illegal services, deals with logistics and keeps clients as hands-off as possible.'

'Contracting killers,' Finn said.

'Among other things, yes, we believe so. If Chaos Reigns is after him, they must think he's either muscling in on one or more areas of their business or he's taken a job that's in some way threatening to the gang or someone within it.'

'Unless they're doing a job for someone else,' Brighton suggested.

He pointed at her. 'Also possible.'

'Do we have any idea what might be in a safe he keeps on his business premises?' Finn asked.

'No, but perhaps a client or contractor list, a record of hits … all of the above?'

'So we get a warrant,' Brighton said.

'We don't have enough on him,' McCabe said.

'And if you go in there with a regular warrant demanding access to the safe, Breen's going to know we played him,' Finn said. 'They're likely to take it out on Desmond.'

'Not to be unsympathetic,' Brighton said, 'but this is one criminal we're talking about as opposed to a lot of lives we could potentially save by getting Blake and his contracted killers off the streets.'

'No life is expendable,' Rachael reminded her coolly. 'And we need Desmond for our homicide case.'

McCabe's phone pinged. 'Hold that thought, everyone.' He read the message on his phone. 'One of the phones located at the scene of the explosion that killed Thomas and Roberts contained proof the two men were dealing with Blake. There are multiple messages to and fro. I'll have to have one of my team do some cross-referencing, but it looks like jobs to me.'

'May I?' Rachael took the phone and scanned the screen, scrolled. 'They're talking about an Ourimbah address here … that's Lexi's. That was definitely a job.'

'These are the guys the Hamills hired to blow up my house?' Lexi asked.

Rachael passed her the phone. 'And now we know they got the contract through Blake.'

Lexi scanned the screen and handed it back.

'So *now* we have enough for a warrant,' Brighton said. 'We just can't use it without risking your witness.'

'What if …' Rachael stared thoughtfully at the far wall for a moment. 'I could ask Ed to petition the Supreme Court for a covert warrant. There's got to be a good chance of swinging one on this.'

'That would suit us both,' McCabe agreed.

'Remind me?' Lexi asked Rachael.

'A covert warrant lets us impersonate anyone we like to gain entry to the premises and allows us to conduct our search without Blake's knowledge.'

'Meaning you could use your existing cover to get inside Blake's unit,' McCabe said. 'No one watching on needs to know the police were ever there.'

'Hold on,' Lexi said. 'I said what I said last night to get us out of there alive, not so we could walk right back in. Breen was one step away from killing us. I might not have studied up on undercover 101, but I'm pretty sure we can't be playing the bad guys one minute, then running back to the police station the next. How do you know he didn't have us followed? Dawny gave them our names. I had news stories written about me over the Spider case. These people aren't stupid. We already took a huge chance trying to get Desmond back. Besides, Breen wants Blake dead. Won't Blake just cooperate?'

'No, you don't know this guy,' Brighton said. 'Blake is as dirty as it gets. Has a rap sheet as long as your arm and hates the cops. He has no idea who you are. None. And there's so much that could be gained. If you can get Blake and the contents of his safe out quietly, we could have him in custody, Desmond safe and a case building against Breen by this time tomorrow night—and you won't help?'

'If Breen finds out Blake's not dead and we go back in there, Desmond's anything but safe and neither are we.'

'So you stage the flat to look like a murder scene before you leave,' Brighton said, 'and you tell Breen you hid the body.'

Lexi took her time thinking about that. 'Let me get this straight. You want me to lure Blake into his unit, arrest him, convince him to open his safe, keep him under control and quiet while I stage a murder scene, then sneak him out of the unit very much alive under the noses of Breen's men, who are already suspicious and will no doubt be watching like hawks. Then I get to put myself right back in the same situation I barely got out of yesterday and hope that, this time, Breen keeps his word. Is there anything I've missed?'

'I'd be there to help,' Finn said.

Cass watched with interest. Lexi generally didn't let anyone get to her, but she wasn't herself today. The case had to be weighing on her, too, and as Brighton had only just stopped short of calling her a coward, Cass could understand the pissed-off expression and long-winded retort.

Lexi took a phone from her bag and slid it across the table. 'Why don't we take a look at this first, see what we find.'

Brighton caught it. 'What am I looking at?'

'I cloned Skink's phone.'

'When did you manage that?' Finn asked in astonishment.

'I wasn't playing with his crotch for fun. I had to slip my phone over his so it would work.'

McCabe laughed. 'Who can we get on that?'

'Neutron and I will sort it,' Lexi said.

'And the rest?' Brighton asked.

'No pressure,' Rachael said to Lexi.

'I'm in,' Finn said, earning an approving smile and a 'Thanks, Finn,' from Brighton.

Oh, could you be more obvious? Cass's gaze accidentally hit Lexi's and she saw her own thoughts mirrored there. The silent communication was almost amiable. A first for them.

Lexi stood abruptly and said, 'I need to think about it.' She walked out.

'What's wrong with her?' Linc asked. 'She's always up for this stuff.'

'It is a big ask,' Rachael said with a pointed look at Brighton. 'She's still recovering from the last case.'

Linc inclined his head in acknowledgement. 'You think she's lost her nerve?'

'She held it together pretty damn well last night,' Finn said. 'But she was as nervous as I've ever seen her going in.'

'She's still injured, still grieving a friend, still hasn't been cleared for general duties and here we are, throwing her straight back in the deep end of a joint homicide–organised crime investigation with ties to a past I'm sensing she'd rather forget,' Rachael said.

How much weight did Rachael's last point hold with Lexi? Cass wondered. Was Lexi as scarred from that time as she was? Lexi didn't even remember Cass, but Cass remembered Lexi. She remembered every detail of the people, that club, those events; they were as vivid in her mind today as they'd been when they happened. Lexi couldn't want her past dredged up any more than Cass did.

Unfortunately, Cass's time on the Cronin case with the Raptor Squad was a matter of public record. If she didn't divulge at least the bare facts, Rachael would no doubt find out during the course of the investigation and wonder why.

'Honestly, I think Lexi's right to want to stay out of it,' she told them. 'Are you aware Breen used to be vice president of Combat Crew?'

'How do you know that?' Finn asked.

'I came across the club on my first case in the Raptor Squad more than a decade ago. If Lexi's previously been involved with them, she wouldn't have to be scared to want to stay out of Breen's way, she'd just have to be relatively smart.'

'You're sticking up for Lexi?' Linc asked in mock shock.

'I'm voicing an opinion based on my experience with Breen and the previous MC.'

'We can't plan anything until we know that covert warrant's approved anyway,' Rachael said. 'Let her think it over. I'll talk to Ed.' She got to her feet. 'Excuse me.'

'We'll get out of your way,' McCabe said. 'Let us know when you have an answer.'

McCabe and his team filed out after Rachael, but Brighton hesitated in the doorway.

'Is everything all right, Olivia?' Finn asked.

'Yes, of course. I had a couple of questions jump out at me this morning after looking over the events of last night. If you have any time today, could I run through them with you?'

'I'm not sure what else I can tell you, but sure. When?'

'Ah … how about now?' she asked hopefully, tossing her hair prettily over one shoulder.

He checked his watch. 'I can do that.'

'Great, do you mind if we talk over some morning tea? I skipped breakfast.'

Finn got to his feet and collected his things. 'Lead the way.'

'Coffee date already,' Cass muttered. 'The woman moves fast.'

'What are you worried about?' Linc said. 'You're not interested in him.'

'She's a bit … full on.'

'And a lot attractive. Go, Finn.'

Cass couldn't help but laugh. 'I'm surprised *you* haven't pounced on the new detective.'

'I'm waiting for Lexi to figure out we're meant to be together.'

She blinked at him in surprise. 'You think Lexi … *really*?'

His grin was a mile wide. 'All the ladies get there eventually.'

'God help us if you ever develop an ego.'

Linc's banter kept the smile on her face as they settled down at their desks to work. There were hundreds of missing persons reports to go through in the hope their victim could be identified, and she wanted to do some digging into Breen. All she remembered was a mean, shifty-eyed bull terrier of a man, with thick-set musculature and a menacing, unhinged presence. She'd been lucky enough to only cross paths with him once, after her superiors in the Raptor Squad had interviewed him.

That had been her first day in the squad and her introduction to Gordon, the leader of the team, and his best mate and partner, Wallis. They'd had two other detective constables working with them, and she'd been the most junior member. The only female.

Gordon and Wallis had come out of the interview room that day and shaken hands with the man who had scared her from across the room as she'd been waiting to introduce herself. Then again, Gordon had been a living legend and his arrest record had been unmatched. She would have expected no less from the man than complete confidence in the face of any foe. She'd been in awe, ridiculously excited to be—albeit temporarily—working with him. So when, at the end of that first day, he'd invited her to get to know the other members over what they called their Humpday Drinks, she'd accepted.

The bar had been an obvious cop hangout, and she'd recognised a few faces as she'd entered through its oak and stained-glass doors. It had been busy, loud, and it had taken her several moments to work her way to the far end of the room to find Gordon outside in the beer garden. He'd been sitting on the top of a picnic table, jacket off, no tie, top buttons undone and sleeves rolled up. He'd had a beer in one hand and a cigarette in the other. Wallis was seated on the bench chair on one side, two other men she guessed were the rest of her team on the other.

When Gordon spotted her, he'd waved her over.

'Cassidy! You've met Wallis, this is Penham and Duke. Gentlemen, Lisa's going to be on the team while Mike's on leave. She's gonna help us bring down Cronin,' he added with a smirk.

She opened her mouth to say hello, was beaten to it by Penham's snuffled laugh into his beer.

'They really gave us a chick?' Duke asked Gordon. 'I thought you were taking the piss!'

'Nice to meet you, Cassidy,' Penham said, though his tone was suggestive rather than friendly. 'Is it true?'

An uncomfortable sensation settled in her stomach. 'Is what true?'

'Are you one of them les-bi-ans?'

Shock had her stumbling over her words. 'Wh-where did you hear that?'

'Well, are you or not?' Penham pressed.

They were all watching her expectantly. She wanted to shrink back, hide, run away. Why were they treating her like this? 'My private life doesn't have anything to do with my position here,' she finally managed.

Penham lifted his beer hand and pointed his finger at Wallis. 'That's a yes!'

'In the hand!' Wallis wriggled his fingers at Duke, who reluctantly slapped a twenty dollar note into them.

'Fine, but I'd like to argue that she probably just hasn't met the right man yet. That's right, isn't it, love?' Duke said.

Humiliation burned her cheeks. 'I … um …'

'Oh, yeah? Why don't you change her mind then, Dukey!' Penham teased.

Duke stood up, putting him in unnervingly close proximity to Cass. 'How 'bout that, love. Want me to change your mind?'

'I'll change it,' Penham said, knocking Duke out of the way.

She stepped back, tears threatening to erupt from her eyes. They were ruining everything. She looked to Gordon in helpless disbelief. He winked and grabbed both men by their shirts and pulled them away, forcing them to sit down as the backs of their knees hit the bench.

'Keep it in your pants, boys. You'll scare her off.'

Cass stood rigid, embarrassed, not sure what to do next. She reasoned they'd had several drinks. There was a chance they'd be mortified at their behaviour tomorrow. She hoped so. But what *now?* She needed a moment, just one, to pull herself back together.

'I'm thirsty,' she told them. 'How about I buy you gentlemen another round?'

Gordon smiled in approval and lifted his beer. 'That's the spirit! Four of the same, please, love.'

She headed over to the bar on shaking legs and ordered more beers for the men—she couldn't quite bring herself to think of them as her team—and decided that no, she couldn't go back out there. She was shaking enough to drop the beers and that would be mortifying.

'Is there any chance you could take these out to the men in the smoking area outside?' she asked the waitress and received a look suggesting she was dreaming.

'Yeah, in my spare time,' she was told before the flustered blonde moved on to her next customer.

'You'd better take those back yourself,' a voice said from beside her.

She recognised the woman from headquarters. Another team, a detective sergeant. 'Ah … I've got a headache. Been a big first day. Thought I'd get an early night.'

She smirked, shook her head. 'They giving you a hard time?'

'Actually,' Cass perched on the next stool, 'a bit. I think the beers might have gone to their heads, that's all. They're not being very appropriate.'

'They take the piss out of each other, they're gonna take the piss out of you. Worse, because you're a woman and a newbie. You want to prove you belong, you're gonna have to be able to handle more than a bit of drunken mouthing off.'

Maybe. She'd fought hard to get that position with Gordon. Was she going to blow it all by being a bit sensitive? Her parents had warned her she'd had too sheltered a life for what they called 'that cop stuff' and Cass was determined to prove them wrong. The only way to do that might be to toughen up. Fit in.

'It's happened to you?'

'When I started out. Not saying it's fair, not saying it's right, but you complain about these guys, you'll be taken off the team and good luck getting anywhere after that. My advice? Fit in as best you can, dodge as many bullets as possible. You get some rank behind you, you'll start to hold some sway. Just don't expect it to take you anywhere as far and as fast as it would a man. You can't handle that, you're in the wrong job.'

Cass dragged her consciousness back to the room. No, it hadn't been the job that had been wrong. Just the team. And what had followed had been some very dark days. That team, that case, had taught her a lot. She'd learnt that some cops will do anything to get convictions, will steamroll over anyone who threatens to get in the way of another star or another stripe on their shoulder. And she'd learnt that the consequences of working with those cops could be devastating.

But she'd put it all behind her and done her best to move on. Now Combat Crew were coming back to haunt her and Lexi was right in the middle of it. It had been bad enough that Lexi had been an unwanted constant reminder of that time for too long, but at least she hadn't made the connection.

But would she now? Would all this be enough to trigger in that sharp mind—Cass had to admit the woman had one of those—a memory of a young officer, much, much younger, before her hair changed to blonde and her figure filled out? And if it was, would she remember that day? That one, fleeting moment?

CHAPTER TEN

'This is not what I was expecting,' Finn heard Lexi tell Neutron. They were sitting in one of cyber's conference rooms with their heads in their computers and hadn't yet noticed him. 'Nice to know he loves his mummy though.'

'And women in general and … whoa!' Neutron said, sitting back and narrowing his eyes.

Lexi glanced at his screen. Did a double take. Frowned. 'That …' Her head slowly tilted sideways as though to see a different angle. The frown cleared. 'Oh, yeah. That's possible.'

Neutron didn't look convinced. 'But you wouldn't … haven't …'

Lexi winked. Neutron blushed.

Finn cleared his throat. 'Morning. Thought I might find you here.'

'Ah, hi,' Neutron said, sitting up straighter and closing something on his screen. 'Lexi and I were just, ah …'

'Going through Skink's phone,' Lexi said. 'He's a strange one—no surprise. His favourite things in the world are his mum, kinky teddy bears and unusual sexual positions.'

Neutron got to his feet, still blushing. 'I'm going to get a cup of water—tea—coffee, I mean. Anyone want one?'

'Yeah, sure, thanks,' Lexi said, a teasing gleam in her eyes. 'The coffee. Not the water or the tea.'

'I'm good,' Finn said, then dropped into a seat opposite to Lexi. 'Do you really have to embarrass him?'

'I love messing with him. He's so cute.'

'You tell him that, he'll probably pass out. Did you find anything useful on that phone?'

'Bits and pieces. Nothing on any drug importation—so far. Mostly just contacts, a pathway into a couple of private MC social media sites and some fight club talk. There'll be illegal betting attached, if anyone wants to go down that path. Nothing of any interest to the homicide investigation. But we're just beginning.'

'You think you could leave this to Neutron and come join our meeting?'

He caught the briefest flash of anxiety before she masked it. He could read her so well now that he often noticed the tiny giveaways she tried so hard to hide.

'Once I have my coffee in hand,' she said. 'But I'll have to get back to it. I'm not sure he can get through all this on his own. He's flat out on a really cool new program to stop some recent cyber-hacking attempts at HQ.'

Finn got to his feet. 'I heard several squads have been targeted in the last couple of weeks by people that seem to know what they're doing. I don't think homicide has been affected. Good to know he's working on it though.'

Lexi stood and picked up her computer then followed him to the door just as Neutron returned with two coffees in hand. 'Thanks,' Lexi said, taking the cup offered. 'I have a meeting but I'll catch up with you later? Good luck with Mario.'

'Mario?' Finn asked as they walked down the corridor.

'Like the little computer game guy that goes through all the different screen levels. That's kinda what Neutron's program does. It—'

'Never mind. I probably won't get it.'

'Where are we going, theirs or ours?'

'Ours,' he said, stepping into the lift to press the button to the eighth floor. 'How's Dawny?'

'Right at home. I'm already feeling like I'm the house guest.'

'I meant about not getting Desmond back.'

'It's hard to say. She doesn't do emotional. She just eats.'

As they were running out of time before the meeting, he decided he should bring up the issue of the warrant now. 'So … we got the covert warrant.'

Lexi's gaze dropped. 'Thanks for the heads up. I assumed you would.'

'What do you want to do?'

'Huh?'

'I'm not going to walk into that meeting and play let's gang up on Lexi. If you really don't want to do this, let me know and we'll work something else out.'

That surprised her and he wondered why. He didn't have to wait long for the answer.

'What would *Olivia* have to say about that?'

'I don't really care.'

'But she was so proud of you for saying you were in. Her face lit up all pretty and her eyelashes fluttered …'

'Oh, shut up,' he said. 'Yes or no?'

He heard her resigned sigh. 'Are you going to try and handle this by yourself if I say no?'

'Probably.'

'Then what do you think I'm going to say?' she asked and opened the door.

When they stepped into the room, McCabe's team and the rest of Rachael's were already waiting.

'Right,' Rachael said. 'Now that we're all here, we'll begin. First, I have a few general updates thanks to Cass and Linc from yesterday. Fingerprints from the gun came back with three matches. John Clarke,' she said, pinning a photo to the board. 'I'm assuming that's our Woolly. Then we have Daniel Carter, who I'm hoping Finn or Lexi can confirm,' Rachael said, putting another image next to the first, 'is Skink?'

'Yeah, that's him,' Finn said.

'Okay, and the third set of prints was obviously yours, Finn. So what do we know about these guys? Clarke left the navy back in 2018 after fifteen years of service as a helicopter mission commander. His wife got sick, the navy refused to pay for some of the more experimental treatments he applied for funding over and she died. He blamed the system. His social media records suggest he joined Chaos Reigns a year later, in 2019. Then we have Carter. Eighteen years old, a few speeding and one dangerous driving offence on record, along with two counts of petty theft and an assault charge while still a minor. We now know our prime suspect in our victim's murder is known as Rocco, but we have nothing else on him yet. The property at Eraring. It's a rental under Breen's name and has been for almost a decade. Speaking of Breen.' She put his image above the other two in the middle of the board. 'Fifty-year-old ex-army, ex-Combat Crew member. Medically discharged from the ADF after suffering from PTSD, depression and drug dependence issues following his service in the Iraq War. Known to suffer from severe violent episodes. He ended up doing a couple of years in prison from 2010 to 2012 for a glassing incident involving another Combat Crew member. A year after his release, Combat Crew disbanded and he was integral in reshaping the club under its new banner, Chaos Reigns, mostly using Combat Crew members that hadn't been implicated in the drug smuggling and gone to prison. Since then, it seems, he's stayed out of trouble.'

'Until now,' McCabe said.

'Until now,' Rachael echoed. 'So, we have the covert warrant if we need it. It's just about figuring out the best way to move forward from here.'

'I think it's pretty clear—' Brighton began.

'For *everyone*,' Rachael said.

Lexi looked around the table. Shrugged. 'Okay, whatever. I'll do it.'

A 'Thanks,' came from McCabe, along with general nods and agreement.

'I have no doubt at all the MC will have their spies in that wine bar, making sure Lexi and Finn are the real deal and that the job gets done,' Rachael said, 'so we need to make this look absolutely legit. We need to figure out the best way to get Finn and Lexi into the office with Blake. They will then issue the warrant and leave through the back with Blake and the contents of the safe. We'll take Blake into custody and copy any files we find in that safe before Lexi hands them over in exchange for Desmond.'

'I'm supposed to kill him, not take him for a drive,' Lexi pointed out.

'So you took him away and then killed him. We can mock up an off-scene death shot if they want proof. What you won't be doing is messing around onsite trying to stage anything,' Rachael said firmly.

'I've done more looking into Blake, which might help with that plan of attack,' McCabe said. 'Breen was on the money with his take on Blake. He's a well-known womaniser. He had several affairs while in government. Openly bragged to a colleague that he likes them, and I quote, "drunk and horny and preferably someone else's". It's the power trip for him as much as a conquest.'

'That makes things easy,' Lexi said.

'He's not pretty,' Brighton said, sliding Lexi a photo.

Finn looked over Lexi's shoulder to see a pock-faced, two-chinned slug. 'You're not kidding,' he muttered.

'So if you wander in there and do your thing on him, Jabba's gonna be suspicious,' Linc said.

'Her thing?' Brighton asked.

Finn ignored her questioning gaze.

'You're right,' Lexi said. 'He doesn't want a paid escort. He wants a challenge.'

'Your thing is being an escort?' Brighton said.

Lexi's smile was tight-lipped. 'Not anymore. Supposedly.' Then to the room, she said, 'So we give him his challenge. I'll take Finn in with me to start with, he can call me dumb again, I'll get all upset and Blake can cheer me up over a few too many drinks.'

'Then I'm going to have to somehow get into that office,' Finn said.

'We'll work on that,' Rachael said. 'Okay, let's get on with our morning and we'll meet again this afternoon with final details.'

When McCabe's team had left the room, Rachael continued addressing her team. 'Cass and Linc, I need you to keep going with missing persons. We need that ID on our victim. Lexi and Finn, you two should work out a plan of attack for tonight, run through a few possible scenarios.'

'Will do,' Finn said.

'Lexi, are you sure you're comfortable to go ahead? I don't want any outside pressure making you feel like you need to do anything you don't want to do.'

'It's all good,' Lexi said. 'But you're going to need to hand over a credit card. I need to go shopping for something classy with a touch of slutty.'

Rachael smiled. 'Give me five. I'll come with you.'

CHAPTER ELEVEN

The shoreline of this section of Erina Creek was shady and tranquil. The hanging branches of trees touched the water and a winding concrete path cut through a neat lawn, drawing in kids on bikes, dog walkers and joggers. Spanning a good length of the space between the waterfront and the road sat a long line of pretty two-storey accommodation units attached to a fancy-looking bar that spilled out into a patio space for drinking and socialising. A family haven by day, a functional strip for the loud, drunk and obnoxious by night.

Cronin took it all in, wandered the path, studied the buildings. Council workers had been here earlier cleaning up the bank, but their machinery now stood empty, resting in the shade. Between the passing of two joggers moving in unison and the approach of a teen with some sort of ancient white dog, he let himself into the unit closest to the bar and looked around.

'Ah, Mr Blake. You have a good office.' A decanter of something amber sat on a cabinet shelf and he poured himself a generous helping, then walked around a solid oak desk, shifted a carelessly thrown jacket with an expensive-sounding label and made himself at home in the executive office chair. 'Very nice.'

'He's going to catch you,' she warned him.

'He won't.' Cronin waved his glass around the empty room. 'He's not here.' He sipped his drink, decided it was whiskey—something smooth and mellow; expensive, like the furnishings: the tasteful leather lounge, the delicate carved woodwork on the library, the large TV with its pretty screensaver artwork by da Vinci. The man considered himself cultured. It was a lie. Still, the façade was pleasant.

He pulled the clay heart from his pocket and turned it round and round in his fingers. There would be no paint left soon, just the memory of it. Sometimes, a memory was all one was left with. Where should he place the bomb? Under the desk? Blake may see it as he comes in, whatever time that would be. Traditionally, Blake would spend Friday nights prowling for an easy-to-impress fuck. A woman drawn more to money and the illusion of power and danger than the man himself, as the man himself was a fat, salivating worm with small eyes and a big mouth. Blake had always had a lust for blood—other people's—and the money it made him. Blood money, dirty money.

There was a code, even among criminals. The fat worm had broken it. 'So the fat worm must pay,' he told her, raising his glass in a toast.

'You won't feel any better.'

'Maybe upstairs,' he said, ignoring her and heaving himself out of the chair. Perhaps she was right—he had never enjoyed killing. But there was satisfaction to be found in knowing Vic and Seth were dust. That they would no longer enjoy their families or destroy anyone else's. It was justice that they died by their own explosives.

He walked heavily up the stairs—he was always tired these days—and found himself in the bedroom. A king-sized bed, neatly made, curtains drawn, lights dimmed. He touched the black satin fabric, rubbed its smoothness between his fingers. Everything was staged for a lover, from the tight hospital corners, no doubt prepared by the cleaners who serviced the holiday accommodation suites, to the plump pillows and unlit candles lining the dresser. He spied an ensuite larger than most bathrooms and a smile touched his lips as he considered placing the bomb in the cistern. At least part of the man would find its way into the sewer, where he belonged. But he had no wish for this man to die not knowing what had hit him. That was too quick. Too kind.

Cronin made his way back downstairs to where she was waiting for him. 'There'll be too many people nearby. He'll call for help.'

No. He wouldn't have that opportunity. 'He'll wet his pants and do as he's told. You worry too much.' He decided on the desk after all. He'd tape it underneath the expensive jacket. Blake wouldn't find it until it was too late.

CHAPTER TWELVE

I arrange the long red dress Rachael picked out into a modest enough state and carefully step out of the car into the carpark of Gosford Police Station, where Rachael's organised some space to work out of during the operation. It's where Blake will hopefully be spending whatever's left of the night before being transferred straight into interrogation tomorrow morning.

I adjust the dress again after collecting my purse and closing the door. The slit up the sides is almost waist high and I can't bend over without it hugging everything almost indecently. There's nothing I can do about the bandage on my hand but I should check my make-up; it's working hard to cover the remnants of bruising on my face.

'Good?' Finn asks.

'Yep,' I say, and follow him to the station doors. I'm on edge, not really talking. It's not that I don't trust him—I know he's more than capable of keeping us both alive—but his acting skills could do with some serious work.

He's shot me a couple of quizzical looks on the way over, so I'm not surprised when he says, 'You're quiet. Are you worried about Blake?'

'More the situation in general,' I answer carefully.

'Which part?'

I sigh. 'The acting part.'

'Because of what happened with Breen? I thought it ended up fine. And look, about the dumb thing. I wasn't making any reference to you at all when I said it. You know that, right?'

I glance sideways, and because annoying him might just save our butts, keep my tone cool. 'Do I?'

He frowns. 'I was trying to be convincing in the heat of the moment and I didn't think through my answer.'

'You're right about that.'

He holds me up at the entry and looks me in the eye. 'You're being petty. What gives?'

I remove my arm from his grasp. 'Oh, so now I'm petty *and* dumb?'

The frown deepens, then clears. His lips twitch. 'You're trying to piss me off.'

I roll my lips over my smile. 'We're supposed to have the sort of argument two people madly in love who currently think they hate each other have. That's as mean as it gets. I want to see if you actually own an argue.'

'Oh, I own an argue,' he says dramatically, following me inside.

'Sure? Because I don't think I've ever really seen it.'

'Because it's vicious,' he whispers. 'I tend to keep it locked away.'

'Well, you need to set it loose because I need to be able to piss you off and you have to get mad. Think of something that really does piss you off about me. I don't care. This needs to be believable.'

'You're generally able to piss me off with no trouble at all.'

'And yet we don't argue,' I say, then pause to ask the constable on the desk where we need to be.

'We're not arguing now?' Finn says as we're shown through.

'A mild warm-up, maybe.'

'Mild? Would you prefer I raise my voice a little?' He does, earning a startled glance from the officer taking us to the back of the station. 'Would that help, Miss Director of the How-to-Argue Police?'

I choke out a laugh. 'I think you're beyond help, honestly.'

'I hate your shoes.'

'Wh— Because your taste completely sucks! I hate your tie—because again, your taste completely sucks.'

'It might suck but at least I own some.'

'If that were true your hair wouldn't look like that.'

The constable pushes the door open, obviously keen to escape.

I say, 'Thank you,' as Finn gasps.

'Now that's a step too far. There's nothing wrong with my hair!'

I spot a couple of dozen police gathered in the room. Rachael and McCabe are perched on a desk, looking over something on a computer screen and Brighton is talking to Cass. I catch the whistle from Linc, spot him in the corner of the room with some uniformed officers a second before he slaps a hand to his heart and falls to his knees. Cute. I blow him a kiss.

'Man, you get all the good gigs,' Linc complains to Finn.

'You want to go in with her? Be my guest,' he says, still fussing with his hair.

'I'm not sure I could think straight.'

'Hi,' Rachael says. 'Are you ready?'

'I think so,' I say as Finn finally leaves his hair alone.

'Hi, Finn,' Brighton says. 'Lexi.'

McCabe echoes the greeting and points us at a couple of seats. 'Let's run through a few last-minute details.' He shows Finn a printed Google image of the bar and accommodation. 'This is where Blake's office and living quarters are located. There's a back door here,' he says, circling the spot in red pen. There's been council work going on along the riverbank here all week with vehicles and heavy machinery, so I'll have a council vehicle parked on the grassed area at his back door and he won't blink an eye. Keys will be in it. That's the vehicle you'll take him away in. We'll make sure his back door is unlocked so you slip in and wait for them. You know what to do from there.'

Finn examines the printout carefully. Nods. 'Got it.'

Brighton sits herself on the other side of Finn. 'We've got everything covered from our end,' she tells him. 'You've got nothing to worry about.'

'We'll be fine,' Finn tells her. His phone pings and he checks it. 'Sorry,' he tells Rachael. 'It's Ava. I was supposed to call. I'll just be one sec.'

'Go for it.'

Brighton takes advantage of Finn's daughter's interruption and scoots over onto Finn's seat. 'How are you feeling about tonight?' she asks.

'Fine.'

'I really thought you were going to bail on us.'

'Did you?' It's difficult to take her seriously when she spends all her time simpering over Finn.

'Well, I mean, you weren't keen. Then I found out about your background and I had to wonder if that made things easier or more difficult.'

Oh, for fuck's sake. 'And did you reach a conclusion?'

She's clearly not sure how to take that, but after a brief hesitation, says, 'No. To be honest, I wasn't sure how much to believe. The guys in the team were talking about what they'd been told and you know how these things get exaggerated.'

'Yeah, well, nothing brings a group of arseholes together faster than something that's none of their business.'

She laughs. 'Truth. Look, you're obviously a no-bullshit kind of person, so I'm going to ask straight up. Are you and Finn just friends?'

Ah, of course. 'Yep.'

She smiles. 'Good to know.'

'What's good to know?' Finn asks, coming back.

'That Lexi's good to go,' Brighton says.

'Right, let's make sure we're all on the same page,' Rachael says, following with all the whens and wheres and what to dos, along with contingency plans that convince me everything really is covered.

'Okay,' McCabe says to Finn and me when Rachael's finished and there are no questions. 'Are you two ready?'

Finn gets to his feet and hits me with a wicked gleam. 'Are you sure you understood the instructions?'

'You just worry about your hair. I'll take care of the rest.'

When his hand automatically goes to his head, I smirk. His eyes narrow in on mine. 'Thanks, *sweetheart*.'

The choice of endearment is deliberate. We both know the last person to call me that wanted me dead.

'Ah … What's going on?' Rachael asks.

'I'm just a poor, long-suffering husband,' Finn says with a sigh.

'And I'm not sure what else you expect from me, Rachael,' I tell her. 'I'm shallow enough to sleep with a bashed crab in order to pay back this one because he hasn't told me he likes the dress I spent hours choosing for him.' I wipe away a fake tear.

'Always after the next compliment!' Finn complains as his gaze hits the roof. 'The dress is fine.'

'Careful, baby,' I murmur, stepping in to gently touch a finger to the side of his mouth. 'You're drooling.'

He snatches my hand and tucks it into his arm, then growls, 'Let's go.'

I smile to myself, pretty sure we're exactly where we need to be to make this work.

'Be careful!' Rachael calls after us.

Erina is a busy place, with more entertainment venues and restaurants than you'll find just about anywhere else on the coast, and cheap night at the wine bar is a popular attraction. There's plenty of full booths and tables both in the bar and out in the garden overlooking the creek. Two waitresses flash past with trays of empty glasses but plenty more still line the tables. It's noisy. How are we going to cause a fuss over all this?

'What do you want to drink?' Finn asks.

'JD.'

'It's a wine bar.'

'Ugh. Fine. Whatever you're having.'

He shouts an order to a bartender who's bouncing between customers like a yo-yo and a minute later hands me something white. I take a sip. It'll do. I look around for our target. I can't see the bashed crab anywhere. We move around the room for a few minutes, then head outside.

'What do we do if he doesn't show?' I ask. 'How long do we wait?'

'He'll be here. Enjoy your wine.'

'I'm not, though. I'm struggling to even pretend I can drink this shit.'

'You— Right. Wait here, keep looking.' He takes my glass and disappears.

I feel conspicuous just standing on the spot, no drink, no partner, so I wander some more, move closer to the river. There's a roar of laughter from a group of young men sitting on the bank, a shouted drink order from one mate to another, then a squeal draws my attention to my left and oh, there he is. By the looks of things, he's just touched up the giggling redhead, who seems more flattered than furious. No clue how that's possible. I keep my eye on him until another glass is pressed into my hand.

'What the—what is that?' I ask of the flamboyant pinkish-orange work of art.

'They also do cocktails. That one's based on scotch.'

'My hero. Oh, and our guy's over there with his back to us.'

Finn follows my gaze to where Blake's moved on to chatting up another couple of female patrons.

'Let's see if you can divert him from the brunettes.'

The look I shoot at him is pure offence. I take a long sip of the cocktail—not bad—and saunter over.

It's marginally quieter here. I sit on one of the sandstone blocks that separate the garden from the river and continue to sip my drink. How long has it been since I've had a cocktail? I had a client who used to buy them for me. A long, long time ago.

Blake is checking me out as he talks to the other ladies and I deliberately shift so that my dress slides away to expose the length of my leg. Finn sits close by and follows the movement with his gaze, his eyes heating to molten as they settle on mine.

Uh … I didn't know he was capable of that look and, fuck, it's like being hit by a cricket bat.

He leans in, his fingers teasing my exposed thigh, sending sparks shooting in all directions. 'Think you'd like to play along?' he whispers.

I blink, almost choke on my cocktail and refocus. Blake is still watching with interest.

'Do you think I could have another drink?' I ask.

Finn pulls back, his expression a thin-lipped snarl of disapproval. 'You're not even finished that one yet. Really?'

I change the plan, decide to play the damsel in distress from the get-go and in contrast to Finn's raised voice, keep mine quiet. 'I … yes, please.'

'Oh, what a surprise, we've been here all of five minutes and you're already doing your best to drink the place dry.' He gets to his feet, waving his hands around to illustrate his temper. 'Did you come here to spend time with me? Or drink until you pass out? As usual!'

He's attracting plenty of stares, including Blake's. 'I—I just wanted one more.'

'It's never just "one" more! You're a bloody alcoholic and I'm sick of it!'

I look down at my glass, my chin coming up. 'It never bothered you before!'

'It *always* bothers me! I thought the drinking and the drugs … I thought it would stop. But it hasn't! And it won't, will it? Not even for me. You're going to kill yourself and you couldn't care less!'

Wow, his acting skills seem to have improved dramatically. Or is this the 'something' I told him to choose that really does piss him off?

'Please don't make a scene.'

He looks around as though he hadn't noticed he was, then shakes his head. 'You know what? Drink all you want. Make your own scene.'

'Where are you going?' I call as he turns to leave.

'Somewhere else.'

He stalks away and I stare dejectedly back into my glass.

'Mack, the lady needs a refill.'

I look up, pretend to be startled and see a waiter rushing off to comply. 'Oh. Thank you. But I shouldn't.' I look back in the direction Finn took.

'Why not? He told you to drink all you want,' Blake says, sitting in the spot Finn had vacated. 'Enjoy yourself.'

I consider him through my lashes. White teeth flashing a big smile, arrogance written all over him. I smile back shyly. 'Who are you?'

'Evan Blake,' he says, holding out his hand. 'I own this place.'

My eyes go wide. 'Really?' I take his hand, allow his sweaty palm to caress my fingers before letting it go. 'I—I'm Lexi.'

Mack reappears with another cocktail and hands it to me. Fuck, not sure how many of these I can drink.

Blake lifts his own drink and I tap mine to it. 'A pleasure to meet you.'

I let him ramble on while he supplies me with a third cocktail. I'm developing a pleasant buzz but whatever sugary mix is in them is trashing my stomach. I need to move this along. Surely Finn's in place by now. I deliberately start to sway on my makeshift seat, stumble over my words, then object when yet another cocktail is placed in front of me. Blake puts it in my hand. I giggle and take it, my mock-drunk gaze moving between his beady little eyes and his big mouth like he's Christmas.

'How does such a gorgeous woman end up with such an arsehole of a husband?' he asks me.

I sigh. 'He seems to have lost interest in me. I think he might even be having an affair.' I bang my glass down drunkenly. 'Sometimes I feel like I should pay him back.'

He rubs a hand up and down my arm in a creepy, comforting gesture. 'Sounds fair to me.'

'But then … oh, I don't know. I wouldn't have the confidence to go looking for someone for that. Besides, it's wrong.'

I make him work on changing my mind for another few minutes before I decide to let him win and we stumble along a well-lit path to where a row of units sit along the water's edge. He leads me to the first one, marked 'manager', then straight past his office and up the stairs to his bedroom like it's a done deal.

Finn appears behind us as Blake swoops his head down to kiss me.

'Not a chance in hell,' Finn says, weapon drawn. 'Get your hands off her.'

Blake spins. 'What are you doing in here?'

'Back. Up.'

Blake lifts his hands and takes a step. 'Now listen, mate, she came on to me. You know what these women are like! She told me you two were over. You can have her! I've got plenty more on the line.'

'Appreciate that, but my name is Detective Sergeant Finn Carson, homicide. You're under arrest. Turn around and put your hands behind your back.'

'What? What is this?'

Finn repeats the instruction when Blake doesn't immediately comply.

'Okay! Just don't fucking shoot me.'

Blake raises his hands as Finn steps in, then at the last minute crashes into him, sending them both sideways. I lunge at Blake and, in his rush to escape, he trips and tumbles back down the stairs. I fly after him, Finn on my heels. I hear a thud and see Blake in a heap on the ground. With too much momentum to stop, I leap over him, only to be caught jarringly around the throat as I land and am dragged back. A gun digs into my cheek.

As I gasp for breath I hear, 'Be good, little Lexi. And you'll live.' At the same time as I register there's only one person on the planet who ever called me that, my mind argues that it's impossible. Cronin's supposed to be in prison.

Finn appears at the bottom of the stairs and, spotting us, freezes. 'Just … stay calm.' He slowly lifts his hands, gun dangling from his fingers. 'Don't hurt her. I'm putting the gun down.' He bends slowly and places it on the floor, then kicks it out of the reach of Blake in case he wakes up.

'Cuff your hand to his through the stair rail and toss the keys!' Cronin orders.

'Okay.' Finn does as he's told. 'I don't know what beef you've got with this guy, but we've got one too. Why don't you let her go?'

Cronin ignores the request and nods at Blake. 'Give him a kick. I need his attention.'

'Hey,' Finn says, nudging Blake. 'Blake!'

Blake gets himself into a sitting position, swaying slightly as his eyes open. They lock onto the man behind me and the swaying stops. Everything stops.

In the silence, Blake breathes out, 'You!'

'Who ordered it?' Cronin asks quietly. 'Who was it?'

Blake's stunned face closes up. 'Dunno what you're talking about.'

'Kick him again! Make him tell you!'

Finn lifts Blake's head up when it starts to loll. 'You might want to answer him.'

Blake grins drunkenly. 'Fuck you.'

The gun barrel is removed from my cheek and pointed at Blake. Cronin fires.

'Fuck!' Blake shouts, coming to with a jolt as blood spills from his thigh. He clutches at it, does his best to stop the bleeding, but it's pouring out from under his hands and pooling around him at an alarming rate. Cronin's hit the femoral artery. I figure Blake's got minutes, if he's lucky, to live.

'Who ordered it!'

I can see Finn looking at his weapon and I widen my eyes to tell him 'No!' with my gaze.

'You got those two bombing bastards,' Blake pants. 'How much blood do you want on your hands?'

'Only the guilty ones.'

'I'm just a businessman.'

'You're just scum! Who was it!'

Blake huffs out a laugh, his pale, sweaty face contorted with pain. 'You'll never know.'

'He's bleeding out,' Finn says. 'If we don't stop it, he'll die.'

'Oh, he's going to die!'

My neck is released as the gun shifts position to the back of my head. I hear a whoosh, see a jacket hit the floor. There's a beep. Finn's whole body tenses, his eyes looking somewhere behind me.

I risk turning my head and my heart stops. I see the clay-like block that's rigged to a timer set to trigger in 58, 57, 56 …

'Tell me who ordered it!' Cronin roars.

But Blake's eyes close and he falls over, unconscious. As his hands fall from his leg, blood pumps from the wound in decreasingly powerful bursts.

'Wake him up!'

Finn leans over Blake, but the blood flow is stalling, becoming a dribble. Finn struggles to find a pulse. 'He's gone.'

'Arghh!' Cronin complains. 'We need to go.'

I'm being towed towards the back door.

'No—wait! What about Finn?' I scream. 'Cronin, please! He's not guilty of anything!'

There's a moment of hesitation, then I'm pushed forward. 'Go, then!'

I hear the back door open but I'm too busy searching for the keys to take notice. Where did they go? Under the dresser. I risk a glance at the bomb. Thirty seconds.

'Lexi, there's no time! Get out of here!' Finn orders.

I try and move the dresser but the thing is attached to the wall. I slide onto my stomach and look, see the keys right at the back. I stretch my arm out as far as I can. It barely fits under there and manoeuvring is next to impossible. 'I've almost …' I touch them with one finger, try to pull them towards me, lose them, try again.

'Lexi! I said get out!'

'Got them!' I scramble back to my feet and get the key into the cuffs with my trembling fingers. They click open.

I'm lifted off my feet as Finn grabs me and bolts through the open back door. He only makes a couple more strides before the world explodes.

CHAPTER THIRTEEN

'Is he dead?'

'I dunno.'

'Push him off.'

A heavy weight lifts off me and suddenly I can breathe.

I feel an annoying tapping on my cheek. 'Hey! You alive?'

The words slowly penetrate as I try to make sense of what happened. I become aware of heat and smoke, of noise, sirens, yelling. I'm lying in the grass. My ears are ringing and aching. I feel like I've been hit by a truck.

'Hey!'

'Yeah,' I rasp and wonder if Finn is okay. He must have taken the brunt of the explosion. 'Yeah. I'm—'

'Good.'

I'm dragged to my feet. Something that smells of dust scratches my face as it's shoved over my head. I reach for it in confusion, realise my arms are trapped by whoever's on either side of me. 'Hey! What are you doing? Let me go!'

I dig my heels into the ground as I'm towed towards the sound of an idling vehicle, but I'm shoved inside. I crash onto the floor, my face hitting what feels like rubber matting as a door slams.

'Careful!' a voice snaps but I'm thrown again as the vehicle takes off. I hear police cars whizz past. My dazed mind struggles to keep up with what's going on as my arms are wrestled behind my back. I hear the zip of a cable tie and do my best to bridge my hands a second before the plastic bites into my wrists and I'm dragged into a sitting position.

I force back my rising panic. I need to think. I take some breaths, slow them down.

I'm in a vehicle with what I think is a long bench seat against the side. Possibly a van? That idea alone has my terror skyrocketing again. Last time … No, don't spiral. *Think*. What else? I smell diesel, leather, cologne, sweat. I hear the rasp of a booted foot as someone shifts in the space with me. I see nothing. Can I get my hands free? I push my wrists together as tight as I can and start to saw my hands backwards and forwards.

What do these people want with me? My heart is pounding heavily in my chest and I can't breathe under this bag or whatever it is. It's claustrophobic.

'Get this fucking thing off my head!' I half-demand, half-panic.

'Or what?' comes the deep-voiced reply.

There's humour in that voice. It pisses me off. The anger helps with the fear. Marginally. I rub my jaw against my shoulder in an effort to dislodge the bag. 'Or I'll get the fucking thing off myself. What do you want?'

'You sure it's her? We didn't get a real good look,' another male voice asks.

'You're not even sure you've got the right fucking person?' I gasp. 'What kind of morons are you!'

'Yeah.' The original voice, a laugh. 'That's her.'

Okay, I'm pretty sure I know *that* voice. An image flashes in my mind of a blond giant in black leather. A few too many tatts, way too many muscles and rough good looks that have no doubt been ruined from too much fighting in the intervening years. Cronin's old sergeant-at-arms, his right-hand man. As I've just been rudely reunited with Cronin, that would make sense.

'Zander?'

The bag is ripped from my head. 'I see joining the cops hasn't settled you down any.'

I blink rapidly against the darkness of the space then a torch is focused on my face. I squint to shield my eyes. 'What am I doing here?'

'Nice to see you too.'

'You shoved a bag over my head, threw me in here and tied me up. There are nicer ways to say hello!'

'Still breathing, aren't ya?' the one beside me rasps out. I think it's Woolly. What's Woolly doing with Zander? 'Get that bag back on her head.'

His breath is in my face. It smells like beer and something garlic. I shift as far sideways as I can to escape it. 'Fuck off,' I snap. The torch is still on me but Zander's fallen silent.

'Where's Cronin?'

'How would I know?' Zander asks.

'How would … You were just there!'

'I was there to make sure you did the job on Blake. I saw you go in, saw the place go up. That's it.'

I suspend my disbelief in an attempt to get myself out of this. 'You're gonna have to let me go if you want those files. A block of C4 got in the way of the retrieval.'

'We've got our orders. You're coming with us. Breen wasn't happy to find out you're a cop.'

The breath halts in my chest, chokes me. This is as bad as it gets. I wince as the bandage on my hand shifts and I manage to pop a thumb out of the tie. 'How does he know that?'

'It wasn't difficult to find out.'

'But you were Crew. You're telling me you're in this—what was it? Chaos Reigns, now? With *Breen*?'

There's a short silence before he says, 'I'm with the club.'

'The club created by Breen after screwing Cronin—ow!' I exclaim as Woolly smacks me over the head.

'Have some respect!'

'Do you ever brush your teeth?' I complain.

'You want another one?' he growls.

'So where are we going? To see Breen or straight to some swamp somewhere to sink me in?' I wish I was joking, but the possibility is real.

'Family reunion,' Zander says after so long I don't think he's going to answer me.

The panic has turned to a sick roiling in my gut. I decide I'm probably still dead, it'll just take a bit longer and some nasty conversation first. Then again, the more rational part of my brain argues, Breen still needs those files. Maybe I can use that.

Everywhere I look I'm seeing an afterimage of that damn light. 'Can we lose the torch? Please?' I ask.

'You want to sit here in the dark?'

'I want the damn light out of my eyes. I think being blown up might have given me a headache.'

'Stop bitching,' Woolly says.

Fuck this. Zander and I were friends once. Close friends. That was more than a decade ago. And even then, I'd never have been stupid enough to try and get between him and the club, but I need to at least get him onside. I take a chance and spring from my spot, do an awkward spin, stumble and fall down next to him.

'What the fuck!' Woolly objects.

'Leave her be,' Zander says. 'She's not going anywhere.'

Though I still have a dark spot bouncing around in my vision, now that I'm facing him and the torch is off me, I glare at Woolly. If someone dressed Hagrid in leather and shrank him a couple of feet, Woolly would be his doppelgänger. He's snarling at me and I can only hope I'm not left alone with him at any point.

'So are you all right or what?' Zander asks.

'Oh, now you care?' I feel sick, my ears are hurting and my head's a bit woozy, but I think most of what hurts was from Finn landing on me when the bomb went off. That life-saving tackle didn't do my already injured ribs any favours. 'Did you see Finn?'

'We pulled a guy off you.'

'Was he alive?'

'No clue.'

And could you care any less? I've got my right hand out of the tie as far as my knuckles. One more wriggle and it'll be free. I'd rather jump from the moving vehicle than face Breen as a cop. I seriously consider it, wonder if the door would open, how fast I could get through it. But the brick walls guarding me are too close. I doubt

I'd even get my hand on the door. I try to think of something else I can do, come up blank.

By the time the vehicle crawls to a stop I'm sick with dread. I tamp it down as best I can. Showing fear or weakness won't do me any good here. I know how these people work. The old club had been home for a while. Not that I was ever a member—women aren't allowed that privilege. Can't wear the colours, can't ride. But I'd hung around, tagged along, and those of us who worked for the club or had partners in it were part of a larger family of sorts. A fucked-up family, but the only one I'd ever known.

I hear voices and the rattle of metal, a gate opening. Then we're rolling through. I take a covert look at Zander. His face is neutral, no emotion, no hint as to what would come next. I have the sudden desperate urge to beg. To remind him he had been the one who'd started me on cyber. Who'd sat me next to his brother Nate and told him I had skills, to teach me, before backing me for a position with Cronin. He'd played in a band that had never gotten further than the corner of the old clubhouse and had made his money through club fights, and when I'd needed to beat the shit out of something, he'd taught me how to do it on drums. It's all flooding back. Some of it was hell, but it wasn't all bad. And lots of what was good had come from knowing Zander and Nate and their father.

So, yeah, as pathetic as I know it is I want to beg, I don't. Because Zander was also the guy whose first loyalty had always been to the club. To Cronin. The one who'd follow his brothers to the grave, the one I saw shoot a friend because of a disloyalty to the president. The one Cronin had always got to handle his problems. And cops have always been problems.

Woolly stands by the door as it opens. He jumps out first then Zander gets up and I have no choice but to step out. Gravel crunches underfoot and the large security gates scrape through it again as they close.

'Let's go.' Woolly grabs my arm with biting fingers while Zander stops to talk to someone by the gate.

Woolly drags me—there's no point making it easy—towards a long green shed. Light spills out from an open roller door. Where are we? I should have paid more attention to how long it took to get here, the stops, the turns.

'Move, bitch,' he warns as I dig my heels in to take stock and work out what to do.

My plan's not great, but as no other option exists, I slide one hand the rest of the way out of the cable tie and deliberately trip. I slip off one heel, surge up, send it hurtling towards Woolly's face. He manages to get a hand between his eye and the spiked heel but lets me go in the process.

'Hey!'

I kick off my other heel before sprinting barefoot through the sharp stones to a stretch of grass that recedes into darkness. Ahead of me is an eight-foot mesh fence that divides the property from the silhouette of trees against the night skyline. I hear footsteps and throw a quick glance over my shoulder to see Zander coming at me like a rugby forward. He's on me in seconds. As he snags my dress, I try every evasive move I learnt at the academy to get free. But nothing's working.

'Is that the crap they teach you when you join the cops?' he says, easily overpowering me.

'Let me go!' I gasp, my ribs complaining about being driven into his shoulder as he picks me up and starts walking back.

'Anyone worth their salt knows those drills you've been taught backwards, knows where to expect you to strike.'

'He didn't!' I say as Woolly approaches, holding one of my heels like a weapon. He's swearing at the top of his lungs.

'Bitch fucking cunt I'm gonna—'

'Learn how to hold on to a girl?' Zander cuts in. 'Give me the shoe, Woolly.'

'I nearly lost a fucking eye!'

Zander swoops down with barely a hitch in his stride to collect the second one. 'The instep's hard to avoid even when you know it's coming,' he carries on conversationally. 'But you need to alter your routine from there.'

'What?' I gasp. 'You're about to get me killed, what the fuck does it matter?'

He puts me back on my feet in front of the shed and hands me my shoes. 'You want to put these back on and walk in there like a lady?'

I snatch them and glare at him before slipping them back on, then I'm marched under the open roller door and faced with a very basic clubhouse. A bar at one end, pool table, darts, a couple of lounges, some tables and chairs and bench space packed with supplies, a barbecue and a spa in the far corner. It has nothing on Combat Crew's old place. Then I spot them: Breen and Rocco at the bar, getting to their feet.

Zander's chatter had me wondering if maybe I would survive this, but the look on Breen's face tells me I'm dead.

CHAPTER FOURTEEN

Finn heard the sirens above a roar that snapped and popped and emitted an uncomfortable heat. He opened his eyes to a confusing red glow and felt the burn of smoke as he sucked in a sharp breath. He rolled onto his side and groaned as his body complained, trembled, with the effort. A few more breaths and everything became steadier. He clasped a hand to the side of his head where a tender lump radiated painfully from his skull and forced himself to sit up.

The bomb. He focused his eyes and shielded them against the inferno. Parts of the structure had collapsed, debris, mostly glass and splintered wood, covered the area around him. The fire was spreading quickly, the heat becoming unbearable. He got to his knees and braced his hands on the grass to help him get to his feet. He stumbled back several steps, still unsteady, and dropped down again to sit and get a better look around.

Lights and sirens dominated the space as fire trucks arrived and instructions were shouted. The roar of the blaze intensified. People were running in all directions, off the street, out of restaurants, from the motel across the busy road. Cars had double parked to stare and police ordered them to move on. The running and screaming converged with the curious carrying phone cameras in hand.

They'd gotten out just in time. As the fog in his brain began to clear, he looked around.

Lexi. Where was Lexi?

'Finn!' Brighton threw herself down in front of him and took him by the shoulders to look him over. 'Are you all right? You're bleeding.'

'Oh.' He touched a finger to the ridge of one stinging eye and it came back sticky. 'It's nothing.'

'What happened? What was that explosion?'

'Bomb.'

'Bomb? I need to tell Rachael. She's frantic.'

'I'll tell her myself. Help me up.'

'You should stay put. I'll bring a paramedic over.'

'Are you a doctor?' a woman called out from behind them.

'No, I'm with the police,' Brighton said. 'Do you need medical assistance?'

Finn turned his head and spotted a middle-aged woman hunched over a child.

'It's my son! We were cutting through here to get something to eat and the explosion … He was hit by something …'

'Finn, are you—'

'I'm fine. Go help her.'

Brighton called for assistance on her radio and dropped down beside the boy as Finn got himself on his feet and joined them. 'Hey, buddy. What's his name?'

'Jason,' the mother said through panicked tears.

'Hey, Jason, hey, can you hear me, bud?'

'My head hurts,' the boy mumbled as he came round, then started to cry loudly, to scream. 'My shoulder! My shoulder hurts! Ow! Ow!'

Paramedics came running. Two more treated patients extracted from nearby units.

Where was Lexi? She'd been right under Finn. He'd done everything he could to shield her from the blast. Had she been dazed and wandered off?

'Finn!' Rachael called out, running over.

'Where is she?'

'Medic!' she called.

Two paramedics rushed over and got in his way, introducing themselves as Jeremy and Linda before they began fussing over him.

'Were you inside or outside when the explosion went off?' Jeremy asked.

'We got clear. Outside. I'm fine.'

'You sound like you're wheezing a bit,' Linda said. 'Any trouble breathing?'

'He'll need to get a chest X-ray,' Jeremy said with a nod. 'Sir, do you have any chest pain?'

'No.'

'Any pain in your abdominal area?'

'No, look, we got outside before the bomb went off. I maybe felt a bit of a jolt and banged my head on the ground as we landed, that's all. I had a friend with me. She's—I can't find her.'

'Blast wave injuries can be tricky. We'll get you down to the hospital and run some tests. Make sure nothing's going on, okay?'

'Absolutely not, but thank you.' Then, because no one was answering his question and he was starting to panic, he tried again, louder. 'Where is Lexi?'

'Wasn't she with you?' Rachael said, spinning to check the area.

'She was.' He thanked the objecting paramedics again and stumbled around to the front of the building, the flames and the firemen keeping him well back from the building.

'Finn!' Rachael objected.

'I had her, Rach,' he said, thinking back as his head began to clear. 'I got her out … She was right underneath me when we landed … Someone—someone rolled me off her and … Damn it. I don't know what happened.'

'Okay, then someone's probably taken her to an ambulance. Just calm down.' Rachael got on her radio, got people searching.

Linc jogged over, his expression uneasy. 'You can't find Lexi?'

'Do you know where she is?'

'I don't want to jump to any worst-case scenarios but I've got a couple of witnesses over there who claim they saw someone taken away in a light-coloured four-wheel drive—could have been a LandCruiser—that took off out of here right after the explosion.'

'What? Where are the witnesses?' Finn asked. Linc pointed to two guys hanging back, watching with interest.

He limped over. 'Tell me what you saw.'

'Not much, man,' the taller of the two said. 'Car was parked just over there.' He pointed to one of four car spaces behind the building. 'Bomb went off, everyone scattered. The car hung outside there for a minute, then … it was hard to see but it looked like two guys dragged someone in from the grass and took off.'

'Could you describe them?'

'Nah, sorry. Only saw outlines, really.'

Brighton reappeared. 'Finn, the paramedics said you're refusing treatment.'

'I don't need it. Lexi's been taken.'

'Taken where?' Brighton asked.

'I don't know.'

'Breen's men?' Rachael asked sharply.

'Maybe … The guy with the explosives. It was … shit. I can't …' Why couldn't he think? 'She called him by name. Maybe one of Breen's men, I don't know!'

'You need to calm down and tell us what you do remember,' Rachael said.

'The bomb was meant for Blake. Whatever made this guy want to kill Blake, it was over something … a job I think. A hit. He had Lexi at gunpoint. I was handcuffed. Blake was dead, or close to it, and the bomb was on a timer. He let Lexi go then took off and she got me out of the cuffs. We were only just clear of the building when the bomb went off. Damn it, she should have left me there and got clear.'

'Wait, back up,' Brighton said. 'The bomber let her go?'

'So she could get me out. I wasn't one of the guilty ones, whatever that meant.'

'So she knows the bomber and she went with him.'

'She was dragged into a car,' Linc repeated. 'That doesn't sound consensual.'

'Linc, make sure everyone available is looking for that car please!' Rachael ordered.

'On it.'

'There was a beige-coloured troopy parked at Breen's place last night. That could be what the witnesses described,' Finn said.

'Then that's where we go next. We'll take as many cars with us as we can.'

'And Desmond?' Brighton asked.

Rachael's lips formed a thin line. 'Desmond will have to take his chances.'

'We're getting an escort, let's go,' Rachael said, climbing into the car where Finn, Cass and Linc were waiting. 'We'll have two cars converging on the property with us. That's all I could muster for now.'

Linc started the car and slipped between two patrol cars, lights and sirens pointed towards Eraring.

Rachael's phone rang almost immediately and she put it on speaker. 'Yes?'

'It's McCabe. I heard you need support. We're coming out to assist.'

'Thank you.'

'Just wanted to clarify a few things en route,' McCabe said. 'Lexi knows the bomber?'

'She called him by name,' Finn said.

'Friendly?'

'I'd hardly call a gun to the head friendly.'

'The gun could have been more about controlling you and your responses,' Brighton said.

'I was handcuffed to a dead man and the staircase. What was I going to do?'

'And the witnesses said she was dragged into a vehicle matching one you saw at your meeting with Breen?' McCabe asked.

'Possibly the one I saw. I can't be sure.'

'So this person Lexi knows is likely a member of Breen's MC that was formerly involved with Combat Crew,' Rachael said.

'That would make sense,' Finn said.

'But why would Breen send someone in to blow the place up when you were there getting him what he wanted?' Brighton said. 'I doubt Breen would sabotage his own project.'

'I'm hoping it's not because he found out we were cops,' Finn said.

There was silence while everyone considered the repercussions of that for Lexi.

Then Brighton said, 'If that was the case, why not take you too? You're a cop.'

'How would I know? I was knocked out, too hard to move? More trouble than Lexi? I don't have the answers.'

'In the club's eyes, she'd be a traitor,' Cass said. 'They know her, she dealt with them and she betrayed them. If they were going to make a statement about that, an example of anyone, it would be Lexi.'

The idea only chilled Finn more because it made sense.

'Unless she willingly got in that car,' Brighton said.

'Witness reports don't paint that picture,' Linc replied, impatience leaching into his tone.

'Finn, did she have the contents of the safe?' Brighton asked.

'No.'

'Are you sure?'

'Are you trying to piss me off?'

'No. Sorry. It's my nature to examine all the angles. It's not a personal attack.'

'Then do me a favour.'

'What?'

'Explore another angle. She's in trouble.'

CHAPTER FIFTEEN

'Nice to see you dressed for the occasion.' Breen's piggy eyes give me a slow once-over before he smiles nastily and closes the distance.

I hold his gaze. I won't give in to the part of me that wants to cower. Not to him.

'Lexi, Lexi,' he says, walking around me in a circle. 'What have you done?'

'You're gonna have to be a bit more specific.' My legs are shaking but I keep my chin up and my eyes cold.

'Zander tells me you became a cop.'

Zander did? Every last hope I have dies. I have no friends here. None. 'Is there anything else I need to know about me?'

He chuckles. 'Smart mouth. I always thought of cops as more … sedate.'

'I got a job, not a lobotomy.'

'One has to wonder, going into that line of work.' He lifts a stray lock of my hair, plays with it. 'Shame.'

I tip my head to tug my hair free.

'What happened tonight?'

'Cronin was there.' I see the shock in his eyes, enjoy the idea there may have been a flash of fear, but I probably imagined it. 'He bailed us all up while we were doing the job on Blake. Took us by surprise. He wanted a name. Blake took a bullet because he wouldn't cooperate.'

'What name was that?'

'He wanted to know who ordered the hit on his family.' I mean, I'm guessing that's what he was talking about. Pretty obvious.

Breen swallows, jaw tight. 'Did he get it out of him?'

'No. Blake bled out before Cronin could make him talk.'

Breen turns on his heel and walks a few steps away as though lost in thought. Then he nods. 'So he's acquired the C4. Seth and Vic must have had looser tongues before they died. Did you get the files?'

'What part of "Cronin blew the place up" did you miss?'

'I needed those files!' Breen pulls a gun from his lower back and raises it dead centre to my forehead. 'Such a waste.'

Two guns pointed at my head in one day is too much. My legs begin to buckle.

'Breen,' Zander snaps. 'We need her, remember.'

Breen fiddles with his grip on the gun, eyes boring into mine. I don't breathe. 'I'm not sure we need another cop.' The gun lifts an inch from my temple. 'I'm not sure we can trust this one.'

Another one?

'You let me worry about that,' Zander says. 'We still need the stuff from the safe. She can get it.'

'Can you?' Breen asks me.

I swallow, try to get some moisture back in my mouth. I'm not sure where the idea comes from but I run with it. 'Deal hasn't changed. I get your shit, Desmond's off the hook. I get more work.'

His eyes bulge. The gun returns to my head, makes jarring contact. 'You're a fucking cop!'

'I was a fucking cop when I did the deal!' I spit back. 'When I made several other deals. Did anyone crash your joint? Had you heard of me?'

There's plenty of suspicion, zero belief, but perhaps a glimmer of interest. 'Keep talking.'

My mind scrambles to find the right words. 'Being reeled into the Spider case gave me an instant in with the big guns. They gave me access to the cyber stuff. It's a fucking goldmine.'

'So you joined them.'

I shrug, try to make my tone less panicked, more casual. 'I was sick of fucking strangers for a living. It was too good an opportunity to waste. I knew what some of that intel I could dig into would go for. They trust me. I can already access most of their systems. I pass a detective exam in another couple of years and I could be at HQ full time. It's perfect. There's very little I can't find out, manipulate or destroy.'

'And your friend. He's a cop?'

'He's a fucking psycho, but he's good. He'll do anything for me, so don't be surprised if he uses the cops to crash that house you sent us to last night. He's gonna want me back.'

More anger flares in Breen's eyes but I shrug. 'Another advantage of joining the cops. Manpower.'

'You gave up the location on the body.'

Fuck. 'Hey, all I was asked to do was get proof of death. I did that. How the fuck was I supposed to drag a body encased in concrete out of the water by myself? I do police work too. That's how I keep my job.'

Several expressions pass over his face, none of them reassuring. His gaze flicks to Zander and back. This guy really wants to kill me. 'We had a policeman working for Combat Crew once,' he growls. 'You remember?'

'No.'

'His name was Dennis. Dennis decided to double cross us. Dennis is dead.'

'Then Dennis was stupid. Zander, am I stupid?' I ask.

'You never were. No.'

'So get the fucking gun out of my face,' I tell Breen, 'and I'll get you what you want.'

'I want what was in that safe.'

I nod. 'That was the deal.'

'How are you going to get it back?'

'I'll figure it out.'

'How!'

'Geez, the best laid plans take time … but okay.' I think for a moment before answering. 'I'm going to go back and tell them *almost* everything that's happened. I'm going to tell them all about the "pretend" deal I did with you to stop you putting a bullet in my head and I'm going to tell them you have someone else on the inside. I'm going to make out I'm playing you, and then, just when they think I've given them everything they need to nail you on whatever it is you're worried about, the information will disappear and they'll have nothing. Of course, we'll have to blame that other pesky inside cop that no one will ever find for ruining their case, but there'll be nothing they can do about it. And that,' I tell him with a victorious gleam, 'is how I keep rising through the ranks and getting away with whatever I want. This is good for me, and in this instance, it's good for you.'

'If the police copy those files I need any trace of my name removed.'

'Too easy.'

He leans in close. 'You fuck me around, I will kill you.'

One side of my mouth tips up in a smile. 'That would be a waste, remember?'

He leans in even closer with a look on his face that has my skin crawling. 'Yes … maybe I don't want to kill you. Yet.'

I hope I don't have to go there. But I play the game, warm my gaze. 'Great, 'cause I don't want to be dead. See? We're on the same side.'

He stays where he is, so close he's almost out of focus for several more seconds, then he steps back. 'You're a witch. You play me, you're a dead witch. I'll send Zander back for you tomorrow.'

'Friday. If the cops have found what you're after, it'll be with forensics and if I push too hard to get it, it'll look suspicious. I don't take those sorts of chances.'

Breen debates that silently before looking at Zander. 'She's your responsibility. She fucks up, I'll blame you.'

Zander nods, then angles his head towards the door. 'Let's go.'

I'm put back in what I now know is a car with a weird rear set-up but, for whatever reason, I'm spared the damn hood. It's not like I can see much anyway, just a few scratch marks illuminate the black-painted windows. I consider opening the front curtain, but I know Zander's right there and I don't think I should push my luck in the slight hope I'll spot a landmark. Instead I give in to the need to curl up in a ball, close my eyes and let myself shake.

It takes me several minutes to calm down, several more before the car stops. I've given up trying to keep track of time or direction, there's so many bends and turns.

The door finally opens to almost total darkness. I have no idea where I am. Zander stares at me, jaw tight, face dark.

'That bullshit story you spun for Breen … if he wasn't thinking with his dick he'd never have bought it. Make sure you stick to the deal. He needs those files.'

I remind myself Zander's not my friend. Not anymore. 'Is that the only reason you cut in? You wouldn't have stopped him, would you? If he'd decided to shoot me.'

'I'll see you soon. You fuck this up, I'll shoot you myself.'

'Zander—'

'Get out.'

I step out onto the side of the road. The door snaps back into place and he's gone.

I look around to get my bearings. My eyes gradually adjust to the dark, make out the bend of the road and the shapes of the trees in the light filtering down from a half-moon. Do I follow the direction of the car or go the other way? I decide heading back the way we came would be stupid, so I mark this spot with a few twigs and walk the other way.

The road seems endless but I keep going. Surely Zander hasn't dumped me too far out into the middle of nowhere? I have no bag, no money, no phone, no ideas. The dull headache I've been too busy to acknowledge is gaining momentum. I need a drink. I need to figure out what to do next. Rachael's probably got half the NSW Police Force out looking for me. Finn. Damn it. I hope he's okay.

Not one car passes by. I roll my heel and wince, stumble on. High heels and gravel roads don't mix, but I can see a light up ahead so I guess I'm closing in on some sort of civilisation. The light turns out to belong to a house. There's a glow from somewhere further ahead that could be from streetlights. I'm on the edge of … somewhere. So what now? Do I knock on this random front door? I have no clue what time it is, but it's not early. If there's a light on they're probably still up, but who's 'they'? I decide not to find out. It's still secluded enough here to spook me. I don't think I've got another drama in me tonight.

I second-guess my decision as I keep walking, my feet now well and truly complaining. I'm thirsty, my head is pounding and I'm getting less and less choosy about whose night to interrupt by the second. Next house, I'm stopping. I pause as I see red and blue lights flashing in the distance and hope shoots through me. I follow their progress, hear the sirens and watch four cars fly by at light speed on a road further up ahead. It's a T intersection and once I reach it, I see the glow of police lights way off through trees. They're a long way ahead, but they've stopped. A quick read of the road sign and I know where I am—and that those patrol cars have descended on Breen's rental. Relief floods through me. That's got to be Rachael looking for me.

The sound of a car approaching slowly from behind has the hairs on the back of my neck prickling. It passes then pulls over just ahead. I stop, not sure what to do. In the glow of the brake lights I make out a rear-window sticker promoting ICU nursing and try to reassure myself I'm most likely dealing with someone who saves lives rather than takes them, is likely calm in stressful situations, and is no doubt used to being interrupted for emergencies. All good things under the circumstances. Still, I hesitate. Knowing my luck, the car's been stolen by a homicidal maniac with a thing for dark hair and red dresses.

A head finally pokes out of the driver's window. 'Are you okay, love?'

I take a few cautious steps closer. 'Ah … sort of.'

The woman gets out, a matronly type who squints as though to get a better look at me in the dark. 'What are you doing out here? What happened?'

Yeah, not going into that. 'Bit of a … domestic dispute. That's all. I'm heading for those cop cars,' I say, waving into the distance.

'Are you hurt? I'm a nurse.'

'Only my feet. Damn heels.'

'Where did you come from?'

'That way,' I say, pointing a thumb over my shoulder. 'My, ah, boyfriend got the shits and made me get out of the car.'

'And left you out here? Some boyfriend!'

'Yeah, well, not anymore.'

'You said you want to get to those police? Looks like some sort of operation going on.'

'Someone there will get me home. I work with the police. Constable Lexi Winter,' I tell her, because I've decided I really don't want to walk all the way over there and this woman might feel better knowing my title. 'I'm based at Wyong Police Station. I'd be happy for you to give them a call and check me out.'

The woman visibly relaxes. 'Oh, that won't be necessary. Let me give you a lift over.'

I thank her, shoving any last doubts away. I can't be sure if she's an Annie Wilkes or a Mother Teresa, but either way, I don't have to walk any further.

CHAPTER SIXTEEN

Finn stepped out of the shed, looked around helplessly. Now what? Lexi could be anywhere.

'There's nothing up here,' McCabe told Rachael from the house.

'Down here either,' Rachael replied from behind Finn. 'They've cleared out. That's not surprising if something was going down tonight.'

'We're going to head back to Erina to check on our crime scene.'

'Thanks, McCabe.'

Finn stared out over the darkness of the lake, his mind racing to figure out the next best step to take. 'There must be CCTV of that car somewhere,' he told Rachael. 'We need to get the plates.'

'Already on it,' Rachael said. 'We'll find her. Right now you need to have a proper examination by a doctor.'

'It's just a headache. We don't even know if she's still alive.'

'They could have killed her then and there. They didn't. She'll be okay. She's resourceful.' He wasn't sure who she was convincing: him or herself. 'We'll secure the property, keep some officers on it overnight and get forensics in first thing, see if they can find any clues while we look into that CCTV.'

'Inspector!' A young officer jogged down the drive. 'A car just pulled up out front containing two women. One's claiming to be a police officer but has no ID. She's asking if you're onsite.'

'Did she give her name?' Rachael asked, but, like Finn, she was already walking quickly up the driveway.

'Not sure. The officer attempting to keep her off scene asked me to find someone in charge. She doesn't look much like a police officer. All dressed up. Might be on something.'

'That's got to be Lexi,' Finn said, picking up his pace. He overtook the others, hurried through the garage and out to the road. At first he saw an older woman with a plump figure and his hopes fell. Then he heard her.

'I *told* you. I'm Constable Lexi Winter and I need to know if Inspector Langley is here.'

'And I told you, I'm *Senior* Constable Matt O'Hurley and without ID, you're not getting through.'

'Listen, Cheezel, I'm not going to stand here while you turn this into a pissing competition over rank, so check your fucking ego. Is Inspector Langley here or not?'

'Lexi!' Finn called out.

'Oh, thank God!' Rachael said. 'Are you all right?'

'Yeah, I'm fine,' Lexi said. 'However, can we all just please ensure—' she turned back to O'Hurley, '—that *Senior* Constable O'Hurley is satisfied I'm clear to pass?'

'Ugh, yeah. Just doing my job,' O'Hurley muttered, stepping back.

'I'll let everyone know,' Rachael said, and got on her radio.

'Are you hurt?' Finn asked Lexi. Her slight squint told him that, at the very least, she had a headache on par with his. He couldn't imagine tackling her had done her damaged ribs any good either, but he couldn't see any new injuries.

'Now you mention it, how much do you weigh?' she complained with a grin that fell as she looked him over. 'Have you been checked over?'

'Yeah. Nothing serious.'

'Are you right now, love?' the woman she'd arrived with called from a nearby sedan.

'Give me a sec,' Lexi said and walked to the car. She said something to the woman and waved her off.

'Who was that?' Finn asked.

'Random, kind, lift-giving stranger.' She wrestled off her heels and stood barefoot on the grass. 'I'm not sure where I've been but it wasn't here. Did you find anyone?'

'Place is cleaned out. What happened to you?'

'Breen's men—'

'Hold that thought,' Rachael said, joining them. 'Let's get out of here and sit down with the team back at Gosford. I'll let McCabe know to join us and you can tell us all together.'

Finn placed a coffee and two painkillers in front of Lexi as she took them through her evening. She paused to thank him. She was obviously exhausted, but the questions were flying at her faster than she could get the details out.

'How did this Zander person know you were a police officer?' McCabe asked.

'He just said it wasn't hard to find out.'

'Why didn't he say anything earlier?' Brighton asked.

'He wasn't there for the first meeting. Maybe he was wherever Desmond is.' She yawned. 'I don't know.'

'And this other cop he mentioned they'd executed—Dennis—there wasn't any further information on him?' Rachael asked.

'No. But Breen might have someone else working for him who's still very much alive. He told Zander he wasn't sure they needed another cop. I guess he could have been referring to the dead one but it didn't come out that way.'

'Linc,' Rachael said, 'can we try and find out if any police named Dennis have gone missing recently? I know the reference to Combat Crew makes it seem like an old homicide, but let's be sure. I'm wondering if he could be our body in the bag.'

'Of course.' Linc opened his laptop and logged in.

'So they took you to the clubhouse, gave you all this information and then they just … let you go?' Cass asked, unable to conceal her scepticism.

Lexi turned tired eyes on her. 'On the condition I get Breen the contents of that safe by Friday.' Her tone darkened. 'He's sending Zander back to collect. If I don't have it, I'm dead.'

'Has the safe been found?' Rachael asked.

'Not yet. We'll have someone in there as soon as the firies clear it,' McCabe said.

Rachael nodded. 'Let's hope it survived the blast.' Then to Lexi, 'Finn said you called our POI inside Blake's unit by name. Who was he?'

'It was Arthur Cronin. Former president of Combat Crew.'

'It can't be!' Cass blurted.

Finn was surprised at the tone of her voice, a thread of almost panic.

'We'll look into that,' McCabe said. 'I wasn't aware he was out, either.'

Cass opened up her computer.

'So both Breen and Cronin wanted Blake dead?' Linc asked. 'Is it possible Cronin was after the contents of that safe too?'

'No,' Finn said. 'He was only interested in knowing who ordered what I'm guessing was a hit.'

'He was released five days ago on parole after serving ten years,' Cass interrupted as she looked up from her screen. 'That's only half of what he should have done.'

'He received an extreme sentence at the time,' McCabe said. 'I'm not surprised it was reduced.'

Rachael stood to stretch then perched on the edge of the table. 'What do you know about him, Cass?'

'Quite a bit. As I mentioned, the first case I worked with Raptor Squad as a detective was on Arthur Cronin, and as Lexi said, he was president of Combat Crew. The club was founded by nine former army, navy and air force soldiers who served in various conflicts and peacekeeping missions only to return home with different psychological traumas from their experiences. They met in an online forum where returned servicemen shared similar stories. Each felt they'd been let down by the government on their return in regard to support and welfare. Their apparent reason for founding the club was simply to share a love of motorbikes and support each other. But their collective anger at the system made them quickly buck it.

'Despite dealing with complicated PTSD symptoms, Arthur Cronin was a very savvy businessman who was able to establish a crack cocaine importation business with an estimated total income in the millions, most of which was never located. He's an intelligent, disciplined individual who was widely respected within his world, even by many of his rivals. Until 2013, when, as you know, he was caught with, arrested and charged for trafficking a commercial quantity of illegal drugs. The club was disbanded by the police.'

'He also had ties to a local brothel and illegal cage-fighting ring and some high-profile crime families,' McCabe added. 'When he took the stand, someone police believed was connected to the drug cartel kidnapped and murdered his wife and child in retaliation for testimony he gave in exchange for dropping further charges that would have extended his sentence.'

'Oh, hell,' Linc said.

'Yeah,' Cass said quietly. 'His testimony led to a couple of arrests but we never came close to shutting down the operation or finding the ringleaders. And his family were blown up over it.'

'Blown up?' Rachael asked, looking between Finn and Lexi. 'Do you think that's the hit he was referring to?'

'That would make sense,' Finn said. 'Given the form of retaliation. Blake was already dying of a gunshot wound. There was no need to trigger that bomb, but he did anyway. As though Blake's method of death was significant.'

'If we're talking about the hit on Cronin's family being ordered through Blake,' Brighton said, 'there's a good chance Seth Roberts and Vic Thomas could have carried it out.'

'Would Cronin have known that?' Rachael asked. 'Because if he did, their deaths might not have been accidental after all.'

'And that could explain how Cronin got his hands on explosives,' McCabe said.

'I'm pretty sure …' Cass said, hitting keys on her computer, '… yep. Both men were members of Combat Crew at the time. Why would they have killed the family of their own president?'

There was silence as everyone thought about that, so Lexi's sigh sounded louder than it should have. 'Some of what the police said is true, some of it's crap and a whole heap more is missing.'

Every head turned towards her.

'What do you know?' McCabe asked.

Lexi didn't answer immediately. She stared at the table as though mentally preparing herself for whatever she was about to say, then took a deep breath. 'Cronin didn't do drugs. He didn't take them, didn't buy them, didn't deal them. That was Breen's thing. He pushed that agenda at Cronin several times, tried to turn the club against him by spouting off about how much money they could be making. Cronin shot the idea down every time, said that wasn't what the club was about. Then the next thing everyone knew, Cronin was caught alone with that million in crack cocaine.'

'You're saying Breen set Cronin up?' McCabe asked with interest.

'I can't prove it but everyone at the time thought it. Breen wanted the president patch, wanted the drug business. So he got Cronin out of the way.'

'Cass, could that be true?' Rachael asked.

Cass shook her head adamantly. 'We did a very thorough investigation. There was no evidence to suggest that's true. Cronin never accused Breen of anything.'

'I don't know how many bikie gangs you've had experience with,' Lexi said, 'but members don't rat on each other, least of all to the police.'

'He admitted guilt! He gave himself up!'

Lexi's face curled into a snarl. 'His wife and son were in danger because he was locked up and he didn't trust the club to protect them, especially with Breen at the helm. He traded his guilty plea for their protection because he knew there was a strong chance he'd end up going to prison anyway, and that Breen had put him there. He did that and his family were murdered regardless of those bullshit police promises.'

Cass nodded sadly. 'I know.'

'If Breen was responsible for crack cocaine coming into the country back then,' McCabe said, 'and this new club with Breen at the helm has re-established trading with this same company, the chances he's still doing it have just skyrocketed. Why can't we catch him?'

'How do you know all this about Cronin, Lexi?' Rachael asked.

'I was about to ask the same question,' Brighton said. 'You seem pretty well versed in club business for a visiting pole dancer.'

'Hey!' Finn said.

Brighton sighed and nodded. 'I didn't mean for it to come out that way. But I'm curious about the answer.'

'I was more than that.' Lexi clasped her hands in her hair and visibly exhaled. 'Okay. Cronin didn't need to import drugs to make money. He had plenty. Made plenty. He had a whole team working for him digging up dirt—or planting it—for whoever his latest client was to do with as they pleased: bribery, blackmail, business deals, manipulating votes, whatever.'

'How did they do that?' McCabe asked.

'By whatever means necessary. But a lot of it was done through hacking into target computers for personal information, emails, bank accounts, business records …'

'Hacking?' Rachael asked warily.

'Yeah.' Lexi's eyes hit Rachael's. 'And, yeah, I worked for him. He—actually, one of the members of his club—taught me how to do it.'

'Wait … that's the job?' Finn asked incredulously. 'That was the mystery job you refused to tell anyone about?'

Lexi's chin came up. 'I never made a secret of the fact I was involved in cybercrime.'

'Hang on,' Brighton said. 'You worked as a cybercriminal for a drug-dealing outlaw motorcycle gang and you're sitting at this table as a member of the NSW Police Force?'

'I told you,' Lexi said tiredly, 'Cronin didn't deal drugs.'

'Oh, well, thank goodness for that!' Brighton hurled back.

'How did this come about?' Rachael asked with her fingers to her temples.

'That's a … really long story.'

'Just give us the basics,' McCabe said.

'I was hanging around the club, got to know some of the members and bugged them enough to teach me.'

'That's not something you learn in a day,' McCabe said.

'Years. A few years. Honestly, they were like the first family I ever had. Good or bad, whatever. It was better than nothing.'

'You must have been very young when all this started,' Rachael said.

'Yeah, but I worked hard at it. And it helped that I was a girl.'

'Why's that?'

'You've got to understand the culture. Women aren't usually all that important in bikie gangs. Motorcycles hold a higher rank. Women aren't equals, can't ever become members. They're either party girls or partners. Entertainment or property. That's not to say there's not a hierarchy among partners but generally in outlaw MCs, women are something to look at and boss around ... play with. You're expected to be brainless bimbos without a thought between you. You act smart, someone's gonna knock it out of you real quick.'

'Your point?' Brighton asked.

'Cronin used that. Other gangs would never send a woman in to do their work, so he did. He'd use girls in all sorts of situations. He'd have them chat up rival gang members in bars and dig for information, even send them into clubhouses or target homes and businesses to download spyware onto phones and computers. He treated his wife like a queen, his girls with respect. And he taught me how to be something other than a—' she looked hard at Brighton, '—visiting pole dancer. The training I got at Cronin's club is how we beat the Spider.'

'I see,' Rachael said. She looked deflated, maybe even disappointed.

Finn wasn't sure how to feel. It was impossible to blame the person Lexi was now for the one she had been, but it did change how he saw her. He couldn't help it.

'Lexi, how well did you know Cronin?' McCabe asked. 'How much worse do you think this is going to get?'

'I have no idea. The Cronin I knew was never violent unless he had to be. He was always more brains than brawn.'

'So Cronin's been out five days and blown up three people, but he's not violent?' Brighton said with a humourless laugh.

'He's after very specific targets,' Finn said. 'This is revenge. I doubt he's a danger to the wider community.'

'But not everyone injured tonight was guilty,' McCabe said.

'He's not the same man he once was,' Lexi said. 'There was something less calculated and more desperate about him.'

'So this guy's wiping out everyone who wronged him and he believes Breen set him up and indirectly got his family killed,' Linc said. 'I'm guessing Breen's feeling pretty nervous about now.'

CHAPTER SEVENTEEN

Thursday, March 24

As the talk around the table continued, Cass checked the time on her watch—12:37am. Surely they could have done this in the morning? The *proper* morning. The overtime on these back-to-back cases was killing her home life. Meera had been shouldering all the responsibility with Noah and she had her own legal business to run. It wasn't fair.

'Rachael, would you mind if we continued this in the morning?' she asked.

Rachael checked her watch and grimaced. 'Of course. All right, everyone, let's call it a night. We'll resume at a reasonable hour back at headquarters, say, nine?'

'I'll second that,' said McCabe. 'See you at nine.'

Cass stepped outside with Brighton and Linc. They immediately started chatting, but Cass had her mind on Breen. She had to agree with Linc. Breen should be very worried. She was sure he'd set Cronin up. She'd known from the start of that first case he was out to overthrow his president. She thought back to that first moment after Cronin's arrest. Inspector Gordon had been on some sort of crazy high.

'We've finally got the bastard in custody!' Gordon called out in a toast as Cass walked into the meeting room. There was a round of high fives and some back slapping between the men as beers were passed around. She hadn't been at the arrest, had been stuck doing some paperwork Gordon wanted finalised. She'd only come in now as she'd left a computer charger behind. No one had bothered to invite her to this little celebration.

'Now the fun begins. We're going to put him away for a very long time, shut down that club and wrap up a major drug importation deal. We're going to be very popular.'

'Have you interviewed him yet?' she asked Gordon.

He looked at her over his shoulder. 'We've had a brief, official chat. First real interview is scheduled for eight am tomorrow. Let him stew on his own demise tonight. Bottoms up, lads! Cass, grab a glass.'

No, she wouldn't drink with them again. 'I have to get home, but congratulations. Will I have a chance to sit in tomorrow?'

Penham, the king of the snuffling laugh, nearly choked on his beer.

'Ah, I've got a different job in mind for you,' Gordon said. 'Cronin's already told us he's not going to cooperate until his wife and kid are safe. He's got this idea they're gonna get knocked off if he talks.'

'They're going to a safe house?'

He nodded and waved a hand at her. 'I've got them en route to the place on Hamilton Street. I'll need a few cops to rotate shifts. I'd like you on that.'

'For how long?'

'Until everything blows over. A few weeks, tops. You'll have to go out to the clubhouse this evening and find someone to pack some stuff up for them. Then you'll do the ten-till-ten day shifts with a uniformed officer.'

'But I was hoping to see the interviews. Be involved in the case.'

'Were you? They'll be recorded. And you are involved.' At her devastated look, he rolled his eyes at his mates, then sighed. 'Look, you're a woman. Be nurturing and stuff. Cronin's old lady might open up to you, talk to you, feed you information—even if it's accidentally. Strike up conversations, get to know her … earn her trust. Anything you can feed back to us could be useful, okay?'

'All right,' Cass agreed unhappily. 'I think I'll get started on that then. They'll need their things for tonight.'

But he'd already turned away. 'That's her out of the way,' she heard before she'd even left the room. 'Let's get on with the good stuff.'

'What about Breen?' Penham asked.

'He'll get what he was promised.'

She'd had no doubt that Breen was responsible for the tip-off they'd been given in order to catch Cronin with the drugs, had wondered what had made Breen turn on his president. She would have liked to put that question to Cronin, but having been relegated to babysitting, she'd be lucky to even see an interview.

Cass said a brief goodnight to Linc as he moved to his car.

'So this case is bringing back some old memories for you then?' Brighton said, walking in Cass's direction.

'I suppose so. I was only starting out at the time. I didn't have a lot to do with the guts of the investigation.'

'Oh? What was your role?'

'I was a junior detective in a team led by Gordon. So, as you can imagine, he had it pretty well under control.'

'Which translates to you weren't taken seriously and were treated like shit because you were a woman.'

That surprised her. Everyone knew who Gordon was, but he was generally revered as an ace cop. 'What makes you say that?'

'I'm right, aren't I?' Brighton said with a knowing look.

'Yeah. I just didn't expect to hear anyone say it.'

'Both my parents are cops. Being a detective runs in the family. My mother worked under Gordon before he transferred to Sydney in the eighties. There were a lot less women in the force back then, especially among the higher ranks. He treated my mum like a general dogsbody. Never gave her anything more important to do than transcribe interviews and make coffees. She's deputy commissioner of the WA police now. You can imagine some of what she's put up with, clawing her way into that position, but she still claims Gordon was the worst she ever worked with.'

It clicked. 'Your mother is Deputy Commissioner Brighton?'

'That's her. I had to move all the way across the country to escape her shadow, though, so maybe don't point it out to anyone, okay?'

'You don't get along?'

'We're ridiculously close, our whole family. We get together a few times a year. But that doesn't mean I want to be known over here as Carol Brighton's daughter.'

'That's understandable.' They reached Cass's car and she stopped and dug out her keys, wondered why the woman was still standing there. 'It was nice talking to you,' she said, attempting to end the slightly awkward silence.

Still Brighton hovered. 'Would you mind if I pick your brain about something?'

'Now?'

'Or in the morning, but privately, if that's okay.'

'Pick my brain about what?'

Brighton frowned. 'Lexi Winter.'

CHAPTER EIGHTEEN

It was almost half-past nine before both teams sat back down together. Finn had skipped breakfast and his stomach growled at the smell of McCabe's raisin toast and the sausage muffin Linc was demolishing. McCabe yawned. It had been a late night and they were all feeling it.

'Right, where are we with this mess?' Rachael said. 'With two investigations into this club going on, the lines have gotten a bit blurry. We have our initial, unidentified victim we believe was murdered by Rocco, Breen's sergeant-at-arms, and we have Arthur Cronin, former president of Breen's club, who has killed Blake, Thomas and Roberts.'

And Lexi's past involvement with Combat Crew, Finn thought, noticing the omission.

'So let's start with Rocco. We need to get a legal ID on this guy.'

'He might work at the shop,' Lexi said. 'That's how Cronin used to pay everyone. By making them mechanics or sales staff. At least on paper. Maybe we could access employee records through the tax department.'

'Excellent idea. Linc, how did you go with that search on Dennis in relation to any murdered cops?'

'There were three Dennises killed in the line of duty in New South Wales between 2000 and 2022, but none of them fit, so I kept looking. The most likely candidate I found was a Detective Senior Constable Dennis Wagner. He worked out of Newcastle Police Station and was found dead of an apparent drug overdose in his home in 2005. It was ruled suicide, but it was a cocaine overdose and his family were unaware of any drug habit.'

'I see. It doesn't sound like there's much chance of tying Breen to that.'

'Unless someone in that club remembers it,' McCabe said. 'We need to know who's in there, their backgrounds, skills, jobs. And I want a location on this clubhouse. We need eyes on it.'

'Lexi, is there anything you can tell us about where you were taken?' Rachael asked.

'It looked like a farm shed. Um … a long metal shed, green or grey. There were four roller doors front and back. An awning on the front, a couple of small windows on the side. It was fitted out like a typical clubhouse inside.'

'What about around it?'

'A large gravel yard—I think it went all the way round, cyclone fencing, a serious gate. I saw some trees beyond that but it was too dark to make anything else out.'

'So no lights? Other than from the clubhouse?'

'I didn't see any, but I wasn't given much chance to look around.'

'What about sounds?' Brighton asked. 'What did you hear?'

Lexi shook her head. 'Nothing ambient, sorry.'

'Any traffic?'

'I don't think so.'

'Do you know how long it took to get there?'

'It felt like forever. I'd guess it took less than an hour, but not by a whole lot. I did mark where Zander dropped me off with a stack of sticks—forgot to mention that, sorry. The trip back to that location couldn't have been more than half an hour.'

'So it's not too far from Breen's rental,' Finn said.

'Is that really all you can give us?' Cass asked impatiently.

'I don't think you understand how close to dying I was!'

'Cass, do you have something useful to add?' Rachael asked.

'On the Cronin case, yes. I think it might be worth talking to the detectives I worked with. I remember they mentioned Cronin had several houses up and down the coast, some boltholes, but I can't find that information in the online case files.'

'Right. You and Linc go and talk to them today. Find out about those properties and ask them if they have any ideas where he might be, what he might do next, any family or acquaintances who might be willing to help him.'

'Got it.'

'I have an idea too,' Lexi said. 'The club may still be using Suzie's services from the brothel. If so, she'll know where the clubhouse is.'

'Good idea. We'll chase that up.'

'I'd be happy to go out there.'

'We'll see,' Rachael said after an obvious hesitation. She wasn't underplaying Lexi's past involvement after all, Finn decided. 'I'm also concerned about this possible crooked cop on Breen's payroll. Lexi, are you sure Breen didn't give away anything else about him or her?'

Lexi shook her head slowly. 'Breen had the gun to my head. Zander reminded him they needed me. Breen said he wasn't sure they needed another cop. That's it.'

Rachael sighed. 'Okay, everyone, bear that information in mind. Hopefully more will come to light during our investigation into these guys.'

'And Brighton has an update on Blake's safe,' McCabe told the room.

'I do. The safe was located and we've recovered some files. But before I go any further,' Brighton said with a tight expression, 'I have to formally state my objection to Constable Winter being witness to the information I'm about to disclose.'

'Brighton!' McCabe grated, in a tone that suggested they'd already been through this.

'As do I,' Cass said, her face a closed mask.

'Noted,' Rachael said with an icy glare aimed entirely at Cass.

Finn silently fumed. It was one thing for a member of another team to raise an objection, it was another for Cass to second it. Lexi was here at her team leader's discretion. To object to that was to object to Rachael's leadership.

'This is not about you personally,' Brighton said to Lexi. 'The fact is you have been approached by a motorcycle club under direct investigation to act on their behalf. This is a club full of members you yourself referred to as family. This puts you and this investigation in a very compromising position, especially if this case goes to court.'

'While I agree in theory,' Rachael said, 'Lexi has no choice but to be involved. We put her in this situation by pressuring her to go undercover.'

'I know that,' Brighton said, 'but to be fair, the full extent of the history between Lexi and the club had not been revealed at that time.'

'She was only in there to get Desmond out of trouble,' Linc said.

'Which now involves handing over sensitive information that, as it turns out, would be quite valuable to any criminal organisation. Her motives could come under fire.'

'What's in those files?' Rachael asked.

After one last, concerned glance in Lexi's direction, Brighton said, 'Blake's entire criminal world, including the evidence that Breen ordered the hit on Cronin's family and that Thomas and Roberts carried it out.'

Lexi and Cass gasped in unison. 'Breen ordered Laura's and Mikey's deaths?' Lexi said. 'Are you sure?'

'It's all in here. There are names, contact details, hits, client lists, evidence of decades of criminal activity. If this guy wasn't dead, he'd be facing multiple life sentences in prison. As it is, there's more than enough names and details in here to keep us on our toes for weeks if not months. This information is going to get a lot of bad people off the streets. I can't thank you enough for working with us on this. Especially you, Lexi and Finn. You both took great risks to get us to this point.'

'Does it contain contact information on Breen?' Rachael asked.

'An email. Generic.'

'And Cronin?'

'Nothing.'

'You've copied the information?'

'What we can. Some of it does appear to be heat affected so we've got technicians working on anything else that might be salvageable.

I realise you still have a homicide in play, but if Lexi hands this information over, Breen will know what we have on the people in these files. He could warn them. Everything could be for nothing.'

'Nothing can change the evidence you have,' Rachael said. 'You may just need to work a little harder to hunt down your POIs. We have another twenty-four hours. I'd suggest you start mopping them up fast.'

'You don't like her,' Finn said as he and Rachael left the meeting room.

'I do,' Rachael objected. 'Enough to play the bad guy when it's warranted. But she oversteps the line. She is not her mother. She is a new senior constable in a new team and she needs to learn her place. If she's allowed to run roughshod over everyone, no one will work with her. And that would be a shame. Because I think she has a lot of potential.'

'Her mother?'

'Deputy commissioner for the WA police.'

'Family in high places.'

'What you see in Olivia Brighton is the raw talent her mother Carol has polished. She just needs to try and fit in before she tries to take over.'

'Better be careful, you'll end up with another protégé. You're not worried about her attitude to Lexi?'

'She wasn't picking on Lexi. She made the reasons for her objections clear and they're valid. The truth is that the same issue has been bothering me. It's a dicey situation. I would prefer to be able to keep Lexi out of it.'

'Fine. Whatever,' Lexi called from the next room as they walked by.

Finn stopped and stuck his head in. She was spreading out at a table with her computer, a couple of notepads and different coloured pens for some sort of spreadsheet she was doing on A3 paper.

'Lexi—' Rachael began.

'Peace! I totally get it,' she said. 'I've been trying to stay out of it from the beginning.'

'What are you doing?'

'Neutron's got a hiccup with his new program. He's meeting me here to work on his latest glitch and track some— You don't really want details. But I will need those files for Breen so I don't die. I can't stay out of it until after that.'

'You'll have them,' Rachael said. 'We'll see you later.'

'Yeah, bye,' Lexi replied, already getting back to work.

Finn continued to the lift with Rachael. 'Do you …' He wasn't even sure how to broach it. 'Do you feel any differently about Lexi, knowing about her involvement with the MC? All that stuff she did?'

Rachael gave that some serious thought before answering. 'No, though I'm kicking myself it didn't occur to me. In terms of her career, it's unfortunate. But she came to us with that past and she is the sum of her experiences. She wouldn't be able to do what she can do otherwise. Cybercrime is rampant and sophisticated in outlaw MCs. We really should have been able to put that piece of her past together ourselves. Where else could someone with her background have learnt to be that good?'

'I guess you're right.'

'It bothers you.'

'Yeah. No. I don't know. Every time I think I'm getting to know her there's some new and crazy revelation.'

Rachael's lips twitched. 'I don't think she can fit too much more in. Let's just get through this next bit and hopefully we can put it all behind us. What are you up to now?'

'I thought I might go check out Lexi's idea: Madame Suzie's. See if anyone knows where that clubhouse is.'

'Good idea. I have a quick meeting with Ed to catch him up, then I'm free, if you'd like some company.'

'Sure, I'll grab some late breakfast, meet you at the cafeteria.'

He made his way down in the lift, Lexi's revelation still bothering him. While he'd shared plenty of conversations over the years with bikers and considered them overall good guys, the one percenters disgusted him. They were little more than thugs wearing patches, their deviant culture revelling in its own blatant disregard for mainstream society. Their overrepresentation in criminal activity, cybercrime, drug addiction, weapons, violence and homicides was unquestionable. They destroyed lives, both directly and indirectly, and their warped sense of brotherhood seemed built on their own egos and utilised as an excuse to carry out heinous acts against perceived rivals. Lexi's involvement in that world would take a while to get past.

He nodded at a colleague entering the lift as he stepped out, then made his way to the glass-walled cafeteria that echoed with busy chatter.

'Finn! Hi.'

He spun around, found Brighton waving at him from a nearby table. 'Hi,' he said. 'Looks like you had the same idea.'

'I never eat breakfast,' she admitted, 'I prefer brunch. Grab something and sit with me.'

'Ah … okay. Sure.' He got himself a sandwich and coffee and went back to her table. 'I imagine you've got a busy day ahead sorting through those files.'

'Yeah.' Brighton cleared her throat and took a sip of her drink. 'Maybe we shouldn't go any further until I've apologised for getting your team offside about Lexi earlier.'

'You had a point. Rachael's concerned too. Lexi's happy to drop out.'

'Okay, then, that's good. But I also shouldn't have pressed you on that line of questioning last night.'

'You mean on the way to the Eraring property?' He shrugged. 'You have every right to ask questions. That's how we figure things out.'

'You were annoyed.' Her hand reached out and long slender fingers with glossy red nails covered his. 'I didn't mean to upset you.'

'You didn't.' He pulled his hand away and opened his sandwich. 'I mean, the questions didn't. I was worried about Lexi. It was a tense situation and my pet hate is someone accusing any of my team of being dirty.'

'I understand. But that's not what I was doing. Lexi was gone, without an opportunity to explain. She may have been relying on us to work out a detail that could have proved vital to finding her. I was asking questions for her sake as much as the investigation.'

Really? he wondered, but decided to let it go. 'Then I apologise.'

'No need. Cass told me you and Lexi are close.'

'Did she?'

'It sounds like Lexi's overcome a lot.'

'Talked about that too, did you? Maybe if you want to know something about Lexi, you should ask Lexi.'

Brighton looked at the table. 'To be honest, I find her difficult to talk to. She's a very closed book and … a bit blunt.'

'She can be.'

She looked up again. 'But not with you.'

'Not now.' He chewed on a grin as he remembered their first few encounters. 'Look, if you want to befriend Lexi, be prepared to earn it. She's not easy to win over.'

'Right now I'm just trying to figure her out. Did you know I studied psychology?'

'No.'

'Becoming a police officer was a given, but I also had a real interest in psychology and I studied that part time while performing general duties. I had an idea I might even leave the force to become a psychologist. Then, in my last year of study, I started hearing first-hand a lot of screwed-up stories from patients who had been victims of crime. It was then I decided I was too much like my mother to sit by and try to fix the results of the trauma. I wanted to get in there and stop it happening in the first place. So I finished my degree and then became a detective instead.'

'That's impressive.'

'And I'm finding this whole Lexi–Breen–Cronin dynamic fascinating.'

'In what way?'

Brighton's face fell, became serious. 'Looking at Lexi's past, listening to what she said … I think you need to be worried about how this might turn out.'

He didn't bother to hide his scowl and she quickly pressed on.

'Just … hear me out. From what she recounted, Lexi believes Cronin was wrongfully imprisoned, and his wife and child murdered, because Breen set him up. She doesn't just believe it—she's still mad about it. She'd only be mad after all this time if that hurt her in some real way.'

'You think she knew Cronin's family.'

'I'd bet money on it and, at least at some point, that she had a close relationship with Cronin.'

'What do you mean by "close"?'

'Rescuer, mentor ... or in her profession, even more than that. I'm not sure yet. And then there's this Zander. The way she speaks his name suggests to me they were also, at the very least, friends. And Zander has just reasserted that by talking Breen out of killing her.'

'So?'

'I know the club has evolved, changed name and gained some new members, but at its core, that club took Lexi in, gave her, in her own words, a family. Gave her training, a job, a purpose, respect, had a massive hand in shaping who she is. It's there she learnt the skills she values most highly in herself. From a psychological perspective, that's powerful. Especially coming from someone with Lexi's background. She hates Breen, that's obvious, but what might she be tempted to do, if asked, for the club? Because we know they want her for something.'

'They want her to steal some files and erase Breen's information from our system. So what?'

'Do you really think that's it? Lexi suspects they already have a cop on their books and just about any cop can find and erase files in the system. I think they're planning something bigger.'

'It doesn't matter. She's not going back in. When Zander comes to collect the files we're tracking him back to the clubhouse. Then we're raiding it and taking Desmond into custody along with Breen. If we can get Desmond to talk on the recent murder, that's gold, but either way, Breen will be charged with conspiracy to murder over Blake.'

'That'll interrupt any take-down McCabe is hoping for over imports.'

'You can't have it both ways. You wanted Lexi out, she's out. And listen, has it occurred to you to wonder how Breen is going to know Lexi has removed his name from those files? Someone's going to have to access them to check. When they do, we'll know who our dirty cop is. You should focus on that.'

'Of course. Oh, there she is.' Brighton smiled and waved over his shoulder.

Finn turned and spotted Lexi and Neutron heading to the counter. Lexi sent a brief, cool nod back in Brighton's direction then met his eyes. The slight tilt of her head and twitch of her lips said it all. He sent her back a silent, *What?* Her eyes darted from Brighton back to him, one eyebrow lifted. He visibly sighed. She shrugged, smiled again, went back to talking to Neutron.

When he picked up his coffee, Brighton was shaking her head. 'Did I miss something?' he asked.

'I don't think you missed anything. That was quite the silent conversation.'

'I suppose you're going to tell me what we said.'

Brighton dusted off her hands. 'She's teasing you for having coffee with me.'

He grinned into his mug. 'Why would she do that?'

'Because I checked with her yesterday that you two were just friends.'

'Why would you do that?' he asked, this time surprised.

'Because I was hoping I could convince you to take me out, show me the city.'

CHAPTER NINETEEN

Cass walked through the carpark with Linc in silence, and it wasn't a companionable one. Linc was generally difficult to shut up and his smile rarely left his face. Neither trait was currently in evidence.

'Something on your mind?' she asked when it got too much.

'Where are we off to?' he asked, reaching the car and unlocking it.

'Gosford Police Station.'

'Some detective that worked in Raptor is now at Gosford Police Station?'

'He's now the Brisbane Water Police District Commander. But the files are at Gosford. He thinks. Can't be sure.'

Linc started the car. 'Okay.'

'Okay, what?' she asked impatiently.

He shrugged. 'Nothing. I mean, maybe I'm worried if I open my mouth I'll incriminate myself in something and you'll jump on some morally questionable bandwagon with an outsider from another team and have me removed from my case.'

Defensive anger burned in her throat. 'I happened to agree with Brighton!'

'I don't care!' he snapped. Linc never snapped. 'If you really have to keep up this gripe you have about Lexi, keep it within the team.

Rachael makes the decisions and you siding against us, questioning her judgement in front of McCabe's team, was very poor form.'

Cass let that sink in, dragged her fingers across her eyes. Maybe he was right. She wanted Lexi off the case, for personal and professional reasons, but perhaps that had been a step too far. 'Okay, okay. I didn't think it through. It's this damn case. The sooner it's over with, the better.'

'Why?' he asked, still mad.

After a brief hesitation, she replied, 'It wasn't the most rewarding time in my career and talking to Gordon is not going to be my favourite part of this investigation. It's been hanging over my head all night since I found out Wallis wasn't available.'

'Why?' he asked again.

'Gordon was pretty famous around here back then. Intimidating.'

'Yeah, I've heard of him. He made an impression on you?'

'They all do when you're just starting out.'

'Good cop?'

Cass thought about the best way to answer that. 'His arrest record was outstanding.'

'So no good?'

'I just said—'

'You qualified your answer.'

'Okay, he was a cop that thought the end justified the means no matter what the cost. I can't imagine he's changed much.'

'Less positive.'

'He was also a narcissistic, misogynistic, immoral old bastard who thrived on his own self-importance and spent more time looking after his own interests than he ever did serving the public.'

'So safe to say this won't be a happy reunion, then.'

'Honestly, I'd hoped he was rotting in hell by now.'

'Takes a bit to get you going but look at that, there's no stopping you now, is there?'

She pulled a face at him. 'You were so desperate to know.'

'How long did you work with him?'

'I didn't really. I was only on the team for twelve months. In that time, he gave me every crap job he could throw at me while he and his best mate ran the cases.'

'Sounds like fun.'

'He wanted me kept out of the way of the serious work. That was for the men.' She stared out the window. It hadn't been fun, but looking after Laura and Mikey hadn't been as bad as she'd expected it to be. And she had gotten Laura to open up to her. Not that it had made much difference—Gordon had told her to pass on any information Laura told her, but when it wasn't what he wanted to hear, he'd shut her down before she could even get all the words out.

'Laura said drugs aren't Cronin's thing,' Cass had told Gordon as he sat at his desk sipping the coffee she'd just brought in. It was the only way she could get a second of his time. 'He didn't organise any deals. Breen was the one who wanted to bring in the cocaine. He sent Cronin to the workshop to meet him over a so-called urgent matter then didn't show. Instead, we did. Laura's convinced he was set up.'

Gordon laughed. 'Of course she said that! What did you expect her to say, her husband is guilty?'

'It wasn't like that. She mentioned some of the other illegal—'

'Good. Make a report on that. The more ammo we've got, the better.'

'But surely it's worth bringing in Breen and questioning him before jumping to conclusions?'

'I've already spoken to Breen.'

'Yes, I saw him here that first day I came in. Just before you arrested Cronin. You know he set him up, don't you?'

Gordon rose from his seat slowly, his face turning scarlet. 'Don't tell me what I know, little girl. And if you ever question my policing again, you'll be out on your arse. Got it?'

She wiped the spit from her cheek and took a nervous step back, all trace of confidence abandoning her. 'I was just trying to understand … I don't know what's going on.'

'You're right. You have no idea what's going on. No idea what it takes to win a case like this. I have thirty years of policing experience and I know how to pick who has a future in this field and who doesn't. The ones that do know how to keep their heads down and follow orders. So keep your mouth shut on what you think you know, keep your head and your uterus in the office, keep the coffee hot and leave the real detectives to it. Maybe you'll learn something. Now get out!'

She'd left his office shaken and tearful and Laura's words about her husband had come rushing back. 'Arthur's not a naturally violent man. He's loving. Loyal. You won't believe it, but he has a strong sense of right and wrong. Arthur's all about justice; his definition of that is just different from that of the police. He leads his club by a code and it's very fair.' Cass remembered wondering if it was possible that the outlaw motorcycle gang leader had more honour than Gordon, the seasoned detective.

She'd been so wrapped up in escaping that she had almost careened into Wallis.

'Cassidy!' she heard and glanced up, quickly stepping sideways to avoid him.

'Yes?'

'Wait there.' Wallis entered Gordon's office.

A minute later Gordon appeared. 'Have you got a drawing Cronin's kid made for his father?'

She'd forgotten about that. Mikey had asked her to give a picture to his daddy. She had been meaning to pass it on to Gordon before she'd copped it. 'Yes, I do.'

'Cronin wants it. And he wants to meet the woman looking after his family. I'll tell you what to say as we're travelling.'

The entire way to the remand centre, Cass held Mikey's picture and listened to Gordon tell her how he thought the conversation between her and Cronin should go. How she should flatter him, flirt a little, while they tried to trip him up. As Gordon and Wallis shared some inane joke about flat breasts, she looked at the colourful picture of three stick people with big round heads standing in front of a house, the sun shining in a sky scribbled with blue clouds. Above the figures' heads was a big red love heart. Such a sweet little boy. He'd so carefully and proudly lifted the drawing to her: 'Please give this to my daddy?' She'd taken it, oohed and aahed over how beautiful it was, and he'd beamed at her. She remembered thinking that surely a man who'd had a hand in raising that child couldn't be all bad.

And as it turned out, she'd left believing he wasn't. Cronin was a formidable man, with his bushy Van Dyke beard, tattoos, a piercing, steely gaze and large stature, but while Breen had scared her, Cronin had been charming, had looked her in the eyes as she spoke, and had listened to what she'd said. Even Gordon and Wallis hadn't managed to do that.

They were staring at her as she spoke to Cronin now though, hard, because she wasn't following the script. She wasn't saying what they wanted her to say. She could feel the annoyance of their gazes burning into her, but she kept her attention on Cronin. On his almost aristocratic face, the way his intelligent eyes softened when he spoke of his family.

'How is Laura coping, locked away in that house?' he asked.

Cass answered as honestly as she could. 'She's a bit bored, but she's okay. She knows you want her to be safe.'

'She likes to keep busy. She likes to cook.'

'Oh, yes, I know! I've been bringing her everything she needs for that. She made some delicious blueberry muffins yesterday.'

Cronin's face lit up. 'Ah, she makes the best muffins anyone has ever tasted. You get her to make you her sausage rolls. You'll never taste better!'

Somehow she'd gotten completely engrossed in their conversation, had enjoyed it. She'd forgotten he was a criminal, talked to him as a man with a wife and child he adored. He'd been charismatic, no question. She supposed a man in his position would have to hold a certain amount of charm and charisma. But he'd been genuine, too, had wanted to know everything she could tell him about his family's days, had thanked her for looking after them. When Gordon had given up on her being useful and all but dragged her out of the room, Cronin had called out a goodbye, that he would like it if she could come back soon with more updates.

And she had. Twice more, Cass had visited him with photos and messages, cooking adventures and drawings from his son. She'd begun to feel a part of that little family. A trusted one.

'You're thinking about Gordon?' Linc asked.

'I was thinking about how much nicer the outlaw bikie gang leader was to talk to than my boss at the time.'

'You got to talk to Cronin?'

'Gordon and Wallis thought a female chest might help.'

'They both sound like creeps. They wouldn't get away with that shit nowadays.'

'They're both still in the organisation. There's still those out there that would prefer to keep this a boys' club.'

'An unfortunate fact. But they'll die out.' He slowed as they reached the station. 'Park on the street?'

'Yeah. I can make a faster exit when this is over.'

He found a spot. 'Do you want me to handle this?'

'No!'

'Okay, then lose the anxiety and get mad, Cass. You have every right to be. You're not that young, insecure cop anymore. You're a kickarse homicide detective. Go in there and prove it. There's no need to bow down to the likes of Gordon ever again.'

She wished there wasn't more to it than that. But in a way, Linc was still right. She'd made a mistake all those years ago, but Gordon had forced her hand. If she went down, so did he. She wasn't scared of this man. And he was about to find that out.

'You're right,' she said. 'Thanks.'

'Cassidy!' Gordon greeted her a few minutes later, his tone reminiscent of meeting a long-lost friend. 'It's been a long time.' The smile turned to Linc. An arm was extended. 'Superintendent Chris Gordon.'

'Senior Constable Jack Lincoln.'

'So, Cassidy, homicide, eh?' Gordon said, moving around a desk to sit down. 'How the hell did you swing that?' His emphasis on 'you' and 'that' was subtle but didn't go unnoticed.

'Hard work and dedication, sir.'

He gestured for them to sit. 'Thought you might have found yourself a decent bloke by now. Been at home with a couple of kids.'

'I do have a son but otherwise your memory isn't as good as it could be.'

'Oh, I don't forget as much as you might think.'

Definite threat there, she noted.

'So you're looking for the files on Cronin. They're online, you know.'

'Not the ones I'm after. I know you had a record of his assets including homes and somewhere he considered his bolthole.'

'Hmm. I'm sure we did. There wasn't much we didn't know about that scumbag by the end of the investigation. We did still do a lot on paper back then.'

'You said you thought the files would be here.'

'Perhaps. I've had these boxes brought in,' he said, pointing to at least ten large boxes piled in the corner. 'If they're going to be anywhere, this has got to be it. You're welcome to take a look. I'm sure you can appreciate I have more important things to do these days and I do value my Sundays off.'

'I'm sure you're a busy man,' Linc said and because Cass knew him so well, she knew he was doing his best not to put a boot in Gordon's arse.

But Gordon went on, oblivious. 'After Cassidy's phone call I thought I'd call in anyway, show some support for your investigation into Cronin.'

'We appreciate that,' Linc said. 'We should get started.'

'Yes, yes. Good to meet you, senior constable. Cassidy.'

He was three steps away when he stopped and turned around. 'Actually, I didn't think to ask the constable helping me if he'd checked upstairs. Cassidy, let's find out. You go on ahead,' he said jovially to Linc. 'We won't be a moment.'

'Okay,' Cass said and followed Gordon out the door, steeling herself for whatever was coming next.

She was immediately guided into another empty room.

'What are you doing working this case?' Gordon demanded.

'I'm homicide and Cronin's committed three recently,' she said as though he was slightly dull.

'Watch the attitude, Cassidy. I'm just looking out for you.'

'Yeah? Like you did years ago?'

'Exactly like that!' he spat. 'You'd have no career left if we'd—'

'And neither would you!'

He laughed. 'No one would have believed you.'

'They might now, though. So do your worst or fuck off,' she told him calmly. 'But I'm going to find Cronin. If the truth comes out, it comes out. I'm tired of living with it.'

'We all agreed on what the truth was a long time ago.' He jabbed a finger in her face. 'I'm one year off retirement. I don't need this shit falling down around my ears now!'

'Maybe you should be more worried about your mortality than your reputation. Cronin's already killed three people. He's promised to come after everyone guilty of what happened to his family. Do you ever feel guilty, Gordon?'

'I'm not the least bit worried. I didn't kill them! Blake and those other two arseholes killed that woman and child, and they got what was coming to them. End of story. If you catch the bastard, put a hole in him. There's no reason for any of this to become a problem unless you fuck up.'

Cass opened the door. She was done with him.

'Cassidy?'

'Yes?'

'Don't fuck up.'

'Mummy!' Noah fell from the lounge and raced over, throwing himself into her arms.

'Ugh!' Cass groaned as she caught him and pulled him up into her arms. 'You're getting too big for this, mister!'

'Nuh-uh.'

She breathed him in as he clung to her, squeezing him before setting him on his feet. 'You have a good day?'

'Yep. We made dinosaur masks! I'll get it.' He scooted off, thumping up the stairs.

'Hey.' Cass touched her lips to Meera's and caught the wine glass she pressed into her hand.

'Glad you're home.'

'Me too.' She sipped the light, fruity sangria as her wife of four years moved back to the kitchen to tend to whatever divine-smelling food was on the stovetop.

'Smells amazing!'

'I'm experimenting with some Asian fusion recipes. We're starting simple with curried coconut sausages.'

How on earth Meera had the time and energy to cook with her job and their four-year-old never ceased to amaze Cass, but she was grateful Meera saw cooking as cathartic, because Cass was no good at it, barely had time to do it. Still, they always ate well.

Cass wrapped an arm around Meera's waist and popped her head over her shoulder to take a peek. 'Looks as good as it smells. From this book?' she asked, noticing one by the stove.

'No … That's another present from my mother,' she said, turning it over so Cass could see the front. 'Fifty more modern Indian dishes to add to my already overloaded yet seemingly inadequate bookshelf.'

'Your mother cooks the best Indian food on the planet.'

'Excuse me?'

Cass's grin spread. 'Other than you.'

'That's better.'

'How is she?'

'Fuck cancer,' Meera responded.

'Rooooaaaarrr!' Noah growled, running into the kitchen with his coloured-in T-rex mask.

'Oh no, it's a T-rex!' Cass shrieked.

Noah giggled and lifted his mask. 'It's only me, Mummy!'

Cass sat dramatically at the already set table. 'I think I need another cuddle!'

Noah skipped over and plonked himself on her lap, then proceeded to tell her about every step involved in creating his mask while Meera dished up dinner.

'More weird food?' Noah complained as he looked at the brightly coloured dish.

'Remember what we agreed,' Meera told him, placing Cass's in front of her then her own at her seat.

'Taste it before you waste it,' Noah said in unison with her. He picked up his fork and blew most of the curry from the small piece of sausage in an attempt to cool it down. On autopilot, Cass took a serviette and mopped it from the table.

'Tough day?' Meera asked.

'Am I that transparent?'

'Only to me.'

She tried for a smile. 'Just a nasty old case coming back to haunt me.'

'Ghosts aren't real, Mummy,' Noah said through a mouthful of sausage.

'Don't talk with your mouth full …' Meera looked past Cass through the window and frowned.

'What's up?' Cass craned her neck around and heard a car start up and drive away.

'That's the third time I've seen that same ute in front of our place in the last few days.'

'The one that just left? What did it look like?'

'I don't know … white, dirty.' Meera shrugged. 'It's probably just someone checking out the house for sale across the street.'

'Probably just that,' Cass agreed but a sudden chill had her taking a large gulp of her wine.

She didn't kill Cronin's family. There's no reason to think he would come looking for hers.

CHAPTER TWENTY

I shift on my stool and throw back a JD. I've been ready to commit murder for a drink for several hours. Dawny could well be my favourite person in the world, but she's also the one who'll send me insane. I fed her an hour ago and she's finally called it a night. Feeling like some regular company, I called in on Tom, but Tom's Joint is a popular bar, even on a Thursday night, so Tom's left the bottle on the bar for me to help myself while he works hard. He's good like that.

'You want any food?' he asks, finally coming over.

'Nah, thanks. I'm good.'

'You don't look it.'

I pull a face in objection. 'Well thanks, handsome. You know, you've seen better days yourself.'

He grins. 'I mean, that look on your face suggests trouble,' he says with a grimace, then looks over my shoulder. 'Is that why your detective's here?'

My eyebrow shoots up. '*My* detective is here?'

He winks. 'There's gotta be some reason I'm not the love of your life.'

'Who says you're not?' I object, then look behind me. Finn's approaching. *Here we go*. 'Mind if me and this other love of my life head over to a table with the detective?' I ask, waving the bottle of JD.

'Go for it.'

'Thanks.' I'm tired and I force my legs across the room. I don't need a third degree over the MC stuff and I don't know why else Finn would've tracked me down tonight. I caught a couple of looks on his face earlier at headquarters that suggested he hadn't been happy to hear about my past, but what can I do about that?

'Hey, thought you might be here,' he says. 'Just let me grab a drink.' A moment later he returns to the table with what looks like a lemon squash.

'So?'

'So I wanted to let you know we got nowhere with Suzie's. They haven't been involved with the club since it was Combat Crew—apparently.'

'And I needed to know that tonight why?'

'*And* to give you these.' He hands over a bag that a quick check tells me has drives in it.

'That's unfortunate,' I say, lifting one out to look at the blistered, melted mess.

'There's some info on three of them, the other two are toast.'

'Right.'

'Itchy?'

'What? Oh.' I hadn't realised I was scratching at my bandaged thumb. It's been irritating me. 'I get the stitches out tomorrow and this thing can finally come off.'

'That's great.'

'It'll make typing a lot easier. Not that I have anything pressing I need to be doing.'

'You're not upset about all this, are you?'

'I told you I wasn't. And I would have said goodbye earlier but I didn't want to interrupt.'

He frowns at that. 'There's no reason you couldn't have come over.'

'Solid pass. Has she gotten around to asking you out yet?'

'She wants me to take her sightseeing.'

'Well, that's nice, and hey, she's cute and … appropriate, so whatever.'

'Appropriate?'

'For you. Talk about peas in a pod. Right upbringings, right families, right positions … you could be quite the power couple.'

His expression is pure incredulity. 'I'm playing tour guide not proposing marriage. I barely even know the woman. However, I do know she's concerned about you. So am I. Can we talk about that?'

Fuck, really? I take a decent swallow of JD and set it down. 'What are you burning to know? Or should I say, what did she instruct you to find out?'

He frowns. 'Olivia didn't send me here to talk to you.'

'And here I was, feeling special.'

He chuckles. 'Come on. I want to know the story.'

'Because my former MC affiliation makes you uncomfortable.'

That's exactly how he looks again now. Got him.

'It was a shock.'

'I don't see why. I told you all along I'd done it.'

'But not for who.'

'Why does that make a difference?'

'It's just one more thing you kept from us. A big thing.'

I sigh. 'It's hardly something I wanted to go around bragging about.' I give a one-shoulder shrug. 'Like it or don't. I can't change it.'

'I want to know details.'

'There's not much more to tell!' I object. 'Okay, I was working at Madame Suzie's. Cronin used to pay her to send girls over on Saturday nights. They'd dance and entertain the guys. Hang around, hook up, whatever. I was only fourteen the first time I went over there.'

He gasps. 'You worked at a brothel at fourteen?'

'I worked at the brothel at twelve. Not as an escort; I needed somewhere to sleep so I did odd jobs: cleaning, washing, cooking, manning the phone. After a while, Suzie showed me how to take care of simple stuff on the website. I kinda had a knack for it. Zander would come and pick up the girls, chat to me sometimes.'

'Who is this Zander person?'

'He's the son of one of the founding members of Combat Crew. He was nice to me, so I knew him a bit when I turned fourteen and snuck onto the bus with the other girls to start dancing. I thought it would be easy money. But one of the members wanted more than a dance and Zander came to the rescue. He sat me down in another room with his brother Nate to keep me out of trouble until the bus went back. Nate was Cronin's cyber expert. Zander told him I liked computers and showed him the website I was learning to do for Suzie, so Nate showed me a little way I could improve it. From then on, I got on the bus each week to find Nate and learn more stuff. I watched him coding. It made absolutely no sense to me and I've always hated not understanding shit. So he taught me some basic bits and pieces.'

'Let me guess, you had a knack for that, too.'

'I did. I ended up spending all the time I could there when I wasn't working for Suzie.'

'And this Nate guy didn't mind a girl hanging around, bugging him?'

'He made me useful. Nate would break into computers, then make me read through files for what he needed. I had some trouble with reading and spelling—leaving school in year six will do that—and that slowed me down. Nate thought it was great because his dad, Freddie, is three parts blind and he used to make Nate and Zander read him the paper. Nate got me to read to his dad so he didn't have to. I hated it at first. I was hopeless, but Freddie has even more patience than Nate and I got better. The better I could read and write, the more time I got to spend helping Nate. The more time I spent with Nate, the more I learnt about hacking. Fast forward a few years and I was good enough and trusted enough to do it myself. I was working at the brothel and escorting clients, but I was also on Cronin's payroll. When he started paying me enough, I quit Suzie's.'

'What exactly were you hacking into?'

I shrug. 'Rival gangs' businesses, finding out what they were up to, where they were growing or producing their products, how they were laundering their money, who they were buying weapons from … all of it. Then Cronin would find ways to bring it all down or steal it or whatever. He wasn't the gun-them-down-in-the-streets type. He preferred destroying his enemies from the inside out.'

'So just bikie versus bikie stuff?'

'And their contacts, people in high places, people with a reputation to maintain. He'd sometimes do a bit of blackmailing—he'd call it bribery—by hacking into their involvement in illegal activities and holding it over them.'

He leans his arms on the table, sighs. 'And that didn't worry you?'

'Honestly, it was fun. "Hey, Lexi, here's a name, dig up some dirt on this arsehole." Or "Hey, Lexi, this woman's husband's cheating on her. Find some evidence for me," that sort of thing. I got out of the brothel, rented a townhouse, bought a cheap car, learnt to read, to hack. I was independent and being paid to do something challenging, something I was good at.'

'So … you feel like you owe Cronin a lot, huh?'

'Is that what Brighton—sorry, *Olivia*—thinks? That I'm all conflicted?' I know I'm right when I see the look on his face.

'She said it would be perfectly normal to be. I think she's feeling guilty she pushed you into that stuff with Breen.'

'So she should. It's dangerous playing pretend with you.'

'Says the woman who completely spaced out halfway through our act in the wine bar.'

I can't help the laugh that gurgles out. 'I wasn't spaced out just … surprised. Did you practise that look in the mirror or something?'

'What look?' he asks, taking a sip of his drink.

'The one you hit me with after you checked out my legs!'

He chokes back a laugh, swallows. 'I was playing a part.' Then, amused, he says, 'You liked the way I looked at you?'

'It totally threw me. Teddy bear Finn has a hot look.'

'Ouch on the teddy bear … And they're good legs.'

I make a show of uncrossing those legs as I stand, then lean in to whisper, 'I know.' I smile over my shoulder as I say, 'Come on, drive me home. I'm tired.'

He skulls his drink, still grinning. 'Yes, ma'am.'

I sneak into the apartment because I don't want to wake Dawny, then nearly jump out of my skin at the man sitting on my lounge with a JD in hand.

'Your security is shit, you know that?' Zander asks.

'What the fuck?'

'I don't like hanging out on the street too long. Hope you don't mind.'

'I mind! Where's Dawny?'

'No idea. Progress report?'

'I told you to give me until Friday.' But I toss the bag at him and he peeks inside.

'Maybe I thought you might have bolted.' He swallows the rest of his drink. 'I can't believe you turned cop.'

'I can't believe you're working for Breen.'

'Why?'

'You were loyal to Cronin. What the hell are you doing, bowing to that bastard?'

'I'm loyal to the president. That's how it goes.' He looks so at home, lazing on my lounge. So familiar and yet not.

'You're not the person I thought you were.'

That earns a scowl. 'The club's Dad's life, all right? He was supposed to have only had a few years left, but the stubborn old bastard just keeps going. Nate and I kept things running smooth for him. I didn't want Breen having an issue with him. Then everything just kinda calmed down and rolled along.'

'It was just easier,' I reply sarcastically. 'All that loyalty bullshit.'

'I'm loyal to the club *and* family.'

'Right. How is your dad, anyway?'

'Older. He misses you.'

'So what? You're all still together ... doing what you did before, or is it just drug imports these days?'

'Is that the cop asking?'

'Sure, let me go get my handcuffs. Call this in.' Instead, I snatch my bottle from the coffee table in front of him, grab a glass and pour myself a drink. Sit down.

'What's in the files?'

'Nothing too engrossing.'

'They're melted.'

'Yep. That's what happens when they're inside a metal box under extreme heat. There's still recoverable stuff on most of them.'

'And I'm just supposed to believe they looked like this when you found them?'

'Believe what you want, I don't give a shit.'

He huffs out a laugh. 'The old Lexi's still in there.'

'Don't know who else you were expecting.'

'A badge and a uniform can't change a person?'

'It totally can. I'm a lot bossier these days. And I know how to shoot.'

He holds up the drives and shakes them. 'Anyone going to miss these?'

'No. I told them I'm giving them to Breen. What's he want them for anyway?'

'Club business. You did what?'

'I told you—and Breen—how I was dealing with this. It's fine. Chill.'

'I hope you know what you're doing.'

'Why don't you ask Breen's other cop to check up on me if you're so worried.'

'Maybe we already have.'

'So am I allowed to know who it is? Could come in handy.'

'If Breen thinks so, he'll tell you.' He lights up a joint and I stare at it longingly.

'Got another one of those?'

'Where's Mojo?' he asks of the marijuana plant I used to own.

I pull a face. 'I pissed someone off. He got blown up.'

'That sucks,' he says, taking a long drag then handing me his joint.

'It was supposed to be me.'

'That what happened to you? You're all messed up.'

'It's related. Speaking of blowing people up, is Cronin finished spray-painting walls with bodies yet?'

He studies me carefully. 'Wouldn't know anything about that.'

'Yeah, sorry, I just don't believe it. You're happily working for Breen, Cronin's out and his best friend—your father—doesn't know where he is or what he's up to *and* you just happen to turn up at the wine bar as Cronin's leaving and don't know he's there.'

'That's right.'

'Hmm. What about Davo?' A member Breen glassed in the face. 'Is he part of this happy new club family?'

'Davo's dead. His bike took on a truck on the M1 and lost.'

'Damn.'

'It was a lot of years back.'

'Nate?'

'Of course.'

'Any other Crew still in there?'

'Majority are. Pulled a few from other clubs, bunch of prospects. Breen doesn't care so much about the military thing. Long as they're useful.'

'Like your new sergeant-at-arms?'

'Rocco's pretty useful.'

'At killing people? How's Desmond?'

'Dunno. We cut him loose. He only ever came and went for deliveries. Hopefully he'll come back.'

'If he does, can you bring him here?'

He huffs. 'What do I look like, a fucking Uber?'

'Dawny wants to see him.'

'Yeah, so do the cops. He'll turn up here if he wants to, but I don't think he's keen.'

'He did dump a body in a bag full of concrete into the ocean. I can't imagine why.'

Zander laughs. 'They got him out yet?'

'Last I heard they were still chiselling. Who was he anyway?'

'Some guy who'd tried to get in as a prospect. But he asked too many questions, got a bit too curious, so Breen didn't like him. Next thing, he's back trying to record what we're up to through the window.'

'I doubt we'll be able to ID him for you. I can't imagine Desmond left any teeth or fingerprints on him.'

'Wouldn't want to have.'

'So … is Breen doing the crack cocaine or what? What's his vision for the club?'

He snatches back his joint, takes a drag and just stares at me.

'Let me guess, club business.'

He shrugs.

'Well, as nice as it's been catching up, I don't seem to be able to pry any incriminating information out of you, so you may as well fuck off.'

He puts out the joint and stands, then pulls me to my feet. 'I missed you, you know.'

'And you're usually such a good shot,' I say sympathetically.

He laughs, then says, more seriously, 'Please be on the level. I don't ever want to have to hurt you.'

Finally I'm getting a glimpse of the old Zander, but I'm not fooled. 'That's how it goes though, right? You don't get to choose, you just do as you're told. Even if it's murder. Say hi to Cronin for me.'

He drops his hands and walks to the door then pauses, hand on the doorknob. He presses his head against the door and swears under his breath before turning back. 'Ten years have passed. A fucking decade. I walk in here and nothing's changed. You're still my fucking conscience. I don't have anything to do with blowing people up.'

'Good to know.'

He throws a 'But maybe you should tell your cop friend to watch her back,' over his shoulder as he leaves.

'Cop friend? Which—'

The door closes. Damn it … 'tell your cop friend to watch *her* back'. Hers. Rachael? Rachael had nothing to do with Cronin. Wait … Cass? Cass had been on the Cronin case. But what would Cass be guilty of?

I grab my laptop and take a look at the case files. I know I'm not supposed to but smaller things have caused me to break the rules. I find out Cass was on a team with a Gordon and Wallis and a few other lesser mortals. A bit more research into Gordon and Wallis shows me they were pretty damn good at what they did and attained serious promotions for their work on Cronin's case. I scroll on. Cass was in charge of one of the shifts on Laura and Mikey. Several other cops took turns. At least one female on each shift. There were no recorded incidents or errors or reasons I can see why Cronin would be targeting any female cops. Everything seems pretty straightforward. That doesn't mean there's nothing to find, it just means I'm not going to find it here.

CHAPTER TWENTY-ONE

Friday, March 25

Finn studied the picture of the body recently liberated from his concrete coffin. It looked a little worse for wear and certainly not like any bikie he'd ever seen. The man had been well groomed, no facial hair or tattoos or jewellery; regular clothes … So who was he?

'McCabe's team is busy this morning making an arrest on a hitman listed in Blake's files,' Rachael told the team, bringing his attention back to the room, 'so we're on our own. Linc, Cass, have we gotten anywhere with an ID on our victim?'

'Nothing,' Cass said. 'He doesn't match any records.'

'Steven has promised to call at any moment. Hopefully he can shed some light. How did you go looking into Cronin yesterday?'

'We found some files and brought them back but haven't finished going through them yet.'

'Any clues as to where he might be?'

'Potentially,' Linc said. 'That list of properties Cass remembered was in there, but it looks like a lot of those properties were repossessed as proceeds of crime. We'll be able to tell you more shortly.'

'You're visiting the prison next?'

'Yep, we have an appointment this afternoon. The warden has a few ideas on who we should talk to about Cronin. Apparently, he made some friends in there.'

'Great. Why don't you head off— Sorry.' She took out her phone and answered on speaker. 'Morning, Steven.'

'Rachael. The victim had had his teeth removed and his fingertips were missing. DNA came back with no matches. I'm sorry.'

'Not your fault,' she said with a disappointed sigh. 'Thanks.'

'And are you aware the Federal Police have put in a request to take possession of the body?'

'No,' she said, frowning. 'That's highly unusual. Can they do that?'

'They stated "cross-agency investigation" on the paperwork.'

'That's news to me. Thanks, I'll chase it up.'

'Perhaps McCabe knows something about it,' Finn said. 'I'll find out.'

'Thanks. Linc, Cass, you should get going. You've got a long drive ahead of you.'

'Right, then,' Linc said. 'We'll let you know how we go.'

Rachael dropped into a chair and opened up her computer. 'Did you find Lexi last night?' she asked Finn. 'Give her the files?'

'Yeah, she was happy to go ahead.'

'Where is she today?'

'Getting the bandage off her hand and the stitches out. Do we know what time Zander is supposed to be collecting the files?'

'No, but I have two cars on her place all day. Did I hear tone when you mentioned Zander?'

'If Olivia's right, he'll be the one.'

'If Olivia's right about what?'

'She thinks the club might have something bigger in mind for Lexi than what they told her.'

'That occurred to me.'

'She hates Breen, but the majority of that club at its core is still Combat Crew. They trained her, employed her, basically shaped her. Olivia said that for someone with Lexi's background, psychologically, that's really powerful. That Lexi might be drawn back in or pressured into making bad choices.'

'Okay,' Rachael said levelly, 'I've heard what Olivia thinks. What do you think?'

'Honestly, Rach, I don't know. Lexi's crazily loyal to anyone she cares about. I think if that scenario was possible, it would be because of this Zander guy. But regardless, if the people she cares about are on different sides, she's going to be torn.'

'Hmm. Interesting. But you're forgetting one thing.'

'What's that?'

'For someone with her background, she's pretty damn good at picking right from wrong. Oh, and we have the employee records for Breen's business. Rocco's real name is as it sounds. Rocco Murtola. Latest stint in prison was eight years in Supermax for wounding with intent to cause grievous bodily harm after he amputated part of a brawler's hand with a fire axe during a bar fight. Multiple priors for assault, intimidation, drug possession, dangerous driving, you name it. We couldn't find a current address or registered phone, but I thought we should pay the shop a visit, see if he or Breen are there. I want to get a feel for the players. I can't do it staring at pictures on a wall.'

'On what excuse?'

'We spotted Blake had dealings with the club, et cetera, et cetera.'

'Lexi was supposed to have removed those.'

'I'll talk our way through that. You can play good cop. It'll strengthen Lexi's cover if you seem to be onside.'

The Chaos Reigns Motorcycle Repair and Restoration business was about what Finn had expected: industrial park, shopfront, workshop behind, lots of driveway space and a couple of shipping containers parked up the back. The shop was glass fronted, tidy and packed with stock, and a desk sat in the corner between the merchandise and the front door.

'This looks nothing like where Lexi described she'd been taken. She wasn't here.'

'No. Let's go straight around to the workshop,' Rachael said.

'Why?'

'So the guy at the front desk can't tell us not to.'

'Good plan.'

Two roller doors were open, bikes in various states of disrepair carefully tended by sweating, jean-clad mechanics sporting tees, tattoos and company caps. A young Asian couple, distinctive due to their smaller stature and lack of ink, were polishing bikes that looked ready for collection. They froze when they spotted Finn and Rachael, looked at each other nervously, then put down their cloths and went through a back door to the shop.

'Something going on there?' he muttered to Rachael.

'Not sure.'

'Help you?' a guy with a lot of facial hair and none on top asked.

'I don't suppose Breen's around?' Finn asked.

'Who's asking?'

'Ah, Finn!' Breen said, coming out of the door the young couple just entered. 'And?'

'Inspector Rachael Langley,' Rachael said. 'Homicide.'

'I take it you don't need a bike repaired. You must have missed the shopfront.'

'Just looking around,' Rachael said. 'Nice place.'

'Thank you. What can I do for you?'

'Your name popped up in an investigation into a man by the name of Evan Blake.'

'Did it?' He flashed Finn a meaningful look. 'I'm surprised by that.'

'Did you know him?'

'Yeah, I knew Blake. Nasty piece of work but a client's a client, right?'

'Blake had a bike?'

'A motorcycle, yes. Trashed it more times than not trying to control the damn thing. Too powerful for a pencil pusher.'

'Told you that would be it,' Finn said to Rachael.

'Hmm. From the number of transactions between you, he must have damaged it almost monthly.'

'I'd be happy to account for all those bits and pieces, but I'd need to see the records.'

'And I'd like to show them to you, but unfortunately, after our initial search, some of the downloaded files further corrupted.'

'Oh, shame.' Another glance at Finn, this one less aggressive. 'I wonder how that happened?'

'Looks like there was water sitting in the drive that was continuing to do damage without our knowledge,' Finn said. 'The information we had on your transactions was all lost.'

'So that's why we're here,' Rachael said. 'To clarify. I'm sure you'd keep records?'

'We'll have to take a look for you. Get back to you on that.'

'I'd appreciate it.'

'Any reason you're interested in his business dealings? You're homicide.'

'We're interested in why someone would want him dead. Looking into his business dealings is part of that. Oh, hello,' she said to the man who had come out to stand, arms folded, behind Breen. Finn didn't need to read the sergeant-at-arms patch to recognise Rocco. 'Inspector Rachael Langley, how are you?'

Rocco gave the barest of nods.

'So if that's all?' Breen asked.

'Inspector, I don't think we need to bother these gentlemen any further,' Finn said.

'But …'

'They've cooperated fully. Thank you for your time, Mr Breen.'

Breen was looking way too confident now, almost beaming at Finn.

'Of course. Ah … I don't suppose you have a restroom I could quickly use?' Rachael asked apologetically.

Breen looked annoyed but pointed to the door on the back of the building. 'Rocco.'

'Thank you.'

Finn moved to the bikes and looked them over. 'So what does one of these go for, anyway?'

'Depends on the model,' Breen said. 'You ride?'

'I haven't yet, no, but you can't look at one of these and not want to, right?'

'They're beautiful machines.'

Finn made a show of checking Rachael had disappeared then said, 'They're not going to find anything on you. Lexi did a good job. You got the originals?'

'I did. Appreciate it.'

'Yeah? Good. Because we almost got ourselves blown up. You find out where Cronin is, I'd appreciate a heads-up.'

Breen's brow shot up. 'You've got it. You find him in the meantime, let me know. I'll make sure you're well compensated for your work.'

'That's a deal,' Finn said and shook the man's hand. They stepped away from each other quickly when the back door opened.

'Sorry, couldn't find the hand wash,' Rachael said. 'Finally spotted it under the sink. I refilled it for you.'

'Great,' Breen said like he couldn't care less.

'We appreciate your time. Oh, one more thing.'

'Yes?'

'Your clubhouse. Where is it?'

'Why?'

'I'd like to see it.'

'It's on private property. Cops aren't welcome. Not good for morale.'

'That's not very cooperative.'

'Because I know how this will go. We cooperate, show you around, next thing you're raiding the place, searching everyone and locking us up on those stupid fucking consorting laws. Used to be if someone did their time, it was done. Nowadays, you're not even allowed to talk to each other over a beer.'

'If you're not doing anything wrong, Mr Breen, there's no reason to be concerned. We may be able to wield those powers, but that's at our discretion. Now, I know I'd feel better if I'd seen that clubhouse and knew once and for all for myself that you guys were just a friendly bunch of motorcycle enthusiasts enjoying your bikes and some company.'

'That's exactly what we are. I'll think about it,' Breen said.

'Of course,' Rachael said. 'Thank you for your time.'

Finn followed Rachael back around to the car and got in. Neither spoke until they were on the road.

'That sergeant-at-arms is a scary piece of work,' Rachael said.

'Yeah, he's a big bastard.'

'I counted five others, you?'

'Yeah, and Skink was there. See his eyes nearly fall out of his head? He seems easily spooked by authority.'

'So did the couple that bolted inside. I tried to talk to them but they didn't seem to speak English—or didn't want to. You talk to Breen?'

'Just a quick, reassuring chat. He'll let me know if he hears anything on Cronin.'

'Excellent. Let's hope he has more luck than we're having.'

CHAPTER TWENTY-TWO

'Looks good,' the specialist says as he examines the thumb he'd stitched back together. It's throbbing lightly. I wish he'd stop moving it. 'But just because the stitches are out doesn't mean it's completely healed. It's going to take a few weeks before you're back to normal, so take precautions.'

'No worries, thanks,' I say, checking out the framed family photos on his desk as he goes through all the what to expects and do's and don'ts and … why is there so much talking? My thumb's better.

I zero in on a photo of a smiling mother and toddler. Sweet. The boy has the same dark curls Mikey had. But he's missing Mikey's huge blue eyes. It's not that I want to think about what happened to him, but I don't seem to be able to get it off my mind. Everything I do is triggering memories, things I'd blocked out or just forgotten. Mikey's little Superman outfit, the silly songs he sang. One memory in particular of a day he carefully tried to help me put a Band-Aid on my finger had hit me way too hard last night. He'd been the sweetest kid. Gorgeous. I can't help but wonder what he would have looked like as a teen. Probably would have had girls falling all over him.

'Okay?' the doctor says.

'Yep,' I say, not having a clue what he just told me.

'Make sure you do. It's important to your healing.'

Oh, damn, what was? Too late, he's already given me my hand back and gotten to his feet. I'm sure I'll live.

'I'll have everything emailed over to you in case you forget.'

Saved. 'Thank you.'

It's a hell of a lot easier to drive without the bandage. I carefully scratch around the scar at the traffic lights. It's also rather awesome my hand is no longer itchy and sweaty.

So what now? Someone's life is very possibly at risk. Probably Cass's. I might not like the woman very much—or at all—and I'm not that keen to try and raise it with her, but I can't sit on this information and do nothing.

As soon as I'm home I grab a coffee and jump back onto the police database in case I missed something. What other female officers were involved? Do I know any of them? Are any of them at headquarters? A time-consuming check tells me no on all fronts.

'And I'm back to square one,' I murmur to the screen.

'Good morning,' Dawny says, coming out of my bedroom with a yawn. 'I see you got yourself a coffee.'

'I didn't know you were up. Sorry,' I say, even though it's ridiculous. It's almost eleven.

'Oh, you have your hand back. That's lovely,' Dawny tells me after flicking on the kettle. 'Is it sore?'

'No. All good,' I tell her, distracted.

'What are you up to?'

'Messaging an annoying twat.' I pick up my phone and text Zander: *Which cop friend?* I ask and hit send.

I force myself to look at the photos in case there's something there. The crime scene, the dead officer, Laura and Mikey pre-abduction. Laura's kind, gentle face, Mikey's big grin, big personality.

'What a lovely family,' Dawny says.

'Yeah, they're dead.'

'Oh, tragic! How?'

Because my anger was right there, I snap, 'They got locked in a shipping container with a bomb and blown up.'

'Who would do such a thing?'

'An arsehole who was pissed off at the father.'

Dawny tuts. 'I assume you're going to catch them, then? Shame it's the police doing it. I'm sure there are others out there that could do a bit better on the justice. Want me to put some feelers out?'

'Dawny!'

'Just trying to be helpful,' she mutters, and gets back up to make her tea.

I check my phone and can see Zander has read my message and isn't replying. I hate being ignored. I retype it and send it again.

Which cop friend!

I flick through a few more photos, then stumble across the video of Laura's and Mikey's deaths. I swallow hard and skip it. It wasn't enough for those bastards to kill Cronin's family. They had to record it and make sure Cronin saw those final, terrible moments. I'm not surprised at the hate festering in Cronin. I think I even understand it. I'd want the people responsible dead, too. But the cops were just doing their jobs. They didn't kill Laura and Mikey. Why target a police officer?

I pause on a photo that stabs me in the chest. A melted ice cream on the front steps of the safe house. It's a hideous shade of green with little multicoloured lollies poking out of it. Mikey's favourite. I rack my brain for the name. What was it? 'Goodie Gum Drops,' I murmur.

'What was that?' Dawny asks.

'Never mind.' I close my laptop. I've had enough. 'I have to do something.'

'Like go to work?' Dawny suggests.

'I can't. I'm not on the case anymore.'

'Why aren't you on the case? It certainly looks like you are!'

'Politics,' I mutter.

Dawny sits back down and settles in her chair, hands on the table as she focuses on me. 'Go on, get it off your chest; you look like you're going to head off and step under a bus.'

'I'm so over all this police bullshit! I signed up thinking maybe I could help people, because of the skills I learnt in my past. They gave me a free pass on that past so I could join the police force for the same reason. Yet when I have the chance to use those skills, I get kicked off the team because of, guess what? That past. It's fucking ridiculous.'

'Oh, dear. Is this because of Desmond?'

'It's because they found out I used to hang with the MC.'

'Did you just? This one? You didn't say.'

'No, the one before. When it was Combat Crew. More than a decade ago, for fuck's sake.'

'Then who were you talking to last night?'

'You knew about that?'

'I'm in the next room, dear. Not New Zealand.'

I huff out a sigh. 'Zander's an old friend from the club. He dropped by because the cops wanted me to pass on some information.'

'And do you think they'd better know that he did, and you did?'

'I guess. Probably. They were going to put surveillance on this place today so that when he showed they could follow him back to the clubhouse and find Desmond for you.'

'Oh, I see.' She's suddenly on her feet. 'Best you go sort all that out then.'

'It's fine. I can call from here.'

'Better to do it in person. Keep your nose in the door,' she says.

'I think it's foot.'

'That too. The more body parts, the better, I say. Go on, off you go. You already look lovely. Just stay in the frame until they remember they can't solve crimes without you.'

'In the picture— Enough already!' I complain but get up and head for the bathroom, because I'm pretty sure I don't 'look lovely' and I really should go and speak to Cass.

I take a moment to freshen up and Dawny's waiting at the door when I come out.

'I filled your water bottle up for you and made you a nice sandwich in case you get hungry. Cheese and lettuce. You really need to eat more greens.'

'Ah … thanks.'

'Off you go.'

'But …'

'Bye-bye, dear. Look after that hand.'

If I'd have said more it would have been to the closed door. I'm pretty sure I've just been run out of my own apartment. Dawny's up to something. That mention of surveillance has got her freaked. Impending Desmond visit? Wouldn't put it past her. Zander had said they'd cut him loose.

Headquarters is still a mess. I can't even get into the meeting room. Rachael spots me and moves to the door, pushing debris out of the way as she opens it. 'Excuse me, can we get some of this moved?' she asks a guy with his back to her. He ignores her.

'Excuse me!' Rachael says.

I hop over some boxes and foam and get in his way. 'Hey … Ron!' I say, reading his badge. 'You're being spoken to.' He doesn't answer, just hits me with some creepy eyes and nods and steps around me. 'Loony,' I say to no one in particular.

'Come in,' Rachael tells me.

Finn, Brighton and McCabe are seated around the table. 'How is it?' Finn asks, nodding at my hand.

I hold it up and turn it around. 'All good,' I say and sit, dropping my laptop bag to the floor.

'What are you doing here?' Brighton asks me.

'Zander turned up last night for the files.'

Brighton's mouth falls open. 'You told us that was organised for today.'

'Because that's what we agreed. But I got home and he was sitting in my lounge room. What am I supposed to do?'

'Sounds cosy. Did you warn him we were going to follow him?'

'Olivia,' McCabe says in disapproval.

I try not to sneer at her because I know how hopeful they were of getting a location and I think her stupid comment was a reflex. But still. 'I guess if I did I wouldn't tell you, would I?'

'Lexi.' Rachael addresses me in the same tone McCabe had used on Brighton.

'No, I didn't warn him,' I say. 'He no doubt suspected we'd have something organised and took a chance coming early.'

'So you gave him the files?' Rachael asks.

'Yep.'

'Did you get any useful information out of him?' Brighton asks.

'Nothing that I can remember, though he did let slip that Desmond's been released. We were drinking and smoking pot so I'll have to have a better think about it.'

Rachael's hands go to her head as a pained look crosses her face. 'Lexi, please.'

I shrug. 'It'll make for a more interesting psychoanalysis.'

Brighton's lips hint at a smile. Maybe Miss Perfect does have a sense of humour. 'Do you know why Breen wanted the files?'

'I was told it was club business. Which is the code for "keep the fuck out of it" with very strong tones of "and don't ask again". But I know what would happen if the club found out he ordered Laura's and Mikey's murders. I think once Cronin was released, Breen was worried it would come out and he wanted all the evidence gone.'

'I see. Do you think he'll be back?'

'Zander? I don't know. Zander does what Zander wants. I've somehow been sucked back in and I don't know where it will end.'

'It will end when we bring down the club,' McCabe says, and signals for Brighton to get to her feet.

'Thanks again for your assistance,' Brighton says. I don't miss the warm look she shoots Finn, but I'm surprised when she returns her attention to me. 'Be careful, Lexi. Remember who your friends are.'

'She doesn't know you,' Rachael says when Brighton and McCabe walk out.

'It's fine. Whatever. If it was anyone else you'd be asking the same questions, worrying about the same things. I don't suppose Cass is around?'

'Cass and Linc are out trying to track down Cronin, why?'

Damn. 'Never mind. I might go see how Neutron's getting on with his program.'

'I'm sure he'd appreciate the help.'

'Until someone decides I'm not fit to do that either,' I can't help but mutter before almost ploughing into the man in the suit attempting to come in past the construction mess. The guy with the bland features and sharp eyes does a double take when he spots me and holds my gaze.

'Can I … help you?' I ask.

'I'm looking for Inspector Langley.'

'Yeah, she's in there,' I say, pointing my thumb back through the door.

'Thank you.'

Another weirdo, I think, glad to be heading to cyber.

CHAPTER TWENTY-THREE

'I wish she didn't feel that way,' Rachael told Finn. 'Not so soon after threatening to quit.'

'I think she's okay,' Finn replied.

'On the surface.'

'Inspector Langley?' a voice asked from the doorway.

Well groomed, nice suit … Federal agent, Finn decided.

'Yes?' Rachael said.

'Apologies for turning up unannounced. I had a last-minute opportunity to call in. I'm Commander Patrick Lloyd, Federal Police. I wanted to introduce myself and explain the situation regarding your victim at the morgue.'

'Nice to meet you. This is Detective Sergeant Finn Carson.'

'Pleasure,' Lloyd said and shook Finn's hand.

'Please, take a seat.'

'I imagine you're wondering what's going on?'

'Yes. I have both called and emailed requesting an explanation.'

'Apologies. I can inform you your victim was a man by the name of Haitao Chen.'

'You have an ID? Nothing came up on the national database.'

'That's because Chen was a seafarer on shore leave from a shipping company that had recently docked at Newcastle.'

'I see. What would he be doing spying on a motorcycle club?'

'He was an enthusiast with grand plans to skip China and join an MC. We can't know for sure, but it was more likely he was trying to take photos of bikes or women than carry out surveillance. He was known as a bit of a party guy to his colleagues. If there was trouble, he was in the middle of it, apparently.'

'That's cost him dearly.'

'It has. We're sending the body back with the next outbound Chinese vessel.'

'What? It's part of an active investigation!'

'You have everything you need for that. All the forensics are complete. Of course, we need to bring someone to justice over his murder as quickly as possible. The Chinese Government is demanding answers. They deserve them. They've requested the body be sent home. We need to handle this diplomatically and with sensitivity. Refusing to release the victim's remains is not the right move.'

'I disagree.'

'We'll also need to keep this quiet.'

'We haven't released any details to the public, if that's what you mean.'

'Well, that's something you're doing right.'

'Excuse me?'

'It's been reported you sent officers in undercover on Breen, one of whom has no training whatsoever, which led to a kidnapping of this constable who, if I have this right, has a long and close relationship with certain Chaos Reigns MC members. Could you explain that?'

'Certainly,' Rachael said coolly. 'Constable Winter is an excellent officer and I have no doubts as to her loyalty to the police force and if you've read my reports, you'll know exactly how that undercover assignment came about. It was not through any initial set-up on our part, though once established, we saw it as our best chance of extricating a hostage from the MC.'

'Except it didn't work.'

'I said best chance.'

'You located Breen at his workshop recently. You could have arrested him but you didn't. Why?'

'There are a few objectives in play here. First and foremost, we're after solid evidence our victim was killed by the MC and that requires retrieving our witness. Once we have Harris in custody, our aim is to obtain testimony implicating Breen and Rocco Murtola, his sergeant-at-arms, in the murder. We've also been working with organised crime on their case against Blake, which ties in with the undercover operation on Breen and has successfully uncovered decades of valuable information, which will solve potentially hundreds of crimes and put some of the worst behind bars. On top of that, we're attempting to track down Arthur Cronin, a recently released ex-MC crime boss who is currently running around blowing up everyone he believes has wronged him. Breen is the common thread in all of this and he still believes Lexi and Finn are onside. He's actively looking for Cronin and when Breen finds out, Finn will be the first to know. We need that in play so, no, I chose not to arrest him for the time being.'

'I believe there's also a suggestion he has a dirty cop on his books?'

'We're looking into it.'

'And Winter?'

'She is no longer actively working this investigation due to those ties you mentioned. She voluntarily stepped back.'

'I'd argue she shouldn't have been here in the first place.'

'Noted. And I'd argue you should look at the work she did on both the Spider and the Hamill family cases and consider rethinking that assessment.'

Lloyd cleared his throat. 'Regardless, due to the serious, time-sensitive and transnational nature of the case, my superiors have recommended to the commissioner that your team receive operational support while handling the case on Chen from here on in.'

'That's not necessary.' Rachael's voice dripped ice.

'It's done. Agent Justin Matthews will be here first thing tomorrow morning.'

'And the commissioner didn't see fit to tell me this himself?'

'I offered to handle it. I wanted to meet with you, address any concerns you had personally.'

'While that's very thoughtful of you, the only concern I have is wasting your agent's time, because he will not be interfering with our investigation. And while we're running it, that body will not be going anywhere.'

'Assisting. Not interfering. We're on the same side. And I can give you two more days with the body, that's it. The ship docks tonight, leaves port on Friday.'

'Commander, if you're so concerned about our work on this, why not take the Chen case over entirely? You're welcome to it. We have enough on our plate.'

He shook his head. 'Your investigation into Breen is well underway. You're making progress and I'm satisfied with your explanation of the events to date. We need a solid conviction on the man who killed Chen as quickly as possible and I believe your work into Breen is the fastest route to that conclusion. Let my agent help, inspector. You're in charge, he'll follow orders.

'I'd like to think so. I suppose we'll see.'

'I'm sure you'll find him useful. Thanks for your time.'

As soon as the man was out the door, Rachael marched back to her office. Finn followed.

'They've got to be joking,' he said.

'I don't think they are. So today, I think we need to attack—' She changed direction and he realised why when he spotted Linc and Cass coming in.

'You're back. I'd like a word in my office.'

'So who is this Agent Matthews anyway?' Linc asked after Rachael explained.

'I know nothing about him,' she said.

'Except he's been brought in to spy on us,' Linc complained. 'Seriously, we've got the best record in homicide and they give us a minder? What kind of political bullshit is this?'

'It's a transnational case and they want to keep their finger on it. I worked with the Feds on the Vaughn case and I have nothing but respect for them after that experience. Yes, I'm peeved this was sprung on us the way it was, but I think we need to be open to the idea Matthews might be an asset. Now, we need to move on. How did you go at the prison?'

'Cronin's been planning this for a long time,' Cass said. 'He talked to other inmates about a grand gesture that would show the world that justice was possible.'

'I'd say he's pulled off two.'

'No, this grand gesture was only going to take place after he'd killed the men responsible for killing his family,' Linc said.

'But if they're already dead, what other gesture is going to show the world justice?' Finn asked.

'No one seemed to know or was willing to tell us,' Linc said. 'We also found out he was close to an inmate who was released twelve months prior. A Ronald Kar. He'd done time for murdering the man who killed his wife in a hit and run. I have an address for him. He lives on the coast. We thought there might be a chance Cronin was holing up there.'

'Head out there, do some surveillance. Any sign he's there and I'll get tactical in.'

'Will do. The other interesting bit of information is that Cronin kept a photo of his mother in his cell.'

'Why is that strange?' Rachael asked.

'Cronin's mother was one of the first people Cass and I looked into. She refused to speak to us, but her sister, who happened to answer the phone, had a good chat to me. She said Cronin's mother won't talk about him because they're estranged. They have nothing to do with each other.'

'Perhaps he feels remorseful about that. Could that be what the photo's about?'

'Maybe. But as well as her home, she owns a second property at Holgate. There's a building on it but it's sitting empty.'

'Then Finn and I will take that one. Oh, and Cass, Lexi was looking for you.'

Cass seemed taken aback. 'Why?'

'Not sure.'

Finn's phone rang. 'Excuse me,' he said and walked outside the office. 'Carson.'

'It's Olivia.'

'Hi, what's up?'

'Firstly, that you haven't saved my number yet,' she teased.

He sighed out a laugh. 'I'll get right on that. And second?'

'You've left me hanging on the sightseeing.'

'Yeah. There's this case I'm working. It's time consuming.'

'Ooh, shame. I could help you with that, but where would we meet? How about … the Harbour Bridge?'

'You want to meet on the Harbour Bridge?'

'I want to climb it. You in?'

'You want to … oh, hell. Really?'

She laughed. 'Scared you won't make it?'

'I don't do heights. You're going to have to get someone else for that one.'

'Okay, then what about the Opera House? Unless those stairs are too steep?'

'Funny. I think I can manage the steps to the Opera House.'

'I'm holding you to that. Tomorrow?'

'As long as—'

'The case doesn't get in the way. Right there with you. We can grab some dinner after. I'll text details.'

She ended the call and he panicked a little. Dinner after? Was this a date? It sounded like a date. That's not what he'd meant.

'You ready?' Rachael asked.

'Huh? Oh, yeah. Got the address?'

Rachael frowned at him like he'd grown another head. 'Of course.'

The lift travelled down a couple of floors before stopping and opening.

Lexi hesitated in surprise before entering. 'Oh, hi.'

'This is a nice coincidence,' Rachael said. 'Did you find Neutron?'

'He's not in. I'm heading home. Where are you off to?'

'We have a potential address on Cronin. A property in Holgate.'

Finn's phone pinged. It was confirmation of a restaurant booking. A good one close to the Opera House.

Lexi peeked over his shoulder. 'Nice.'

'What's nice?' Rachael asked.

'Nothing,' Finn said, putting his phone back in his pocket.

The lift opened and they stepped out onto the parking level.

'Make sure you wear a suit,' Lexi tossed over her shoulder then, with a wave, headed in the opposite direction.

'What's going on?' Rachael asked as they got in his car.

He debated not telling her, then thought, *Why not?* 'Just a dinner … thing.'

'Like a date?' Rachael's eyes lit up. 'Is that what you two were being secretive about?'

'What? We weren't being …' Then he caught her meaning. 'You think Lexi and I … No.'

'No?' Could she sound more disappointed?

'Lexi doesn't date.'

'And you've decided it's time to get back out there.'

'I've been thinking about it, sure, but there's no official *date* involved here. Olivia just needs someone to take her sightseeing. She doesn't know many people on this side of the country yet.'

'Olivia. Oh, that's nice,' Rachael said, losing interest.

Finn huffed. What the hell was wrong with taking Olivia sightseeing? She was attractive, engaging, smart, they had loads in common and it could be fun. In fact, if he was looking for a date, this would be a great start.

'Do you want me to drive?' Rachael asked.

'Huh? No.'

'Then would you?'

'Yes, right.' He started the car and got his mind off Lexi—shit, *Olivia*, and onto the job.

'Okay, here we are.' 'Here' was not much more than a post box, a rusty gate and a dirt track. A sign on the gate had been spray painted in orange and read PRIVATE PROPERTY. 'So … what now?'

Rachael was looking at an aerial map of the property on her phone. 'The house is just over that rise, but the property runs right back into the bush. I'll get the gate.'

'Aren't we just here for surveillance?'

'I don't think we can see much from here, do you?'

They drove along a rutted road and pulled up outside what Finn could only describe as a shack. If anyone lived here, they weren't comfortable. The place was run down enough that a strong wind would end it. But he got out cautiously, looked around.

There was no sign of life. An old shed stood on a definite lean in knee-high native grass, old fencing, a few dying gum trees.

'No … I doubt this is it,' Rachael said after walking the perimeter of the shack with her weapon at the ready.

Something odd in her voice caught his attention and he stopped to look at her. She indicated one of the windows with her eyes. He nodded, got a better grip on his weapon and went close to the side of the house, then moved in. Rachael joined him.

'There's food on a picnic rug in the middle of the room. Looks fresh.'

'What do you want to do?'

'We can't be sure it's Cronin, could be a squatter. But if it is Cronin, I don't feel like walking back out in the open and potentially getting shot in the back now he knows we're here. Do you?'

'Guess we're going in.'

'Be careful, Finn.'

He nodded, stepped up onto the creaking old veranda and tried the door handle. The door opened without resistance. He led the way inside, doing his best to watch his footing and his surroundings at the same time. He found the food Rachael had spotted from outside, a sleeping bag, a radio. Several bottles of water. And on the wall …

'Rach.' He pointed at the photo of a pretty woman with a curly-haired child; another, older one of a woman who could be Cronin's mother.

Rachael nodded in understanding, tension lining her face. They'd found him.

Every sense straining for the slightest sound or movement, Finn led the way around the building. They cleared the last room. He wasn't there. Rachael put her hand on her radio, but two gunshots in quick succession had them ducking for cover. A third shot kept them down. Then a car engine roared to life, its tyres spinning as it took off.

Finn lifted his head above the window line to see a ute disappearing from behind the outbuilding down the drive. A few seconds later a crash suggested it had gone through the gate without stopping to open it first.

'Damn!' he said.

Rachael went outside, her eyes drawn to the car. 'Looks like he took out the tyres on our car so we couldn't follow him. Did you get a good look at what he was driving?'

'White ute, filthy number plate. NR something, I think.'

Rachael sighed. 'Call it in. I'll get us a ride out of here.'

CHAPTER TWENTY-FOUR

As I push through my door, I half-expect to find Dawny and Desmond here. There had to be some reason I was all but kicked out of the apartment earlier. But no one's home.

I kinda feel like I've wasted my day. All the way in to headquarters and no Cass, no Neutron and a whole bucketload of suspicion from some lovesick police blue blood who's been here five minutes. Agitation fuelling my hunger, I head to the pantry and stare at the lack of food. Close it in disgust.

I need something to do. Something useful. I check my phone again. Zander's read all my messages. No answer. In a fit of temper, I send the message again. Then again. And again.

I hear the door unlock and Dawny comes in with some sort of bag on wheels.

'Just thought I'd do some baking. You don't mind, do you? Didn't think so. Thanks so much. I'll just be over here making a pie. Had a thing for a lemon meringue. I got a mixer too, a few other bits and pieces. Bit of a struggle bringing it all up here.' She unloads her trolley. Two round baking trays are the last to emerge from the bag. 'Oh, damn, got any spray oil?'

'No.'

'Butter will do.'

'I think there's some margarine.'

'What about milk? We were getting low. I really don't want to have to go out again. My knee's killing me. I'll take some pills.' She rifles through her bag and locates them.

'Okay, well … enjoy,' I tell her.

'Don't go too far, dear. I wouldn't mind a bit of help. Maybe a cup of tea. You may as well learn how to do this. I won't be around forever, you know. And you're so fond of pies.'

I flick the kettle on and tell the universe this was not what I meant by needing something to do. 'So you're taking off again?'

Dawny sends me an enigmatic smile. 'Why don't we let the future take care of itself while you unwrap that mixer and figure out how it all goes together, eh? How did the cop stuff turn out?'

I get to work on the mixer. 'Not great.'

'We feel terrible. Truly. Didn't mean to get you in all this trouble.'

I stop opening the box to stare at her. 'How exactly would you know how Desmond feels about it, Dawny?'

'Did I say "we"? Oh. Habit, I suppose. Though I'm sure he would.'

'Right.' I guess I'm relieved Desmond's okay.

I spend the next hour and a half making pie. It's almost fun. I'm just putting the final touches on my wonky pastry when I hear the unmistakable roar of Harley pipes outside and go to the balcony to look down at the street.

Zander. His body language screams pissed off: shoulders hunched and arms taut against the handlebars, his mouth a thin line. He's holding an extra helmet and peering up at me through his sunglasses as though expecting me to get my arse down there.

'Ah … Dawny? I need to go out for a bit.'

'Just pop this in the oven and you're free.'

'Can't you—' It's quicker not to argue and she has been coaching me along all afternoon. I take the dish and slide it in. 'Are you going to be able to take it out? I might be back in time but …'

'Off you go. We'll eat it when you get back with dinner. I wouldn't mind Thai. I'm partial to a red curry. Duck. Just steamed rice. Not that fried stuff. Ruins the flavour.'

'Sure, Dawny.' I grab my bag and get down to the street as quickly as I can. Zander hasn't changed position. 'What are you doing here?'

'You're being fucking annoying,' he tells me, lifting his sunnies to glare at me.

I press my lips down against the smile. 'Oh, I can be way, way more fucking annoying.'

'Get on the bike.'

'Why?' I ask, suspicious.

'You want an answer, don't ya?'

I catch the helmet and slide on behind him, hear the bike roar to life and hold on.

I'd forgotten the feeling of flying along on the back of a bike. It's somehow exhilarating and relaxing at the same time. Back when every other moment of my life had been dictated to me, it had been freedom. The smile on my face when he pulls off the road into The Entrance Memorial Park carpark is real.

'Forgotten what it's like?' he asks with a grin of his own.

'I guess I did.' I look around and walk to the water's edge. I'm greeted by a sheltered stretch of shallow water protected from the ferocity of the ocean surf by a long sand bar. I haven't visited The Entrance since I was with the club and it's changed a bit. The tourist town spears out to a point dividing Tuggerah Lake from the ocean. A bridge connects The Entrance to The Entrance North. There's plenty of beachfront. In the setting sun, the colours are breathtaking. Behind me the foreshore is a maze of shops, clubs and parks. Units line every other inch of space. There's a slight, welcome breeze and I release my hair from its band and shake it free to cool down. Helmets are necessary but not comfortable.

'You gonna stand there for what's left of the day?'

'Why not?'

He trudges over and stares at me for one, two, three beats, then shakes his head, mutters 'fuck' under his breath and grabs my hand, towing me away.

'Why are you cross?'

'Because you. In the sunset.'

'Ah … Sorry?'

'So you fucking should be.'

My, 'Where are we going?' comes out on a laugh. I know this isn't the past, we're not friends anymore. But the ride, the place … It's lifted my mood.

'I thought this might jog your memory.'

'Memory of what?' I ask as he leads me through the park, past some play equipment and towards the shops.

'Do you remember the cop Cronin allowed in to pick up the stuff from the clubhouse for Laura and Mikey? The extra clothes and toys you brought back from the house—Goatee, remember? You helped her load the damn boxes into her car.'

Goatee—the stuffed, patched goat. Mikey's favourite toy. He wouldn't sleep without it. I think back, search my memory. Cronin had been arrested and charged. He'd done the deal to keep Laura and Mikey safe and the cops had shown up. Laura and Mikey had been taken straight from the clubhouse, hadn't had a chance to get home for the rest of their things. The cops had asked me to pack some up. Told us they'd be back for them. Zander and I had collected them. As promised, another cop had shown up to get them. A young woman—dirty blonde hair, serious expression, obviously out of her depth but determined to pretend otherwise. I try and bring her face to mind. It's hazy but … could it have been Cass? It's the memory of her voice, that same serious expression that comes most easily. Yes. Yes, it could have been.

'That's right! Damn it, I *knew* I remembered her from somewhere!'

Zander leads me towards a long line of shops. 'We'd pulled up in the carpark. We were going for a swim, hanging around to pick up the pizzas for Dad's birthday and you spotted her. She was right over here, at this ice-cream shop.' He stops in front of it. 'The only one that sold that damn flavour Mikey loved so much.'

I shake my head slowly. 'I don't remember.'

'You made some smartarse comment about the cop needing to buy an ice cream to chill out or something.'

'Okay, and?'

'She had a cup of green ice cream in her hand and we thought it had to be for Mikey so we were going to follow her to see where the safe house was, but she lost us in traffic.'

The memory takes shape in my mind. 'We were going to come back and look for her the next day …'

'But then whoever framed Cronin implicated the rest of us, the clubhouse was raided and I got arrested.'

'Yeah, I remember that part. But what do you mean "whoever"? You know it was Breen.'

'I don't know that!' he says a little too emphatically. 'Come on.' We walk into the shop, see that the girl behind the counter is cleaning up in preparation for closing. She takes one look at Zander and her eyes widen in appreciation. Zander doesn't seem to notice.

'There it is. They still do it. You want one?'

My heart sinks into my stomach as I see Goodie Gum Drops. 'No, thanks.'

'Yeah, you do. Hi, darlin',' he says to the girl behind the counter. 'Can we get two of these Goodie Gum Drops in cups? Double scoops,' he adds with a wink.

The girl blushes and nods. 'Sure.'

'Why are you doing this?' I hiss, officially pissed off.

'Tribute,' he tells me, taking the first from the girl and handing it to me, before taking his own. He hands her a note. 'Keep the change, darlin'.'

I roll my eyes when she blushes deeper and looks up through her lashes with a breathy, 'Thank you.'

I follow him back over the road to the reserve and sit on the steps of the pelican feeding area. Zander takes a mouthful. Pulls a face. 'It's … sweet.'

I try it and have to agree. But it's more than sweet. It's painful. I can't swallow it, so I put the cup down.

'You all right?'

'I don't want to remember. I don't want it so fresh in my mind.'

'That's how Cronin's feeling every day.'

'You know this how?'

'You don't think he would be?'

'So it's okay then, what he's doing?'

'Didn't say that. But I've got nothing against people getting what they deserve, either.'

'But why go after Cass?' I brush away an ant intent on finding out what's in my cup. 'Those cops were just doing their jobs. And

Cass, she was barely even a detective back then. She didn't make any decisions.'

'Cass? Oh, Lisa Cassidy, right.' He stares over the channel. 'I thought about it later, when I saw the picture of the ice cream on the safe house steps. I was in remand by then so I got Nate to chat up the young chick behind the counter.'

'Much as you just did?'

'Baby, that was not chatting up. He asked if she remembered a blonde in a suit buying ice cream the day they were taken. She told him yeah, the lady had been coming in right on ten every single morning to buy a cup of it. Double scoop. And yeah, she'd come in the morning Laura and Mikey were abducted.'

'She was taking Mikey his favourite ice cream every day? I like her a little bit more than I did now.'

'Yeah, well, don't. Think about it. She got that ice cream at ten every day. Reports said police were called to the house at one thirty in the afternoon. That the police guy they'd found upstairs had been dead for several hours. How is that possible, Lexi? This bitch picks up the ice cream at ten. It's a five-minute trip. The ice cream ends up on the front step. It's baked into the fucking cement by the time anyone knows what's going on. What happened in that three and a half hours?'

'Cronin's testimony.'

'And what did that hinge on?'

'Laura and Mikey's safety … Oh, hell, no. You think the abduction was deliberately covered up until after Cronin talked?'

He shrugged, an exaggerated move accompanied by a *got any other suggestions?* look.

'How do you even know about the ice cream?'

'It was the media's favourite fucking shot! They kept showing it while they reported on the murdered cops and the abduction. The poor little missing boy, his ruined fucking ice cream melted all over the scene of the fucking crime!'

I stand up and move to the water's edge, the darkening skyline no longer appealing. I spin back around, not able to believe it. 'You think Cass saw something happening and just … ran away? That she cared enough to bring him his favourite ice cream every day then left him to a bunch of monsters? Didn't even call it in? No way.'

'What do you think happened?'

'I don't know!'

'You're a cop. Look at the facts. The ice cream Cass bought that morning was dropped on the steps and a half-hour later she looked Cronin in the eye before he got on the stand and told him his family were safe. She knew, Lexi. She knew they'd been taken and she lied to Cronin so he'd talk. If she hadn't delayed the search, Laura and Mikey might still be alive.'

'I just don't see it. Cass is quite literally referred to by other cops as the human rule book.'

'Maybe something made her that way. Maybe this did. Cronin trusted her and she lied to his face for a conviction. As far as he's concerned, she's as bad as the arseholes who activated the bomb.'

'And he told you this even though you haven't seen him and don't know where he is.'

Zander's face closes up. 'I don't.'

'Then I'll talk to your dad.'

'You fucking will. He's dying to see ya.' He gets up. 'But not today. And not about Cronin. Let's go. I've got shit to do.'

I contemplate the afternoon as I eat red curry duck and steamed rice with Dawny. Perhaps Zander doesn't know where Cronin is, but someone does and I'd bet my life it's Freddie.

'This is lovely, dear,' Dawny says, spooning in another mouthful. 'I don't think they've got the heat level quite right but the flavour's very nice.'

'Glad you're enjoying it, Dawny,' I say distractedly. I have to believe Cass is in danger. But I just can't get my head around the story. She was supposed to have been watching the house that day, but she'd ended up at the courthouse for Cronin's testimony against the cartel. Why? For what reason could she have been needed there?

I get my laptop and place it on the table next to my food.

'You know it's rude to use electronic devices at the table,' Dawny says. 'What's on your mind, anyway? You're off with the fairies. Are you thinking about that rather dangerous-looking young man who's been calling?'

'More about something he told me.'

I dig into all the records I can find on Cronin's day in court and find a photo of him being led from the courtroom. Cass and another officer are beside him. She's so much younger there. She looks so different.

'It's this case, isn't it?' Dawny prods. 'You're still looking into it.'

'Yeah.' Something catches my eye. A ladder in Cass's stockings? That's almost funny. Cass is always immaculate. Curious, I zoom in.

'So I guess then you wouldn't mind being involved. If you were asked to be.'

'They don't want me, Dawny. I'm too close to this.' No, it's not a ladder. It's a small, dark smear. Just as unheard of. Maybe Cass wasn't born perfect.

'You could use that to your advantage, you know.'

There's another smudge on the hemline of her skirt. Two, actually, if you include the minuscule dot beside the smudge. 'I know that, you know that, the police …' I blow the photo up as much as I can but it becomes too pixelated. My stomach drops. Could it be green? Could it be an ice-cream stain?

'Fuck, Cass,' I mutter. The evidence points to Zander being right. A furious anger boils in my gut. 'How *could* you?'

CHAPTER TWENTY-FIVE

Saturday, March 26

'So Cronin didn't actually aim at you?' Cass asked Rachael.

'No, he shot out the tyres and took off.'

'Lexi said he was never violent unless he had to be,' Finn reminded them, spinning his chair gently from side to side. He seemed restless this morning, maybe frustrated by their near miss on Cronin. 'And Cronin himself said he was only interested in the guilty parties. I think this proves he has a code. Even if it's a warped one.'

'Agreed,' Rachael said.

They were interrupted by a knock on the door and the appearance of a tall, ramrod-straight thirty-something man in a black suit. Short brown hair added definition to a sharp angled face and serious green eyes.

'Inspector Langley?'

'That's correct,' Rachael said, getting to her feet.

'I'm Agent Justin Matthews. Nice to meet you.'

'And you,' she said, shaking his hand. 'Let me introduce you to my team.'

He shook each hand and at Rachael's invitation, took a seat.

'I imagine you're familiar with the details of the case?' Rachael asked.

'Yes, ma'am.'

'We were just going over yesterday's events. I'll catch you up,' Rachael told him.

'Appreciate it.'

He's nothing if not polite, Cass thought. She wondered what the suit cost. Looked expensive.

'Morning,' Brighton said, entering the room. She wasn't smiling. 'I heard about yesterday. All okay?'

'Yes. We're fine,' Rachael said, before introducing Brighton to Matthews. 'You don't look happy about something. What's up?'

'Look, there could be a perfectly good explanation. Maybe you already know about this, but in case you don't, I thought I should bring these over.' She handed Rachael some photos.

'What is this?' Rachael asked, taking them.

'McCabe put some men on Lexi's place hoping Desmond would turn up. They took these just before five pm yesterday. I told McCabe I thought we should follow up with you.'

Rachael spread the photos on the table. They showed Lexi meeting with an MC member on a bike, getting on the bike and taking off.

'This is Constable Lexi Winter?' Matthews asked.

'That's right,' Finn said, clearly unimpressed.

'They came back about an hour and a half later,' Brighton continued. 'He dropped her off and left.'

'Do you know who this is?'

'No. Too much of his face is obscured with the helmet and sunnies for facial recognition. Even if he is in the system.'

Cass turned a photo around, studied it. 'I think that's Zander West. Do we know where they went?'

'That'd be right,' Finn said, exchanging glances with Rachael. Cass wondered what that was about.

'Only that they headed out towards East Gosford,' Brighton said.

'I know you're not going to want me to ask this,' Brighton said, and Cass noted the apologetic glance she flicked Finn. 'But did Lexi know where you and Finn were going yesterday?'

'I think we mentioned it,' Rachael said. 'Yes.' Her eyes narrowed. 'And you're right. I don't like where you're going with this.'

'It needs to be acknowledged as a possibility, that's all.'

'Lexi would never endanger Finn or me. Besides, this was later in the day and she was with one of Breen's men. They wouldn't warn Cronin, they want him dead.'

'But I don't think she would. Can we be sure others in the MC don't feel the same way? That they might not have found him somewhere else to hide?'

Rachael picked up her phone and pressed a number. Waited. 'Lexi, it's Rachael. Can you give me a call, please?'

'Why? I'm right here,' Lexi said, striding in.

'Perfect timing. Though what are you doing here?' Rachael asked.

Cass flinched at the look Lexi sent her. 'I had a visit from Zander and—'

'We know,' Finn said and waved a hand at the photos on the desk.

Lexi's gaze dropped to the photos and her eyes bulged. She looked back at Rachael. 'That's why you wanted to see me?' she asked sharply. 'I'm under surveillance?'

'Not you, your apartment,' Brighton said. 'In case Desmond shows up.'

Lexi thrust a finger in the direction of the photos. 'My *apartment* is not in a single one of these photos and I'm certainly not Desmond!'

'The officers were there, they saw you with a guy on a motorcycle, they took a couple of shots, that's all,' Brighton said calmly. 'Why was Zander there?'

'He was— Who are you?' Lexi asked, spotting Matthews at the end of the table.

He stood. 'Agent Justin Matthews. I'm assisting with the investigation.'

'Agent? Why are the Feds here?' she asked Rachael.

'Our murder victim was a foreign national. Agent Matthews is assisting with the transnational element of the investigation.'

'I see.'

'Rachael and Finn found Cronin yesterday,' Brighton said, watching Lexi closely.

'You got him?' she asked. 'Congrats. Where is he?'

'We didn't get him,' Rachael said. 'He was holed up at the Holgate property. Squatting. He had a picnic blanket, a sleeping bag and some pictures of his wife and child and one of his mother on the wall. That's it. We went in to check it out and he shot out our tyres and took off.'

Lexi's face fell. 'Damn. Got plates?'

'Partial.'

'CCTV?'

'Nothing yet.'

She thought about that. 'If you didn't pick him up on any cameras at Erina, Gosford or Lisarow, he might have snuck over the Ridgeway into Tumbi?'

'Possibly.'

'Did you find any explosives?'

'Nothing. He might be done. Roberts, Thomas and Blake might have been his only targets.'

Lexi's gaze jumped back to Cass and darkened. A chill ran through Cass.

'Hey, long shot,' Lexi said, 'but if he has nowhere to go and you're watching the stuff he has in storage … those photos, they could be the only ones he has. He's a sentimental guy. He might go back for them.'

'Everything has been taken by forensics.'

'Damn.'

'I'm glad you came in to talk to us, anyway,' Rachael said, but she was looking pointedly at Brighton. 'Instant transparency. Can't ask for more than that.'

Brighton inclined her head in acknowledgement and Lexi glanced from one to the other in confusion. 'Sorry?'

'Never mind,' Rachael said. 'What happened with Zander?'

'As you apparently know, we went for a ride on his bike.'

'Where to?'

'The Entrance.'

'Why?'

Lexi's gaze hit Cass's a third time. 'That's something I was hoping to talk to Cass about.'

Definite anger there. Cass felt her stomach start to churn.

'Also, I think Zander's father might know where Cronin is likely to have gone.'

'Why do you say that?'

'Freddie's been in contact with him. He made out Cronin believed he was treated unfairly by the police. I thought Cass might have some ideas on that.'

Panic threatened to choke Cass. 'Of course he claims he was treated unfairly!' she snapped. 'It's always someone else's fault with those sorts of people.'

'I think it's more than that. I'm wondering if procedure wasn't followed or promises were made and broken … something,' Lexi said. But it sounded like a lot more than wondering. It sounded like an accusation.

'Cass?' Rachael asked.

'You're wrong!' Cass snapped. 'The man is a criminal who refuses to take responsibility for his own actions. That's it.'

Lexi's face reflected disbelief. 'Cronin is a crime boss through and through. But even these guys have rules, standards, unspoken codes you don't break. If you do, you deserve to die, and very few people, sometimes even your own club, will get in the way of justified retaliation.'

'I think recent events have proved at least some of that is correct.' Rachael's gaze was now focused on Cass thoughtfully.

Cass felt her discomfort crank up another notch. She shifted in her chair as she scrambled for something to end this. She couldn't let this woman ruin her career. *Wouldn't.* 'I was on that case! Are you saying I'm a dodgy cop? Because that's bullshit! Some ex-lover has you under his spell and you're trying to blame the police for a madman's behaviour.'

'Zander?' Lexi laughed in surprise. 'Zander's not an ex-lover.'

'Oh, sure. And we should all just believe you.'

Lexi's expression went blank. 'Cass, I don't have any.'

Cass huffed in disbelief, then looked around the room, desperate to rally some support. 'How can you stand there and tell us that? You were a prostitute!'

Lexi's eyes flicked to Matthews and back, her mouth a cold, thin line. 'If men wanted to sleep with me, they paid me. End of story.

I didn't do relationships. An ex-lover—especially back then—is a joke.'

'Yeah, right. Poor Lexi.' Totally on the attack now, Cass laughed. 'You're so full of shit!'

Lexi lunged so fast Cass jumped back in her chair, but Lexi stopped just short, slamming her hands on the table. 'Being abused as a kid, working for a brothel and being owned by a bikie gang leader didn't leave any time or inclination for a personal relationship, even if I had wanted one. Even if I'd been *allowed* to have one. And I didn't. I wasn't. The only men I even actually liked back then, I liked because they didn't expect me to spread my legs for them. Satisfied?'

Shaken by the heat of Lexi's attack, Cass shook her head, then stammered, 'Even if all that's true, you have a clear bond with this man and that means we can't trust you.'

'You can't *trust* me? You're just damn lucky after what you did that I'm willing to help you!'

'I don't need your help!'

'Oh, you *think*?'

'Let's just all cool down, okay?' Finn interrupted.

'Yeah, okay,' Lexi said, stepping back but still glaring at Cass. 'Let's cool down, maybe go get an ice cream.'

The words hit Cass like a ton of bricks. Any further arguments died in her throat. There was no question left that Lexi knew. She'd put it together. And she understood what had happened.

She waited for Lexi to go for the kill.

When she didn't, Cass stood on shaking legs and said, 'I'm not listening to your shit.' She walked out.

She was halfway down the hall when she heard a snapped, 'Cass, wait!'

She reluctantly stopped to face whatever was coming next. 'What?'

Lexi caught up. 'Just tell me why.'

'I did my job!' she hissed. 'I followed my orders to the letter. But you wouldn't understand that, would you? Because you're incapable of it.'

'He's going to come after you. You need to explain to everyone so they can help.'

'I don't know what you're talking about!'

'But you knew I'd remember you. You've been worried about it ever since I first turned up in this place.'

'All I remember about *you*,' Cass shot back, 'is that you were one of several little gutter whores who congregated around a bunch of filthy packrats. I don't need your kind of help!'

Lexi threw up her hands, her expression loathing. 'Okay, I'm done. Good luck.'

Only after Cass had watched Lexi stalk down the corridor did she see Rachael in the doorway.

'Cass?' Rachael said. 'A word?'

She walked back, every step more difficult than the last, feeling the heavy weight of their stares as she entered the room.

'What was that about?' Rachael asked.

Cass raked her fingers over her hair, got them caught in her bun. 'My main role in the Cronin case was to mind Cronin's family. I used to buy the kid ice cream, okay? But I wasn't there when they were abducted. That wasn't my fault. She doesn't know what she's talking about.'

'Is there any reason Cronin might think it was?'

'How would I know?'

'You seem very upset over a baseless allegation.'

'Because an ex-MC groupie just accused me of not doing my job properly!'

'You said you remembered Lexi from the MC. Any reason you never, in all this time, mentioned that?'

Shit. 'I … I didn't realise, until this came up, that it was her. I'd … forgotten. Now, are we done?'

The look on Rachael's face suggested she wasn't convinced. But she nodded, face tight. 'If you're sure that's all it is.'

'I have a stack of work to do. I'll be at my desk.' Cass hurried out to the pod and dropped into her chair, staring into space and blinking back tears. *What now? What do I do now? Lexi's bound to tell them the truth.*

With no answers, she steadied her breathing, buried herself in work and didn't lift her head for an hour, until she heard footsteps behind her.

'Sergeant Cassidy, are you okay?'

Agent Matthews? What was this about? She glanced up. 'Yes, why?'

He sat in a nearby chair. 'You seemed upset before.'

'I don't like my integrity being brought into question. Least of all by a criminal who has no right being a cop, let alone inserting herself into an investigation revolving around her old friends.'

'I don't think any of us would.'

'And?'

'And I'm here to make sure the investigation into Chen's death reaches a satisfactory conclusion. So if you have concerns about Constable Winter that might threaten that conclusion, I need to know.'

'You've been following the case. You know about Lexi's involvement with the MC. I'm not surprised she's pointing fingers at police, siding with Cronin. Her views are tainted and she's a liability to the case. She's not even supposed to be on it yet she's here, influencing it again.'

'Perhaps it might be worth putting something in writing?'

She remembered Linc's words, couldn't stand the thought of him turning against her on top of everything else. 'Thanks, but my team and I can handle it.'

'Sometimes it takes someone from the outside coming in with an unbiased view to see things clearly. Here's my card. If you want to talk about it some more, confidentially, call me.'

Cass cuddled her son on the lounge, heard the telltale deep breaths that told her he'd fallen asleep and tilted her head to check, smiling at the peaceful face.

'Want me to take him?' Meera asked, still wrapping her robe around her from the shower as she walked in.

'Let him stay here a bit longer. I feel like a snuggle.'

Meera sat down on the rug in front of her. 'I know you don't like to talk about your cases, but something's up. You haven't been yourself for days. Whatever's bothering you, if I can help …'

'Thanks, but you can't. It's an old case. I can't go back in time and even if I could, I'm not sure I could have changed the outcome.'

'If it's an old case, it's behind you. Let it go.'

'It's resurfaced. The thing is, I made a mistake.'

'Everyone does.'

'Someone at work seems to think maybe the guy that was put away …' She trailed off.

'That the guy that was put away what?'

Was she really going to tell Meera some story Lexi had thrown at her during an argument? Worry her like that? She'd decided on the drive home that if Cronin was going to go after any cops, it'd be Gordon and Wallis. Cronin didn't know what had really happened, at least, not her part in it. Lexi was just causing the usual drama to justify her presence in the team. So why bring it up with Meera?

'That he might have done some more shit things. We're going to find him.'

'Well, that's good, isn't it?'

'Yeah, I guess. It's just that mistake. It's stuck in my mind.' She tried for a smile. 'You know what I'm like.'

'Better than most,' Meera said with a wry grin. 'I don't know what happened, but one mistake against all that good you do every day? Don't dwell on it.' She got to her feet. 'Put him to bed, I'll get us some wine.'

Does it balance out? Cass wondered as she carefully carried Noah up the stairs. Can all the good deeds in the world ever make up for one serious error? One lapse in judgement? She lowered Noah into bed, watching him curl up as she laid the Spider-Man doona over him and placed a gentle kiss on his forehead. Then she straightened and went to the window to close the curtains. Instead, she leant on the sill and stared out into the night.

Yes, Lexi, she said silently. *I'd gone to the ice-cream shop that morning, just like every other morning. Ice-cream o'clock.* She smiled, remembering she and Mikey had come up with the term after the night cops had repeatedly joked that ten am was no time for ice cream. Laura hadn't seemed to mind. She'd said better morning than evening—he had all day to get the sugar and food colouring out of his system before bed. She'd loved seeing her son happy, had lived for it.

Cass remembered the ice-cream shop well, though she'd never so much as driven past it since. Its brightly coloured front with the crazy, happy signage, the rows and rows of ice-cream flavours she never bought, because Mikey always wanted the same one. The cashier had gotten to know her, had greeted her that morning by name as usual.

It had been a perfect morning. Full sunshine, cool breeze. As she'd walked back to her car she'd thought about her plans for the day ahead. Yesterday, she and Mikey had played with moulding clay and cookie cutter shapes. Today she'd brought a jigsaw puzzle for him to do. Playing games helped the day go by and gave Laura a break to cook or read or write to her husband.

Cass was heading back to her car when she heard the Harley. A long glance across the carpark revealed Combat Crew's sergeant-at-arms parking in the end spot. He got off his bike, a skinny young woman with long dark hair climbing off behind him. Lexi, she remembered, the one that had handed over Laura's and Mikey's things. She hadn't had much to say, but she'd seemed to care about the kid, about Laura, made a point of handing her Mikey's favourite toy, asking Cass to make sure she put it in his hands. Not that she'd been overly friendly. Cass had hoped to create a rapport. She was just a young, uneducated girl with limited prospects and turning her as an informant hadn't been out of the realm of possibility. Might have impressed Gordon. The offer of some cash, a way out of trouble when the shit hit the fan with the club … But Lexi wouldn't have a bar of it. So Cass had left that evening with Laura's and Mikey's suitcases and nothing else.

Zander, on the other hand, frightened her. Most of those large, tattooed MC giants did. But Zander was Cronin's standover guy, the one that took care of problems. He was also involved in the illegal underground cage-fighting club, she was sure of it. So far they hadn't been able to crash a meet, but they'd get them.

She watched the pair take off their helmets, hang them on the bike's handlebars. What were they doing here, anyway? Strutting around like they didn't have a care in the world? Didn't they know their whole club was about to fall down around their ears? By the time Gordon was finished with Cronin, he intended on having the entire club implicated in the illegal activity. Maybe with Cronin in prison and the club dismantled, Laura and her son would have a chance at a normal life. The idea pleased Cass.

She watched Zander and Lexi remove towels and lotion from a saddlebag. Zander ripped off his vest and tee, revealing a fighter physique and tribal-looking tattoos, one of which stretched between the broad expanse of his shoulders. Lexi happened to look up. Their eyes met. She said something that had Zander looking over.

Time to go, Cass had thought, suddenly nervous. She hurried to reach the car and placed the ice-cream cup in her drink holder. It was only a five-minute drive to the house, but she aimed the air-con at the ice cream anyway before negotiating her way through traffic. She hoped she wasn't being followed.

Cass closed Noah's curtains and stared down at her sleeping son. She'd made one mistake a decade ago. Hadn't she suffered enough for that? She couldn't let Lexi take her career away. It meant too much, not only to Cass, but to her family's security. There was only one way to stop it. She thought about the card Matthews had placed in her hands that was now safely tucked away in her wallet. She told herself this wasn't just about protecting a lie. Lexi was a liability. She had to get rid of her and protect her family. Once Lexi was gone, the truth could remain buried.

And Cronin? He didn't know. Couldn't. Unless ... Surely Lexi wouldn't tell him? Did Zander know? Better to play it safe.

With that thought in mind, Cass went into the bedroom, reached for the gunsafe on the top shelf and removed the Beretta. She loaded it and slipped it back within easy reach.

Just in case.

CHAPTER TWENTY-SIX

Monday, March 28

'Commissioner Cranbourne will see you now,' Cass heard the secretary tell Rachael. Cass shifted in her chair and sucked in a deep breath, prepared herself for what would come next. Rachael likely had no idea what this summons was about, a thought that was quickly backed up by the puzzled look on her boss's face at finding Cass and Matthews already seated by the commissioner's desk. Cass really wasn't sure how one written complaint and a meeting with her and Matthews had caused things to move so quickly. She'd only lodged the complaint yesterday, on a Sunday, and yet here they were.

'Sir,' Rachael said. 'Cass. Matthews.'

'Inspector, please take a seat.' Cranbourne had always struck Cass as more hot air than action, a glorified pencil pusher who'd taken over two years ago from a very talented leader and was already, if the rumours could be believed, on his way out of the top job.

Rachael sat stiffly, crossed her feet at the ankles and eyed Cass. Cass swallowed her nerves. Rachael would be angry, but Matthews had convinced Cass she was doing the right thing.

'How are you, Rachael?' the commissioner asked.

'Well, thank you.'

'Good. Good. Sorry for all this formality,' he said jovially. 'I couldn't be happier with your performance, so I'm sorry to have to broach this with you.'

'What's "this", sir?'

'I'm afraid I've received some complaints.'

'About me?'

'No, of course not. About an officer you have had working in your team. Constable Winter.'

'Lexi? Then respectfully, sir, why am I here?'

'I'm discussing this with you first out of courtesy because I happen to know you've been a mentor to Winter and brought her in on a couple of homicide investigations. I thought it would be better if you were aware of the situation in advance.'

'All right. What are these complaints regarding?'

'Winter has shown a pattern of misconduct—arguably corrupt misconduct requiring serious disciplinary action. As such, after reviewing the complaints and doing my own research, I'm afraid I'm left with no choice but to terminate her employment.'

'Now just hold on a second!' Cass watched Rachael jerk impossibly more upright in her seat. 'What misconduct has she been accused of?'

'Her past involvement with an outlaw motorcycle gang is concerning, to say the least.'

'And?'

'And it seems that involvement is ongoing. It's completely unacceptable for a member of this organisation to be associating with an outlaw motorcycle gang under any circumstances, least of all one that is currently under the microscope in a homicide investigation.' He turned one of Brighton's photos around and slid it to Rachael.

Rachael looked at the photo and took a moment, as though striving for calm. 'We know why Lexi was on that bike. She's been involved in undercover work for us. We put her in a very difficult situation and she's doing her best to get out of that without jeopardising the case, all the while collecting valuable intel.'

'It was my belief she'd been told to stand down since those undercover events took place.'

'It's not that simple. The MC know who she is and where she lives. You don't just say no thanks to these people. Her life could be at risk if she doesn't tread carefully.'

'If her life is in so much danger, why not put her in a safe house until you get this gang off the streets?'

'I've found in the past it's better to utilise Lexi's skills rather than try to lock her up.'

'Because that results in rogue, vigilante behaviour?'

'And whose words might those be?' she asked coldly, glaring once again at Cass.

'Please don't take this out on Detective Cassidy,' Matthews said. 'She's not the only one who holds these concerns.'

'You've been here five minutes and you think you have a handle on this?' Rachael snapped at Matthews. Then her eyes narrowed into slits. 'Your commander was very interested in Lexi when he was in here. What's going on?'

'Careful, Rachael,' Cranbourne warned.

'As you know,' Matthews said, 'Commander Lloyd looked into your team. The commander was concerned with Constable Winter's colourful past and requested any further concerns be flagged. Once they were, I was instructed to bring them to the commissioner's attention.'

Rachael's eyebrows shot up as she turned her attention back to Cranbourne. 'Sir, as the attorney-general saw fit to clear Lexi of any repercussions from her past, I hardly think a Federal Police commander has the right to dictate otherwise. And on this latest complaint, I'm sure if you'll allow me to brief you fully, you'd understand it's completely unwarranted to—'

'I'm sorry, inspector. Apart from anything else, Winter failed to disclose her gang affiliation when applying to the police force. You know as well as I do that puts applicants out of the running for the police force permanently.'

'*Former* affiliation,' Rachael clarified. 'And perhaps it puts applicants out of the running, but once they're in, it won't normally result in a current officer's employment being terminated.'

'That's at my discretion. I won't have officers with criminal pasts working under my leadership.'

Cass shifted uncomfortably, then regretted the movement when it drew Rachael's scorching glare.

'Really?' Though her tone was carefully measured, Rachael was emanating rage. 'Because I was under the impression one in every forty officers currently serving under you not only has a criminal past but the conviction to prove it.'

Recognising his mistake, Cranbourne cleared his throat and averted his gaze. 'I'm not sure that figure is accurate but—'

'Then look it up!' Rachael snapped. 'Drink driving, major traffic offences, serious assaults, illegal use of guns, fraud, stealing, break and enters—the list goes on. They're *all* working for you, right now! Lexi has never been convicted of anything. This is an unfair dismissal and you know it!'

Cranbourne's face reddened at the attack, his scowl fierce. 'I have the power to terminate officers that I believe are no longer suitable for the position of police officer due to a lack of integrity or questionable conduct and that's the end of it!'

Rachael shook her head. 'Lack of integrity and questionable conduct. Isn't that what your head is on the chopping block for? Are you really that scared of the Feds?'

He shot to his feet. 'Get out of my office before you lose those stars, inspector!'

Rachael got up slowly, disdain leaking from every pore as she silently left the room.

Cranbourne stared at the door for several seconds after she'd left, his face a regretful mask.

'Appreciate your stepping in, sir,' Matthews said.

'This had better not come back to bite me,' he said. 'Now get out of my office. This has taken up enough of my time.'

Cass followed Matthews to the lifts.

'You did the right thing,' he told her. 'Rachael will get over it.'

Cass wasn't so sure. Had she done the right thing? She rode the lift in silence and when Matthews stopped walking to take a call, stepped into the ladies room. She felt sick. Needed to pull herself together. Ridiculously, tears sprang to her eyes. She splashed water on her face. Rachael's fierce expression had shaken her badly. All she'd wanted to do since joining the team was emulate and prove herself to the woman. She'd have to face her again, get that first, horrible follow-up out of the way. She stared at her reflection in the mirror. Why, oh why, had she made such a stupid mistake?

It had been just a few days after she'd spotted Lexi and Zander at The Entrance. She'd bought the ice cream as usual. She never got sick of seeing the look on Mikey's face when she handed it to him. He wasn't difficult to please. She parked her car behind the unmarked patrol car already in residence, unstrapped her seatbelt and stepped out. It was a cool, overcast morning and no neighbours seemed to be about. She was running late, so she hurried up the path. Noticed the front door was ajar. It should've been closed. Locked. The ice cream fell from her fingers as she stopped mid-stride, a sick panic swelling in her chest.

She strained to hear something, anything. Where was Mikey's excited little voice? Why was Laura or her colleague, Constable Lucas, not ordering him away from the window where he always stood, jiggling on the spot to watch Cass arrive? Her hand shook as she removed her gun from its holster. It felt strange in her hand; she'd never drawn it in the field. She peered in through the narrow opening of the door. Still no sound. Nothing to suggest anything other than the door had not closed properly. She touched it, the lightest bump. It swung open a couple more inches. 'Hello?' Her voice sounded odd in the heavy silence.

Another bump of the door. Now she could see the evidence of chaos inside: two overturned chairs; a broken glass. Orange juice covering the table, leaching into Mikey's drawings and pooling around the set of clay hearts he'd made the day before. More juice dripped on the floor. Okay, okay. Perhaps Mikey had cut himself. Perhaps they'd taken him to the hospital. They might have been in a rush, forgot to notify her.

She breathed slowly to try and calm her heart pounding in her chest. She looked around, saw nothing else to suggest anything more sinister had happened. But her gut told her something was wrong. Then it occurred to her: Lucas's unmarked car was still out front.

Two more steps inside, gun leading her movements around the table, into the lounge room. An overturned lamp. Side table upended. She moved to the stairs, looked up and stopped breathing. There was blood spatter on the wall of the landing.

She forgot her own safety, her terror only for Mikey and Laura as she sprinted up the stairs. She frantically checked each room. Found nothing.

She opened her mouth to call for assistance but her phone rang, catapulting her heart through her chest. Gordon.

'Sir.'

'Cronin would like to see you before he goes in for his hearing. I need you down here—'

'Sir, I'm sorry but I've just reached the safe house. There's evidence of a struggle. There's blood on the stairs. Sir, they're gone.'

The line was silent for several beats, then, 'Calm down, constable. Who's gone?'

'The door is wide open, there's been a struggle, someone has been injured and I can't find Laura or Mikey or Constable Lucas. They've been taken!'

'Take a better look around,' he said calmly. 'Don't jump to conclusions.'

'Sir, I've looked!' She was already moving back to the kitchen. 'I'll call it in, have—'

'No.'

'Sorry, sir?'

'No. I don't want any of this broadcast over the radio. Do you understand me? We don't want to risk the wrong people finding out and potentially putting them at more risk or contaminating the scene. I'll handle it. I'll make the calls and send a team over there immediately. I want you to get out of there and come straight to the courthouse.'

'Yes, sir. I'll secure the scene and when the team arrives I'll be right over.'

'Listen to me, constable. You leave everything exactly as is and come to the courthouse as instructed. Now.'

'But I'm supposed to—'

'What you're supposed to do is follow orders! Do you want a future as a detective or not?'

'Yes, sir.'

'Then do as you're told! I'll handle it!'

Tears of panic pricked at Cass's eyes. Was she really going to walk away from this crime scene? She stood in the kitchen, frozen by indecision. This wasn't right. *Do you want a future as a detective or not?* Gordon had said he'd handle it. She spotted the clay hearts sitting on the table. One had her name on it. Another read *Daddy*. She knew she shouldn't touch anything, but she swiped them up anyway. Raced to the car and got moving.

Tears streamed down her face as she made her way to the courthouse. Poor Mikey, poor Laura. What was happening to them? Shouldn't she have passed the teams Gordon was organising? Who had been injured? And Cronin … he was going to be so upset. She swept her eyes over the hearts. She was glad she'd taken them. A heart might be all Cronin had to hold on to while they found his family.

She spun into the courthouse carpark. Had Cronin already been informed? She hoped she didn't have to be the one to break the news. No, she was barely allowed to make a coffee; Gordon wouldn't leave that to her. Guilt ached within her, even though she knew it wasn't her fault. She was a cop and they'd failed as a collective.

She climbed from the car and stopped, just for a second, while she mentally prepared herself to face a panic-stricken father.

Inside, she spotted Gordon and Wallis, heads down, talking low.

She rushed across the foyer. 'I don't know how long they've been gone, but there was spilled orange juice on the table still dripping onto the floor so I'm guessing not very long at all,' she blurted. 'Has the team arrived on scene? If we alert the media, set up roadblocks—'

'Okay. Cassidy, you need to calm down,' Gordon said. 'Cronin's about to come out and he can't know anything's up.'

That stopped her racing mind dead in its tracks. 'What?' She looked blankly from Gordon to Wallis to confirm she'd heard correctly. 'They're his family! He has a right to know they're in danger!'

'Telling him before he goes into that courtroom is the wrong move. They could have just gone for a walk or something. We don't want him unnecessarily upset. We need him to enter his guilty plea.'

'Gone for a walk?' she asked, shell-shocked. 'Sir, there's been a struggle. At least one person is hurt—or worse! They've been taken. Their lives are at risk!'

'Pull yourself together, constable!' Gordon hissed when some passers-by turned to look. 'There are potentially thousands of lives at risk if we don't get this man behind bars and his drugs off the street! We don't have enough physical evidence to take him down at trial. If Cronin doesn't plead guilty, our whole case is screwed. Understand?'

Her head was shaking of its own volition. 'No, sir, I don't understand at all.'

'I will not let you destroy this case with your hysterics! We've worked too long and too hard. Failing now would be a humiliation to the whole force. Telling Cronin afterwards won't make any difference to finding his family. Now get over there, Cronin wants an update. You tell him nothing or you're done. Understand? You're finished!'

She nodded, felt numb. 'Yes, sir.'

It won't make any difference to what we're doing to find them, she reassured herself. But how could she look Cronin in the eyes and pretend nothing was wrong? She followed Gordon to the court cells as Cronin was being led out.

His scowl lessened when he saw her coming in. 'Ah, Lisa. Hello!' His smile of greeting dropped. 'You look sad. What's wrong?'

She forced a return smile onto her face. 'Nothing. Are you ready?'

'Yes, yes,' he said dismissively but there was concern on his face. 'How is my family?'

Oh, God. Cass glanced over his shoulder at the two men staring at her hard. When her throat clogged on the words, she nodded jerkily and pulled the clay heart from her jacket. 'This is from Mikey.' She cleared her throat when her voice threatened to crack. 'He made it for you. He doesn't really understand why you can't be with them. He wanted you to know he loves you.'

Cronin took the heart and smiled gently. 'You are upset. I am too. But Mikey will be okay. They can visit soon.' He sighed heavily, his own sadness showing. 'I don't like doing this. But you kept your end of the bargain, so I will keep mine.'

She swallowed. Took a shaky breath.

Cronin heard it and frowned, worry creeping into his tone. 'Lisa, it's important to me that you tell the truth. You promise me my Laura and my Mikey are safe.'

Somehow, Cass looked him in the eyes and nodded. 'I promise.'

'Thank you. You are a good person, Lisa Cassidy. You care.' He smiled down at the heart and squeezed it in his palm. 'My good-luck charm. You tell Mikey I love it. I will see them soon.'

As soon as Cronin was led out, Gordon sidled up beside her. 'Well, look at that. You might just have a future here after all.'

'I promised him.'

'Don't get too cut up about it. He's a fucking criminal. And we're about to be very popular.'

CHAPTER TWENTY-SEVEN

Finn looked up from his desk as Rachael stormed towards her office. 'Ah …'

'I see it,' Linc said. 'Are we brave enough to go find out what that's about?'

'You want to go first?' Finn joked, but worry lined his voice.

'You're family,' Linc countered. 'She's less likely to throw something at you.'

'Rachael doesn't throw things.'

'Rachael doesn't charge around with smoke coming out of her ears either. And yet here we are.'

Finn studied Rachael's expression through the glass wall as he approached, saw the fury as she dropped her bag and snatched up her phone. 'Ed, call me,' she said and hung up.

He knocked. 'Hey.'

'Meeting room,' she barked and stormed back the way she'd come.

They'd all just filed in when her phone shrilled. She checked it, hit speaker and gestured for Finn and Linc to sit down. 'Ed.'

'Sorry, just missed you, what's up?'

'Lexi's being fired over some perceived, complete bullshit, misconduct allegation Cranbourne is using to suck up to the Feds.'

While Finn took that in, Ed asked, 'Do they have proof?'

'Only that surveillance of her getting on that bike and her own admission of previous affiliation.'

'Sounds like a weak case.'

'I'll start the ball rolling with Industrial Relations.'

'Lexi needs to be the one to do that. She's not a child, Rach.'

'But I can help her!'

'Okay. Of course. But maybe hold off until I've had a quiet word. I'll see if I can get some more details.'

Rachael sighed heavily. 'Okay. Thanks.' She ended the call and dropped her head back, rubbed her shoulders.

'Lexi's been fired?' Finn asked just to check he'd heard right.

'Yep.' Her furious expression returned and Finn followed her gaze to see Cass at her door.

'Rachael, a word?' Cass asked.

'Oh, I have more than one. And the title is inspector. Bring in another chair. Get comfortable.'

Eyes downcast, Cass nodded and complied. She'd just sat down when Matthews appeared in the doorway.

'Unscheduled meeting?' he asked.

Rachael stepped around her desk, preventing him from moving further into the office. 'Your presence isn't required.'

He scowled. 'Whether or not you like the commissioner's decision has no bearing on how this case is being run.'

'I'll call you when we resume our case.'

When he didn't move, Rachael stood toe to toe with him.

'Get out.'

Finn stood. He didn't know what was going on, but Rachael had asked the guy to leave. He needed to leave.

Matthews lifted his hands, palms out. 'Okay, if you want to be unprofessional … Have your little pity party. I expect we'll be getting on with the case in say—' he checked his watch, '—the next hour?' It wasn't a request.

'Try dictating to me how this team is run one more time,' Rachael said very quietly. 'See what happens.' She shut the door in Matthews's face, locked it and turned around, her gaze settling on Cass. 'Did you or did you not go over my head without so much as doing me the courtesy of letting me know your intentions?'

Cass's face was righteous indignation. 'Yes.'

'And what did you think would be the result of that?'

'Someone had to do something. She's out of control and you won't listen!'

'What are you talking about?' Finn asked.

'Cass and Matthews got together and decided Lexi was a threat to the police force. That she's displayed a lack of integrity and questionable conduct.'

'She has!' Cass exploded. 'And it isn't just us that thinks so!'

'You got her *fired*?' Finn asked in disbelief. Cass's brief flash of victory was almost too much. He didn't like what Lexi was up to, had questioned her actions in his own mind a lot over the last few days, but this?

'Cass … really?' Linc asked, appalled.

'She's a criminal!'

'Oh, bullshit!' Finn growled. 'This is your way of shutting her up.'

'That's a lie!'

'Is it? We overheard your little argument. You knew who Lexi was the first time you laid eyes on her. Whatever happened back then has meant you've seen Lexi as a threat ever since. That's why you never wanted her on the team.'

'I never wanted her on the team because she doesn't deserve to be here!'

'Sure, whatever you say.' He turned to Rachael. 'One of us is off this team. You decide which.'

'I have every right to make a complaint against a fellow officer if I feel it's warranted,' Cass said.

'Yeah,' Linc said, 'you do. But you betrayed your team. I'm not sure how we come back from that.'

The hurt registered on Cass's face a moment before her eyes filled. 'Fine. I'll put in a transfer request,' she said. She got to her feet, opened the door and slammed it behind her.

'I can't believe she went that far,' Linc said.

Almost immediately, the door opened again. Olivia Brighton. 'Ah … sorry, guys, I was just—is everything okay?' She glanced over her shoulder and back.

'Not even close,' Rachael said. 'But please come in.'

'She's really been fired? It's an actual done deal?' Linc asked.

'You're talking about Lexi,' Brighton said. 'I just heard.'

'How?' Rachael asked.

'Details of your big blow-up with the commissioner have been flying around the cafeteria. Matthews seems to have drawn an audience.'

'Of all the stupid, unprofessional— Lexi hasn't even been told yet!' Rachael barked.

'You slammed the commissioner?' Linc asked.

'Both barrels, I heard,' Brighton said.

'I'm sure Matthews has been in his ear,' Rachael said. 'The bastard sat there with this superior look on his face the whole damn time.' She pressed her fingers to her eyes. 'What is going on in this place? The commissioner's a dead man walking, the Feds have moved in, Lexi gets fired and our team's about to fall apart because I don't have the first clue what to do about Cass. To go over my head like that because of personal gripe and a small push from a Fed is inexcusable.'

'So what are we going to do about Lexi?' Finn asked.

Rachael calmed herself and took a steadying breath. 'We follow Ed's advice. We're going to take this further but not until he's sussed out the landscape. My take is the Feds have been in the commissioner's ear so he's panicking, trying to save face. Lexi's already off the investigation and trying to force the issue now in order to bring her back in might not send the right message. It might even work against her when we have this heard. We'll get her representation to build a case against the dismissal and appeal through the Industrial Relations Commission. We'll explain all this to her, advise her that right now the best way to protect her is to not rock the boat. We play by the rules, go through the proper process. And until I hear from Ed, we don't mention any plans in front of Matthews, okay? I don't want him running back to his commander or the commissioner and possibly throwing more spanners in the works. As far as he's concerned, we're sucking it up and letting the dismissal stand.'

'I still can't believe she's been fired,' Linc said.

'Like it or not, Lexi is involved with these people,' Brighton said, 'she has the history. She did get on that bike. This is the right way to handle it. Any other way could jeopardise all your careers.'

Finn was thoughtful, then said, 'Okay.'

Rachael nodded. 'Right, for now, let's get on with the case.'

CHAPTER TWENTY-EIGHT

I reach Rachael's office just as Linc announces 'she's' been fired. A few more comments leave me in no doubt as to who they're discussing. The shock registers first, then denial. Not just over being fired, but by the way they're taking it. Because they all seem to think it's for the best. For their own careers anyway. Rachael doesn't want to lose face? They're worried they'll go down with me?

I'm stunned by the degree of hurt, the betrayal, that grabs me by the throat.

'You're firing me?' I ask. 'Is that why I've been summoned?'

'Lexi,' Rachael says in surprise. 'We didn't realise you were there.'

That's all she has to say to me? 'I can't see how that makes any difference.'

'Come and sit down.'

'I just need a yes or no.'

'It's not that simple.'

'Lexi, you're here. Have you been told?' Matthews asks, coming in behind me.

'Guess that's a yes, then.'

'Afraid so,' he says with an attempt at sympathy that makes me wonder why he bothered. 'The commissioner had a complaint.'

I laugh and shake my head. 'Oh, I'll bet. Where is she?'

They're all looking at each other as if they want to say something but no one does, so I turn on my heel. I don't need the humiliation of standing there in awkward silence, or worse, listening to empty platitudes.

'Lexi, wait,' Finn says. 'We'll take a walk, talk about it.'

I turn back. 'Why?'

He glances at Rachael. 'So you understand.'

I laugh again. 'Believe it or not, I've dealt with more complex concepts.' I lift my shoulders, take a breath, drop them. 'Well, nice knowing you.'

I reach the lift and no one follows. I'm not sure if that makes me feel better or worse. What the fuck? I guess now that Finn's got that blonde fawning all over him, he's distracted.

Maybe they really don't think it's such a big deal to me. After all, I did try to quit recently. But they're my friends—were my friends. Couldn't they have at least pretended to be a bit more cut up about it?

Who cares? Fuck them. Fuck Cass. Fuck the whole fucked-up situation.

I take the lift down and find my car. As I dig for my keys, I realise my hands are shaking. 'Don't be a fucking sook,' I mutter to myself.

Once I get on the road, I turn the music up loud. As I merge into the motorway traffic, I realise I have absolutely no idea what to do next. Not a clue. I don't have a job. No money coming in and the sum total of the people I call friends—other than my sister Bailee, Tom and, okay, I guess Dawny—are all back there in that building. What am I going to do?

Anxiety trickles in. Even if I can figure out my next step, who would ever even hire a person for a legit job once they've been fired by the police? My stomach sinks. I can't believe not so long ago I thought I'd wanted out. I'm going to need money and I don't want to go back to my old life. I just don't.

As I weave through the traffic, I gradually become aware that a dark-coloured SUV is keeping pace behind me. I'm being tailed? I tell myself not to be ridiculous. It could be nothing. I'm on the main road north—it's one of those drivers who likes to pick someone going just that bit faster than they should be to stick behind, to cop the fine if a patrol car is around. I'm probably being paranoid but, just to be sure, I take a left onto a side street that I know will eventually link me back up to the motorway. The car follows and the moment the road widens with parked cars, lights flash from the SUV's dash.

'You're fucking kidding me!' I snarl.

Beyond caring, I pull over, slam out of my car and stride towards the two suited men climbing out of the SUV.

'What the fuck could you possibly want now?'

'Lexi Winter? Federal Agents Patrick Lloyd and Martin Smythe. Can you come with us, please?'

I recognise the first one from headquarters, but I take a cautious step back anyway. 'Why?'

'We have some questions for you regarding your recent involvement with the Chaos Reigns Motorcycle Club.'

I can't *believe* I tried to keep Cass safe. Right now I want to kill her myself. 'If I refuse?'

'It won't take long. Once we've spoken to you, you'll be free to go.'

Three hours later, I push through my door. It occurs to me to wonder if Finn's gonna want his apartment back. But I've paid upfront. Then I snap at myself because despite whatever's going on, Finn wouldn't do that. I don't think. Though the events of the morning have left me wondering if I really know anything about how the fuck things actually work. I spent most of my life hating everyone—turns out I was on to something.

It's pretty apparent Dawny's not here and I wonder where she's gone. I'm betting it's to see Desmond and suppose it won't be long before they both disappear again for good. The police might still want to talk to him, but that's no longer my problem. For all I care, Dawny and Desmond can come and go as they please. I grab my JD and sit with the bottle before taking a long swig.

'Haven't lost your ability to drink.'

I almost jump out of my skin. 'Damn it, Zander!' I say, glaring at him as he wanders in from the balcony. 'You do that one more fucking time and I'll ...'

'What? Put it down, let's go. Breen wants to see you.'

I eye him suspiciously. 'Why?'

'He'll tell you when we get there.'

'I don't think so. I'm not in the mood.'

'You're in some sort of mood.'

'For drinking. Fuck off.'

'Yeah, look, you're coming with me. I have orders. So … how hard do we need to make this?'

'You'd enjoy that, wouldn't you?' I sneer at him.

He sighs. 'It was so much easier when I just shoved the bag over your head.'

'Oooh! He made a joke! I fucking told you—I'm not in the mood!'

'I can see that.' He perches on the arm of the lounge. 'What's going on?'

'I'm fired.'

'What?'

'Because you took me for a fucking bike ride. So I can't help you anymore, sorry.'

'Yeah, I reckon Breen will still want you back. Other than Nate, he's got no one particularly cyber-savvy. And you were the best, even then.'

I take another long drink. 'I wasn't better than Nate. He taught me all of it.'

'According to him, by the end you were. Now you've got all this police training behind you, and I'm betting you can still access their shit. If Breen can't use you, he'll kill you.'

'And get you to do it?' I lift my arms out in a welcome gesture. 'What are you waiting for?'

'Baby—'

'I'm not your fucking *baby*, I'm not going anywhere, and just try and put that damn bag over my head again.'

He folds his arms. Smirks. 'You don't think that might be a slightly stupid thing to say?'

He's probably right. He's six-foot-fucking-three, built like Hercules and a trained fighter. What chance do I have if he wants me to do something? I'm not giving him the satisfaction of a wrestling match.

'Fine! Whatever! But I'm riding up front.'

I do ride up front in the truck, but with the damn bag on because—Breen's orders—I'm not allowed to know where the clubhouse is. The fabric stinks, it itches and if I try and remove it, Zander's threatened to get out the cable ties. I'm beyond pissed off by the time we arrive.

'Arsehole!' I snap, giving him and his damn hood a shove for the hell of it as I finally breathe fresh air. The act draws some attention from the clubhouse: a few jeers and whistles.

Zander doesn't even pretend to budge, just laughs at me. 'I really need to teach you how to fight.'

'How about I just shoot you? I know how to do that!'

'Lexi?' a familiar voice calls. 'That you making all that noise?'

I spin around to the clubhouse and scan the small audience. A couple of members drinking at the bar, a couple more at the pool table and some chicks wandering around in swimmers, including one who looks way too young to be here despite all those piercings and—is that a tattoo? When I catch her eye she sends me a filthy look before tossing her hair over her shoulder and smiling up at one of the members. Then my gaze lands on a guy in the corner. Old school ZZ Top beard, bandana, silver rings, neck tatts, black leather.

'Freddie!' I send Zander my worst look then beam a smile as I head off in the old man's direction. My happiness on this occasion is genuine. 'How are you?'

Freddie lifts his beer in salute. 'Just as sour and just as blind. Only older. And a fair bit stupider, seeing as no one's around to read me the news anymore. You giving my boy a hard time?'

'I'm gonna tie that bag around his neck while he sleeps and strangle him with it!'

'Got you here though, didn't he? Had orders to put a bullet in your head if you wouldn't come back. You should go down. Don't want to keep Breen waiting.'

'Down?' I ask in confusion.

'This way,' Zander says, catching up. I follow him to the other end of the shed, notice what I'd thought was a regular row of waist-high cupboards in the corner of the room was not: the benchtop has been laid back on hinges, revealing a staircase. I stop and stare, both impressed by its simplicity and how well something could be hidden in plain sight. But also …

'What is this? A dungeon or something?'

'Nope. Move.'

I'm marched down a set of concrete stairs that end in a small concrete box. Concrete walls, concrete roof. Doors to the left and right. Zander reaches an arm over my head and pushes open the left door. I step through and find myself in a corridor. More concrete walls, ceiling, floor. Four doors on the left, one on the right.

'In here,' he says, opening the first door on the left.

'Here she is!' Breen says as I find myself in a small office. 'Thank you for coming.' He always did have a knack for the ridiculous.

Well, so do I. 'You're very welcome.'

He moves around the desk and perches on its edge. 'I said to Zander, ask her to come back. She doesn't come, kill her. You're a cop, that's reasonable.'

'Actually, I'm not. They booted me. What do you want, Breen?'

His face reflects his surprise. 'You're not a cop?'

I hope the knowledge doesn't get me killed. I'm so shitty I'm probably not as nervous as I should be. 'They don't trust me.'

He thinks about that. Then says to Zander, 'It probably makes no difference now. Give her a room to sleep in. She can stay here where we can keep an eye on her.'

'What makes no difference?' I ask.

'We'll talk later,' Breen says. 'Make yourself at home.'

'I have a home!'

'For now, this is it.' The tone in Breen's voice and the look in his eyes suggest maybe I shouldn't push too much further, so I shut up until I'm out of the room.

'Make myself at home? What even is this place?' I ask Zander as we walk further down the corridor. There're some old black and white framed photos to break the grey void, but that's about it. I stop to stare at one. Looks like some sort of military base.

'Okay, listen. This whole place is a rectangle. Around the outside on three sides you've got various rooms. Any doors on the inside are for one central lounge area. If you turn right at the bottom of those stairs we came down instead of left, you'll see another bar and fight area takes up the fourth side.'

'Okay.'

'So this side, you know Breen's room was that first one. Next to that is the boardroom. Never, ever set foot in there, got it?'

'Sacred men's territory?' I whisper in awe.

He rolls his eyes. 'Then we've got a … storage room and this last one holds all the mechanical shit that makes this place run.'

'A storage room, huh? Why not just tell me you don't want me to know what's in there?'

'Okay. I don't want you to know what's in there. Keep moving.' We turn the corner and I'm met with more corridor, more concrete, more doors. He waves at the next row of doors on the left. 'Bathrooms—male *and* female—and an adequate laundry. Keep up.' I'm marched around the next corner to another identical corridor. He stops at the first door. 'This row is bedrooms for anyone who needs to crash. In here.' We enter another small room. A single bed takes up almost half the space, a straw mat, an old Ikea-style chest of drawers and—ew—a pair of men's undies chucked carelessly over the bedframe. Zander drags them and some unmade bedding from the bed then picks up an empty cigarette packet, two long necks.

I screw up my nose in disgust. 'It smells like a bottle of bourbon took a dump in here.'

He flashes me a grin. 'Bourbon? Or tequila?'

'Can't really tell over the cigarette stench. Zander, if I have to stay in this box, I'm gonna puke. There's not even a window to open.'

'Let's get all this stuff out, leave it to air. I think we've got some Glen 20 in the bathroom.'

That's not gonna do it. 'How about bleach, a flame thrower—don't think I won't burn this shit—and an insect bomb, to start. Can we rip up the mat? My head is not going anywhere near that pillow. Don't suppose you've got a UV light? Luminol?'

He stops in the doorway. 'UV light?'

'To pick up any semen, saliva, urine, narcotics … bone and teeth fragments …'

'And Lumiwhatever?'

'Blood.'

'Hmm. Not sure about bone and teeth fragments.'

'Okay, just shoot me.'

He's amused; I'm close to serious.

A familiar face checks us out as he walks past with the multi-pierced girl I'd spotted earlier.

'Hey, Skink,' Zander calls.

'Yeah, bro?'

Zander drops the large bundle of bedding and rubbish in a pile at his feet. 'Clean this shit up.'

'You got it. Hey, it's you,' he says to me. 'Hi, again.'

'Hi, Skink.' The girl is now staring at me like she'd enjoy running into me with a truck but I don't have time to contemplate that because I'm being dragged to the next room. Another bedroom. It's cleaner. It doesn't stink, but there's a definite hint of men's deodorant, maybe aftershave. Harley pictures on the walls, mostly naked women draped over some of them. A wardrobe, roughly made bed, bar fridge full of water bottles and snacks.

'Better?' he asks.

'Marginally. About that UV and luminol …'

'Don't push it. Sleep here. I'll fix up the other room.'

'This is your room?'

'When I don't go home, yeah.'

It might be cleaner but it's still tiny, claustrophobic. 'So … it's not that I'm not grateful, but am I stuck in here or what? It's only early.'

'Nah, come and have a drink. Oh, the lounge area …' He pushes open the door opposite his bedroom. Huge TV, kitchenette, lounges, beanbags, some magazines and few arcade games.

I stick my head in. 'Hmm.' Step out.

'Where are you going?'

'This end door.' I want to know if there's another way out. I doubt it, but it's worth a shot. I open the door and find a dedicated training and fighting area complete with an eight-sided cage of padded red vinyl and mesh with a black canvas mat.

'Those things look like oversized kids' playpens,' I tell him.

He grins. 'That's kinda what they are.'

Along the side of the room are training mats and freestanding bags, and shelves full of gloves, mitts and other training equipment. He walks through it all to the bar. The set-up's not dissimilar to the clubhouse above us, just much, much nicer and more comfortable.

'Why do you need the bar up top if you've got this?'

'Cops come looking for a clubhouse, they can check out the top one. They don't need to know about down here. And it lets us spread out a bit more.' He goes behind the bar and pours me half a glass of JD. 'Here.'

'Thanks.' I sit myself on a red vinyl stool and take a better look around. 'What exactly is "here"?'

'I'll let Dad explain it to you. He'll love it.'

'Fuck, it's something military that requires a long, long, *long* explanation.'

Zander grins and taps his beer bottle to my glass.

'So I can just hang wherever?'

'Sure, why not?'

'What's to stop me walking out?'

He looks like I've just made a joke then says, 'Me.'

Piercings and tatts girl comes in wearing tight shorts and a tank top, and four members follow close behind and rack up balls for a pool game. Because I've almost skulled my drink, Zander gives me a top-up and points me at a lounge. I sit and he flops down beside me, arms along the back. More people pour in.

'What are you looking at?' Zander asks in my ear.

'That girl in the gold shirt. What's her deal?'

'Dunno. I think she's crashing here. Lots of girls hang around, you know that. Can't resist us.'

I turn my head to pull a face at him. 'Uh-huh. That girl that can't resist you, how old do you think she is?'

He frowns in thought as he looks at her. Shrugs. 'Too young for me, that's for sure.'

'Glad you think so. She seems to have a problem with me. I'm guessing it's because she has a thing for you.'

'They all do,' he teased. 'It's a curse.'

'Well, well, well.' A woman's voice, vaguely familiar. 'I see you found your way back.' She comes around from behind us and I'm faced with the ICU nurse.

'What …?'

'Lexi, Jan.' Zander introduces us with a wave of his beer. 'Woolly's old lady.'

'Zander sent me after ya,' Jan tells me. 'Wanted to make sure you found your way home.'

'I did wonder if you were an Annie Wilkes or a Mother Teresa.'

She has a big laugh and she uses it. 'I don't do any breaking, but there's always plenty to patch up around here.' She looks from me to Zander. 'Guess that domestic dispute sorted itself out then.'

I shrug when Zander laughs. 'I had to come up with some reason for being out there.'

'Dodged a bullet there, quite literally. Breen wouldn't have been happy if you'd sprouted off the truth to the first stranger you could find. Still, can't believe he'd tolerate a cop sitting here.'

'Former cop,' I amend.

'Well, nice to meet ya. And I don't say that to cops very often. I'm off to get a drink.'

'Former,' I growl again.

'You're way too cut up about this,' Zander tells me. 'Why did you even want to become a pig in the first place?'

'I became a *cop* because I was sick of escorting, and because I got to use what I learnt from Nate to help solve the Spider case. And I liked solving problems, liked using my brain to make a difference.'

'Is that really the best way to solve problems? To make a difference?'

I drop my head back against the lounge. 'Honestly, I was never quite convinced. But having the decision taken away from me wasn't fun. Neither was learning how quick so-called friends are willing to dump you. Rachael, what she said … I wouldn't have believed it if I hadn't heard it myself.'

He whistles and when everyone in the room looks up, he waves over a cute little blonde in a blue leather top and tiny denim shorts. 'This is Taylor. Her husband used to beat her up.' Then to Taylor, he says, 'What'd you do about it, honey?'

'Called the cops. They took him away for the night to cool down.'

'Then what happened?'

'He came home and beat me harder. Called the cops again, they arrested him. Charged him. He got bail. Came home again, beat me up again.'

'That one put her in hospital. He took off, cops couldn't find him, not that they seemed to try very hard. When Taylor got out, he was waiting. Only difference was, so were we.'

'What did you do?' I ask.

'Exactly what he did to her. Eye for an eye.'

'And?'

'He spent some time in hospital. Cops caught up with him but that was a joke. He never ended up doing any time, but he's never come near her again either.'

'Walked past me in the street one day, took off across the road faster than I've ever seen him move. Fucking coward.' She high-fives Zander and wanders off.

'Okay, so?'

'Not finished. The guy over there in the black tee with his head in a beer is Tony. He used to own a million-dollar business. His wife and her secret boyfriend decided to strip his accounts. Cops told him he had to provide proof. He recorded a conversation, got the wife to admit it. Got that *absolute* proof. Courts threw the case out—you're not allowed to record conversations without the consent of all parties. They walked away, he was left with fines and ordered to pay court fees. All that took months. One sit-down visit from us—twenty minutes tops—Tony had his money back. The system's a joke, Lexi. You used to get that. You used to help Cronin make sure people got what was coming to them all the time without wearing a uniform.'

'I'm not sure they all had it coming to them. What Cronin did, he did for profit. No system's perfect.'

'You're not one of them, with their privileged lives and expensive suits and one rule for them and another for everyone else. The system will use you and spit you out.'

'I think it already has.'

'This is who you are. Who you always were. You can help people right here. Under your own rules.'

'As a prisoner. How do I know Breen's still not considering putting a bullet in my head?'

'When Breen knows he can trust you, you can come and go as you like. Just like before.'

'Yeah, but what's he want?'

'You'll find out soon enough.'

CHAPTER TWENTY-NINE

Tuesday, March 29

Cass stared up at the ceiling and shifted in a vain attempt to untangle the mess her sheets had gotten into from a restless, sleepless night. Her team hated her, saw her as a traitor. It had all seemed so straightforward when she'd called Matthews. So cut and dried. He'd told her she had a responsibility to tell the truth. To voice her concerns, as he was. He'd told her Olivia Brighton had already spoken to him, had mentioned the chat she and Brighton had had regarding Lexi and her irresponsible approach to rules and order. Lexi's history, especially with the club. Brighton had also agreed Lexi was a liability, at least to this case. After months of no one wanting to listen, of being shot down in flames whenever she questioned Lexi's behaviour, Cass had felt so damn validated.

So she'd written the complaint and Matthews had taken it to the commissioner and their case had been strong enough to convince the commissioner to take on-the-spot action. That proved she was right. Nothing she'd said had been a lie. Maybe she had exaggerated a few points, bent a motive here or there, but that was her interpretation and she'd challenge anyone to prove otherwise.

Lexi was fired. Mission accomplished. But she could hardly celebrate. Cass might have won on one front, but she'd badly lost on another. It had been easy to jump on the Matthews/Brighton bandwagon, but she didn't work with them day in, day out. They weren't her team. Now she wasn't even sure she had one.

She had been going to lodge her transfer request this morning. Instead, she'd done something she'd never done in her life: she'd called in sick. Lied to get out of having to go in, face everyone. She'd have to be there when they didn't want to work with her. The discomfort of that scenario had kept her in bed. Transfers weren't instant. Then again, her brain reminded her, they didn't happen at all unless you lodged them.

She buried her head in her pillow. She wanted to scream into it. Everything was falling down around her. Damn Lexi! Cass's position in homicide had been her dream job. At least, it would have been until she had the opportunity to run her own team one day. She'd loved working under Rachael. The woman was as good as it gets. Except when it came to Lexi. Couldn't Rachael see all the controversy she caused? How Lexi's mistakes reflected on her? There was nothing stopping Rachael from reaching the very top of the organisation. Except for her treatment of Lexi. And she refused to see it. Cass would never understand it.

A ping on her phone had her picking it up to check. Maybe Linc had forgiven her, was wondering where she was. Of all of them, he was the one who was most understanding. His condemnation yesterday had been the most difficult to take.

But it was Meera. She'd taken a photo of Noah pulling silly faces outside daycare. The message said, *Cheer up and feel better! Xoxoxox*

Cass touched the screen, ran her fingers lovingly over the faces of the two people she cared about more than her own life. In terms of family, she'd hit the jackpot. If nothing else, that was solid. Last night, she'd briefly explained the events of the previous day to Meera. Meera hadn't pushed, had told her to take some time, do what's best for her. She was used to Cass not wanting to discuss work and she had always been so damn understanding. So kind.

For some stupid reason, the thought that Meera would never have done to Lexi what Cass had done to her popped into her head. Hell, if things were different, maybe she would have cut Lexi a bit more slack. But that's not how it was. She dragged her hands over her face and through her hair. Blew out a breath. None of that mattered. She needed to protect herself, her family. That had to come first. What was done was done.

The same could be said about Cronin's case. He hadn't come after her. Wouldn't. Because he didn't know. She wanted to believe that, desperately. But what if she was wrong?

He'd been led from the courtroom in handcuffs after having given his testimony on the drug cartel as part of his deal. It was that agreement that was supposed to have reduced his sentence and guaranteed Laura's and Mikey's safety.

Cass had almost chased Gordon and Wallis, had had to wait while they received pats on the back, slaps of congratulations from high-ranking officials and talked of promotions. When she'd finally managed to get their attention on the courthouse steps, she'd been treated like a pest for interrupting them. Gordon had ordered her to the parking area where he and Wallis had stood over her and shattered her belief in human nature.

'Go back to the safe house,' Gordon said. 'And call it in.'

Confused, she'd simply stared, not able to fathom the full ramifications of the request.

'Anyone home?' Wallis had taunted.

'It's her first big win,' Gordon said. 'She's stoked.'

'No one's been looking for them?' She checked her watch. Three hours had passed. 'You said you'd take care of it! I was to come straight to the courthouse and you would deal with it.'

'And I did. I dealt with it the way I knew was best for the case. Better for everyone if you go back and call it in now. You weren't there earlier; you came straight to the courthouse this morning and when you went back to check on the family, they were gone.'

'But … but that's not what happened! Of course I was there. You know I was there!'

Gordon's expression was calculating and cold. 'Then why didn't you call it in?'

'I— You told me not to. You said you would call the teams to get out there.'

'Did I?' He looked at Wallis, who shrugged. 'Why would I tell you to break protocol? Your career could go down the toilet over something like that.'

The sickness in her gut built and built. 'I was following orders …'

Gordon leant in close enough she felt his breath on her face. 'Who's going to believe you?'

'But—'

'Okay, I'm going to do you a favour and tell it like it is. The wife and brat of a career criminal got pinched by more criminals. That's what they do to each other. You live the life, you pay the price. They were already gone and you can't be sure for how long. If we'd acted earlier, Cronin wouldn't have testified and a whole lot more criminal arseholes would have continued to get away with breaking the law. It was our duty to secure his testimony to incriminate those cartel arseholes, to get them off the street for as long as possible. Now that we've done our duty to the public, we'll go after the criminals who pinched the other criminals, but honestly, we've already won this one. If you're going to be a detective, you need to know how to work a case. How to get the right outcome. It's greater good.'

'Laura and Mikey aren't criminals. Nor is Constable Lucas!'

'You go, you call it in, just like I told you. I need detectives I can trust on my team. Let's make sure you're one of them. 'Cause, Cassidy, if you made a mistake, if you stuffed up and left the scene of the crime, didn't call it in, ran away and forgot your training and a cop is injured or dead, I can guarantee trying to make excuses by blaming highly decorated superior officers is the kind of bad look that gets you booted from the force. Understand?'

Head spinning, mind racing, Cass didn't have time to think things through. She had to get back to the scene as fast as she could to call that help. That had to come first. Even though she knew, once she made that call, there was no going back.

She was still in her pyjamas when Meera called home for lunch.

'I thought I'd keep you company,' she said. 'And bring you some of that pasta you like from down the street.'

'Thank you,' Cass said, forcing a smile. She didn't feel at all hungry but as Meera had made the effort, she opened the container, poured some into two bowls and sat.

'Still bummed about yesterday?' Meera asked when Cass remained quiet.

'Feeling a bit steadier, actually,' she lied. 'Pasta helps.'

'Carbs solve everything,' Meera joked.

'You know,' she said, 'I've been thinking. You should visit your mum.'

Meera put down her fork and stared. 'Should I?'

'We keep talking about it but we can never take time off at the same time.'

'Can you take time off now?'

'Not with all this crap going on, but I don't think you should wait indefinitely for us all to go together. I have some time that I can take later in the year. We can go then. I'd love to, but your mum's not well and I worry …' She watched Meera's eyes go glassy. 'I think you should take Noah to see his nani. While she's still well enough.'

Meera stared at her plate, took a couple of breaths and shook her head. 'I'd feel guilty leaving you when you're going through this stuff with work.'

Cass reached out and squeezed Meera's hand. 'Don't. I wish I could come, but this is the next best thing.'

Meera's concerned expression turned into a smile. 'If you're sure … Okay. I am worried. I need to see for myself how she is. She says she's fine but she'd never tell me otherwise. I know she'd love to meet Noah in person. Zoom's not the same.'

'Noah will love it too. I think you should stay a couple of weeks, more if you can manage it. And if I can wrangle it, I might be able to get there for a few of those days.'

Meera laughed. 'I can't take too much time off, I won't have a practice left! But I'll see.' She chewed on her lip thoughtfully and looked at Cass with so much gratitude Cass felt guilty. She'd known Meera had been worried about her mum, she should have said something before this. But it was the perfect excuse to get them out of the city. She was sure Cronin couldn't know what she'd done, but Lexi's warning wouldn't leave her alone and if he had somehow found out, she needed her family out of the way until he was back in custody.

CHAPTER THIRTY

'Lexi, would you please call me?' Finn heard from outside Rachael's office. 'I understand you're upset, but if you'll give me a chance to explain, I know you'll feel differently. Please.'

'I left a couple of messages too,' he said, entering as she ended the call. 'Then I went over there, got Dawny. She hasn't seen her or spoken to her. Or so she says. I'll try again this arvo.'

'Okay, let's move on with our meeting. Our friend Matthews will be waiting.'

'So we take our time,' Finn suggested. It was bad enough the man was on the team—he wasn't running it too.

But sure enough, Matthews was waiting impatiently when they walked in. Linc was already there too—his head buried in his laptop as though deliberately avoiding the man.

'Morning,' Matthews said testily. 'I spent last night in a meeting with my team. They're not happy with the lack of progress.'

'That makes two of us,' Rachael said, putting down her things. 'Had we not had to deal with an unnecessary upset yesterday, we might still have a full team and more progress under our belts.'

'Cassidy's not here?'

'She called in sick. She's accrued plenty of leave. I doubt she'll be back any time soon.'

He shrugged. 'That's her prerogative. Not very professional, though.'

'Nor was your behaviour.'

He leant back in his chair and eyed her directly. 'You think this is my fault?'

'Reading between the lines of the explanation you provided, I believe Lloyd assessed our team, decided Lexi was a liability and encouraged you to do something about that. I think you played Cass to get what you wanted.'

Another shrug. 'Cassidy made her own decision, I simply gave her options. And for the record, I agree with her. Let's move on.'

'So you have something constructive to offer?' Finn asked. 'Because from what I've seen, you're not much more than a fly on the wall.'

'My suggestion would be to go after the sergeant-at-arms.'

'We bring Rocco in and then what?' Rachael asked. 'All we have on him is the secondhand testimony of a woman who wasn't there and didn't see anything.'

'It's called interrogation. You're supposed to be famous for it, right? Do that.'

'I worked closely with the Feds a couple of months back on another case. They were outstanding.'

'Of course.'

'So how did we end up with you?'

He scowled. 'I suppose you've got a better idea?'

'Yes, I do. Linc, the club prospect that goes by the name Skink. Do we have an address on him?'

'Yes,' Linc said after a quick check. 'Dora Creek.'

'He appears to be easily overwhelmed by authority. I think I may be able to turn him. Depending on what happens today, we'll pick him up, see if we can get him to talk.'

'What's happening today?' Matthews asked.

A knock on the door was followed by McCabe entering. 'Morning.'

'Good morning,' Rachael said with a smile. 'All set?'

'What's going on?' Matthews asked again.

McCabe slid into a seat. 'Breen's latest shipping container arrived at the docks last week. It's just been cleared for pick up.'

'Then you're on,' Rachael said.

'On?' Linc asked.

'As we know, Dawny said Desmond's been doing deliveries for the club. But she told us he's been delivering from the port to the clubhouse. That our victim was killed after attempting to sneak in and video what was going on inside.'

'So?' Linc asked.

'So why would they have Desmond deliver motorcycles and parts to the clubhouse when they have to then take them back to the workshop? There's plenty of room to unload a shipping container at the workshop. The place is made for it. They already have a couple on location.'

Finn sat up straighter. 'Of course.'

'We need to make sure customs isn't missing something,' McCabe said. 'We've got surveillance ready to go. We're going to follow them back, find the location of the clubhouse and watch them unload, see if we can't figure out what's going on.'

'And if Desmond is driving,' Rachael said to Matthews, 'we'll pick him up and offer him a deal to give up Rocco. Then we'll have something solid under our belts to build a case with.'

'We'll see you later.'

'Thanks, McCabe.' After McCabe left, Rachael said to her team, 'In the meantime, Arthur Cronin's mother. Linc, you have an address?'

'Yep. She's pushing ninety and lives independently in a house at Forresters Beach.'

'Finn and I will visit the location this morning.'

'Ah … sorry to interrupt,' Neutron said, hovering in the doorway.

'Good morning,' Rachael said. 'What can we do for you?'

'Sorry. I'm looking for Lexi. She's not answering her phone.'

There was silence around the table because no one, it seemed, wanted to tell him.

In the end, Finn blurted it out. 'Lexi no longer works for us.'

Neutron's eyes went wide, his mouth falling open. 'What? When did this happen? What do you mean? Like, not at all? Why?'

'It's a long story.'

'Better offer? I heard the private sector is paying bucketloads.' Disappointment leaked into his voice. 'I just spoke to her the other day. She never mentioned it.'

'It was a bit of a surprise to Lexi too,' Rachael said with a glare at Matthews.

'Well, our loss, right?'

'You got that right,' Finn said.

'Then what do you want me to do with the information we have from the phone she cloned?'

'Had you both finished going through it?'

'No—at least, I hadn't. We got sidetracked by a couple of club chat rooms and didn't get back to it.'

'Neutron, I know you're very busy at present, but if you have another chance to look at it, I'd really appreciate it.'

'I'll ... see what I can do. I might try giving Lexi another call. Make sure she hasn't already done it. Say hi.'

'Thanks, Neutron.'

He paused at the door. 'I keep the name, right?'

'Neutron forever,' Finn said, and watched him walk away.

'That's one sad computer nerd,' Linc said.

'What did he mean he keeps the name?' Matthews asked.

'Neutron was Lexi's pet name for Jim,' Rachael said. 'It stuck.'

Matthews stared then shook his head. 'Why don't you all just build a shrine to the woman and be done with it?'

Finn pushed to his feet. He didn't need to like this guy even less. 'You ready, Rachael?'

'This is it,' Finn said, and stopped the car in front of an impressive sprawling home on the waterfront. The gardens were immaculate, everything was clean and neat and tidy and masterfully presented.

'One ninety-year-old lives here alone?' Rachael queried.

'I'd say she has help,' Finn said, 'and if Cronin's living in a squat when she's living here, I guess they really must be estranged.' He stepped out of the car and did up his jacket.

Rachael followed him through a gate to the double front doors. A camera and intercom sat on the wall. Rachael pressed the buzzer.

'Yes?' came an abrupt, deep-voiced reply through the speaker.

Rachael pulled out her credentials and held them in front of the camera. 'I'm Inspector Rachael Langley and my associate is Sergeant Finn Carson. We're here to see Mrs Cronin.'

Footsteps echoed from the other side of the door, grew louder. A moment later, a slight woman in a nurse's uniform opened the door.

'Follow me, please.'

'That wasn't her voice on the intercom,' Finn muttered.

'Keep your eyes open.'

They stepped onto mosaic floors and followed the nurse through one of the most luxurious homes Finn could remember visiting. They were ushered into a glass-walled sitting room overlooking the ocean and a long sandy beach. A frail old woman in a navy dress and pearls sat stiffly on a white leather chaise longue. Beside her sat a magnificent spray of pink orchids.

'Mrs Cronin. Rachael Langley and Finn Carson. Lovely to meet you.'

Mrs Cronin's lips only pressed tighter, but she nodded.

'Please take a seat,' the nurse offered. 'May I offer you any refreshments?'

'No, but thank you,' Rachael said.

As the nurse nodded and walked away, another set of footsteps approached. Finn spotted a large man in a black suit settle himself by the doorway. Security, no doubt. But for what purpose? They were police.

'Mrs Cronin, we don't want to take up too much of your time, but we were hoping to talk to you briefly about your son,' Rachael said.

Mrs Cronin looked them over, her dislike evident. 'I don't see my son.'

'We heard you were estranged but we thought you may know where we might find him.'

'Estranged?' She smiled sadly. 'My son refuses to see me because he's ashamed, detectives. He's ashamed he allowed himself to be fooled and his family to be murdered. He considers himself less of a man, and for the shame he feels he's brought to his family, he refuses to grace my door.'

'That's a heavy burden,' Finn said. 'Especially as that wasn't his fault.'

Beady eyes pierced Finn's. 'Were you two involved?'

'I'm sorry?' Rachael asked. 'In what?'

'It was evil!' she spat. 'You two were there, weren't you? That's why you're here now. You're scared.' She gave them a smile that had Finn's blood running cold. 'You should be!'

'Mrs Cronin, I'm afraid I have no idea what you're talking about,' Rachael said.

'You put Arthur in prison with your lies and got Laura and Mikey murdered!'

'I assure you we did none of those things. But I would be very interested to discuss—'

'It's too late for discussion,' she said. 'No one believed him, no one would help.'

'We do believe him,' Finn said. It shut Mrs Cronin up, so he continued. 'We have a friend who was close to your son at the time. She told us the truth.'

'What truth?'

'That he was never responsible for the drugs. That he was framed by another member of the club who wanted his position. That that led to the murder of his family.'

'They were my family too! You let it happen! The deals, the lies! You pretended you didn't know. You didn't care. You paraded like heroes when you were nothing but scum!'

'Mrs Cronin, I would turn in my badge before doing any of those things,' Rachael said gently. 'If justice has been denied to your son, we can make sure he gets it.'

'He doesn't need your help. If you are telling the truth, you have nothing to worry about. Now get out. I don't want you in my home.'

Rachael got to her feet and gestured for Finn to do the same. 'We appreciate your time, Mrs Cronin.'

Mrs Cronin's face once again became a rigid mask.

'Well, that was fun,' Finn said as they drove away. 'I wonder if Cronin himself has anything on the evil Mrs Cronin.'

'That woman isn't evil, she's in pain, and has been for a long time. It's turned her bitter, but I don't think she was lying. Something's going on here. Something very wrong went down during that case. Lexi was so young and no doubt impressionable, so I wasn't sure if she was relaying fact or the version of it she'd been fed. But now I think she was right and I think the investigation needs to be reviewed.'

'Honestly, I was convinced of that as soon as she bailed Cass up. I've never understood Cass's behaviour towards Lexi but the idea Lexi knew something that could dredge all this up and ruin Cass's career makes perfect sense.'

'We need to talk to both of them again. As well as Gordon and Wallis.'

CHAPTER THIRTY-ONE

It's almost lunchtime and I'm sitting in the bar with a drink because the tiny bedroom was giving me claustrophobia and there is nothing else to do. Absolutely nothing. I'm bored enough that a confrontation with Breen would almost be a welcome relief from the inactivity. Almost. I'm agitated, fidgety, anxious. I'm suffering real withdrawal symptoms from not having my computer nor contact with the outside world. I may need to find a friend in this place with some pot to chill me out.

I'm giving that thought serious consideration when a rowdy group set up for a game of pool.

'Hey, Skink, you in?' Rocco growls.

'Yeah, coming!' Skink calls from behind me, then says to someone else, 'Hey, Krystal, can you grab us some beers?'

'Yeah, Skink. Sure.'

Krystal, the piercings and tatts girl, moves behind the bar and starts pulling beers from the fridge, popping lids. She eyes me off like a mortal enemy then, in an act that could only be completely on purpose, knocks over one of the bottles, sending the contents hurtling across the bar towards me. To her clear disappointment, I shift just in time to avoid a lapful. Her pinched smile and 'oops' are deliberately nasty. I've gotta hand it to her, the girl has an impressive mean streak.

'*Krystal?* Really?'

'You got a problem with my name?' she demands.

'You couldn't come up with something a little less … done?'

Her eyes narrow with contempt. 'That's my name.'

'And it's cute. Truly. And bullshit. What's your real name?'

Angry eyes flash. 'I just told you!'

'Must be embarrassing then, huh? Like one of those made-up ones no one can spell, or something that can be turned into a bad word. Or—'

'It's Caitlin,' Skink says helpfully, coming over with a wad of paper towel and handing it to the now irate Caitlin. 'Make sure you clean that up good,' he tells her, 'or I'll cop it.'

'Caitlin. Huh. Well, that's a shitload better than I thought it was gonna be.'

Caitlin's still glaring at Skink but as her gaze sweeps back it settles warmly on someone behind me. 'Hi!'

I turn to see who she's looking at. Zander. I pounce on him.

'Want to tell me why I've hung around here all morning doing nothing?'

'Nup. Want some lunch?'

'I want to go back to my apartment. I want clean clothes, my own shower. I need my phone, my computers. I have to take calls. I don't want people running around thinking something's happened to me!'

He considers me for a minute. 'Fine. I'll talk to Breen.'

'Now?'

He gives me that *you're being fucking annoying* look, but he sighs and turns around. 'Okay …'

For all my earlier bravado, I can't say I'm not at least slightly nervous about the outcome of that, so I sit back down to drink.

'He'll get sick of you,' Caitlin says, sweeping past me with the beers. 'You're not that fucking special. Oh—sorry, Dean,' she tacks on as she narrowly avoids crashing into the newcomer.

'No worries, babe,' Dean says.

I'm still grinning into my glass as Dean sits himself down beside me. He's maybe forty, has a terrible goatee but a pleasant enough face and a vest that tells me he's treasurer.

'Hi,' he says.

'Hey.'

'I'm Dean.'

'I'm drinking, fuck off.'

He chuckles. 'Damn, and here I was thinking you'd fall in love with me at first sight.'

'Original.'

'Effective?'

'Sorry, I don't get all those cute, tingly feelings people talk about.'

'Are you a psycho?'

'Are you an arsehole?'

He laughs. 'No, I mean, there's talk we've got some in here. I thought Rocco was; turns out he's a diagnosed sociopath. Big guy over there has something called oppositional defiance disorder. Prisons pay a stack of money to give everyone labels these days. Breen's been recruiting all sorts lately. If you're useful, you're in, no questions asked. So, I like labels. Helps me remember who I'm dealing with.'

'So what are you?'

'Boring. But only as far as labels go,' he says with a smile. 'You?'

My drink dangles from my fingers as I check him out. 'I hate labels, so I wouldn't know. And I've dodged prison so far, so no fancy shrinks. Maybe you'll just have to make up your own mind.'

'I'd like that. Assuming you don't plan on murdering me in my sleep.'

I shake my head. 'Would never happen. I prefer to look people in the eye as I stick the knife in.'

There's a silent 'oh,' and he studies his drink. He looks up once, twice, hoping to see a smile or any other hint that I'm joking. I manage to keep my face blank, my stare empty. On the last look I can tell I've spooked him and, sure enough, he gets off the stool.

'Well, nice meeting you.'

'I'll see you around.' It's not quite a threat. I have to avert my face before I give myself away. Too funny.

'One down, twenty-three to go,' Zander says, coming back to sit beside me.

'Apparently Breen's bringing all sorts into the club.'

'Well, you're back.'

'Oh, so funny!'

'Come on, he wants to talk to you.'

'Okay.' And then I notice the exodus, the beers Caitlin had just served being quickly downed and pool cues being returned to their holders. 'Where's everyone going?'

'Club business.'

'Let me guess, drug shipment?'

'Close. Got an alcohol delivery to unload. Won't take 'em long. What made you think drug shipment?'

'Organised crime thinks you're doing deals with some shipping company to smuggle shit into the country.'

'What?' he asks in surprise. 'Come with me.' He leads me to Breen's office. 'Hey, Breen, Lexi said the cops are on to our pick-ups.'

Breen's eyes narrow. 'What do they know?'

'I'm not really up to date. They were suspicious because you started trading with that same company Cronin was supposed to have been importing from. They were talking about intercepting one of your shipments.'

He doesn't look particularly surprised. 'They won't find anything.'

'I'm guessing you won't mind if they make an appearance then.'

Breen's thoughtful for a moment. 'Do you think you can still get into their computers?'

'What do you need?'

'To know if you can still get into their computers.'

I shift on the spot. 'Breen, that's a lot of computers and networks you're talking about. Be specific. What do you want?'

'I want you to tell me if there's any plans in place for tonight,' he snaps.

'Okay … Got a computer I can use?'

'Follow me. Zander, is Nate here yet?'

'Everyone's just headed upstairs, so I reckon. I'll get him down here.' Zander gets out his phone and I follow Breen to the 'storage room'. I watch him unlock the door. Inside is a network of computers, screens, servers and other hardware large enough to run a small country.

'Wow!' I say in real admiration as I look around.

'Yeah?' Nate says. 'You wanted to see—Lexi!'

I'm gathered up in a bear hug that steals my breath. I shove him off but smile. 'Hey, handsome.'

'You didn't tell me!' he says to Zander.

Zander shrugs. 'Surprise.'

'I've been here all night, where have you been?' I complain.

'Busy. Just arrived back from the city. I heard you'd turned cop.'

'I had. It was handy. But not anymore.'

He beams at Breen. 'We're gonna do this job easy with both of us.'

'One step at a time,' Breen warns. 'Lexi, find me that information.'

I look at Nate for guidance. 'Which computer can I use to log into police HQ?'

He puts me in front of the one I was hoping he would and lets me in.

'Okay,' I say. 'Let me give it a go … Hey, what do you know? I'm not locked out yet.'

'What are their plans?' Breen asks again, impatiently.

'I can't go in from here. I have to cover my tracks or they'll know it's me.'

'Does it matter?'

'I'd prefer to remain anonymous so I don't have to go into hiding for the rest of my life. If I haven't had my credentials tossed it could be to keep an eye on me. I've had every level of cops questioning me over you guys. They've probably already flagged my log in. I'll check my work email, nothing suspicious in that.' I check it, ignore all the messages, then log out.

'Now what?' Breen asks.

'Now I break the computer,' I say and create a small issue, log a service request with IT and drum my fingers on the desk. 'Because I'm still in the system this should be fairly straightforward but I have to be careful. Cyber has been developing this new program because everyone wants to break into police databases these days … Give me a sec.' I silently praise the efficiency of IT when I'm called almost straight back.

'Thanks so much, Daniel!' I purr into the phone ten minutes later and end the call. 'Okay, I'm in.'

'Because of Daniel? Who's Daniel?' Breen asked.

'He's one of the IT admins at headquarters.'

'You were talking to headquarters? Why?'

'Because why hit the system guns blazing if you can tiptoe through it?'

Breen's annoyed growl is followed by his hands being tossed in the air. 'You make no sense to me!'

'She does to me,' Nate said, sliding into the chair beside me. 'She got IT support to access the computer to help with this self-created problem and while they were doing that, she used the vulnerability of that connection to access the IT admin's account.'

'Then I used admin's account privileges to reassign all file permissions to my account.'

'Which means what?' Breen asks impatiently.

'Which means I can get in and see what's going on without anyone knowing I've been there.'

'We should let her in on the plan,' Nate tells Breen as I spend some time locating McCabe's files. 'While she's got access.'

I glance up, interested, but Breen's undecided, shaking his head. 'I don't trust her yet. Let's see what comes from this.'

I'm into McCabe's emails so I check them out. 'Ah … Breen?'

'What is it?'

'They've got surveillance on your shipping container. They're planning on following it home.'

Breen spins around. 'Nate!'

Nate furiously types away on a nearby computer. Swears. 'She's right! Sorry, boss. The information came in an hour ago while I was doing the alcohol run.'

Breen looks over my shoulder. Swears. 'I need to warn people!' He's already dragging out his phone as he leaves.

'Nice work,' Zander says.

'You told me I had to be useful so I could get outta here.'

'You want to get out of here?' Nate asks. 'You only just got here!'

'It would be nice to come and go at will,' I say, looking at the equipment. 'Can I just say, Nate, this is amazing.'

'My life's work,' he mutters. I think he's worried he's pissed off Breen.

I wander around, open a cupboard and find it stacked to the roof with what looks like police equipment.

He shrugs. 'Comes in handy occasionally.'

'So what is this big plan, anyway?' I ask.

An annoyed expression flickers over his face. 'Can't tell you till Breen okays it.' Then a ping has him checking his phone. 'I need to move. You coming for a ride?' he asks Zander.

'Nah, I'm babysitting,' Zander tells him. 'Enjoy.'

'I'll see you later,' Nate mutters again, before jogging out.

'So, babysitter,' I say as we walk back to the bar, 'where were you all morning when I could have just wandered off?'

He lifts his gaze to the roof. 'Up top working on my bike. You wouldn't have got far. Drink?'

'Didn't you offer me lunch?'

'Yeah, I'll organise something.'

I give the lab one more envious look as he closes the door. 'I wish you'd let me know about that *storage* room earlier.'

'You don't go in there unsupervised until Breen clears it.' He grins at me. 'I'd forgotten what a nerd you were.'

'A nerd that just saved your arses!'

'Yeah,' he says and pushes open the door to the bar. It seems everyone has returned, some are busy restocking fridges. 'Didn't take you long to switch sides.'

I shrug. 'I'm on my side. And I'm broke. I can't afford to feel guilty.'

'That's a good philosophy.'

I drop heavily into a seat with a sigh. 'So why *do* I feel guilty?'

He chuckles. 'Programming. They've rewired your brain. We'll fix you.'

'There's nothing wrong with my brain!' I object. 'Two days ago these people were my friends. McCabe didn't get me fired and I've just blown his whole operation.'

'Yeah, I reckon you're done with the cops. You could always go back to escorting.'

'I've probably forgotten how.'

His brow shoots up. 'It's been that long?'

'I think my virginity is growing back.'

'Lexi!' Breen shouts over Zander's snigger. He's standing in the doorway with his phone pressed to his chest.

'Yeah?'

'What else did the cops have on the club?'

I contemplate him. Bastard. Weren't we supposed to have had a talk about my freedom? As I've just been useful and he wants more, I play my advantage. 'I can probably find out. But if you want me to risk my arse going back in there, you're gonna have to start paying me. I need money.'

He stares at me thoughtfully. Nods. 'You work with Nate. We'll be watching you carefully. I want you keeping tabs.'

'And I want to come and go. I want my computers and my phone. I'm not going to go running back to the cops. After what I just did, I'd go to prison. I told you I joined the cops for what I could get out of it. That wasn't a lie. You're going to have to trust me—or not. But there's only one way you'll get my best work and that's not by locking me up in here.'

He doesn't like being spoken to like that. I can see those mean eyes considering his next move. He tells whoever's on the phone he'll call them back, then closes the distance between us to talk quietly. 'You know her better than I do,' he says to Zander. 'What do you think?'

Zander shrugs. 'We need her. Loyalty's not her strong suit but she's out of options and she's broke. I'll keep an eye on her. Nate can monitor her online activity, her phone. But I say we give her what she wants and lock her into working for us before she ends up working for someone else.'

Breen leans in and stares at me hard. 'You can come and go with Zander, have your stuff, but until I've got what I want out of you, you spend your nights here.' He straightens, says to Zander, 'She fucks up, it's still on you. Got it?'

'Loud and clear.'

I watch him stalk away. 'Thanks for the fabulous rap.'

'You think he'd have believed it?' Zander huffs. 'And from now on, can you please tell your face to use its inside voice?'

'If I'd smiled and simpered, do you think he'd have believed *that*?'

'It's Breen,' he mutters, taking a look at some commotion going on at the pool table. 'You never know.' He snags a beer from the bar. 'You want anything?'

My stomach growls. 'Yeah. About that food?'

He nods. 'Hey, Skink!'

Skink puts down his pool cue and races over like an obedient puppy. 'Yeah?'

'Go get us some fish and chips. Grab yourself something, too.' Zander throws him a fifty. 'Make sure I get the change.'

'You got it. I've just got to sink one more ball.'

'Skink?'

'Yeah?'

'We're hungry.'

'Ah … sure. I'll do it now.' He calls out to his friends that he's gotta go and scurries out.

'The way you talk to him is not cool.'

'I was going to take you out and get it, but Skink was winning that game. Rocco doesn't lose to prospects or it gets ugly. I just saved Skink some teeth.' He leans forward to put his beer down and I wonder if those arms are any less than quadruple the size of mine. The tattoos just make them look even bigger.

'Are you still fighting?'

'I'm fighting *again*.'

'You stopped.'

'For a bit. Got a regular gig playing at the leagues club for a couple of years while the club was in a mess, band I was with got a following, played a few venues. Too much drinking, not enough training. Got fat.'

A laugh gurgles out of me. 'Yeah, right. I can't imagine you fat any more than I can you playing at the leagues club.'

'We got good. But also fat.' He sits back and grins. 'Got slammed for the first couple of fights. Took ages to get fit again.'

'Well, you weren't that good to start with.'

He gets me in a headlock and scruffs my hair. 'Mouthy bitch,' he says affectionately. 'Go get a drink. After Skink brings back our lunch, I'll take you home to pick up your stuff.'

I get up. Realise I'm smiling. Breen's an arsehole, but the rest is so much like it was at the best of times. I force the bad memories to the back of my mind. I dealt before—if I have to, I will again.

Two hours later we're at my place. I let us in, find Dawny eating pizza with Desmond at the table. Both freeze like caught-out teens. 'Well, well,' I say, amused. 'There you are.'

'Lexi,' Desmond says in greeting, then gives a nod to Zander. 'Boss.'

'You got the message then,' Zander says, flopping down on the lounge.

'Yep. Got someone taking the stuff straight to the shop like Breen asked.'

'Good job.'

I fill in the blanks and shake my head, then grab my laptop.

'Lexi, dear, it is good to see you,' Dawny tells me. 'Finn's been around looking for you. Don't think he believed me when I said I didn't know where you were. He said he might pop in again this arvo.'

'Long as he doesn't come round for pizza and spot Desmond,' I tell her, plugging in my phone. It's completely dead. 'Remember they had surveillance on this place a few days ago. You'd better be careful.'

Dawny waves her pizza behind her as she chews a mouthful and I see a curly grey wig and a padded dress hanging from my bedroom door. 'Meet Deirdre. My new friend. She visits often and we play bridge.'

That cracks me up. 'Creative.' Then, 'You two aren't getting up to anything creative in my new bed, are you?'

Another wave of the pizza. 'We'll get you another one.'

Zander's got his head in his phone but he snuffles with laughter.

I start up mine and there's a whirlwind of sounds as I'm notified of too many missed calls, voicemails, emails and messages. Shit. It's only been offline since yesterday. I walk into the spare room, which is still full of boxes of my stuff, and collect clothes to toss into a bag.

'You off somewhere again?' Dawny asks.

'Just staying at the clubhouse until Breen decides he can trust me off-leash. Do me a favour. If anyone else shows up looking for me can you tell them I'm fine? To stop with the messages?'

'Best you tell them yourself, dear. Like I said, I don't think they believe me.'

I sigh. 'Fine. I'll—'

The knock on the door has us all stopping to stare at it. Wordlessly, Desmond gets up and takes the disguise from the door, disappearing into the bedroom. Zander hops over the back of the lounge to sit in Desmond's vacated chair in front of the abandoned plate of food.

'So tell 'em yourself,' Zander says.

I go to the door and peek through the peephole. Finn. My stomach sinks. I don't want to do this. I look back over my shoulder to where Dawny and Zander are watching expectantly. Fuck, fuck, *fuck*. I take a deep breath, prepare myself and open the door.

'Finn. Hi.'

'Lexi! You're back,' he says with obvious relief.

'Yes, she came back. Isn't it wonderful?' Dawny says.

I almost groan because now he's looking around me. I open the door all the way and he steps in. I know the moment he spots Zander because everything about him tenses.

'Did you want something?' I ask.

'You weren't answering your calls. We were worried,' he says. But he's still sizing up Zander.

'Hey, man,' Zander says, lifting his hand in a friendly enough wave.

'Ah … Finn, Zander, Zander, Finn,' I say.

'We were just having pizza,' Dawny says. 'Would you like to join us? There's plenty of food.'

Oh, God. *Please*, no. I think desperately. If these two stare any harder at each other, one of them is going to explode.

Finn looks like he's actually considering taking a seat, but not because he's hungry—he wants to know what's going on. But he shakes his head and I think my sigh of relief is audible. 'I've already eaten. Thanks.' Then he says to me, 'You sure you're okay?'

Zander gets up and walks with deceptive casualness over to stand beside me. He drapes a possessive arm across my shoulders. 'She's fine.'

Finn takes that in and stands his ground. 'I think I'd prefer to hear that from her.'

I huff because honestly, they're fucking children.

I step out from Zander's hold to stand in the doorway. 'I'm fine.'

Damn it, I wish Finn wouldn't look at me like that. Like I'm somehow betraying him. Then I remind myself of the conversation I overheard and I don't feel quite so bad.

'Can you come into work tomorrow?' he asks.

'Work?'

'Headquarters.'

'Yeah, I don't think so. I don't work there anymore. Petrol's not cheap, nor's my time.'

A muscle works in his jaw. 'I have something to discuss with you about the job and I'd rather do it in private.'

'I'm not sure Breen's going to want you doing any side jobs for the time being, babe.'

I realise Zander's still not clear on the full truth about what Finn and I have been up to. I decide not to clarify.

'You're working for Breen?' Finn asks in disbelief.

The look on his face, the disappointment and condemnation, is more than my fragile emotions can take. 'Don't you dare fucking judge me! You lot dumped me faster than you could click your fingers.'

'That's not what happened.'

'I *heard* you, Finn. I heard every fucking word, so I'm not really sure why you're here.'

'Yeah, okay,' he says, looking from me to Zander and back. 'I'm not so sure now either.'

He walks out, doesn't even look back. Not that I deliberately wait to see if he would. Well, maybe I do. I feel like I've been punched in the gut. Fuck it.

'Close the door, babe.'

I look at the empty corridor one last time, then let the door swing shut.

CHAPTER THIRTY-TWO

Finn slammed into his car and gripped the steering wheel hard. What the hell was that? After everything Olivia had said, everything Lexi had 'fessed up to about her past, he'd never fully believed Lexi would choose the club. He'd thought about it, worried a little, but now he wasn't sure what else he could believe.

He shoved out of the car again and stalked to the waterfront. He needed to calm down before getting behind the wheel. It had been a long time since Finn had been furious enough to want to punch something, to pulverise it. How could she be so stupid? And what was with that thug Zander staking some kind of claim?

He walked some more, took some time to calm down. His phone pinged and he noticed Rachael had tried to call three times.

'Finn,' she said when he called her back. 'Did you find Lexi?'

'Yeah. Look, Lexi's fine.'

'She is? Where is she?'

'Home.'

'Is she all right? Did you talk to her? What did she say?'

'She and Dawny and Zander were enjoying pizza,' he said, hearing the bitterness edge into his voice.

A pause then, 'Zander was there?'

'Yeah. Get this: she's working for Breen now.'

'What?'

'Zander seems to still be under the impression Lexi and I have done those side jobs we pretended to have been doing and he said Breen wouldn't like it if that continued. I concluded she must be working for him and she slammed me about not judging her.'

'We'll fix this.'

'I doubt it. How's McCabe's team going on surveillance?'

'That's why I called. The container was picked up and taken straight to the shop.'

'They knew?'

'Lexi did say we had a dirty cop at headquarters.'

'But who? No one has logged in to check the info on Breen. Who was this latest information shared with?'

'Just the two teams. We'll keep digging into it.'

'I've got another call coming through,' he said, hearing the alert. 'See you tomorrow.' He ended Rachael's call and took the next. 'Carson.'

'You *still* haven't got my number saved?' Olivia teased.

'Oh. Hey.'

'I tagged along with McCabe on the dock surveillance this arvo. Anyway, I'm feeling a bit like a toddler and I'm wondering what you're up to.'

'Because you're feeling like a toddler?'

He heard her laugh. 'Hungry and tired. I've made it halfway back to the city but I don't want to drive any further without fuelling up and getting something to eat and I'm not great on Central Coast options. Feel like some dinner?'

'I don't know if I'd make very good company right now.'

'What's happened?'

'Looks like Lexi's decided to go work for Breen.'

'Oh, damn. Okay, well I can handle grumpy if my stomach is full. I'll eat, you can tell me what happened.'

'Sure,' he agreed with a reluctant laugh. 'Why not.'

Finn got into headquarters late the next morning. Despite a nice dinner with Olivia and a shared bottle of wine, he hadn't slept well and had had to drag himself through his morning routine. Olivia had not been all that surprised about the situation with Lexi. 'I did try and warn you,' she'd said. 'She thinks we've dumped her so she's gone back to what she knows.' Then she'd talked about the psychology of abused children and a whole bunch of consequences and disorders, but he'd switched off after a while. None of it had taken all the anger away. Not completely.

'There you are!' Rachael said, winding her way through to the pod. 'Everything okay?'

'Yeah, fine. Just … overslept.'

'Okay. You ready? Morning meeting with McCabe and Brighton. Linc's already in there, Neutron's popping over too. Apparently he's found something.'

He followed Rachael to the meeting room, found McCabe and Olivia poring over something on a laptop screen.

'Good morning,' Olivia said to Finn, then when he slipped into the seat beside her, she added, 'How'd you sleep?'

'Okay. Fine.'

'Is something the matter?' Rachael asked, overhearing.

'Finn and I had dinner last night,' Olivia told her. 'We were discussing Lexi.'

Rachael's lips pursed. 'I see.'

Wanting somewhere else to look—did Olivia really have to bring that up with Rachael this morning?—he spotted dock surveillance on her screen. 'What's this?'

'Just going over and over the footage we have on Desmond's pick-ups from the docks. Customs haven't found any drugs so I thought they may have been coming in another container and being transferred, but there's nothing to see. Everything's done exactly the same way on each visit and it's clean. On this last one there was a different driver and we know he dropped off the contents at the shop, but the process at the docks didn't change.' She played the recording and Finn watched the comings and goings of various dock workers as the container was loaded onto the waiting truck. Then again, on a previous date, the same procedure. Yet again, on an earlier date, same again.

'Morning,' Neutron said. Olivia closed the screen.

'Neutron, what have you got for us?' Rachael asked.

'You wanted me to let you know if Lexi logged in,' he said. 'She checked her emails yesterday.'

'Sorry, that message must have gotten confused. I wanted to know if she still had access to the system,' Rachael said.

'Okay, then yes, she does. It can take a couple of days for these things to take effect.'

'And you said she was in yesterday?' McCabe checked.

'Yes, she checked her emails.'

'Did she do anything else?'

'Ah … Not that I know of.'

'Someone knew what we were up to. Is there any way to tell if anyone hacked into the organised crime emails?'

Neutron frowned. 'The hackers that have been plaguing us are good. Really good. I didn't pick anything up yesterday but I guess I could have missed something.'

'But why would random hackers go looking for and interrupt a specific operation?' Finn said.

'Maybe to prove a point. To hold us to ransom over the next big find.'

'I don't believe that,' McCabe said. 'This person went in looking for this information and had less than an hour to warn that club and stuff things up for us. It was too specific, too fast.'

'What time did Lexi log in to check her emails?' Rachael asked.

Neutron checked. 'Eleven fifty-seven, was off a minute later.'

'Could she accidentally have been copied in on the operation?' Rachael asked McCabe.

'Absolutely not.'

'You're suggesting Lexi ruined an op?' Neutron asked in confusion.

'She's working for Breen,' Olivia said.

'And still has access to the system,' McCabe added. 'Who else in that club could get in to know what we're up to?'

'Let's not jump to conclusions,' Rachael said.

'So we kick her off the force and she goes running to the other side,' Matthews said from the doorway. 'Guess you were wrong about her.'

Rachael frowned. 'We don't have any proof this was Lexi. Hacking attempts have been rife lately and we know the earlier attempts weren't her.'

'Do we?'

'Yes,' Neutron said. 'Absolutely.'

'So arrest her,' Matthews said, 'and question her on suspicion of hacking a government facility. Does she know the penalty for that?'

'On what? A hunch?' Rachael glared at him. 'You go at Lexi with a sledgehammer and you'll get nothing.'

'What would you suggest then?'

'I'd suggest we move on to plan B while Neutron takes a better look into this. We'll bring in Skink. See what we can get from him.'

'Why don't we just tack surveillance on a few key members of the club and follow them around?' Matthews asked.

'One, because they'll be expecting it; two, because we don't have the manpower; and three, because we don't need to. Give me Skink, I'll do the rest.'

'You're very confident.'

'Interrogation's her thing, remember?' Finn said. 'You said so yourself.'

'All right, but if this doesn't work, I want Winter in here answering questions.'

'Linc, we need to get started on the files relating to the investigation Gordon and Wallis ran on Cronin. But I also want Skink in here asap and we're a team member down so—'

'If you need Linc, Finn could take Brighton,' McCabe said. 'She'll be up for a field trip.'

Rachael glanced at him in surprise. 'But what about your own work on the Blake files?'

'Churning along nicely, and I need to chase this up too.'

'No objection here,' Finn said.

'I'm good with it,' Olivia said. 'What are we bringing him in on?'

'He's got an outstanding warrant for a DUI, let's run with that.'

Finn stood. 'Text us the address.'

CHAPTER THIRTY-THREE

Wednesday, March 30

As the boardroom is right next to the computer room, I can hear the yelling going on inside, despite the concrete walls. Breen is in the throes of a massive dummy spit.

'We're seventy-five k down and our business partners aren't happy!'

'We should have gone through with it, just dropped off at the shop. They could have waited there,' someone said.

'And if we were caught, the whole thing would have been screwed! Nate, you've been on this for weeks, why did it take a chick coming in here to find out what we should have already known?'

'Your cop is supposed to give us plenty of warn—'

'What are we going to do about this?' Breen barrels on. There's a thump I imagine is his hand hitting the desk, then the voices start to die down and I have trouble making out anything more.

I get back to work and am startled when the door opens.

'There you— I told you you're not supposed to be in here alone. What are you up to?' Zander hisses.

'Trying to get a head start on Breen. From the rant I just heard, I'm guessing he's about to find me and demand I give him access to everything organised crime.'

'You're not far off, actually,' he says in a way that leaves me curious. 'Come on out, before you're sprung.'

'I may as well still be working for the cops,' I grumble.

Zander stops suddenly and I have to look straight up to see why. The expression I see on his face is scary.

'That's not even close to funny.'

'Chill,' I say, brushing past him. Nate spots me and I cop a filthy look. I reluctantly head over to where he's sulking at the bar.

'Am I in trouble?'

'I don't need a chick walking in and showing me up. Especially one I trained.'

'If that was my fault, I'm sorry. If you had an insta-in you could have done the same thing. Breen's pissed off but he's not stupid.'

'Yeah.' He drains his beer. 'Look, forget about it,' he says and walks off.

'Everything okay?' Freddie rasps.

'Hey, where'd you come from?'

'Around. What's going on?'

'Nate's pissed at me over Breen.'

'You know he likes to grumble. He'll get over it. You busy?'

'No. I'm bored!'

'Good, you can help. I need you to figure out some wall hanging things. Here.'

He leads me over to a table holding a packet of sticky wall hooks and a framed black and white photo of a sea plane.

'Where's this one going?' I ask, looking around the room as I rip into the hook packet.

'Hallway.'

'Lead the way.'

He shows me the spot and I do my best to line up the hook with others on the wall before sticking it firmly on and hanging the picture. I stand back to check it's straight then study the line of RAAF seaplanes. The scribble at the bottom says, *Catalina flying boats.*

'What is this place? And what the hell is a flying boat?'

'One of those things,' he says, pointing to the picture.

I move to another picture. *RAAF Rathmines.* 'There was a base around here?' I know what I'm in for, but whatever. Freddie loves his stories.

'Set up in 1939 with Wing Commander JE Hewitt in command,' Freddie tells me. 'That point you can see in this photo is ten minutes down the road. The base held loads of Catalina flying boats and other aircraft. Was the largest flying boat base in the southern hemisphere. Lake Macquarie was perfect 'cause it's the largest saltwater lake in the country. Four times the size of Sydney Harbour—did ya know that?'

'No, I didn't,' I say, indulging him.

'Was almost three thousand personnel here by 1944. It was the military personnel bringing in their families that meant houses, schools, post offices and the like got built.'

'So what's this place?'

'This place? It's a bunker. Built during the war as part of the RAAF base. Mostly got used as a communications building and for storing ammunition. This is Breen's grandfather's property. The one he always talked about.'

'The sea captain.'

'Sea *plane* captain.'

'Yeah, I think I kinda zoned out whenever he started on about his family's multigenerational war hero shit.'

'He bought this land when the base was abandoned and lived out his days in the house that used to sit above us.'

'Dad, you boring Lexi?' Zander asks, appearing through the door from the bar.

'She's interested!'

'I am,' I say and poke my tongue out.

'Then it's a shame I have to snatch you away. You need any more help?' he asks Freddie.

'Nup. I'm going home to have a sleep. Skink's gonna drive me.'

'Okay, I'll see ya.' Then to me, Zander says, 'You coming back to the bar?'

'I can't believe I'm asking this, but is that all you do around here?'

'It is while I'm in charge of you. But I'm not going back there to drink. I have to train. Come and watch.'

'Pass. Sorry. Human slaughter is not my thing.'

He grabs my hand and tows me away. 'It's mixed martial arts.'

'It's fighting in a cage. And you should give it up.'

'I told you, the band made me fat.'

'You've got a brain!'

'So do you. And look what you fell back on when the club went to shit.'

'That wasn't a choice.'

'Of course it was.' He stops at the door and taps my temple. 'You and me, most of the guys here, we've been through some serious shit. It fucks with everything. The way we act, the way we think. The way we see the world. Besides, you don't want to just sit around here all day doing nothing, remember? I've got a surprise for you.'

'I hate surprises,' I say suspiciously.

'Come and meet Rodger. He's my trainer-slash-life coach.'

'And his wise advice is to put you in a cage with monsters so you can tear each other apart?'

'Mixed martial arts is an outlet for my risk-taking behaviour. A controlled one. I have to eat right, train right, think right. Look after myself. So do you.' He holds the door open. 'Let's go.'

'Fine, but I'm not doing anything.' I reluctantly follow him to the cage, where a compact man in black tee and track shorts is setting up.

'Hey,' Zander says, fist bumping him. 'Rodge, this is Lexi. She needs help.'

'What!' I object in true horror. 'I do not!'

'This is the one you want coached?' Rodger rasps, looking me up and down with an assessing eye.

'I absolutely am not the one!' I snap.

Zander grins at me as he secures his gloves. 'You can't fight for shit.'

'Nice to meet you, Lexi.' Rodger greets me with what I consider surprisingly intelligent eyes. He goes to the cupboard and chooses some gloves. 'Here,' he says. 'Chuck those on. I can show you a few things while Zander warms up.'

I'm already backing away. 'Yeah, I don't think so.'

'Oh, come on, scaredy cat,' Zander teases. He locks me in a sideways hug and shuffles me towards the mats laid out at one end of the room beside the cage. There are freestanding bags on them. 'Let him show you some moves.'

I shove him off. 'Let go. I'm not a hugger.'

'Never were. Because of all that serious shit you should be working on.'

I snarl at him. 'Bailee already spends too much time trying to psychoanalyse me. I haven't murdered her yet, because she's my sister.' I smile threateningly. 'You're not.'

His grin just widens. 'There's the big mouth. Better learn some moves so you can back up those scary threats of yours.'

'Are we training today or not?' Rodger says with a clap. 'Let's go. Pick up those gloves.'

I stare at the gloves like they're going to jump up and hit me of their own volition. 'There aren't enough bad words in existence to call you right now,' I complain with one last scowl at Zander, but I pick the gloves up.

'Right,' Rodger says. 'I'm gonna show you how to do a simple punch.'

I huff. 'I know how to punch.'

'Rodge, I'm telling you straight,' Zander says. 'She has no idea.'

I slide my hands into the gloves and do them up. I'm not sure this is what the specialist had in mind by taking it easy on my hand.

'Okay, over to the bag. Watch. Then you can practise.'

For what feels like an hour but is probably closer to five minutes, I half-heartedly hit the bag. 'Okay, I did it!' I call out, because Rodger's moved over to where Zander's trying to disembowel a bag with his fists.

'We've just started,' Rodger counters. 'Do another set of reps.'

'No, we've just finished. I had stitches in this hand a few days ago.'

'And now they're out.' Rodger is staring at me with his arms folded. 'Ten more reps of ten jab crosses. Go.'

Fuck. I start again, saying lots of nasty words in my head.

'What happened to your stance?' he calls out. 'Fix it!'

I pretend the bag is Rodger's head and whack it a bit harder while I try and remember where my feet are supposed to go. As soon as he turns his attention back to Zander, I drop my arms. They're killing me.

'I can still see you,' he tells me.

'Like fuck you can,' I mutter.

'And my hearing's not too bad either. Start again.'

'Who made you the boss? Zander! He's not the boss!'

Rodger charges over and I take a reflexive step back.

'Listen, little girl, those bruises on your face? They shouldn't be there.'

'These are from a truck hitting me!' I object. 'I'm not boxing a truck! Zander couldn't box a truck!'

'Then you both need to toughen the fuck up. Stop whining and get back to it.'

Zander's laugh is followed by a kick that topples the bag—the same size and weight bag that I can't get the slightest wobble out of with my hardest punch.

'Show-off!'

He winks. 'Bring on that truck.'

When Rodger finally decides to stop torturing me, I'm dying. I can't lift my arms and I may never walk again, but I manage to stagger off the mat before I collapse.

Caitlin and a couple of other girls have been watching Zander train for several minutes. When I finally decide I need to get myself to a shower and drag myself off the floor, Caitlin leaves her friends and gets up too. I'm just on the other side of the door when I feel her body smash into mine.

'Sorry,' she mutters and continues past.

Yeah, right. That bump was anything but accidental.

I follow her down the hallway then snatch her shirt and tow her backwards. 'Give it back.'

'Get the fuck off me!'

I pull her bag from her shoulder and take out my phone. 'Thanks.'

Standing there with her mouth open, she says, 'How did you know I took it?'

'Honey, there was a time I was the queen of this shit. You're good, but you're not that good.'

Three members walk past chatting and look us over with mild curiosity.

'You're not gonna say nothin', are ya? I won't be allowed to hang around if you rat on me for pinching stuff.'

'You shouldn't be allowed to hang round here anyway. How old are you?'

Her chin goes up. 'Eighteen.'

'You are so full of shit.'

She tries to snatch her bag back. I wriggle it at her just out of reach. 'How old are you?'

After a frustrated hesitation she snaps, 'Nearly sixteen.'

I toss her the bag.

'Like it's any of your fucking business. If you get me kicked outta here I'll stab you in your fucking sleep!'

'If you steal from me again you won't be around to stab me. Deal?'

'Whatever.'

She stalks off and I laugh, decide I kind of like her. She reminds me of someone. Smiling, I head for the shower.

CHAPTER THIRTY-FOUR

'Wow, nice place,' Olivia said, screwing up her nose as she checked out the rental Skink had listed as his residential address. There was little wrong with the small, older-style brick home itself, but it was in dire need of some maintenance and a good clean-up.

'I'd be pissed if this was my investment,' Finn agreed. Over the top of a short fence he could see an overloaded washing line, mostly men's clothing in various sizes but a few female pieces. The house was only small. He wondered how many people were crammed in there.

They walked to the front door, stepping around three milk crates of recycling before Finn knocked. Music, some sort of headbanging crap, was playing so he knocked again, harder. The music flicked off and footsteps stomped to the door. It opened.

'Yeah?' It wasn't Skink, but the kid was the same sort of age and looked as much in need of maintenance as the property.

'Skink around?' Finn asked.

'Uh. Why?' the kid said, taking in the suits.

Finn introduced them. 'We'd like to speak with him.'

'Uh. Um. Nah. I don't reckon he's here. Hang on.' The kid shut the door, the lock clicked over and footsteps receded.

Finn could hear a discussion going on, some sort of ruckus of footsteps and thumps, then the kid returned.

'Nah. Couldn't find him.'

'You're alone in the house, sir?' Olivia asked.

'Yeah. Why?'

A screen door banged from somewhere out the back.

'Maybe now he is,' Finn said, and moved around the side. He spotted a bare-chested Skink, tee in hand and wild hair flapping, as he darted towards a backyard shed. Finn leapt over the fence and went after him.

Skink looked around as he opened the shed door and spotted Finn, changed his mind and sprinted around the other side of the house. Finn made some ground but heard the thud before he made the corner.

'Get off me, bitch!'

Finn rounded the corner to see Skink sprawled on the ground under Olivia as she wrestled his hands behind his back.

'You good?' he asked.

'Oh, yeah.' A few strands of her hair had fallen loose and she was puffing lightly as she got Skink to his feet and read him his rights, but there was a victorious smirk on her face.

'Nice work,' he said.

'She fucking tackled me!'

'Yeah,' Finn said. 'I'm impressed.'

Olivia flashed him a grin. 'Thanks. Let's go, Skink. Someone wants to talk to you.'

Finn found Rachael in her office working with Linc on the Cronin case. 'Hey, we're back,' he told her. 'Olivia's got Skink for you.'

'Excellent,' Rachael said and got up. 'Keep going on this,' she told Linc. 'See if you can find any direct evidence that Cronin organised that shipment.'

'All good. Ah …' Linc pointed behind them and Finn turned to see Neutron rushing over.

'Inspector!' Neutron puffed, coming to an abrupt halt in Rachael's doorway.

'Slow down,' Rachael said. 'What's the matter?'

'Lexi logged a service request for IT support.'

Rachael looked back, bemused. 'Straight off the bat, that's ridiculous.'

'IT didn't know that. And the only reason I can think of she would do that is to gain access to the file permissions.'

'What?'

'So what happens when you need help with a problem is IT gains access to your system so they can go in and fix it. But to do that they have to open a connection or a portal between computers, okay?'

'We're with you so far,' Finn said.

'So while IT was in her system, she could have used that connection to get into IT's computer. It's kind of like hacking the hacker. And IT have file permissions to access all the computers in the system so, technically, so could Lexi now. She could have used that to access McCabe's computer.'

'So she's in everything?' Rachael asked.

'I can lock everyone out and require them to update passwords and set up two-factor ID before they can get back in. We were about to implement it anyway. That'll shut her down.'

'How fast can that happen?'

'Pretty much immediately.'

'Do it!'

'Okay.' He raced away.

'Surprise,' Finn murmured.

Rachael's fingers went to her temples. 'What has Lexi done with that information, Finn?'

The possibilities didn't bear thinking about, but Rachael didn't need to hear that. 'Nothing we can't undo by bringing down Breen, so come on, how are you and Linc getting on?'

'It's an interesting one,' she said, still frowning over the news about Lexi. 'I can't find any proof Cronin organised the shipment. There was an anonymous tip-off a shipment of crack cocaine had come in through the docks and that Combat Crew would be divvying it up for street sale in the warehouse behind the shop at a certain date and time. Surveillance was undertaken. Cronin was observed entering the premises, talking on his mobile phone. There's no record of who to. He unlocked the workshop and walked in. Thirty seconds later, police entered the building and made the arrest. They caught him with the goods but failed to prove anything else. Without Cronin's own admissions they would never have got a solid conviction. They relied on him giving himself up.'

'Which Lexi said he did because he knew he was likely to do at least some time behind bars and he wanted his family put under protection.'

'This whole thing seems shoddy to me.'

'So are we talking to Gordon?'

'Tomorrow. He's already had one weekend interrupted and would prefer to talk to us during working hours.'

'Well, that'll give you some time with Skink anyway,' he said.

'Remind me of his real name?'

'Daniel Carter.'

'Thanks.' Rachael opened the door to the glass-walled room where Skink was waiting and strode in, nodding to Olivia. Finn followed.

'Mr Carter. Thank you for coming.'

'Look, I just forgot all right? I'll get another court date. I was only just over the limit anyway. Waste of fucking time.'

'We'll get to that. Would you like anything to drink?'

'Nah, don't want nothin'.' He looked around. 'This is no interrogation room.'

'Heavens, no!' she said nicely. 'But as would have been explained to you, you're welcome to call a lawyer if you'd feel better having one here with you.'

'Do I need one? I don't know any lawyers!' he said in a panicked voice.

'Again, it's purely up to you, Daniel. May I call you Daniel?' Rachael soothed.

'Don't care. I should sic a lawyer on them,' he said, nodding at Olivia and Finn. 'They tackled me to the ground!'

'We're allowed to do that if you resist arrest!' Olivia snapped.

'And actually, it was just Olivia who tackled him,' Finn clarified.

Rachael winced. 'Oooh. I understand how being tackled to the ground by a woman might be embarrassing. Olivia, that was very unkind.'

'Apologies, inspector.'

'You must be a very fast runner if they had to tackle you,' Rachael said.

Daniel puffed out his chest and his chin went up. 'Yeah, I am.'

'Good skill. Why were you running?'

'To try and get away from these two.'

'That wasn't very smart, was it?' Olivia said.

Rachael leant forward with a private smile 'She's a bit cross. I think you must have had them on the run.'

'Ducking and weaving,' Daniel said. 'Nearly lost 'em.'

Rachael sent him a smile. 'Clever.'

Finn sat back and watched the women work. Rachael had a few different tactics she employed, depending on her subject. He'd seen her in action enough times to know how this particular game was played, and apparently Olivia knew it too. Good cop, bad cop was a classic for a reason.

'So about this warrant …' Olivia said.

'I think we can help him with that small, silly mistake,' Rachael said.

'Oh, yeah?' Daniel said, interest lighting his eyes. 'Would ya?'

'I wouldn't,' Olivia said.

Rachael considered Daniel for several moments, a slight smile playing at the corners of her mouth. 'There is an opportunity I'd like to discuss with you. One that would get you out of this silly little mistake. It's not an opportunity I'd give just anyone but perhaps …'

He leant forward, eager to hear more. 'Perhaps what?'

'She's good,' Olivia said over her meal. 'When she started talking to him like a five-year-old I thought it was overkill but she was right on the money. She read him perfectly.' The day had run late and they'd only just made the Opera House tour, but they were now seated in the restaurant overlooking the harbour. Yet somehow, even after a full day and a nice tour, they were still discussing the case. 'Even Matthews was impressed. I don't know why we didn't try that earlier.'

Finn washed down a mouthful of lobster with his wine. 'We had other things to tie up first.'

'If we had Rachael on our team, I'd just round up all our suspects on day one and put them in a room with her. We might not have to do any investigating. She'd just talk them into giving it all up.'

He grinned at that. 'Rachael has a thing about taking advantage of people who are a bit lower on the intelligence scale. She'll fight tooth and nail in an interrogation with someone that can hold their own. She enjoys that. But not so much what she did today. It's necessary but not satisfying.'

'You don't need to be a genius to be a criminal,' Olivia argued. 'Most of them are of average to lower intelligence. And look at the horrific crimes they carry out. Statistics show that an IQ score of 91 is average for male offenders who have committed four or more criminal offences.'

'One could argue it's average for male offenders who've committed four or more criminal offences and been caught.'

She acknowledged that with a tilt of her head. 'But look how easily led Skink is. You don't think he'd commit multiple crimes for the club? Whose mother, father, sister or brother is going to bear the brunt of that?'

'Okay, settle down.' He chuckled. 'You'll be giving me a psychology lesson on repeat offending next.'

She sipped her wine. Smiled. 'I can, if you like.'

'I've no doubt.'

'Sorry,' she said when her phone alerted her to a message. 'That's McCabe.' She read the text. Frowned. 'It's just more work he wants me to do on the Blake files before he gets in tomorrow.'

'Something wrong?'

'Not really. I'm not used to the team dynamics yet, how McCabe likes to work. But he's hitting the Blake files hard, loading us with tons of work, some of which I think can wait, but I feel like he's dragging his feet on the MC. I guess you can't do everything.'

'And some people enjoy a work–life balance.'

'They do?' she joked. 'Not in my family.'

'Or mine,' he agreed and looked through the windows to the water. 'This is nice. I don't do this sort of thing enough.'

Olivia smiled. 'Then maybe we should make a habit of it.'

CHAPTER THIRTY-FIVE

The bar is filling up and I don't feel like hiding in Zander's room but I don't want to be forced to socialise either—I've had more than enough of black leather, goatees, body odour and big egos to last me a lifetime. I've been out here for twenty minutes and nurse Jan's talked my ear off for half of those; the other half I've spent deflecting the unwanted attention of members intent on talking me into bed by treating me like I have the brains of a blow-up sex toy. When another potential stalker approaches, I jump from my stool and head off in no particular direction like I need to be there. I end up in the darkest corner of the room where the band equipment is set up and sit behind the drums.

With no one bothering me, I sigh happily and finish my drink, then, spotting the drumsticks, I pick one up, turn it around in my fingers. I used to think the whole band thing was so cool. That the guys that played on Saturday nights in the corner of the Combat Crew clubhouse were superstars. Other than Zander and Nate, I don't think any of those guys are still around. I haven't seen them. Maybe that's why no one seems to bother with the instruments.

I had nothing back then. Life had been working for a roof and food, and fun was sneaking in to Combat Crew's clubhouse to pinch drinks and cigarettes and practise dancing with the older girls who made money out of it. There wasn't anything else to do. Whatever fun I had, had to be free.

I pick up the second stick and wonder if I can remember any of the stupid little beats Zander taught me; I spent so much time watching the band practise that eventually they'd let me muck around with the instruments. I could never figure out the keyboard, the guitar was a complete mystery to me, but the drums … I liked that I could beat something up and kinda make it sound musical.

I very lightly play out two kicks and a snare beat. It's the basis for 'We Will Rock You' and a toddler could pull it off. It was the first beat I learnt.

I jump as two arms come around me, large hands cover mine.

'You can do better than that,' Zander says.

'No, I can't!' I snarl. 'I can barely lift my arms. I hate Rodger, I hate you and you'll be lucky if this stick doesn't end up shoved through your eyeball.'

'Eight notes on the high hat, two and four on the snare. I'll do the kick drum to start.'

He counts out the beats. Slowly at first, until I get a rhythm going. For a moment I forget I'm pissed off. I'm fourteen again and thrilled one of the guys from the band is paying me attention. And what the hell, it's fun.

After a while I glance up and my attention is caught by two drunken idiots watching me with lust-glazed expressions. I don't know what they're saying but one makes a stomach-turning tongue gesture.

'So which one are you taking home tonight?' Zander asks in my ear.

I whack him lightly on the head with a drumstick and his grin just gets bigger.

'I think I need to start shooting people. It's really the only way to stop the pond scum coming after the new face.'

He whistles to get the pair's attention, points from me to him and glares. Two sets of hands come up in apology and the men move away.

'Well that backed them the fuck up.'

'Come on,' he says, 'go again. Add the kick drum.'

As I try not to get my hands and feet confused, four strippers come in and head for the poles to raucous appreciation. Zander unwraps himself from me.

'Gotta move. The ladies are incoming and they need to know I'm available.'

'Where are they from?'

'Suzie's. Why?'

'Just curious.' Rachael really should have let me handle that one.

More women follow, party girls, not here to dance, just to join in, have a good time. Whatever that entails.

'Off you go, Romeo.'

'Unless … I'm not available?' he asks with a hopeful grin.

I squish his chin playfully. 'Oh, you are so available. Go wow 'em.'

Grinning from ear to ear, he takes a few steps away, turns back. 'I'll change your mind.'

'Sure you will,' I mutter, putting down the sticks and stretching.

Music is turned up loud, copious drinks are consumed. I grab another JD and watch one guy slide up to a dancer as she swings around a pole to stuff a twenty in her bikini. She leans down to give him a face full of breasts in gratitude and he howls as he falls back in apparent delirium. Fuck. They never grow up.

As the night wears on I catch Zander leading an average-looking woman with above-average breasts out of the bar. Two guesses where they're going.

'I remember you a little bit,' Breen says, coming to take the stool beside me. 'I think if you had danced up there, I'd remember you more.'

'I wasn't dancing when you were here. I just came along initially to help out. Then you went to prison.'

'You should get up there.'

I look to see if that's an order or a throwaway comment and gratefully realise it's the latter.

'You saved us getting caught today. We lost some money but it could have been much worse.'

'I already had access to the system. I doubt it'll happen again. They don't trust me anymore. But there are other ways.'

'Why'd you do it?'

That surprises me. 'Because you told me to.'

'No. Desmond. What was your motivation for coming to Desmond's rescue?'

'Dawny's a friend. She and Desmond helped me out with a nasty situation with a body once. I owed them. So did Finn. They had some info they got from that body that helped save his daughter's life.'

'All that stuff you told me about why you joined the cops. Was that true?'

'I had a gun to my head, I'm not sure I remember what I told you.'

He seems to find that amusing. 'So tell me again.'

'I joined for lots of reasons. I joined because I was broke and I had an easy in, because I suddenly had access to a whole heap of tech I hadn't had access to before and because I needed that money and that tech to find an arsehole called Damon Vaughn, who I have every intention of ending. I've always hated cops, but I thought I could juggle that. I even thought I had a few friends there. I was wrong about that. They're all the same. They won't step outside of their own self-constructed box and if you do, you're out. And yeah, it was a fucking goldmine.' I look at him. 'It still could be.'

He considers all that. 'You'd better not be lying to me.'

'Why would I lie? If I didn't want to be here I'd find a way to leave. Look, I've got nothing. No friends out there, no job. Just a prison sentence waiting for me courtesy of stuffing up the operation on your container.'

'They don't know that was you.'

'They'll figure it out, if they haven't already.'

'You don't like me. Why?'

If I tell him I know he ordered the hit on Cronin's family he'll kill me. So I go for the next best thing. 'I reckon you set Cronin up so you could rebuild the club your way and take the chair as president. And I think that's fucked up. But what the fuck ever. I don't get to be choosy. This is what it is and I still need money and tech. You pay me, you don't get in the way of me chasing down Vaughn and I'm in. You want reassurance, the best I can give you is I don't have a choice. This is the only way I can do things now.'

'I can live with that. You've got guts talking to me that way, but don't ever do it again. You ever utter that crap about Cronin again,

I'll kill you. I don't care how fucking useful you are. You're loyal to *me*. I don't mind you having a side project, but what I want comes first. Got it?'

'Yep.'

'Then it's probably time you're filled in on our little project.'

'What's that?'

'Nate will explain tomorrow. But we'll pay those bastard "friends" of yours back, don't worry.' He looks me up and down with a face full of lust. 'Let's see if that mouth of yours is good for more than getting you into trouble.' He grabs my hand and tugs me to my feet.

I tug my hand back. 'I'm not an escort anymore.'

'You're whatever I say you are. Move.'

Banging on the door wakes me up. I check my watch and find it's almost nine. 'Go away!'

It had not been a fun end to the evening. It hasn't been that long since I left my past profession behind but I'd had no intention of revisiting it, especially with Breen. I'd showered and scrubbed my teeth for way too long last night but I'm sure I can still smell him, taste him, feel him. My stomach turns.

The door opens and Zander stands in its frame. I'm not happy to see him, but at least it's not Breen back for round two. I sit up and drag my hands through my hair to untangle it. Zander gets that same look on his face he had at The Entrance and—oh no, no fucking way.

'You got a hair fetish or something?' I mutter.

'I've got a stunning sleepy woman in my bed. And, as I have to be back with Breen and Nate in the next couple of minutes, I've now got a problem.' He tries to adjust his jeans at the crotch where his 'problem' lies.

'If you need to fix that you'd better hope that very average brunette you dumped me for last night is still in your other bed. Go away.'

'You're jealous?'

'That's not even close to being it.'

He studies my face, his expression dropping into a frown. 'Something happen?'

'Damn straight.' I'm barely wearing anything, so to be a bitch I throw off the blankets and get out of bed. Hear his groan. I hope he's uncomfortable for hours. I pull on jeans and a tee. 'Why am I up?'

'I'm wondering the same thing.'

'Zander!'

'Breen and Nate are waiting.'

'For this thing they want me to help with but refuse to explain to me?'

'That'd be it.' He's still staring at my chest so I thump him with my jumper as I walk past. Keep going.

I walk into the computer lab without knocking. Zander steps in behind me. He's close enough that when Breen sends me the sort of satisfied smirk that leaves little doubt as to what went on last night, I feel Zander's sharp and instant rage.

I shoot a quiet 'Leave it!' over my shoulder before sitting next to Nate. 'Morning.'

'Hey,' Nate replied.

'So what are we doing?'

'We need secure links to the Drug and Organised Crime Squads networks.'

'Okay. For what?'

'We need to transfer the data onto another server.'

'Right. I think.'

'You think? You have the file permissions.'

'Yeah and Neutron's got a new toy. It's next-level genius and almost foolproof. If I start downloading massive amounts of data from outside of HQ, the activity might get flagged. But I don't know for sure.'

'Why only almost foolproof?'

I shoot up a smile. 'Because he's been letting me play with it.'

Nate grins back. 'Come on, then. Let's see what you've got.' He opens the computer next to his.

'So you need everything?'

'Our business partners are looking to expand their interests,' Breen says. 'They want to know who the competition is, specifics, they want to understand our crime organisations, who's who, who's likely to deal with them or cause trouble. They want to know what the police know about these different organisations and individuals, whether it is high risk or low risk to deal with them—to know of any undercover cops and operations before they take this next step. There are millions and millions of dollars involved here. This information is vital. And they're willing to pay for it.'

'I see.'

'How long?'

'Ah … could be as little as an hour, could be a lot more. I don't know how much there is. I need to figure this out.'

'Which will be when?'

'We can't afford to show our hand until I know for sure we're ready to roll. I'll have to get in, do some digging.'

Breen steps in and plays with a lock of my hair. 'So what are you waiting for?'

CHAPTER THIRTY-SIX

Thursday, March 31

Finn sat holding the piece of paper that would allow them access to the Chaos Reigns clubhouse. He stared at it, wondered what they were going to find in there. Whether everyone was going to come out in one piece.

'Right,' Rachael said, addressing everyone. 'As you all know, I've been talking to Daniel Carter AKA Skink and this is what we know so far. Desmond was released following the proof of death on Chen. He's in the wind, but that doesn't mean he won't be back to do more business with them at some point. Carter witnessed Rocco punching Chen around the head just prior to his death, which falls in line with the official cause of death being head trauma.

'Ah ... the MC has just over twenty members. We have a list of the more senior names and their ranks within the club, so we checked those names out. Breen's spent the last couple of years building numbers and some of the sorts he has in there are extremely dangerous. As you already know, Skink also told us where the clubhouse is. It's on a property in Rathmines and is owned by Breen in the name of a bogus company. There's a house—Breen's—some sheds in reasonable condition. The clubhouse is the green shed closest to the property entrance through a set of locked metal gates. McCabe's team will do a drug search and I want Rocco. With Skink's testimony, I've now got enough to bring him in and question him over Chen's death. So, are we ready? Tactical are meeting us at one.'

'More than ready,' Matthews said. 'Let's hope for some actual progress today.'

'It takes as long as it takes,' Rachael threw back. 'We're not expecting a warm welcome, but we'll have plenty of backup.'

As they all got up, Olivia crossed the room to join Finn. 'It's a hell of a drive. Want to ride with me?'

'We'll stick with our teams,' Rachael interrupted. 'See you there.'

'I thought you said you liked her,' Finn said to Rachael as they stepped out.

'I do. Why?' Then, louder, she said, 'Linc, are you ready?'

'Yep!' Linc stepped around two of McCabe's men and jogged over to catch up.

'Never mind.' Finn didn't think he was imagining Rachael's cool attitude to Olivia, but he decided to drop it. There were more important things to worry about.

One street back from Breen's property, Rachael gave a last set of instructions to the assembled teams. 'You know your jobs. I don't need to remind you there are some very nasty characters in there and to keep your wits about you at all times. We'll hit them with official warnings on consorting so that next time we find ourselves here we can start making arrests. Let's shake this club up. Good luck.'

They followed in convoy down a length of dirt road, found themselves separated from the property by locked gates. Two officers moved ahead with bolt cutters, the chains were cut and fully armed officers swarmed in, shouting orders.

Breen approached with his hands up and shouted, 'This is private property!'

'Here's our warrant,' Rachael said, showing it to him. 'We'll be doing a thorough search of all the buildings onsite. Please tell your members to cooperate.'

'She's right, guys,' Breen called out. 'She's got the warrant. Stay cool. We've got nothing to hide. Cooperate!'

But they already were, Finn noted—like lambs. Bodies were rapidly lining up on the clubhouse floor.

'Would you like a personal tour?' Breen asked them nicely.

'I'd like to speak to Rocco,' Rachael said.

'Ah, well, unfortunately he's not here.'

'I see. Care to tell us where he is?'

'Could be at the workshop. Maybe. He doesn't keep a journal for me.'

Finn took another look at Rocco's mugshot, not that he thought he'd have any trouble remembering the hulk, and walked along the line of men and women on their stomachs, checking the men to make sure he wasn't present.

When he heard Lexi's voice, his head shot around. She was sitting on the pool table, talking to Matthews. He stormed over.

'Want to tell me why you're not on your stomach like everyone else?'

Matthews looked more startled by his bark than Lexi. 'Because I'm questioning her?' he said.

'You're done for now,' Rachael said from behind them in a voice that dared Matthews to argue. 'Lexi, a word?'

'Oh, for fuck's sake,' Lexi muttered before sliding off the pool table. 'What?'

'With me, let's go. Finn?'

Finn sighed but followed as requested. Walking into this pit had just reinforced his disgust with Lexi for choosing to be there, and in that outfit of denim and leather, she fit right in.

'How are you?' Rachael asked Lexi.

'What do you want, Rachael?' Lexi asked, not bothering to answer the question.

Clear of the clubhouse, Rachael stopped walking. 'You know, we only intended on letting the dismissal stand until we could rally the right support to challenge it. To get you reinstated. It was going to take a couple of weeks, maybe a little longer. But we never intended on turning our backs on you. You unfortunately heard the end of a very involved conversation and got the wrong message.'

Finn saw surprise, a slight softening of Lexi's expression. Then it was gone, replaced with boredom and a careless shrug. 'Doesn't really matter now, does it?'

'It matters that you know that,' Rachael said.

'Sure, whatever. Are we done?'

Both gazes followed Lexi's. Breen was watching them.

'You don't have to worry about him,' Rachael murmured. 'You can come back with us now. He won't have a chance to get near you.'

Lexi laughed out loud then stepped away and held out her arms. 'Why would I want to do that?' She spun to walk away.

'Lexi!' Rachael shouted.

'Hey!' Finn snapped, his anger spilling out. 'Rachael's not finished with you, get back here.'

Lexi glanced skyward and dragged herself back. '*Yes?*'

Rachael pursed her lips, clearly unimpressed. 'You're better than this. Why would you stand beside this lost cause? We'll beat Breen. Then what? You'll be implicated. Treated like a criminal.'

'So what's new?' Lexi looked from Rachael to Finn. All he saw there was contempt.

'It won't end well,' he warned. 'We already know he's got you working on some plan to hack into headquarters. That he's after something. But you'll get caught. We know about the stunt you pulled with IT. Do you realise what the penalties are? It starts with a three-year sentence, even if you do nothing with the data. It gets worse from there. Don't do this because you're pissed off at us.'

'Guess you can prove it?' Lexi held her wrists out for cuffs, waited a beat, then dropped them. 'No? Didn't think so.'

'What do you think Breen's going to do with you when you're not as useful as he hopes you will be?' Rachael said. 'Let us fix this, please, before it gets any worse. Even you can't get past Neutron and the entire Cyber Squad.'

Lexi scuffed her shoes and nodded at her feet before looking up with a smile. 'I don't know what you're talking about, but if I did, I'd say: game on.'

'It was like they were expecting us. Like they knew we were coming,' McCabe told Finn as they waited in line to get coffees back at headquarters' cafeteria.

'I agree. Everything was too easy, the place was clean as a whistle. Not a single joint … nothing.'

'And we deliberately kept the details offline. We need to work out what ears Breen has in here.'

'How well do you know your team?'

'I'd say well enough that I don't believe it's any of them. Olivia's new but I can't see that as a possibility.'

'I'd agree with that, too.'

'You would,' McCabe said with a grin. 'I noticed you two have been spending a bit of time together.'

'Nah, we're just friends.' Finn got coffees for himself, Rachael and Linc and waited while McCabe got a few others. 'It's disappointing Rocco wasn't at the clubhouse earlier. What's the bet he goes into hiding now he knows we're looking for him.'

'Pretty good, I'd say. You need to sort that murder so you can lose the Fed. What's he do, anyway?'

'Not much. Spare tyre.' He juggled the drink tray in one hand and looked at his phone with the other. 'Rachael's got Neutron at homicide, said you should pop your head in.'

'Almost done.' McCabe put four drinks into a cardboard tray and picked it up.

'There you are. Thank you,' Rachael said, taking her coffee from Finn as he and McCabe walked into the meeting room. Linc jumped up and grabbed his.

'Sorry, Neutron, I didn't know you'd be here until after I'd ordered,' Finn apologised.

'I have one,' Neutron said and pointed to a large takeaway cup by his laptop.

'So what's this about?' McCabe asked.

'That phone Lexi cloned for you,' Neutron said. 'There wasn't a lot that was useful on it at first glance, but a bit more investigating and I found a Uniden app hidden within a stack of collapsed poker apps.'

'A what?'

'It's cameras.'

'Of where?'

'We've got eyes and ears on the clubhouse,' Rachael said, 'Breen's rental property, the business and I think the rest are at another location. Another home or possibly an industrial building of some kind.'

'Jackpot!' McCabe said and looked up at the wall screen. Twenty boxes appeared, each containing video images of different locations.

'Can we zoom?'

'Of course.' Neutron enlarged and collapsed a few at random.

'Nice,' Finn said. 'Wait—go back. Where is this?'

'That's the location I couldn't identify,' Rachael said.

Neutron played around again and the screen split into six segments. 'This is all of location three,' he told them.

'What are those people doing?' he asked, pointing at one shot. Neutron enlarged it. Two people standing in profile staring at a computer screen, two more sitting in front of it, partially obscured. 'That's Breen and Zander,' Finn said of the two standing. Zander shifted position, unblocking their view of another man he didn't recognise and … 'Is that Lexi?'

Linc squinted. 'Yeah, I reckon. She's at a computer so there's got to be a good chance. Oh, there we go, yes,' he said as Breen sat on a chair, moving out of the way.

'What is she doing?' Rachael asked. 'Can we get in any closer?'

Neutron zoomed the image further but the screen placement was wrong to see anything of value. 'No way to tell.'

'Can we listen?'

'There're audio options on all the cameras but it looks like in this room it's switched off. Same with the room we think might be a boardroom. Wait.' Neutron collapsed the footage to check an alert on his computer.

'What's up?' McCabe asked.

'It's my new security program telling me someone's trying to access my system.'

'The hackers?'

'Has to be.' After some furious tapping, he flopped back in his seat. 'Sorted.'

Onscreen, Lexi stopped and sat back, chewed her bottom lip, then lifted her hands back to the keyboard.

Another alert. 'What the?'

'And that one?' Finn asked, eyes narrowed on Lexi.

'Probably just the same arsehole trying a different tactic. They've been doing it for weeks.'

Neutron stopped tapping. Lexi dived on the keys again.

Another alert.

'It's Lexi,' Finn and Rachael said together. 'Lock her out.'

'Already done.' Another alert. 'Wait. She's back in.'

'Kick her out and keep her out!' Rachael ordered.

'I did! I just …' Another alert. 'Damn it!' Then, 'Oh, that is not funny!' he said when a winking emoji popped up on his screen.

Lexi laughed. Went again.

'What is she doing?' McCabe asked. 'Is she actually trying to find anything?'

'I don't think so,' Neutron said. 'There doesn't seem to be any reason for this. If she wanted anything, she'd hardly be deliberately playing with me.'

'We pissed her off,' Finn said. 'She's proving a point.'

'What?' McCabe asked.

'I told her even she couldn't get past Neutron and the entire cyber team,' Rachael told him. 'I think she might have taken it as a challenge.'

'I think it's more of a challenge for me,' Neutron complained. 'Let me try a couple of things.'

'Damn it, Lexi, this is not a game!' Rachael growled as she watched.

CHAPTER THIRTY-SEVEN

I hear a ping and check the notification. Laugh. 'Come on, Neutron, you're not even trying.'

'What are you doing?' Nate asks.

'Playing games with Neutron.'

'Why?'

'Because while he's busy with this, he's not paying attention to what's really going on.'

'Smokescreen?'

'You bet.' Then, 'Oh, dude, really? You know me better than that. Ha.'

'You're enjoying this shit too much,' Zander says.

'I really am.' Another victorious laugh. 'Ha, again. I could do this all day.'

Zander pokes around in my hair and I shake him off. 'What are you doing?'

'I think your horns are coming in.'

'Maybe they are,' I murmur.

'What exactly are you fucking around with?' Breen asks, coming closer and grabbing a chair.

'Just testing the waters. They know we found out about the operation because I had those file permissions. Neutron will now have organised crime under an electronic microscope. Any unusual activity could be flagged—as you can see from what I'm doing here. I need to foolproof this.'

'How?' Nate asks.

'Neutron's new program is a crazily advanced intrusion detection system. In a nutshell, it's Big Brother on cyber steroids combined with ethical hacking—penetration testing. Imagine a little gremlin running around inside the system keeping tabs on user activity while constantly doing its best to find any weaknesses and break through security. If it succeeds, the weaknesses are identified and Neutron can work on patching the problem up.'

'So he fixes it before anyone else can find the weakness?' Breen asks.

'Yep.'

'So?'

'So I've been spending some time with Neutron. Learning about it.' I flash him a smile. 'Right now, I'm keeping him busy while I talk to his gremlin, commanding it to carry out my evil plan.'

'Which is?'

'First, to map out the networks so I get a better idea of what I'm dealing with and second, to report any weaknesses it finds to me, rather than Neutron, so we know where they are and he doesn't. If I can, Nate and I will exploit those to make more and, bingo, we can get in and out whenever we like.'

'So how long will this take?'

'You know, if you'd just told me in the first place, I could already have had your files. Gotten in and out before they realised there was a reason to be worried.'

'How long?' he snarls.

I guess he doesn't want to hear that. 'Not sure. This is sensitive work. Even with the gremlin, we'll have to be ultra careful. This is not a home PC. Neutron's as good as it gets. I leave one trace, I guarantee he'll figure out a way to bring the whole plan crashing down.'

'But you can get in?'

'Oh, yes, I can already get in. What I'm doing now is ensuring we can get you your data uninterrupted.'

Nate's looking at me like I'm not making sense but he doesn't say anything.

Breen stands to stare at the screen in excitement. 'This is fabulous! I'll tell them. They called me a small-time idiot! Now they'll see.'

I spin around. Stare. 'They called you that? Ah … May I make a suggestion?'

'Anything,' he tells me, still on a high. 'What?'

'Nate said we're transferring the data straight from headquarters to your associates, is that right?'

'Yes. Nate has the information you need to do that.'

'Have you been paid already?'

'Of course not. For what?'

'So you're going to just hand it over and hope they pay? Don't you think that's a little … dangerous? They called you a "small-time idiot". What if they think they can play you?'

That wipes the smile from his face. 'I have no choice! They have it or they don't. They won't pay for nothing!'

'What if you could prove you had what they wanted—even hand it over—but they couldn't access most of it until they paid up?'

'Explain.' I've got his attention.

'I could encrypt it. They'd be able to see the files were there, see they've been delivered. I could even leave some as is so they can see they've got the real deal. Once that's established, you wait for the money to land in your account and when it does, I send the decryption file. Let's see what they think of that for a small-time idiot. And when they want more in future, which is when Neutron's program will come in handy, we can use the same transaction system each time.'

Eventually Breen nods slowly, smiles. 'Yes. Perfect. Do it!'

'Okay.'

'Good work, Lexi,' Breen tells me. 'I'll update my associates.'

'Someone's on a high,' I murmur when Breen leaves the room.

'It's a lot of money,' Zander says. 'You done for now? We have to get moving.'

'Why?'

'You're training while I prep for my fight tonight. Rodger's waiting.'

I test my muscles and every single one of them complains. 'Not a chance in hell.'

'Fine,' Zander says and I have three seconds to relax before he says, 'I'll get Rodger to come get you.'

'I don't want to! I'm sore! I'm not a gym-type person! Even my organs hurt.'

Zander shrugs. 'I didn't want to train once. Rodger dragged me the length of the room by my nostrils. Me. I'm not making that shit up. But up to you.'

The image isn't pleasant. Damn it. 'Okay! But I'm not doing it in jeans again. Give me a minute.'

I get changed, reluctantly step onto the mat and within fifteen minutes my already sore muscles are screaming. And anyway, 'This is boring,' I whinge.

'So we'll throw in some theory,' Rodger says.

I drop my arms in gratitude.

'Imagine you're walking along the street, it's dark, there's not a lot of people around. You're vulnerable. What are you looking out for?'

'A taxi.'

'Cute. Too many people walk along in a daze, not thinking or thinking about what they're going to do when they get where they're going or what they want to eat for dinner. The trick is to pay attention to what's going on around you. Like people walking too close, watching you, pretending not to be watching you. People repeatedly turning up where you are. Trust your instincts.'

'Got it,' I tell him. 'Will do.' Anything to sit down.

'Got it? Okay, question. What's the first thing you notice when someone tries to approach you?'

'The audacity.'

And, wow, bald Rambo actually owns a laugh. 'Okay. You need to gauge a couple of things. What does the guy look like? Is he solid or wiry? A runner or a brick shithouse? You want to watch how they're moving. These cues will tell you the best defence, the best way to react. Let's say I'm a big solid dude.' He walks towards me. 'What are you going to do?'

'I don't know, but if I have to run I'm screwed,' I tell him and grimace as I try and stretch a cramping muscle in my calf.

He knocks me to the floor.

'Ow!'

'Now you're screwed. Most of the really big guys can't fight for shit. They got big young and stood over everyone making scary faces and never actually had to. They're going to want to get you on the ground where they can use their weight against you, rather than rely on stamina. You keep just out of range, make them move their feet around, throw the odd jab cross and you'll see them fade. Fast. You're going to wear them out. When they're a puffing sweating mess, that's when you go in for the kill or leg it out of there.'

'Rodger,' I say, still on the mat, 'I'm already dead.'

He reaches out a hand and pulls me up. 'Let's practise a couple of moves before I let you go. First, a simple throat strike. Easy and effective. Then we'll get you out of a choke, okay?'

This is better. I'm working my brain as well as my body. My struggle with Vaughn during the Spider case sits at the front of my mind as I listen, more interested. Some of this might just come in handy.

Half an hour and a long hot shower later, I head back to the bar. The cage is being given a final clean-up. People are piling in, not just our club. Someone's taking bets, someone else is setting up a couple of cameras. Zander's in one corner of the room, wearing fight shorts and grappling gloves and talking to Rodger. He spots me and waves me over.

'Hey, wasn't sure you'd show. You gonna bet on me?'

'Bet on you getting pulverised? I'd rather not.'

He sends me a huge smile. 'Not gonna happen.'

I see a giant enter the ring and cringe. 'Well, nice knowing ya,' I say with a friendly slap on the back. 'Wish I could hang around to watch the carnage but …'

'How is he any scarier than me?'

'Because he's the opposition.'

Zander's hands go to his heart. 'You care.'

'You moron. Don't die.'

'Zander! Let's go!' Rodger calls.

I'm already nervous. Watching people beat the shit out of each other has never been my thing. But I reluctantly take a seat as the fighters are introduced.

It takes almost the full three rounds for Zander to finally take the giant down and keep him there, and both the conscious and unconscious look like they've been in a car wreck, but Zander's pretty proud of himself. I hang around as music starts up loud and drinks are passed around. Apparently, we party post fight.

Zander disappears then eventually returns—showered, with a taped eyebrow and a slight limp—to rowdy applause and a drink placed in his hand by a blonde who may as well not be wearing anything.

'How was it?' he asks me.

'Yeah, loved it. It's barbaric. You basically both smashed each other in the head until one of you passed out.'

'There's never been a death.'

'Maybe not in the ring, but all that head trauma is gonna kill you eventually.'

Woolly walks past and puts something in Zander's hand. It takes me a minute to realise that what he's taking out of the small Zip-lock are green pills. He tosses one back with his beer and hands me another. 'Just a Molly,' he says.

'I can see that. What happened to all that healthy talk?'

He grins. 'It takes a break on fight nights.'

CHAPTER THIRTY-EIGHT

At headquarters, where both teams had been poring over footage from the clubhouse most of the afternoon and evening, the screen showed Zander swallowing a pill before handing one to Lexi to chase down with her JD.

'Did she just swallow—what was that?' Finn erupted. He turned to Rachael, but she didn't reply, just stared at the screen sadly.

'Where are our dancers?' Breen complained from onscreen. In the clubhouse, at least, they had audio.

'Shouldn't be too far away,' Zander called back.

'Hmph. They're taking too long!' Breen complained. 'Lexi, baby, dance for me!'

'I don't feel like it!' she whined.

Breen snagged her and pulled her onto his lap. Said something they couldn't pick up.

Finn watched Lexi smile petulantly then say something in reply, making his stomach turn.

More talking. Breen was getting pissed off.

Lexi pouted again but stretched like a cat, threw back the remainder of her drink and called out, 'At least put something half-decent on!'

The music changed, something with a strong beat. She leant down in a steamy eye to eye with Breen, tugged her hair free and shook it loose. With a spin and a wink, she started to move.

'Uh … She's good,' McCabe said.

'And, man, with permission to be inappropriate, so freaking *hot*!' Linc added, glued to the screen as Lexi stretched her arms over her head in a sinuous move that had most of her long, toned torso on display.

'Yeah, nice moves. Brothel requirement?' Matthews snapped. 'With what she's put down her throat I'm surprised she's not falling over.'

'So she drinks, smokes pot *and* takes pills … I thought she was smarter than that,' Olivia said.

'Lexi's fallback when she's under stress has always been substance abuse,' Rachael said, annoyance edging into her tone.

'She looks anything but stressed to me,' Matthews said. 'She's off her face and enjoying the hell out of it.'

'Is she though?' Rachael murmured. 'You don't dance like that when you can't see straight.'

'So it takes a lot to knock her over,' Finn snapped. 'What are you suggesting?'

Rachael opened her mouth to speak, closed it and shook her head. 'I don't know. Maybe I just don't want to believe we've lost her.'

Onscreen, Zander stumbled over, reached for Lexi and said something into her ear before pressing a kiss to her temple and continuing over to Breen. She laughed and bowed theatrically, headed for the bar.

Finn turned away in disgust. He wasn't watching any more of this. 'Time to go.'

'Of course,' Rachael said, her face a reflection of his own thoughts. Finn admired her reluctance to admit defeat. But after the events at the clubhouse and now looking at that screen, it seemed the woman they thought they'd known, had cared about, was gone.

'Okay, it's late,' Rachael said to the room. 'We've got evidence of the fight club, Rocco and Desmond haven't made an appearance and Lexi's obviously not getting back on the computer in the foreseeable future. Let's go home.'

'I appreciate you offering me that lift,' Olivia told Finn. 'I wouldn't have asked if I'd known we'd run so late.'

'It's no problem,' he told her, his eyes back on the screen.

He felt the hand on his arm. Olivia smiled up at him.

'Let's go. I'm only around on Phillip Street.'

'Yeah, sure. Too easy.'

Finn wasn't in the mood to talk, so other than for navigation, the short ride to Olivia's Parramatta unit was quiet. He found a park underground and pulled up. 'I'll see—'

'Come up, I'll make us a coffee.'

He would have declined but she was already out of the car, so, with a reluctant sigh, he stepped out and went with her up in the lift.

'This is a nice apartment,' he commented flatly as she let him in and flicked on the lights. It was a modern and functional space; a recent build, by the looks of it. Open-plan two-bedroom, timber floors, stone benchtops and a large balcony.

'Thanks. The rent's a bit high but it's handy and I like the view.' While she fiddled with a shiny coffee machine, he walked to the glass doors and stepped out to look over the Parramatta River towards Commbank Stadium to brood. He was vibrating with anger. How could Lexi be so stupid? Switching sides so easily, swallowing pills, carrying on like that with Breen. The damn dancing that had left McCabe and Linc salivating. Had the Lexi he'd thought he'd known ever really existed? How many times had she told him she wasn't the person they'd all built her up to be? Maybe he should have listened. Maybe he should never have allowed himself to—

Olivia joined him on the balcony and placed two large coffee mugs on the long glass table. Then she stood beside him. 'You okay?'

'Yeah. Just … stuff.'

'You're feeling shitty about Lexi.'

'Is it that obvious?'

'She's your friend. It's difficult to watch a friend go off the rails.' She laid a supportive hand on his sleeve. 'Hopefully she'll wake up soon and step off the self-destructive path she's set herself on, but, Finn, you can't control that. She is who she is and she makes her own choices. Where she is now … that might be her final decision. She's not like us. We grew up in a different world.'

'I know. You're right.' He turned, attempted a smile, fully intent on having his coffee and getting out of there. But he noticed the look in Olivia's eyes. Her hand was still warm on his arm and the other came up to rest on his chest.

'Don't apologise for being human, Finn. I get you. You're a good person. You care about everyone, especially your friends and family. It's one of your most attractive traits.' Her hands slid up to link around his neck. 'Just one of them. There's plenty more.'

'Olivia …'

She pressed her lips to his, nuzzled them. Heat shot through him. His hands went to her hips to support her as she leant in. She hummed in approval, the sound dulling rational thought. When her lips parted under his, he allowed the combination of pent-up tension, ragged emotions and a pretty, willing woman to take him over.

CHAPTER THIRTY-NINE

Arthur Cronin reclined comfortably in his driver's seat and listened impatiently to the loud and drunken conversation going on beyond the tall muraya hedge that blocked Wallis's front veranda from view.

'You're getting too reckless,' she told him. 'Someone will see you.'

'It's late, no one is walking around looking inside dark cars. I need to know when they go inside, when they sleep. Hush now.'

'The hide of that bitch Langley to call us into headquarters over the handling of an old case,' Cronin heard Gordon splutter. 'I'm telling you, women and power, mate, not a good match.'

'You've got that right,' returned Wallis.

'And why now? Just one more year and I could have packed up and left all this shit behind. Moved to a foreign fucking country or something.'

'We'll have to make sure we've got our stories straight. You don't think Cassidy blabbed, do you?'

'Nah, mate. She's too gutless. Knew that from the start. She put on a decent act, but it's all in the eyes, you know that. She was shitting herself.'

'I just can't bloody believe it,' Wallis said, the sound of liquid hitting ice suggesting he was having yet another drink. 'The one man on earth I hoped would rot—or die—in prison gets released after doing only half his bloody sentence! Half! How the hell did he convince the parole board he was fit to walk?'

'I don't know, man.'

It wasn't difficult, Cronin thought. *I kept my head down, was remorseful, a changed man. Everything I needed to be in order to be here tonight. To make you pay.* He'd come for Wallis. Finding Gordon here was a bonus.

'His wife will be in there,' she reminded him.

'She'll be fine.'

'She'll never be fine after this.'

He sighed, because she was probably right. But all he could do was spare the woman a life lived any longer by the side of this animal.

'You don't really think he'll come after us, do ya?' Wallis asked, making Cronin chuckle.

'Mate, he got the guys who did it, and the guy they took the job from. None of that's got anything to do with us. And Langley found his hole. Can you believe it—walks in completely unprepared. Cronin's right there. Then they lose him. Anyway, there were no explosives found. He's used 'em up. Gone to ground.' The creak of a chair and unsteady footsteps on the old front veranda told Cronin they were on the move. A moment later there was a crash, laughter.

'Might be time for bed,' said Wallis.

'Hey, hey, wouldn't it be something if I found Cronin?' Gordon said. 'If I was the one to bring him in right before I retired!'

'That would indeed be something, my friend,' Wallis agreed. Another creak of a chair, more staggering footsteps and the opening and loud, sloppy closing of the door. Had they even bothered to lock up? They were making this too easy.

He waited until the lights went off, then for exactly one more hour before deciding it was time.

'It's not too late to change your mind,' she said.

'You know I won't.' He climbed quietly out, grabbed his bag and walked into the front yard. He'd intended on moving around the back, but the temptation to try the front door was too great. When it opened because, yes, the drunken idiots hadn't bothered to lock it, he walked straight in.

The heavy snoring to his left was courtesy of a passed-out Gordon occupying the lounge. He poked his head in the room to the right, a bedroom. Two sleeping figures occupied a queen-sized bed sporting a floral pattern that shone in the moonlight streaming through the window. More than enough light to see.

He had Wallis's hands and feet cable tied before the man had stirred enough to realise what was going on. By the time he thought to object, duct tape was being slapped over his mouth. The panicked writhing that followed woke his wife, but she was anything but a challenge to subdue.

Satisfied they weren't going anywhere, Cronin made his way back out to the lounge room.

Gordon was gone.

'He knows you're here!' she whispered. 'He could be getting help! They could be coming!'

Quietly, Cronin removed his gun from its ankle holder and listened. Waited.

He crept silently through the lounge, checked the kitchen. Nothing. His pulse was starting to race. What if she was right? He couldn't be caught, not now. He should set up the bomb, leave. Come back for Gordon later.

'You promised you wouldn't hurt the wife,' she reminded him.

Damn. He stood frozen with indecision, then almost dropped the gun at the sudden sound of a toilet flushing.

He released a long, relieved breath. 'We are okay,' he whispered, standing against the wall near the bathroom. The door opened and the room was momentarily flooded with light before Gordon flicked off the switch. The sudden flash of it was disorienting and held Cronin up just long enough for Gordon to realise someone was there. Desperately, Cronin lashed out.

The kick to the back of the knee sent Gordon sprawling flat on his face, the shock of the fall on top of his inebriated state giving Cronin the seconds he needed to bend a knee into Gordon's spine and get the zip ties secured to his hands. The feet were more of a struggle as Gordon began thrashing and shouting. Cronin silenced him by pressing the gun barrel to his head.

'You mentioned you wanted to find me,' Cronin said. 'You found me.' He rolled Gordon into the bedroom where Wallis and his wife were reclined on the bed.

Sweat broke out on Cronin's brow. He was an old man now, and these things were more difficult than they used to be. But he was almost done.

He left Gordon to rip the tape from Wallis's mouth and noticed with disgust the man had wet himself. In the end, what cowards they all were.

'We need to have a chat. I think it would be nice if you explained to your wife why she's tied to the bed.'

'What?' Then loudly, 'Help! He—'

The smack sent Wallis sideways and the gun now pointed at his wife had him shutting up.

'I want you to explain to her how you lied to me, used me, decided my family was expendable in the name of a couple of arrests. I want her to know what sort of a cunning, manipulative, self-serving, heartless bastard you really are.'

Tears formed in Wallis's eyes, trickled out. 'I'm sorry. I'm sorry. I'm sorry.'

'You're sorry for what? That I found you? That your wife has a gun to her head? That you're going to die? Because I know you're not the least bit sorry about any of the rest of it. You've had ten years to be sorry about that. To tell the truth. You haven't.'

'What do you want? A public apology? Money? Whatever you want, just tell me.'

Cronin turned to the doorway, to Laura, and smiled sadly. 'I want my Laura to not be dead. I want her to be more than the ghostly image that haunts me. I want to hold my son in my arms and tell him I love him. I want those things you took from me. Can you give them back?'

'I would if I could. I swear.'

Cronin sighed heavily, then shrugged. 'Do you know what day it is today, gentlemen? It's April Fools' Day. The perfect day to blow two fools sky high.' He replaced the tape on Wallis's mouth then cut the ties on his wife's feet. 'Come with me,' he ordered.

Her eyes widened on her tears and her muffled screams of terror were aimed at her husband. Wallis bounced around on the spot, unable to get free, to help, his eyes pleading.

'No need for all that,' Cronin said. 'I'm only after the guilty ones.'

CHAPTER FORTY

Friday, April 1

Finn looked over the scene and shook his head in disbelief. The front of the house was gone. Inside was the damp, charred shell of a bedroom. Bricks and debris littered the front yard, the road, made heavy indentations in what was left of the neighbour's fence. The front section of roof was mostly adding to the mess underfoot. They signed themselves into the scene and ducked through the police tape, where local police held back the mass of curious onlookers and firemen leant on a shiny truck enjoying breakfast. Van Zettan's forensics team photographed evidence, sifted through rubble and collected samples, and members of the Bomb Squad seemed to be packing up devices and equipment.

'Nice to see you again,' Jake called, rising from where he was bent over his crime scene.

'Hey,' Finn said. 'Long time no see.'

'Hi,' Rachael said, taking in the mess. 'We would have gotten here sooner but we've been talking to Mrs Wallis.'

'How is she?'

'She was tied to a tree in the backyard while she watched her husband get blown up. I think you can guess.'

'Unimaginable. You want to go in? Shoe covers and hard hats. Not sure how stable parts of the roof are. We've obviously allowed forensics in and what's still standing has been stabilised as much as possible, but don't spend more time in there than you have to.'

'Understood,' Rachael said.

'We've got confirmed bodies?' Finn asked as Rachael left to collect her protective gear.

'Bits and pieces.'

'Detective!'

Finn turned and looked back to where a couple of reporters stood waiting with a camera and microphone.

'I've got nothing for you yet,' he told the woman leaning against the tape.

'But if you could just confirm—'

Finn returned his attention to the ruined building, decided he'd better get in there. He stepped around forensics officers working through the black mess with sifters, others shovelling debris into containers. He stuck to the designated path, carefully avoiding an evidence marker and spotted a plastic sheet covering what he guessed was going to be human remains. He found Steven Van Zettan and his assistant Kenja Mei crouched on the ground in the corner behind the remains of a bed frame, examining something biological he couldn't identify.

'Good morning,' he said.

'Hmm, not if you're these gentlemen,' Steven said.

'How's it going?'

'We don't have much.' He lifted a plastic sheet. 'This is what's left of the upper torso of Detective Gordon, who ended up partially out the window.'

Finn's stomach turned. 'And the rest of him?'

'We have some bone fragments from what we think is a thigh bone over there,' Steven said, pointing a short distance away. 'But I'm guessing that's from the other victim, Detective Wallis. That's all we have so far.'

A photographer took a photo of something sticking out of a wall and it took Finn a moment to realise it was charred bone. 'Do we have anyone out the back where the wife was restrained?' he asked.

'Yes, detective. Everything is under control.'

Rachael walked outside to take a call and Finn took one last look around, stepped back as a burnt chunk of roof insulation fell from above and decided he'd seen enough.

'Finn,' Rachael said. 'We need to go.'

'What's up?' Finn said when they were in the car.

'I'll tell you in a second. Hold on.' Rachael called a number and he heard it ring out. The voicemail message let him know the number was Cass's. 'Cass, this is Rachael. I need you to call me. Gordon and Wallis are dead. It was Cronin. If there's any chance Lexi was right about him coming after you, we need to put some protections in place. Call me back.' She ended the call. 'Was it really just a week ago Lexi was working with us?'

Finn didn't want to talk about it. 'What was the other thing?'

'I have to make a statement to the media. We're going public with the links between events, calling on public assistance to find Cronin.'

'That's going to cause a panic.'

'There's only so long we can "no comment". I'll push the "no threat to the wider community" aspect. Also, I had a call from McCabe. That little stunt Lexi pulled with Neutron has—courtesy of Matthews—flagged her with the Feds as a national security risk. They've put a warrant out for her arrest and expect our cooperation.'

'She *is* a national security risk. She needs to be stopped. Also, we're investigating multiple homicides. She's not our problem. There's no reason for us to interfere.'

'She's our problem if she gets back into homicide's files. We're going to assist. I need you to pop around to her place later. See if you can pick her up.'

Finn risked taking his eyes off the road long enough to shoot Rachael a look of disbelief. Her face was set.

It was mid-afternoon by the time Finn and Olivia stepped out of the car just down the road from Lexi's apartment. Olivia stalled on the footpath to look up at the tall cream-brick building, then out to the views over the water. 'Nice spot.'

'I used to think so.' He locked the car, decided he'd better warn her. 'Ah, look ... Before we go up, you need to know that even if Lexi's not there, Dawny might be.'

'And?'

'And she's a bit of a character. So be prepared.'

'For what?'

He smiled crookedly. 'Anything.'

They travelled to the fourth floor and Finn knocked on the door. Sure enough, it was Dawny who opened it, but only as far as the chain would allow.

'Oh, Finn, dear. It's you. I'm afraid I've only got my robe on. Was about to step into the shower. We'll have to talk from here.'

'I was hoping to speak to Lexi. Is she in there?' he asked. He could clearly see Dawny was in a robe. He wasn't sure there weren't long pants hanging out from underneath it though.

'Haven't seen her since you last dropped by.' Dawny craned her neck to see behind him through the few inches of space. 'Who might you be?'

'Detective Senior Constable Olivia Brighton. Lovely to meet you.'

'Ah, the new detective. The one who's so devoted to her job.'

'I ... guess so,' Olivia said.

'Are you two partners now? Wasn't that long ago you couldn't pry him and Lexi apart with a crowbar. You make note of that. He's not very good at looking after people either. You know that lovely boy Zander? I believe he's got a brother.'

'Thanks, Dawny,' Finn said flatly. 'Do you know where she is?'

'Not that Finn's not a very caring young man,' Dawny barrelled on. 'He does have his redeeming features.'

'Yes, I certainly think so,' Olivia said, smiling in amusement.

'Ooh, look at that, devoted *and* loyal. But I'm afraid I can't help you, Finn. So why don't you and your new Labrador get going.'

'Dawny!' He snapped it this time but was distracted when he heard something bang behind her. 'Have you got someone in there with you? Lexi!' he called out. But he didn't think it was her style to hide. Another thought crossed his mind. 'Is it Desmond? Let me in, Dawny. Now.'

'Oh, no problem, dear. Better just show me that warrant.'

'I can come in to arrest or detain a person without a warrant. Are you going to open the door or not?'

'Well, that just depends. Why are you after Lexi?'

He hesitated. If he told her it was to arrest her he was screwed forever.

'We're trying to solve a crime,' Olivia said calmly. 'And we need her help.'

'Can't say I'm surprised. Imagine booting her out then coming back here begging for help. No shame, I say. Give me a moment.' She shut the door.

'Sorry about that,' he said, but he noted Olivia's eyes were dancing.

'My feelings are not that easily hurt. You said she was a character. Besides, you copped more than I did. So it sounds like she's gone to talk to someone. Who do you think she's got in there, Lexi or Desmond?'

'Either? Neither? Both? Hard to tell. She's a complicated woman.'

The moment Dawny had promised was a full five minutes, then the door opened again on the chain. 'What you need to understand, dear, is not everything is how it looks. You do have to watch carefully. It's so easy to sneak people in and out of places these days, even right under the authorities' noses.'

'What—'

'Especially if they're wearing work shirts. Those bright, fluro-coloured jobs. Sounds counterproductive—oh, that's a good word, have to remember that one for Scrabble—doesn't it, to dress in fluro to hide, but you might want to look into that. Ta-ta.'

She closed the door.

'So … do we break this thing down,' Olivia said with a laugh, 'or do we have another plan?'

He stared into space, thoughtful.

'Finn?'

'There's something there.'

'You think Lexi was being counterproductive … or is Desmond climbing down four storeys in a hi-vis work shirt?'

'No.' But something was bugging him. 'We need to get back to headquarters,' he told her. 'I think I might be able to help you with your case.'

'Okay. But what about whoever's inside?'

'You don't understand the way Dawny works. That was a trade.'

'But …'

'It's not going to be Lexi. That hint was about the docks. Do you still have the footage?'

'Yes, of course.'

'We'll get a car back on this place with the heads-up that Desmond might be inside. They can play the waiting game with him. We've got things to do.'

Finn worked his way through all the footage Olivia had from four separate pick-ups. He eliminated the last one, went back over the remaining three. This had to be it.

'I got a ham and cheese and an egg and lettuce,' Olivia said, popping both sandwiches on his desk in front of him.

'Whichever one you don't want is fine,' he said distractedly. 'Come and look at this.'

She pulled over a chair.

'This is the container waiting for pick-up.'

'Yeah, and?'

'Here comes the flatbed. Desmond gets out and lights up a cigarette, wanders off. Then these three workers turn up. They hang around somewhere just out of camera view but if you watch carefully, you can see one guy goes round with a clipboard and opens the container. A couple of minutes later he gets out, closes it up and the container is loaded on. Desmond reappears and secures the container to the truck bed. Then he gets in and drives away.'

'Okay and?'

'Watch.' The truck drives away. 'The guy with the clipboard is the only one there. So what happened to the other two workers who'd been helping?'

'Maybe the camera didn't pick them up walking away.'

'That's what I thought. But in all three recordings the same thing happens. Watch this one again. I think the one on the right that's trying to pull off being a man is actually a woman.'

'I'm sure there are many female dock workers, Finn.'

He pulled a face. 'They aren't really helping though, are they? They look nervous. They both keep their caps on and their heads down but I think there's a chance they could be the pair Rachael and I ran into at Breen's workshop.'

'They could be crew from one of the vessels. If they left with the driver they were probably hitching a ride out for some shore leave. As long as they have a pass, that's perfectly fine.'

'Then why would they get in the container not the truck? McCabe said Oxacot is believed to be involved in smuggling. What if they're not smuggling drugs, but people?'

'Two at a time? That doesn't sound very profitable.'

'If you're running as many ships as Oxacot, who knows how many other operations they have going? The cost of being smuggled from China to Australia is up to $75,000 per person. If the MC are getting a chunk of that on a monthly basis, that's a nice top-up for the accounts.'

'And would explain why customs isn't finding anything in the containers,' Olivia said.

He saw Rachael at the end of the room talking to Matthews. Then Matthews headed for the lift and Rachael turned towards her office. Finn caught her attention and she approached his desk.

'Hi.'

'What was that about?' he asked.

'We're getting serious about tracking Lexi down. Surveillance, the whole works. What are you two up to?' Rachael asked.

'I've got something I want to show you,' Finn said. 'Take a seat.'

CHAPTER FORTY-ONE

'Take your gloves off,' Rodger tells me. We've been at it long enough that I'm hoping that means the end but he takes the gloves from me and drops them on the ground. 'I want you to punch the bag as hard as you can. Just one big whack. Don't forget your stance. Go.'

I do as I'm told, get a kick out of making the bag move.

'Okay, good, now put this in your hand and close your fist,' he says and holds out a roll of Life Savers.

'Weird.'

'Go with it.'

I take them and close my fingers around them.

'Now do it again. Hard as you can. Go!'

Whack! The bag moves a lot more like it means it. 'Wow.'

'Yeah, wow. Holding something in your fist when you punch someone massively increases your punching power. Doesn't matter what it is—as long as it's solid, it'll stop your hand from giving way on contact. Even a Chapstick can make a difference.'

'Lexi!' Breen calls out from the doorway. 'Upstairs.'

'Sorry ...'

'Don't be. You did good. I'll see you tomorrow.'

I leave the room and tiredly take the stairs, wondering why I've been summoned up top.

Breen's out on the grass by the gate.

'What's going on?'

'They've got eyes on us. Since yesterday. They saw you at the computer. They know it was you.'

'What?' I think about that, shake my head. 'They can't possibly. The camera angle's wrong. There's no way they saw the screen. They could guess, but that's it. I'd be more worried about them having recorded it and using a lip reader to figure out what we were saying.'

Breen shakes his head. 'Hasn't happened.'

'How do you know? About the cameras?'

'I told ya. We have someone inside.'

'But that's not something just any cop would know! Who is it?'

'Doesn't matter who. They got the cameras off that phone you cloned.'

Fuck. My stomach sinks. Why am I not already dead? Is that why he brought me out here? So he wouldn't make a mess?

'Some of the shit you've given away has left me pretty fucking suspicious of whose side you're really on, but this? I want to fucking wrap my hands around your throat!' he suddenly shouts in my face.

'I was hedging my bets back then,' I tell him, voice not quite steady and my heart pounding so loudly I'd be surprised if he couldn't hear it. 'Had a couple of sides to play. You backed out of the deal on Desmond so I played the other way. But that's changed. Since we made our agreement, I've been yours. Completely. Cops hate me, no one's gonna pay me better than you do and—the big one—I couldn't go back to my old life even if I wanted to. You've got nothing to worry about.'

'Hmm,' he growls, unconvinced. 'You're just lucky I fucking need you! We're gonna turn those cameras off. You pull any more shit, I'll turn them back on so the cops can watch what I do to ya!'

The breath I release is not steady. 'Got it. But, um … Won't turning off the cameras clue them in to your inside cop?'

He smiles nastily. 'If they figure that out, I'll let our cop know whose fault it was.'

Considering the bullet I just dodged, I spend most of the afternoon out of Breen's way, on the computer with Nate until my stomach reminds me I haven't eaten. With a tired groan and a headache brewing, I get up and stretch.

'I think we're good to go,' I tell Nate.

'You got that cyber program shit sorted?'

'I hope so.'

'Good, because not everything you've been telling Breen makes sense.'

'Such as?'

'Such as why a simple encryption is taking so long?'

I smile. 'Because it's mine. And it's not simple. I need something to eat.'

I leave Nate in the lab and step into the corridor. I can hear a few people in the bar area and someone's mucking round with the instruments. But I go into the lounge instead and head for the fridge. Hopefully there's something in there. I find some milk and some leftovers I wouldn't feed a dog. The pantry reveals some bread that's not too stale and peanut butter. I guess it'll do.

A muffled sound of distress from the other side of the wall grabs my attention. Then another. It's coming from a woman. Then she's crying. Keening.

'Shut up!'

'You're hurting me!'

Fuck that. I drop the peanut butter and charge out of the lounge. Listen. When I pinpoint the right door, I open it. Rocco's back. He's got the tiny figure of the phone stealer—Caitlin—on her hands and knees, his fingers biting into her hips as he pounds himself into her, hard. She's biting her lip, tears are pouring down her pained face.

My vision contorts with rage. I launch myself at him. 'Get off her!'

I grab fistfuls of hair and drag him backwards. He roars with anger and throws me off like an annoying insect. I hit the wall hard enough to knock the wind from my lungs, but he's coming at me. As he strikes I manage to half-fall, half-duck out of the way and when he comes at me a second time, I throw my hand out at his throat the way Rodger has taught me. It sends Rocco back, seems to stun him. I'm stunned too—that it worked. But my relief is short-lived. His face is beetroot red, his eyes furious slits as he charges again.

A flash of movement from the doorway hits Rocco with enough force to knock him off his feet and into the wall. I hear the sickening crack of his head hitting concrete. Then Zander's knee is in his gut, his fist poised in a direct line to Rocco's face.

'You're done!'

'I should rip your fucking balls off!'

'That's enough,' Breen snaps from the doorway. His gaze takes in the crying girl now huddled into an impossibly small ball under a sheet in the corner of the bed, then turns on me. 'What the fuck?'

'She's just a kid!' I yell.

'So? She chose to be here.'

I stand my ground as he steps forward and points a finger in my face.

'You're almost more trouble than you're worth!'

'But—'

'Mind your own fucking business! I don't need my sergeant-at-arms out of order. And you,' he says to Zander, 'should know better. They're chicks. Fucking entertainment! What is wrong with you? Help your brother up!' Breen stalks out and Rocco drags on his jeans before sending me a look that suggests payback and following him.

'Did he hurt you?' Zander asks me.

'Not me, no. Thanks to you.'

He scowls. 'Don't expect me to do it again. Next time, do what Breen says and stay the fuck out of it.'

When he too stalks out, I shake my head and sit beside the huddled mess on the bed.

The silence stretches and though she's well covered under the sheet I'd like to give her the space to shower and dress but I'm not sure Rocco won't come back the second I leave, so I toss her her t-shirt and she struggles into it as I hang on a bit longer.

'You okay?'

'The fuck do you care?' She sniffs. 'You go causing shit, next thing I'll get kicked out.'

'Sorry about that. But would that be the worst thing in the world?'

'Got nowhere else to go. So then what?'

'First time I walked into the old clubhouse I was eighteen too. Except I was actually fourteen.'

She sniffed again, swiped her arm across her nose. 'To party?'

'To work. Cronin used to get girls from Suzie's brothel to come in on Saturday nights. Dance and shit.'

'You can't work there until you're eighteen.'

'I cleaned, organised, took phone calls, booked clients, all that sort of shit in exchange for somewhere to sleep … and I'd sneak on the bus with the older girls to dance to get some cash.'

The slightest glimmer of interest sparks in her eyes. 'You think Suzie'd let me stay there if I did all that stuff?'

'I don't know. You don't have family worth going back to?'

She huffs. 'Could you have gone home?'

I stare down at my hands. 'No.'

'Why not?'

'Ah … My parents were junkie arseholes and my stepfather … died.'

'Overdose?'

'Bullet,' I mutter.

'Who shot him?'

This is not something I talk about. But I want this kid to open up, so I have to give her something. 'Me.'

Her eyes widen in shock. 'Serious?' she asks, turning around to cross her legs and face me. 'You shot your fucking dad? How old were you?'

'Ten.'

'Woah!' She laughs in disbelief. 'He must have been a fucking arsehole.'

'First order. He, ah … helped me get into prostitution.'

'A massive fucking arsehole.'

'Yeah. Yours?'

'My parents died in a housefire when I was nine. I was placed in the care of my uncle and his girlfriend. I became insta-maid to the girlfriend and fuck buddy to my uncle. Couldn't get out of that place fast enough. Wish I'd had a gun like you did.'

'Shooting people's not really the answer. It was a bad moment. I didn't have a choice.'

'What happened?'

'You know, that's not a story I've ever told. To anyone.'

'Whatever.'

'But I'll tell you if you want. On one condition.'

'What's that?'

'If I find you a way out, you'll consider taking it.'

There's a knock on the door. 'Lexi.' Zander's back.

'In a minute!'

'Now!'

He's still pissed off. I turn my attention to Caitlin but she's got her game face on.

'I don't care what you did. Just get out so I can finish getting dressed,' she snaps at me.

I sigh, get up. 'Okay. I'll see you around. Think about it.' I step out of the room and hear her sobbing again before the door is all the way shut.

Zander is waiting. 'She gonna be okay?'

'She's fifteen years old! And that big fucking prick …'

'Find out where she lives. I'll take her home.'

'Do you think if she had a safe place to go she'd be here? I need you to take me somewhere.' I look over my shoulder at his shitty huff and ask nicely, 'Please?'

He drops his head back and stares at the roof. 'Where are we going?'

I direct him to Bailee's, well, most of the way. I walk the last bit and tell him she'll drop me back to my place after. He can hang with Dawny. I'm not sure he's impressed but whatever. He put himself in charge of babysitting.

'I've been worried about you!' Bailee complains when she finds me on the doorstep.

'I don't see why.'

'My sister drops off the face of the planet for a week and you don't see why? Come in.'

'I've been busy,' I tell her, stepping into the welcoming lounge room. Everything in Bailee's house is white beneath flashy coloured furnishings and splashy artworks that add brilliant colour. It's so damn bright and happy it does my head in. I can't make a place look this good and I don't even have two small children. I barely ever come here, but that has more to do with her husband than the decor.

And speaking of: 'Ah … who's home?'

'Just me. Mike's parents minded the kids today and he's going to have dinner there when he picks them up. I only just got home so I passed.'

'Lucky for me.'

'So what's brought you here in spite of my husband's possible presence?'

'I need to talk to you about someone.'

'Okay.' Bailee sits down and tucks one leg under her. 'Shoot.'

'She's fifteen, homeless and needs to go back to school.'

Bailee drags her hand through her hair and stares into space. 'We'll need to do a risk of significant harm report. Because she's under sixteen, I'll need to contact family—'

'Can't happen. She'll bolt. Look, she's *almost* sixteen …'

Bailee sighs. 'Sounds like I need to know more about her before I can know what's best for her. Will she meet with me?'

'Maybe. I might need to work on her a bit more. Soon, hopefully.'

'Where is she now?'

'She's hanging around with an MC. I need to get her out.'

'An MC? Right, I'll make coffee, you can tell me what the heck is going on.'

It's not all that late when Bailee drops me home, but it's been a hell of a day and I hope Dawny doesn't have any dramas waiting for me. I wave Bailee off and start the short walk towards my building; the no-stopping zone prevents parking any closer and the carpark is a pain for drop-off. Beside me, the heritage church basks in the light of the full moon. I find it pretty and a bit eerie at the same time. I push my hand into my bag to find my phone in case Zander chose to take off rather than hang around.

'Lexi.'

My head jerks up. 'Finn.' I look around. Don't see anyone else. I move closer so I can make out his features, but his expression is giving nothing away. 'What's going on? Why are you waiting for me in the dark?'

'I need you to come with me,' he says.

'Why?'

'To answer some questions.'

'You want me to answer some questions at nine o'clock at night? Can't it wait? Why are you shaking your head like that?'

'It's crazy how different you are without an audience of thugs around you.' A tone leaches into his official pitch, but it's not warm.

I pull a face. 'Well to be fair, you didn't start this conversation with "Get down on the ground".'

'It might end up that way.'

'What are you talking about?'

A muscle works in his jaw. 'You're under arrest. Turn around and put your hands behind your back.'

That stuns me. What for? What do I do now?

He reaches out to get a hand on me. Before he can, I take several quick steps back, look left and right, assess my chances if I bolt.

'Don't make me chase you, Lexi. Don't.'

'I won't talk to you.'

'That's your right.'

I don't even know this Finn. He's robotically distant. I take another step back. 'Just let me go. Please.'

'I'm afraid I can't do that.'

'You're going to wish you had,' Zander says, appearing behind him. He has what looks like a fence paling dangling from one hand. *Fuck.*

My pulse pounds in my ears as the men size each other up. There's not a lot of difference in height but Zander's got some extra bulk on him. And he's a trained fighter.

Finn really needs to get out of the way. Why isn't he getting out of the way? He may as well be daring Zander to strike.

'You think I'm scared of you?' he snarls at Zander, contempt dripping from his voice as he tenses for action. 'Take your best shot.'

My heart stops. Because I know Zander will.

'Guess you're not as smart as you made out,' Zander says and lunges.

I rush forward and, without thinking, slip between the two with a split second to hope I don't die. 'Zander, wait!'

He pulls back the paling. Just. 'Lexi, fuck!'

'It's fine. He just wants to talk to me.'

'He wants to *arrest* you!'

'That's just so he can talk to me whether I want to or not. But I don't mind, so it's all good.' I look over my shoulder, glare at Finn and say, 'Stay there!' Then I drive Zander back several steps and hiss, 'They've got nothing on me! They want to try and trip me up but they won't. I *can* handle this. You hit him and you'll be in way more trouble than I am. I'm not going back to that clubhouse if you're not in it. *Please*.'

He eyes me intensely for way too long. 'You sure?'

'I am. I'll call you as soon as I can. Get you to pick me up.'

He looks over the top of my head and the glare he gives Finn is terrifying. Then he tosses the paling and walks away.

I take a deep breath and turn around, my anger straight back to boiling point. I stride to Finn and shove him in the chest. Hard.

'What the fuck were you thinking? Don't ever do anything that stupid again!'

He snatches my wrist, holds it while he looks at me with some sort of probing stare I can't figure out in the dark. Then he twists my arm behind my back and places the cuffs on my wrists.

CHAPTER FORTY-TWO

Saturday, April 2

Finn stared at Lexi through the one-way glass panel. She looked exhausted. She'd been locked in that cold room, sitting on an uncomfortable chair, for hours. And she didn't need to be there. Her alternative had been to let Zander take him out. Right now she could have been happily back at whatever that place was she'd holed up in while Finn was in hospital or dead. So why had she stepped in like that?

'You got nothing?' Rachael asked McCabe. 'She's been in here half the night. You've just about exhausted all the time we have to detain her!'

'Ah … yeah, about that …' He rubbed the back of his neck and shifted uncomfortably then glanced at his tired team as though someone else would tell them. 'They're talking preventative detention. Up to fourteen days.'

Finn scrambled for the meaning behind that. Felt sick. 'They're treating this as *terrorism*?'

'Cyber terrorism,' Olivia said. 'They're claiming Lexi intends on seriously interfering with or disrupting a government system in a manner that could endanger lives. They're using the model of what happened in the US, where police and members of the public were murdered after stolen data was sold, they believe, to Oxacot.'

'Oh my God,' Rachael said thickly.

'They'll be here any minute to take her,' McCabe said.

'You need to get back in there,' Rachael said. 'Tell her what she's going to be charged with! Tell her what'll happen if she doesn't cooperate! She needs to understand that once they've got her, that's it. No help, no deals. It's out of our hands and as bad as it gets!'

'She knows that,' McCabe argued. 'There's only so much we can do to make her talk. It's not Guantanamo.'

'Okay, I know I said I'd stay out of it, but you need to let me in there. Let me push her.'

'Respectfully, Rachael, you're sounding more like a panicking parent than an investigating officer. We agreed it was best for you to let us handle this and Lloyd left instructions no one else was to question his suspect. Even if I said yes, with all due respect to your interrogation skills, I don't think it'll make any difference. She wouldn't even agree to a lawyer. She has no intention of cooperating in any way. Another push isn't going to do it.'

'Then I'll break her!'

'Rachael …' Finn warned. She rarely got emotional and he didn't want her to do anything she'd regret, because they were short on time.

Rachael frowned at Lexi through the glass, her face set. 'Better I do it than they do.'

'You think?'

'Stay out of it, Finn!'

'Okay, fine. Go in,' McCabe relented with a surrendering wave at the door. 'Olivia, keep an eye on the carpark, let us know when Lloyd arrives.'

'Do you really think that's a good— Yes, of course,' she amended at McCabe's cutting look.

Then to Rachael, he said, 'I'll knock on the window when they pull up, give you a chance to get out of there.'

'Thanks.'

Rachael walked into the interview room and stood in front of Lexi. Finn saw Lexi's body immediately stiffen despite her exhaustion.

'Hello, Lexi,' Rachael said, sitting down.

Lexi dropped her head in her hands and closed her eyes.

'You think that'll stop me?' Rachael slapped her palm against the desk, jolted her. 'The Feds are about to come in here and lock you up for as many decades as they can. So open your eyes, damn it! Give me something to work with!'

Nothing.

'Okay, have it your way.' Rachael linked her hands on the table, kept her back straight, expression cool. 'You know how this works. Lexi Winter, we know you're involved in a plot to steal information from police headquarters in order to sell it to an international crime organisation. We know you hacked into an IT connection to give yourself access to government files and used that access to interrupt a sensitive police operation.'

Lexi's eyes opened, focused on the table.

On the other side of the window, McCabe cleared his throat. 'We don't actually *know* that.'

'Deception's acceptable during an interrogation,' Finn automatically said, eyes never leaving Rachael and Lexi.

'We also know you've been upset with the police since you were fired,' Rachael said more gently. 'So does Breen. He's obviously taking advantage of that. Manipulating you. This is not something you would choose to do without some sort of coercion. This is not your fault. We both know that, right?'

Nothing.

'I want to help you,' Rachael said, voice soft as butter. 'Let me help you.'

Nothing.

McCabe's phone pinged and he checked it. 'Shit. They're already here.' He stepped forward and tapped on the window.

Rachael's face tightened. 'Lexi, I don't have time for the usual rigmarole. Look at me.' Another slap of her hand on the table. 'Look. At. Me.'

Lexi's only answer was to drop her head another inch.

'You think you can just sit there and pretend this is not happening? You think you've got this figured out? It doesn't matter that you know how this works. It won't make any difference to me getting what I want. You know that. I don't lose! You are going to tell me what Breen's got you wrapped up in. Just one detail. That's all I need. You are going to tell me whether you want to or not. Do you know why? Because I know every button to push with you, madam, and make no mistake, I'll push them! Understand?'

Nothing.

Rachael sat back in apparent frustration. 'Hmm. Daddy's little girl is good at keeping secrets.'

Lexi's eyes flew up to Rachael's. 'What?' she whispered.

'There we go, you can speak.'

Red-hot anger replaced the previous look of shock. 'You bitch,' Lexi spat. 'Really?'

'Well, she's got her talking,' McCabe said.

'Yeah, but jeez,' Finn said.

'You think I care about hurting your feelings?' Rachael said. 'I don't. All I care about is the truth. So give me something!'

Lexi's head turned away in disgust. 'Fuck off, Rachael.'

'Not likely. We're only getting warmed up. You in a hurry to go? So what … you can get back to that gang? Back to Breen for the relationship you've never had?'

Lexi's scowl deepened.

'I saw you partying on Thursday night, saw you lying all over that cockroach. If that was me, I'd be pouring all those drugs and alcohol down my throat, too.'

'Stop it.' It's the barest whisper through clenched teeth, but it trembles with anger.

Rachael only accelerated. 'Or maybe you like being Breen's bitch. Maybe that's why you don't want to talk to me anymore. You miss your old job and all those hot, sweaty, disgusting gang members are lining up for a piece of you. Is that it?'

'I said stop it!'

'What is she doing?' McCabe asked.

'Started out as the Reid technique, morphed into get her riled and riding on adrenaline, hoping she'll blurt out something Rach can take to the Feds as evidence of cooperation.'

'The name for *that* technique?'

'Desperation.'

'Hmm. Thought so.'

'What's he promised you for ruining your life, Lexi?' Rachael said. 'A permanent gig as the club's most useful whore? Because all of that's over! The only thing you're guaranteed if you don't talk to me is a long-term gig in prison!'

When Lexi's fingers convulsed in her hair, and she finally made eye contact, Finn thought Rachael had done it.

'You don't—' Lexi began.

'That's enough!' Lloyd said, storming the interview room with Matthews.

'It's not too late,' Rachael pressed.

'You think you're helping me? You're not!' Lexi shot at Rachael. 'Those things you said … you'll regret it!'

'This interview is terminated! What the hell do you think you're doing with our suspect?'

Rachael's head dropped back and she closed her eyes. Then, with a curse, she got up and left the room.

'Well, if she didn't hate us before …' Finn said as she stepped out of the way of the entering officers.

'I almost had her,' she said in frustration, watching as Lexi was led out without a glance at either of them. 'One more minute and she would have talked.'

'I think you're right. But all you ended up with was what sounded like a threat.'

Rachael shook her head sadly. 'Lexi wouldn't hurt me.'

'But are you sure that gang she's with wouldn't? She made her choice, went back to what she knew, and you wanting things to be different doesn't change that.'

Rachael rarely ever looked at him with disappointment, but it was there now. 'I never thought you'd be so easily manipulated.'

'Huh?'

'You're a grown man. You can make your own decisions.'

'I don't even know what to say to that. Thank you?'

'Just make sure they're actually yours.'

'Okay, what is that supposed to mean?'

'It means you've always known your own mind. Don't let someone with a fancy degree tell you you don't.'

She stalked out.

CHAPTER FORTY-THREE

Cass saw it on the late news first. The story had exploded, as flashy and terrifying as the C4 Cronin had used to wipe out old injustices. The police had finally formally linked the 'accidental explosion' in Auburn and the Central Coast hotel explosion to the latest incident where two senior police officers had been killed. It was big news. Cronin's face was everywhere. Rachael assured the community the events were targeted, not random, to stay calm, they were close to an arrest. It was only then that Cass decided to listen to the message Rachael had left her the day before.

'Cass, this is Rachael. I need you to call me. Gordon and Wallis are dead. It was Cronin. If there's any chance Lexi was right about him coming after you, we need to put some protections in place. Call me back.'

He's a fucking criminal, Gordon had said.

He's all about justice, Laura had said.

He's only after the guilty ones, Finn had said.

Vic was guilty, Seth was guilty, Blake was guilty. So were Gordon and Wallis. Now they were dead. All dead. Cronin's idea of criminal justice.

She was guilty …

He's going to come after you!

Lexi's words finally invaded the near-impenetrable wall of denial Cass had erected in her mind. She leapt from the lounge, ran into the toilet and threw up.

When she'd cleaned herself up, she went back upstairs and checked on Meera and Noah. They were curled up together in Noah's little race car bed. He'd had a restless night, too excited about his big trip on the plane to settle, and Meera must have fallen asleep while calming him. Cass closed the door and went into her bedroom, took the loaded pistol from her wardrobe and lay against the pillows.

She turned the gun over in her hands. Meera's and Noah's bags were packed. By lunchtime they'd be at the airport. It had been a massive undertaking to get Meera prepared to be out the door in only a few days, but Cass had insisted, and the pull to see her sick mother had given Meera the momentum to make it happen. They'd be safe. And Cass would deal with Cronin.

After several sleepless nights with a plan formed in her mind, Cass's eyes finally closed and she slept.

The quiet shuffling of footsteps penetrated her groggy mind. Someone sneaking into the room. In her dream she had waved her family off on their flight, far away from Cronin and the danger that lurked at home. And in the way of dreams, had seen Noah's excited face plastered to the plane's window, his little hands waving madly down at her as he cruised into the sky. She saw his little frame in the big business class seat, saw Meera handing him the little activity pack she'd brought for him to cut and colour and paste, so his head wasn't in a screen for too many hours. She saw the flight attendant offering him a special lunch on his special tray as he scrolled through myriad movies to entertain him. Happy, safe. Far away.

So who was sneaking into her room?

Her fingers twitched on the gun still loosely held in her hand. In a fast, deliberate move, she surged up, weapon out, her trigger finger tense.

'Cass!'

Meera's shriek had Noah dropping the Spider-Man plate of toast he'd held in his hands. His eyes were wide in his little face.

'Mummy?'

Horrified, shaken, Cass dropped the loaded gun she'd just pointed at her family. Without a word to Cass, Meera scooped up Noah and disappeared. She heard something about 'Mummy must have been having a bad dream, let's make some more toast,' before Meera's voice faded altogether. But her eyes hadn't left the gun.

How close had she been to pulling that trigger? Too close.

She heard *Spidey and His Amazing Friends* start on the television, then Meera was in the doorway, her face grim.

'I'm sorry,' Cass said.

'Put that thing away. Now.'

With trembling hands, Cass unloaded it and put it back in the safe.

'Sit.'

She perched on the end of the bed and stared down at her hands.

'Now you're going to tell me. I never ask, I never push, but now I am. So fucking tell me. Because I'm not getting on a plane without knowing why my wife just pointed a gun at our son.'

'I thought you were gone. I dreamed it. I thought you were him. I thought … I'm sorry.'

She heard Meera's sigh, then curled into the arm that went around her as she joined her on the edge of the bed.

'I need you safe. I need you gone. That case I told you about? That mistake I made. The guy's gone crazy. He's killing the people he blames for it.'

Meera drew back in horror. 'The guy blowing everyone up? The one on the news?'

She nodded. 'Arthur Cronin.'

'And you want me to leave you!'

'There's a safe house right next door to headquarters. I can stay there if I have to and work the case with my team while we get him. But I can't do that if I'm worrying about you and Noah. If you don't go to India, you're both going to have to be locked in a little unit in the city while I'm running around with the team tracking him down. Tiny unit, possibly for days or longer. Or India, with the rest of your family, with your mum and Noah. There's so much for him to see and experience.'

Meera stared into space and shook her head. 'I don't know.'

'You can be back in half a day if necessary, but I need to focus on this case. I'm only in danger if I have to worry about you two being here, if I have to factor that in. At headquarters with my team, I'm as safe as I could possibly be. And I can concentrate on tracking him down. No distractions. Meera. I need you to do this. For me. Please.'

'Okay,' Meera agreed after a long pause. 'If it helps you to focus, helps you to stay safe, I'll take Noah and I'll keep him safe.'

Cass's sigh shuddered out. 'Thank you.'

An hour later, Cass held the second piece of toast Noah had made her between her teeth as she grabbed her things, managed a bite before Noah charged down the hallway to launch himself into her arms. She cringed slightly as the honey bumped the side of her mouth, worried that it might leak onto her suit as he took the toast and cheekily grabbed his own big bite. She'd always presented the perfect professional image to her colleagues, and the idea she did gave her shattered nerves a small, if not fake, confidence boost. But as the most important thing in her world by far was currently in her arms, her smile never wavered.

She placed the toast on the side table and hugged him tight. 'Hey, Superman.'

'It's Spider-Man, Mummy!'

'That's what I meant to say, Iron Man.'

'Spider-Man!' He giggled because her lack of knowledge of Marvel characters was a running joke.

She put him on his feet, managed to evade one very sticky hand and kissed him loudly on the cheek. 'Have you packed all your things, Captain America?'

'Mu-um!' he said, rolling his eyes.

'There you are!' Meera said, lugging a suitcase down the stairs. 'Careful of Mummy's suit!'

'I am!'

She placed a noisy kiss on his forehead. 'Goodbye, baby. Have a wonderful, wonderful holiday!'

He nodded excitedly, then his face fell. 'I wish you were coming.'

'I'll get there as fast as I can! I promise.'

When his face lit back up instead of falling into tears—either had been a possibility—Cass silently gave a sigh of relief. She couldn't handle a sad goodbye today. She swooped him up again and dragged Meera in with her other arm, leant in to kiss her goodbye. 'I will try and get there.'

'Be safe. Talk to me every day. I love you.' Meera took Noah and Cass picked up her things.

'Love you both.' She smiled and, because her eyes had begun to well, quickly stepped through the door, closing it firmly behind her.

Cass sat with her fingers tightly knitted together on the table as she truthfully explained the events of Cronin's case to her team. She'd been a wreck by the time she'd sat down with Rachael, Finn and Linc, had been nervously waiting for hours because most of the team had had a late night with Lexi and weren't in the office at the usual time. But once she'd started, she hadn't been able to stop. The story had poured out of her with a relief she hadn't realised she'd feel.

'I didn't call it in. I left the scene, then went back and called it in, pretending I hadn't already told Gordon about it,' she said, cursing the unevenness in her tone.

'You were manipulated and stuck, under severe stress, young, inexperienced. Gordon played on that,' Finn said, his face filled with rage.

'I wish I'd known this when we went to see him,' Linc snapped.

'No wonder Lexi tried to warn you,' Rachael said.

'I'm sorry. This was never about Lexi. It's just … I hate that part of my life. I've spent every day since trying to block it out. Then she walked in and was a constant reminder of that time, of my stupid mistakes.'

Rachael sighed. 'Cass, you were put in an impossible situation. It's not unusual not to broadcast sensitive information over the radio. You believed it was being taken care of.'

'And Lucas had been shot … he might have still been alive … I should never have left the scene.'

'No, that's true. But hindsight and a decade of experience are wonderful things. You didn't have either. You followed instructions.'

'But then I lied to Cronin and I know, I *know* that if he is coming after me he must have figured that out. He trusted me. Believed me.'

'How could he have figured that out?' Rachael said.

'The ice cream,' Finn said. 'That's what Lexi said. There was one in a crime-scene photo.'

'I bought Mikey an ice cream every day. I had it with me when I got there that morning. Dropped it when I saw the door ajar. Lexi and Zander knew I had been buying him that particular flavour. They'd spotted me just a few days before. They must have seen the photo of one on the step and realised I'd been there earlier that morning.'

Cass saw comprehension wash over her team's features.

'Why didn't you just tell us?' Linc asked.

'Because I went along with it! I went back to that house and I called it in. From that moment, I was complicit! All I was worried about at the time was getting back there and getting people looking for Laura and Mikey as fast as possible, but in the back of my mind, I knew. I knew what I was doing was wrong. I let Gordon's threats push me across that line. I've regretted it ever since, but I can't take it back.'

'Okay,' Rachael said. 'Once the case is dealt with, you'll write a statement containing the full events of that time and I'll discuss what further action should be taken with the relevant parties. I'll be making strong recommendations as to what I believe the repercussions should be and you'll accept whatever reprimands you receive, put this behind you and we'll all move on. Got it?'

'Assuming I'm not fired.'

'Highly unlikely. You were a junior officer following the direct instructions of your superiors. I only wish they could have answered for it.'

'I kind of think they did,' Linc said.

'One way or another,' Rachael agreed. 'Right now, we need to move on with the case. Are you in or not?'

Cass glanced at Finn and Linc. Tried to gauge their expressions. 'If everyone is okay with it.'

Finn nodded curtly.

Linc sighed and shrugged. 'Fine.'

'Right, and Cass, we'll need to get you and your family out of that house immediately.'

Cass's phone shrilled. 'Sorry, speaking of family, that's Meera.' She frowned. 'I sent them away. They should be on the plane by now.'

'Find out what's going on.'

She answered. 'Hi, flight delayed?'

'Cancelled! The email came through right as we were about to step into the taxi. They've rescheduled us for tomorrow morning. I wasn't sure if you'd prefer we went to a motel for the night—hold on, there's someone at the door ... Hey!'

Shuffling, something crashing—Meera's scream. Noah's shrill, 'Mummy!'

The call dropped out.

Cass ran for the door.

CHAPTER FORTY-FOUR

'You right?' Zander asks as I climb off his bike.

'Yeah.'

'Breen will want to talk to you.'

'I know.' I hand him my helmet and head for the stairs. I'm not in the best mood. Haven't been since the Feds let me go. But it wasn't them that had gotten under my skin, it was Rachael. She used that Spider stuff against me. That's unforgivable. She'd still been getting warmed up and I'd been more than ready to wrap my fingers around her throat. Even though I'd known what was coming, she'd dragged a reaction out of me so easily. The bitch has a reputation for a reason.

I head down the stairs. Fuck it. I don't need to worry about it now. I need to concentrate on getting this shit done so Breen doesn't decide I'm too much of a pain in the arse after all.

'Lexi!' Breen calls from the bar as I push open the door.

My stomach drops. Damn it. I'd hoped I'd get a drink in before handling this. There's another guy sitting at a table with him. Kind of reminds me of a brick shithouse. A nervous one. He's tapping a finger on the table and sweating. Then I remember: he's the big guy who'd been taking online bets at the fight on Friday night.

'What happened?' Breen asks.

'I got to spend way too much time with a bunch of fuckwits,' I tell him and pour myself that drink, throwing the whole lot back and feeling its welcome burn in my throat. 'They threatened me with cyber terrorism charges.' I sit down and kick my feet up on another chair. 'Then tried to bargain information out of me on the promise of a reduced sentence. I called their bluff, which left them with nothing.'

'So how'd you get 'em to let you go?'

'They couldn't get the authorisation on the terrorism charges and under regular law, they had to let me go after six hours. So here I am.'

'Right. I want details, but later. My friend needs a favour.'

'Oh, yeah?' I take another look at this friend. 'What kind?'

'He's lost some money. He needs to know where it went. Now.'

'Sure,' I say, kicking back to my feet with a yawn. I'm so tired I already feel drunk. 'Let's do it.'

I check the crypto transaction. *Some* money? In his drunken state on fight night, the guy's knocked a couple of extra zeros onto an already hefty payout.

'Can you hurry up?' he asks, getting more and more stressed the longer it takes me.

I get it. It's a lot of money. But still. 'You're joking, right?'

'I don't joke when my money is at stake. Find it!'

'For fuck's *sake*,' I mutter as he paces around behind me, his noisy huffs and puffs and slight body odour distracting at best. 'Could you back off?'

'What did you say?'

'I said, for fuck's sake, could you back off?'

He grabs my hair and reefs my head back, dotting my vision with pain. 'I could snap this like a twig.' Then to Breen, he says, 'Is she important to you?'

'She's important to you, my friend, if you want your money back. But I apologise for my little hothead. She's had a bad night. Lexi, baby, what's the hold-up?'

'My hair?' I grit out from between clenched teeth.

It's released and my breath whooshes out in relief. I can't help the giant sigh—or the snarl. 'This isn't just some personal account

I need to find, this *person* is an address on a dark-web site dealing in crypto running their transactions through an international mixer service. Can you give me five fucking minutes?'

Breen chuckles. 'You see?' he tells his friend. 'She's finding your money. Five minutes.'

There's some sort of commotion in the hallway and Breen sticks his head out.

'We've got him,' Rocco says.

'I haven't done anything!' Skink's voice echoes through the corridor. 'I didn't tell them about this place, I swear!'

'Five minutes, Lexi,' Breen says and he and his friend walk out.

'Can you do it?' Zander asks, coming in to stand behind me.

'Of course I can. It just takes time.' I press a hand to my head where the hair had almost been ripped out.

'Sore?'

'A bit.'

'You've really got to learn to control that mouth.'

'It doesn't matter how many times you tell me that, it's still gonna do what it wants.'

'Kinda like your face.' Zander's phone beeps and he sighs. 'Dad's got a photo project happening in the lounge. Can't read something. I'll be back.'

'Wait—what's going on out there?' I ask Zander.

'Skink's been talking to the cops.'

Zander leaves and I hear a scream through the open door. My stomach flips. This is not going to be good. There's a couple of faint oofs, some rushed conversation. Breen's yelling. More thumps and oofs.

'Can't you do something about that?' I ask Zander when he returns.

'He ratted on the club, baby. He's lucky I'm not out there.'

'But you like the kid.'

'You betray the club, that's the end.'

Another scream, genuinely agonised, has me standing.

Zander pushes me back in my chair. 'Nope. Get on with it.'

I try, but I can't think. Another scream. Another. 'That's enough! Surely!'

'It's enough when the boss says it's enough. You done?'

'No …' I make a mistake, have to go back. Force myself to focus. After a few more minutes, there it is. 'Got it!'

Bang!

I jolt hard enough to shake the chair. Silence. 'What … what just happened?'

'He stopped screaming,' Zander says, moving to the door. 'Come on, you've got to hand this over.'

I reluctantly walk out behind him. When he pushes through the door to the bar, I see it straight away: Skink on the floor, broken and bloody, limbs in unnatural positions. One eye stares through me, the other is gone, the left side of his head blown out by the bullet.

'Lexi! Are you done?' Breen asks, no sign in his manner of the horror he and Rocco have just committed. He has blood spatter on his face. Rocco looks up from the body, a mean smile telling me I haven't been forgiven.

'Got it,' I tell Breen, swallowing hard.

'Who?' his friend demands.

'Whoever lives here.' I hand the paper to him.

He grunts, nods. 'Thank you, my friend,' he says. But not to me—to Breen. Whatever. They exchange a few more pleasantries and the German wrestler is on his way.

Breen looks disgustedly at what's left of Skink. 'Fucking mess on my floor,' he says and heads for the door. 'Rocco, clean it up. Lexi, make me a drink while I wash.' And then he's gone.

My stomach is churning with revulsion and the shaking in my hands has me shoving them in the pockets of my jeans. I have to step over Skink's body to get to the bar and I take the biggest step I can to avoid the blood that's fanned out around him. I make a whiskey sour.

Nate comes in, pulls a face at the body. 'What's going on?'

'Rocco found Skink,' Zander says.

'Ah,' is all Nate says.

Fuck this shit! I leave the drink on the bar and rush back to my room. Heels of my hands to my eyes, I drop on the bed and will myself not to lose it.

'God, you look like you're going to be sick.' Caitlin appears in my doorway. 'I can't stand it either.' She sits down beside me. 'They just killed him. In front of everyone in there.'

'You shouldn't be here!' I tell her. 'There's someone I need you to meet with.'

'You're pimping me out?' she snaps instantly.

I stare at her. 'What part of taking on Rocco the brick shithouse screamed, "I can't wait to pimp you out" to you? My sister Bailee is a child protection off—'

'Nup. No way! It was one of them put me with my arsehole uncle!'

'That's not going to happen. She wants to discuss options with you. Find a solution you're happy with. She'd never—'

'I don't believe you! I'm not doin' it!' She drops her gaze to the floor and I study her, take a breath.

'What would you do with your life if you could do anything?'

'What's the fucking point of dreaming about shit?' she mumbles. 'Only reminds ya of what you'll never have.'

'Then let's be miserable together. When I was fourteen, I desperately wanted to be the lead singer of Zander's band.'

'You might have been a good singer.'

'I mean, anything's possible. But I decided I couldn't do it, so I never tried and guess what? Now I'll never know. Your turn.'

She looks at me, her mouth moving in a few different directions before opening. 'Café.'

'Huh?'

She looks back down at her hands. 'It's stupid.'

'No, it's not. Let's have it.'

'There's a little café in Toronto. It opens out onto the street. People always seem to enjoy being there. They're sitting over coffee, chatting, eating pretty little meals. The staff always look happy, maybe a bit flustered when it's busy, but making coffees, organising treats onto plates, being in that vibe. The one in charge has these cute little plants she takes care of, and you can tell she loves the place. Loves being there. I think that would be something I'd love, too. To have something that's mine, that I can look after. Where I'm surrounded by happy people.'

'You know, that's a pretty damn reasonable ambition.'

'Not for me. I got no way to get that. Can't barely read, didn't finish school, could never even add up the money. I got what's between my legs and that's that.'

'So let's change things up.'

She eyes me suspiciously. 'What do you mean?'

'Come with me.' I take her into the lounge, where Freddie is still poring over his photos, squinting through his glasses. Zander's helping him make out the captions.

'Hey, Caitlin, how's it going?' Zander asks. Then he looks at me. 'You two friends now?'

'I hate her,' Caitlin says with a grin at me. 'The woman falls for nothing.'

'Ha. That's because she used to be you.'

'Freddie, do you know Caitlin?' I ask.

'Hello, love.' Then he says to me, 'What are you up to?'

'Today is your lucky day,' I tell him. 'I've got someone to read you the paper.'

CHAPTER FORTY-FIVE

A loud and consistent banging wakes me and I blink in confusion. My phone tells me it's almost eight pm. I've slept all afternoon. Rodger'll be pissed I missed training. I might be losing my mind but I'm starting to enjoy it. My attention returns to the banging. I hear a moan. Someone's going at it in the room next door and the bed frame could do with a tighten up.

Choosing not to listen, I yawn and head for the lounge, intent on making coffee. There're quite a few people lazing around watching television, a music video channel.

I've just finished making my coffee when I'm spotted.

'Lexi!'

Caitlin has been talking to some other girls, but she gets up and comes over. 'This shit with Freddie.'

The aggravation in her voice has me grinning. 'How'd it go?'

'I can't read the fucking words! Then he just says, "Course you can, sound it out." But lots of words don't sound out, so then he's all like, "Well, read the sentence and tell me what you think it might be." And I'm like, "Well, I don't fucking know." I mean, sometimes I get it. But other times I've never even heard of the fucking word so he makes me look it up and tell him what it means. And it takes for fucking EVER to read a fucking story and I get five fucking dollars!'

My smile widens. It's almost enough to make me tear up. 'Keep at it, yeah?' I slap her on the back. 'You'll be running that café in no time.'

'Lexi?' she calls again as I'm about to let the door close.

'Yeah?'

'You really think I could, or are you just making fun?'

I look her in the eye, make sure she knows I mean it. 'Whether you choose to put in the time and effort to get there is up to you. But if you do? No word of a lie, Caitlin, you fucking can.'

'Then maybe …' She scoots closer, lowers her voice. 'I was thinking … maybe you might come with me to, you know, talk to your sister?'

I beam at her. 'You bet. Let me get it organised.'

I walk out, still smiling, and stick my head back in my room. All quiet. Excellent. I'm not in the mood for the bar tonight. I'm starting to feel like I have a permanent hangover and I need to get this job done for Breen before I go insane from being pretty much stuck inside this underground prison. I scroll through Facebook and Instagram, find myself checking if any of the team have been posting. Because it feels sneaky, I jump out of my skin when my phone tells me I have a FaceTime call. I check it. Ava.

Fuck. I should ignore it. I'm pretty sure Finn would go apeshit if he finds out I've been talking to her. I wait a few more rings, undecided.

Damn it. She'll just keep calling. I'll have to make up an excuse why we can't talk for a while. I scramble to think of something reasonable as I answer.

'Hey, kiddo.'

'Lexi, hi!'

I sit on the bed and spend several minutes hearing about school and boys and her wicked stepfather, horse riding, dancing and some weird bug she tried to show me that was crawling on her window. I haven't come up with an excuse yet, but something's up, so that plan evaporates. It's more like she's avoiding telling me something than filling me in on everything.

'Tell her!' I hear whispered down the line a minute later, pretty much confirming my suspicions.

'What was that?' I ask. 'Ava, do you have someone in there with you?'

'Um, yep.' The phone swings around. 'This is Megan.'

I see a girl of about Ava's age. Brown hair and a spattering of freckles over her nose, pretty green eyes. 'Hi, Megan,' I say.

'Hi.' She looks shyly back before averting her eyes.

'Is something wrong?'

'Go on,' Megan says to Ava. '*Tell* her!'

'We'll get in trouble!' Ava hisses.

'Not from me you won't,' I cut in. 'Spill it.'

I hear a sigh from Ava, then she turns the phone back around. 'It's … Mr Brown.'

'Who's Mr Brown?'

'Our next-door neighbour.'

'Okay, what about him?'

Ava looks like she's rethinking the whole 'tell me' part.

'Ava?' I try for a stern parent voice. 'Out with it.'

There's a commotion in the hall and a couple are making out and giggling, banging into walls as they claw at each other's clothes. I kick my door shut.

'I'm not supposed to go over there,' she whispers. 'But he has bunnies and they're really, really cute and he has trouble bending down 'cause he has a sore back and so he needs help feeding them or they'll starve in their cages and they'll die.'

'Okay …'

'So— Promise me you won't tell.'

'I promise,' I say, though I have a feeling I might live to regret it. 'What happened?'

'He asked me to help. He told me he'd give me two dollars every day to come over and look after them. But he said to keep it a secret because otherwise the RSPCA will come and take them away and put them down.'

Alarm bells sound in my head. 'Kiddo, we don't keep those sorts of secrets, okay? They're dangerous secrets.'

'He showed me his penis,' she blurts.

I almost lose the phone in my shock. 'What!'

'Please don't tell Mum or Dad. I'll get in trouble!' And now there's tears.

'Okay, calm! Just … calm down.'

She sniffs and swipes at her cheek. 'You're not!'

'No. Because that's bad. That's really bad, Ava—*you're* not bad!' I amend, because she's looking miserable. 'This is not your fault.'

'But I went over there when I wasn't supposed to and if I tell on him he won't be able to feed the bunnies and they'll be taken away and killed and it'll be my fault.'

'Okay.' *Fuck*. 'Okay, let me think.'

'You promised you wouldn't tell!'

'I did, didn't I.' I hear the door creak open and Zander is leaning against my doorframe, arms folded, legs crossed, listening with interest. 'Which house does he live in?'

'Number 32. The white one next to ours.'

'Leave it with me, kiddo. And don't worry. This is not your fault. I just need you to promise me you won't go anywhere near Mr Brown again.'

'But the bunnies!'

'I'll take care of it.'

A teary, hopeful smile. 'Really?'

'Really.'

'You promise?'

Fuck me. 'I promise. The bunnies will be fine. Now, have a fun night with Megan and don't worry about it anymore, okay?'

'Okay, Lexi.' Ava sniffs again and wipes her face. Smiles. 'Thanks.'

'Bye, kiddo.' I end the call then, 'Fuck!' I hurl the nearest pillow at the wall.

'You want to tell me what that was about?' Zander says.

'I need my computer,' I say, reaching for it.

'Why?'

'Because the number of sick pricks in the world refuses to decrease.'

'That's a fact. I'm gonna need more information.'

'That was Ava, she's Finn's kid. Ava's sweet and smart and eleven years old, and some pervert neighbour just lured her over to his place with bunnies and got his dick out.'

'Why does that require a computer?'

'Because I need to find out who he is so I can do something about it.' I scrawl down the address to look up and Zander picks it up.

'Seems pretty straightforward. What would the cops do?'

'Get a statement from Ava, go talk to him, see what he has to say.'

'Then what?'

'I don't know … he's in his own home, dressed—sort of, he says it was a wardrobe malfunction … her word against his on what he was actually doing …'

'Her word against his.'

'Pretty much.'

'Wow. How long would all this take?'

'Depends. If he's on the sex offenders register that would be helpful. Otherwise days, weeks, I don't know.'

'And if it doesn't come to anything, he just keeps living there.'

I clench my teeth. 'Yeah.'

'And Finn won't take care of it?'

'I kind of promised her I'd keep it a secret.'

'Super.' He squats in front of me, his eyes level with mine and considering. 'This kid, is she prone to spinning stories, attention seeking?'

'No. Not at all. I know this kid. She's not making this up.'

'That's good enough for me. What's the address?' He spins my computer around to see what I've just typed in, then straightens and walks out.

I follow him to the bar.

'Nate, Woolly, let's go,' he says. The two men get up without question.

'What are you doing?' I ask.

'Reminding you there's more effective forms of justice than what you just explained to me.'

'Zander!'

'Yeah?'

Everyone in the bar is watching. I'm not gonna try telling him what to do. 'Can I come?'

He grins, nods and walks out with his posse.

As I follow them up the steps, my emotions are mixed. Dread is there, because what is he planning on doing? But that arsehole came after Ava. The kid that's already been through enough shit.

The kid deserves to be safe. And the angry part of me feels an undeniable small thrill that this dick has a nasty night ahead.

When Mr Brown answers my knock at the door I take a good look at him. He's maybe forty-five, fifty. Bald, neat beard, thick through the belly, clean and tidy. Then I look in his eyes and they're flat, cold. And I know what he is.

'Yeah?'

'Hi. Mr Brown?'

'Yeah,' he says again, his mouth moving into a nasty smile as he looks me up and down.

I smile back. 'I was hoping we could have a chat. Can I come in?'

'Uh, yeah,' he says yet again and steps back. 'What about?'

'About keeping your dick in your pants, you piece of shit.'

'Huh?'

I step aside and Zander steps into view and drives him back into the room. Nate and Woolly come in behind and guard the door. Brown's eyes double in size and his mouth falls open.

'Hey!'

Zander pins Brown against the wall with an arm across his throat. 'Make another sound, I'll snap your neck. Got it?'

Brown nods. He's already perspiring heavily.

Zander grabs a fistful of Brown's shorts. The guy squeals. 'You think it's fun to show your shit to little girls?'

He shakes his head violently.

'You a liar too? A liar and a paedophile?'

Another shake. He's turning purple.

'Why don't you go get the bunnies, babe?' Zander tells me. I think that's code for 'Don't watch'.

'Sure.' I walk through the house to the back door. See a cage with a tarp thrown loosely over the top. The breaking of things begins before I step outside.

A quick look under the tarp reveals two brown and white fluffy rabbits. They twitch their noses and sit up on their back legs to sniff at my fingers as I find the handle.

The cage is big and awkward and it takes me some time to shuffle back with it. I have a foot on the bottom of three steps when a bright beam of light hits me in the face. I freeze. I step back and follow the beam to the fence, to Ava's house. Two heads are at the window. It opens.

'Lexi!' Ava whispers loudly.

'Shh!' I say.

'You've got them?'

'I've got them!'

'What's banging?'

'Never mind. Close the window!'

'Okay! Thanks!' As it goes down, I hear, 'See, I told you, she's awesome!'

Hmm. Not sure about that. I'm not exactly setting a good example. I wrestle the cage through the door and put the rabbits down in the kitchen. Something else breaks and is accompanied by an 'oomph'. I wince. Maybe I've gone soft, being a cop. The arsehole deserves it. I walk back into the front room and one look at the guy has me wincing again. Zander's just playing with him like a cat with a mouse. The other two haven't moved, are just leaning on the door with their arms folded, taking it all in.

Zander pauses with a handful of the guy's hair in his fist and flicks his chin at an upended box of old video tapes and DVDs. Paused on the TV is a shot of the man in front of me in bed with a small boy.

Any sympathy I might have felt evaporates. 'You piece of shit!'

'I'm sick! It's not my fault! I can't help it!' he splutters through the blood pouring out of his nose.

I didn't know Zander had the gun until he pulled it from the small of his back. 'Just can't control yourself, huh?'

'I can't!'

He shoves the gun in Brown's mouth. 'Then let's make sure you don't have to.'

CHAPTER FORTY-SIX

Sunday, April 3

Finn stared into the private hospital room feeling helpless. He'd come to see Cass, but he wasn't sure she was up for visitors. She was sitting curled in a ball on the bed, rocking. Her face was devoid of any hint of colour except for the black shadows that encircled her eyes. Her hair was messily pulled back, her expression stunned.

By the time they'd reached her home yesterday the house had been engulfed in fire. Neighbours had raced into the street after the initial explosion and had alerted the fire department. Emergency crews had already been in attendance. He'd never witnessed anything so heartbreaking, so terrifying, as when Cass had run at that wall of flames and collapsed, screaming in utter anguish.

'Can I help you, sir?' a nurse asked.

He introduced himself and asked quietly, 'Should she be sedated?'

'She has been. The doctor is doing his rounds now. He should be here shortly.'

'Thank you.'

'Finn?' Cass's voice was barely a rasp.

'Hi,' he said, and stepped into the room.

'What are you doing here?'

'I came to see how you were doing. Rachael's here too. She's just on the phone. She'll be in in a sec.'

'Why?'

'Because we care about you,' he said, and sat on the edge of the bed. 'We want to help you.'

Cass's eyes were bleak. 'I don't want help. I just want to die too.'

'I can understand that, and I know it sounds like an empty platitude right now, but you will get through this.'

Rachael's voice drifted down the hallway before she came striding in. 'Get as many people as you can on CCTV. And I want their faces everywhere! As soon as we know what vehicle he was in I want it on the radio, the news—I want everyone looking for them. I'll have Cass make a public plea to Cronin. Get a news conference set up. I'll be ready in an hour.' She hung up. 'Cass,' she said, moving straight to the bed. 'They weren't there.'

Confusion marred Cass's already dazed features. 'What?'

'Steven can't find any evidence of any victims. He doesn't think Meera and Noah were in the house when it exploded.'

'But … I heard the shouting, the screams. You heard it!'

'I know. And I don't want to give you false hope, but that's how it looks.'

'You don't think the explosion was bad enough to not leave any trace?' Her voice broke as tears erupted.

'No. More importantly, I asked that same question, and Steven doesn't believe it either.'

'They're alive?'

'I don't know that. But it's possible.'

'Why … why would he take them?' Cass scrambled to get out of bed, the formerly inert, almost catatonic mother now desperate to move, to fight on. 'I'll help. Cronin won't pay any attention to a public plea but I'll do it anyway. At least other people will see it and the more people that know about it, the more eyes and ears we have out there.'

'Slow down,' Rachael warned when Cass stumbled. 'I know this is going to be the most difficult thing you've ever done, but you need to stop and let us take care of it.'

'That's my family! If that sick bastard has them, they're not safe! You need everyone on this!'

'Cass, you need to stay calm.'

'What's going on in here?' a doctor asked, coming into the room trailed by a nurse.

'I have to go,' Cass said, and scrambled to get around everyone to find her clothes.

'Can we have ten mg of Temazepam please?' the doctor asked the nurse.

'I don't need another sedative! I need to go to work!'

Rachael took Cass gently by the shoulders and drew her back to the bed. 'You need to rest. I promise I will keep you updated and send someone for you as soon as we're ready to do the public appeal. Okay?'

'But—'

'We can stand here and argue with you or we can go and find your family,' Rachael said more firmly.

More tears flooded Cass's cheeks and she reluctantly nodded. 'Go. Go find them. Please find them.'

Finn had almost been home when he'd gotten the call from his ex-wife demanding his presence. It'd been a hell of a day and he'd barred dinner with Olivia because he wanted an early night, so he hadn't been happy about running to Viv's summons. And now she was yelling at him.

'Why didn't you tell us!' she said, opening the door wide to let him in.

'Hi, Viv,' he snapped. 'How are you?'

'You didn't check? Didn't know?'

'Tell you what, Viv? What didn't I tell you that I didn't know?'

'Don't be smart! The man next door! We moved in here and you never checked?'

He closed his eyes against the verbal attack and rubbed his forehead. 'I have no idea what you're talking about.'

'There was a pervert living next door. A registered sex offender! Apparently members of the public aren't entitled to know if they have a paedophile living next door to them. Even if they have kids! Apparently even if the police want to warn you, some stupid privacy act means they're not allowed to. That's fucked up, Finn! Why is the law protecting paedophiles and not our children?'

'Back. Up,' Finn said, shocked. 'You had a registered sex offender living next door?'

'Yes! Why does this keep happening to our little girl? How can a man like that live right next door and no one tell us anything? You could have accessed the information! We would never have bought the place!'

That wasn't true. They'd bought the house before he'd even known about it. Still, he was no happier about this than she was.

'Where's Ava?'

'At the movies with Megan. She'll be home any minute. I needed to talk to you before she got back.'

'How do you know about this?'

'The police were at his house earlier. I was in the backyard—yes, eavesdropping—and overheard a couple of them talking about how the guy was on the register. It didn't click with me until they came over here to ask a heap of questions. Did we know anything about an incident that had occurred with our neighbour. He's got to be that sicko they were talking about on the radio this morning.'

'I missed that. What sicko?'

'The one that was left hog-tied in the park opposite the police station in his underwear with boxes of filthy movies and a couple of caged rabbits beside him. Someone had beaten the bastard up. I wish it had been me!'

Movies? Rabbits? His head was starting to spin. 'Let me make a call.'

He spoke to the local police and confirmed the details. When he hung up, he nodded at Viv and sat. 'The guy's on the register. He's been charged. You won't have to worry about him again. He'll be going back to prison for sure.'

The front door slammed and Ava ran in. 'Dad! I saw your car.' She ran over and gave him a hug. 'Hi!'

'Hi, sweetie.'

'What are you doing here?'

He glanced at Viv. She seemed happy for him to handle it. 'Sweetie, do you know the man next door?'

Ava's face closed up. 'Why?'

'He got arrested today. He's not a nice man. I was wondering if he ever tried to talk to you.'

'He said hello to all the kids,' Ava said, staring at the floor. Then she looked up. 'Is he in jail?'

'He will be. He won't be coming back here.'

She grinned. 'Okay. I need to go call Megan!'

'You just saw her,' Vivienne said in astonishment.

'Forgot to tell her something!'

'Make it quick and have your shower. It's dinner time.'

'Okay!'

'I've got to get going,' Finn said. 'We've got an emergency at work and we're pulling long hours. I'll see if I can get an update for you on this guy once he faces the magistrate.'

'Thanks. I wish we'd known. After what she went through with Vaughn the thought …'

'I know,' he said. 'I'll stick my head in on her, say goodbye.'

As Finn walked towards Ava's bedroom, he heard her talking excitedly.

'He's going to jail and the bunnies will be safe now!'

Bunnies. Ice settled over him.

He stepped into her room. 'Hang up the phone please, Ava.'

Ava spun, her eyes shooting daggers at him before she got a better look at his face. 'Gotta go!' she told Megan and hung up.

'Kitchen,' he said, knowing Viv would need to hear this too.

'Finn, I thought you were heading—what's going on?'

'Sit down and tell me what you know about bunnies,' he ordered Ava.

Ava flopped heavily into a chair and her eyes dropped away from his. 'Mr Brown had bunnies.'

Viv's face drained of colour. 'How do you know that?'

When Ava's eyes filled with tears, Finn's heart lurched and he crouched in front of her. 'What happened?'

She shook her head. 'Nothing!'

'Ava,' Viv urged. 'Honey, we need to know.'

'He always says hello!' she blurted defensively. 'He seemed nice. Then last week I was walking back from the bus stop by myself 'cause Mandy from Year 7 who usually gets off and walks with me was on school camp and he said hello like usual. And he kinda groaned and said he had to feed his bunnies but he had such a sore back he couldn't bend down. Could I quickly just give them some food? So I did and he said thank you and I came home. Then the next day I saw him and he said his back was still sore and so I did it again. He said if I could do it every day while his back was sore he'd give me two dollars. I don't need the money but the bunnies were cute and if he couldn't feed them the RSPCA were going to take them away and put them down. That's what he told me. It only took a second. I didn't mind. He even let me pat them.'

She looked down and twin tears blobbed onto her skirt. 'And then yesterday, I was playing with the bunnies because I had nothing to do until Megan came over and he was standing just inside the screen door in a bathrobe and his penis was sticking out. He smiled and said oops and covered it up but then he just stood there and rubbed where it was poking underneath. I told him I had to go and he told me it was an accident and not to tell or the bunnies would be taken away and put down.'

'Oh my God,' Viv said. 'Why didn't you tell us!'

'I didn't want to get in trouble!'

'We need to tell the police handling the case,' Finn said, holding on to his rage. Then to Ava, he said, 'You're going to have to tell the police what happened so he can get into trouble for that, okay?'

'I'm sorry,' Ava sniffed. 'Are the police going to be mad?'

'No, sweetie. But you can't keep secrets like that, okay? It's not safe. We're always on your side. We might get cross sometimes, but we love you more than anything. What happened is not your fault.'

She sniffed and nodded. 'That's what Lexi said.'

Finn's gaze shot to Vivienne, but her look was blank. 'You told Lexi about this?' he asked.

Ava brightened, nodded. 'I was scared of getting into trouble but I had to tell someone so Megan and I FaceTimed Lexi. I made her promise if I told her she wouldn't tell anyone and she said yes so I told her about Mr Brown and the bunnies. And she told me what you just said and she fixed it.'

Vivienne's fingers clutched her hair. 'Oh my God,' she said again.

'What do you mean "fixed it"?' Finn said. 'What do you know?'

'We saw her in the backyard,' Ava said.

'In Mr Brown's backyard?'

'She was saving the bunnies.'

He didn't know what to think, whether to be grateful or furious. Lexi hadn't beaten the guy up. So who had she gotten to do it? Zander? He didn't want that thug anywhere near his daughter. Didn't even want him knowing about her!

'I'm going to go talk to the police in charge. They'll probably want to talk to Ava tomorrow. I'll let you know.'

'Sorry again, Dad.'

He hugged her tight. Thank God it hadn't been any worse. Thank God she was okay. 'Go shower. I'll talk to you tomorrow.'

'Okay.'

'Four houses, Finn, that's how far we are away from the bus stop. How can she not be safe walking four houses from the bus stop!' Viv's voice was thin and shrill. 'How can we not be allowed to know a convicted child sex offender is living right next door? How is anyone supposed to protect their kids anymore?'

What could he say? He didn't agree with the law on that either. Right now he was fuming about it. 'I'll keep on top of this.'

'Finn,' Viv said when he reached the door. 'Don't you dare tell those police Lexi was involved in what happened.'

He hadn't even thought that far ahead. 'She should have told us!'

'I had that moment too,' she said sadly. 'But then I realised there are going to be times as our daughter gets older when she's not going to want to tell us everything. No matter how much reassurance we give her that she can. I'm grateful she can at least talk to Lexi. That she knows she can trust her, and if Lexi had told us, that trust would have been broken. I feel better knowing they've got that connection. I know neither of them handled it the right way, but Lexi looked after Ava. And I think she always will.'

He wondered if Viv would feel the same way if she knew what Lexi was currently up to. 'I'll deal with it.'

'Tell Lexi thank you. I'm so grateful. As far as I'm concerned, the woman's a hero.'

CHAPTER FORTY-SEVEN

'What the hell did you think you were doing *this* time?' I stretch my arm out further from my ear at the volume coming through the phone as I replay Finn's voice message. Clearly he's not impressed. 'Bashing and hog-tying a naked man to a tree? Really?'

He was only almost naked. And it was as close as I could get Zander and the others to the police station. The sick prick was still breathing, wasn't he?

'Of all the stupid, vigilante stunts you've ever pulled … I don't want those gang members anywhere near my daughter ever again! Got it?' There's a long, silent pause then, with less volume, 'But also …' I hear the sort of sigh he always does when he's calming down. 'You came to Ava's rescue even after everything that's happened. I don't like how you went about it but the fact you did anything means something. I'm hoping it means you still care. So I'm asking you for a favour. I don't know if you've seen the news, but Cronin set off explosives at Cass's house yesterday.'

My stomach sinks as crashing guilt slams into me. I should have done more!

'She wasn't home but Meera and Noah were. We believe he's taken them. We don't know why. If you know anything or can find anything out … Please.'

Wait. Cass wasn't there and Cronin's taken Cass's family? Another kind of dread settles over me. I'm glad Cass is alive but there's not going to be any sort of humanitarian reason behind kidnapping her family. This is too much like Laura and Mikey. He's got something planned. Something terrible.

But what does Finn expect me to do about it? I don't know where Cronin is, I can't get involved in that. I need to get Breen's job done and stay out of trouble. What does Finn want? I'm not fucking superwoman.

I open my computer and, after taking a look, see the news sites are flooded with stories on Cronin and the bombings. I watch Cass beg for her family's life, see a photo of another smiling little boy, another innocent, loving mother. The knot in my stomach tightens, then strangles me until it threatens to snap. I can't let this happen.

I shut my computer with a snap. 'Fuck this.' Zander's got to know something.

I find him and the rest of the committee finishing off a meeting. I snag him as he comes through the door.

'I need to talk to you.'

Breen's expression is interested with a touch of suspicious so I smile and return my attention to Zander. 'I have to go shopping. I'm sick to death of these clothes so I need you to take me.'

Breen chuckles. 'Lucky you.' He slaps Zander on the arm and walks away with the others.

'Yeah, look, I've got a few things to do so …'

'So do them later.'

I see the flicker of annoyance cross his face but he sighs. 'This clothes shopping emergency has to happen now?'

'I'm guessing you wouldn't like it if I took off on your bike …'

He bends down to look me in the eyes, hard. 'That would be a step too far. Even for you.'

'That's done it. I'm terrified. Ready?'

He kind of laugh-growls but gestures for me to go ahead. 'Only because I need to get some stuff too.'

I let him take me shopping, briefly, because if I turn up with nothing and Breen sees us come back, he's gonna know something's up. When Zander suggests lunch, I see my chance.

'Let's grab some prawns and chips and go see your dad.'

'Seafood place is back upstairs and you see Dad almost every day. Can't we just get something out the front here?'

'No, because I need to talk to him, and you, away from the clubhouse.'

'I knew there was something going on,' he complains, looking longingly at the Mexican place. 'What's this about?'

'I'll tell you when we get there.'

A half-hour later we're peeling fresh prawns on the back deck of Freddie's old weatherboard cottage. It's tucked into a mess of mangroves in Tacoma on the edge of Ourimbah Creek, which I remember is always mosquito paradise in the hotter months. They're not a whole lot better in April.

'So this nice surprise,' Freddie says, chomping down on a prawn, 'what's it about?'

'You're so suspicious,' I tell him.

'That's why I'm still breathing. Come on, let's have it.' He sits back in his chair with his beer perched on his knee. 'What's going on?'

'I need to know where Cronin is.'

He exchanges looks with Zander and the temperature drops several degrees. 'Can't help you.'

'Don't bullshit me, Freddie. It's important.'

He goes back to peeling prawns. 'And why would that be?'

'He's taken Cass's wife and little boy. There's only one reason I can think of why he'd do that.'

'Fuck,' Freddie tells the prawn in his hand.

'You know that for sure?' Zander asks me.

'I know he blew up their house and they're missing, so yeah. I doubt they're off sightseeing.'

'Revenge is all he's got to live for,' Freddie says. 'You won't convince him to stop.'

'Then I'll make him stop!'

Both Zander and Freddie seem to think that's funny.

I have one card I can play. I *know* I shouldn't use it; I deliberately haven't. But I won't let anything happen to Meera and Noah if there's any chance I can stop it. 'You said revenge is all he's got to live for, so I guess he'd be interested in the name and location of the person who ordered and paid for the hit on Laura and Mikey.'

Both men's hands still.

'You know?' Zander demands. 'You fucking *know* and you haven't said anything?'

'Why would I? You haven't seen him.'

Zander sucks in a noisy breath and his hand closes into a fist. I flinch, but he smacks it down onto the table rather than into me, making everything on it jump. 'Smart fucking mouth …'

'Who was it?' Freddie asks quietly.

'I'll tell him when he lets them go.'

Zander pushes up from his chair and it clatters over behind him. 'Are you fucking out of your mind?'

'I need that family safe. I can't watch another—'

'He'll kill you! He'll get the name out of you and strap you to the nearest block of C4. You don't tell Cronin how it's going to play!'

I swallow hard because he's probably right. 'I'll take the chance.'

'No, you won't,' Freddie says. 'I'll take the information to him, talk to him about the woman and kid. If I can't talk him around, no one can. That's the best I can offer and it's the only chance you're going to get.'

I don't like it but I need Freddie to deliver the message and I can't force him to say what he doesn't want to.

'Okay,' I agree reluctantly.

'Okay,' Freddie says, 'so who was it?'

I'm well aware I'm about to set something in motion that I can't control, even more aware I'm probably handing Breen a death sentence. But what choice do I have? I see a broken Cass begging for her family, a little boy's smile. And I see Skink, lifeless on the bar room floor, his murderer casually wiping the blood from his face and demanding a drink. I have to choose and it's not a difficult decision to make.

'It was Breen.'

His eyes close on a curse. 'Do you have proof?'

'Yeah. I do.'

Freddie turns to Zander, who has walked off with his hands on his head. 'Cronin's already been looking for an opportunity to get his hands on Breen. Breen knows it too. He never goes anywhere except the clubhouse and the shop, carts Rocco everywhere. Without the support of the members, he's screwed.' Freddie takes time to swallow another prawn before continuing. 'Lotsa members still loyal to Cronin. Lots that would like him back. We take the evidence to the club, put it to a vote. Breen's done.'

'He's not interested in being president again!' Zander says. 'He's already got one foot in the grave with Laura and Mikey. He'll destroy the club over this mission of his. Don't be stupid, Dad, he's nuts!'

'He's got a right to know who killed his family,' Freddie says sternly. 'The rest is up to the club.'

CHAPTER FORTY-EIGHT

Monday, April 4

'We're good to go,' I tell Breen. 'I've sorted the encryption. Night would be best, when the cyber team isn't in the office. Just in case.'

'I'll tell them.' He grabs my cheeks and presses his lips to mine. 'We are about to make some serious money!'

I smile at him, manage not to gag. My smile fades as Zander, Freddie and Rocco walk into the room behind us.

'Breen,' Zander snaps.

He turns. 'Yes?'

'You're needed upstairs.'

'What's this about?' he asks, but leaves the room. I catch Zander's look and follow. Behind me, more members emerge from the bar, follow us up.

'Who are these people?' I hear Breen ask as I reach the top of the stairs. I step out of the way for the members still filing up behind me to see four men standing just outside the clubhouse, legs apart, arms folded. No colours, just jeans, black tees and plenty of tatts and muscle. Then Cronin steps around them, gun dangling by his leg.

'Hey!' Breen shrieks. 'Get him!'

No one moves.

'They don't take orders from you anymore,' Cronin says.

'What? There's been no meeting, no vote.'

'Last night,' Freddie says. 'When you weren't here.'

'You can't hold a vote without your president present!'

'Under the circumstances we voted, we could,' Zander says.

Breen's sneering at Zander, but he's fidgeting, nervous. 'What is this? What circumstances?'

'You were vice president when you set Cronin up on those drugs charges,' Freddie says. 'And when you ordered the hit on his family. You attack the president's family, you attack the club.'

I think that's the moment Breen knows he's going to die. I can see it in his face. With nothing more to lose, he lashes out.

'That's right!' he tells Cronin, 'I got you! I got your whore! I got your kid! I got your club! Laura should never have run to you. She'd still be alive!'

'She didn't run to me,' Cronin says, 'she ran to the club. It was all she knew. All the family she had.'

'You're full of shit! You married her!'

'Yes, I did. I took care of her and Mikey for years. I fell in love with her. Who wouldn't have? She didn't deserve what you did to her, never deserved to be a punching bag. She was a good woman. I loved her more than you ever did.'

Breen charges at Cronin. 'Loved her? *I* loved her! All I ever wanted was a family. A son! And you couldn't even let me have that, could you? You had to go and put your own little bastard inside her.'

Cronin laughs humourlessly. 'You fuckwit. Why do think she finally ran from you after all she'd put up with? After all those times she'd stood by you and made excuses for you? All those times she'd convinced herself she could save you?'

'Because of you!' Breen spits, shoving a finger into Cronin's chest. 'You took her from me!'

'Not because of me. Because she was pregnant. She wanted to protect the baby she'd found out about a half-hour before you beat the shit out of her that last time. Yeah—that's right,' he says when

Breen stumbles back, his expression shocked. 'She was already knocked up when she got herself out of there. If you'd bothered to do the maths, you'd have figured it out. Mikey was never mine.' Cronin steps forward as though to ram the point home. 'You killed your own damn son!'

'Liar!'

Another step. 'That beautiful baby boy you blew to pieces was your own flesh and blood. The one you'd always wanted.'

Breen's shaking his head, still moving back as Cronin advances.

'He's telling the truth,' Freddie says. 'Even says so on the birth certificate. Where did you think those blue eyes came from? Should've been pretty damn obvious, really. To anyone in his right mind, anyway.'

Breen's face turns from blind denial to ashen misery. 'I killed my son?' Other words are forming on his lips but not leaving them. He collapses bonelessly to the ground.

'And now all that shit you thought you had, it's gone,' Cronin taunts. 'You've lost your club, the mother of your child is in the ground with your little boy and I'm back in business. Tell me, Breen, was it worth it?'

Breen turns a tortured face to Cronin, to the gun still dangling from his side. 'Kill me. Just do it.'

Cronin sneers and drops his gun at Breen's side. 'Do it yourself.' He turns on his heel.

Zander pulls me away and gives me a gentle shove towards the stairs. 'Go.'

I'm halfway down when a single shot echoes around the carpark.

'Lexi. I wanted to thank you,' Cronin tells me. I've been summoned to the office and was wondering what the hell to expect. None of those possibilities involved a thank you.

'There's no need.'

'I'm told there is a plan in place to steal some information from the police. That you are ready to go ahead.'

'That's right.'

'I don't care about the money. But the club, they want it. So we go ahead with the plan. You want to do it late.'

'Better when no one's at the office.'

'Then be ready.'

'Sure. What about Meera and Noah?'

'I've worked that out.'

'What does that mean?'

'We can do both.'

'Both ... What? You can't kill them! I gave you that information so you'd let them go.'

Cronin's expression cools. 'Last I checked, little Lexi, you don't tell your president what to do.'

'But you said you were only going after the guilty ones. Cass's family is innocent.'

'Yes. So was mine. I think it's called guilt by association.'

I struggle to find the right words to change his mind. 'The people that did that to Laura and Mikey were monsters. Evil grubs who deserve to rot in hell. You got them. They earned their deaths. But you're not evil. How can you think killing an innocent woman and child will make you feel better? You've always been a man of strong principles. Your wife was proud of that. Your son—'

The smack sends me to the floor, dazes me with its intensity. When I look up, he's purple with rage.

'Do not quote my Laura's words at me! Do not tell me what I am! I was that man when I had my wife, when I had my son. He died with them. Ten years in prison prepared me for what I need to do. Now I will show the police and the country what happens when justice is not served.'

'But Cass—'

'That bitch looked me in the eye and promised me they were safe. She promised me! Then I had to watch my family die. Now she will watch her family die. That's justice!'

I get back to my feet, half-expecting another blow to my throbbing cheek. 'How is Cass going to see anything? You're going to broadcast it?'

'A grand gesture to show what happens to anyone who messes with me. We'll do it at the place you'll steal the information from.'

'Police headquarters? You've lost it.'

He grabs me by the throat and the pain is incredible. 'The only reason you're not dead is because you gave me Breen. Understand?'

I can't speak, try to nod. He releases me and I drag in a painful breath.

'I didn't know that night you were a cop or you and your friend would have died with Blake.' He spits at my feet. 'Freddie explained your story to me. I either taught you too well or you're lying. But I will never trust a cop again. Ever. So. You will not leave the grounds. You'll hand over your devices and no one will give you access to one. You will not be on the club computers unless someone is looking over your shoulder. You are breathing because I allow it. That's all.'

He leaves the room with a snap of his fingers to the thugs he'd brought with him.

Zander shrugs. 'I told ya. He's fucking crazy.'

I try to clear my sore throat, not really sure what to say. 'He can't be serious. How does he think he's going to get Meera and Noah and a bomb inside headquarters?'

'He's gotten away with everything else, hasn't he? Remember, this is his grand gesture. He's been stewing on it for a fucking decade. Anyone can blow up a woman and kid, but to get into the heart of police territory and do it right under their noses … That's a powerful statement.'

'He must know he won't get away with it. He'll be the most hunted man on the planet.'

'I don't think he cares what happens after. Do you? He's going ahead with the info trade to keep the club onside and happy, but I don't think he has any plans as a long-term president.'

'You can't be good with this. You have it within you to be an arsehole of epic proportions from time to time but you're not a child killer.'

'Thanks, I think. I need your phone.'

'Huh?'

'He told me to get it off you. Hand it over.'

I reluctantly put it in his hand.

'And no computer lab. Seriously, don't fuck with him. He's mad enough to kill you by accident. Let's go get your laptop.'

This time the loss of contact with the outside world is much more dire, because I have no way to warn anyone about Cronin's crazy plan. We reach my room and I hand over my computer.

'You might want to ice that cheek.'

'Nope. I'm going to train.'

'Bit early for that.'

'I need to hit something. Get out while I change.'

I beat the shit out of the bag until my arms and legs are jelly. I will not believe I'm out of options. I can't accept that there's nothing I can do. There has to be *something*. Why the fuck can't I think of anything?

Mikey's face merges with Noah's and I hit the bag again, hard, and feel a painful twinge in my shoulder suggesting I've swung one punch too many. I grab hold of it. 'Fuck.' Pissed off, I kick the bag and stub my toe. I growl loudly in aggravation.

'That's enough,' I hear Rodger shout.

I spot him and Zander at the bar and wonder how long they've been watching. I roughly throw the gloves back on the shelf and clutch at my shoulder as I walk over to get a bottle of water. Rodger comes around with me and takes my arm, starts manipulating it painfully. 'Ow!' I complain, doing my best to escape.

'Keep still.'

'That hurts!'

'Where? Here?' He presses two fingers into the muscle and nearly sends me through the roof.

'Yes! Fuck!' I swear again when he digs more fingers into the spot in some sort of sadistic massage.

'It's just a strain,' he says when he finally gives my arm back. 'Get some ice on it.' He swings down to the freezer under the bar and hands me an ice pack.

I put it on and sit, sulking. But I think whatever he did actually helped.

Zander laughs. 'Feel better?'

'Are you just going to sit there laughing or are you going to make me a drink?'

He takes pity on me, grabs the JD and pours me a tiny glass. 'What, are we on rations now?'

'You've got a job to do tonight.'

'As if I could forget.'

'Hey,' Nate says, appearing at the bar. 'Bro, who's the cop that's been working for the club?'

'You don't know?' I interrupt in confusion. 'I thought they messaged the club about stuff.'

'Yeah, and they use their name and police email.' Nate's eyes are wide with sarcasm.

And okay, I should have realised the who and where from would be deliberately kept untraceable.

'So?' Nate asks Zander.

My ears prick up but Zander shrugs. 'Only person who knows that is Rocco. Why?'

'Cronin wants to know. He needs someone to detonate—' Nate looks at me. 'Look, I know this is fucked up, but whatever. He's gonna set the timer so it'll countdown like it did with Laura and Mikey, but it's all show. Control over the bomb will be remote in case anything goes wrong and the cops get in there too early. So he can blow it anyway.'

'You're gonna have to find Rocco.'

'He wants to know *now*.'

Zander puts down his beer. 'Guess I'll help.'

Zander wanders off with Nate and I pour myself a proper glass of JD. How can they all be going through with this? No one seems comfortable with it, but they're not so uncomfortable that they're doing anything to stop it. I desperately want to but …

Again the helplessness hits me. What's left to try?

CHAPTER FORTY-NINE

'She did what?' Rachael asked with a laugh of disbelief. Finn hadn't had a chance to talk to her about the incident with Brown until halfway through the day. The morning had been another frantic search for Cass's family that had seen them running in different directions. A large number of police and analysts were in residence, tracking down Cronin, Meera and Noah. The number of calls to the hotline alone had been astronomical, hundreds of hours of CCTV was being monitored, forensic evidence and witness statements were being analysed and reviewed.

'It's not funny!'

Rachael's face instantly sobered. 'I know but it … certainly … got the job done.'

He stared at her. 'You're impressed.'

'I'm never impressed by vigilante behaviour, Finn. I just can't believe she did it.'

'Why not? Nothing would surprise me anymore.'

'She could have done nothing.'

'Sure. She didn't have to come to Ava's rescue, she didn't have to come between me and a gorilla swinging a wooden fence post. She didn't have to come at me afterwards like a raving bloody lunatic as though she's been terrified I'd been about to die.'

'She did that?' Rachael asked, tone softening.

'Yes! But she also chose a motorcycle gang over her friends, hacked into a government database, refused to answer questions, has been harbouring Desmond—I'm sure of it—has gone into hiding so we can't find her and is likely working on some plot to wreak more havoc on national security.'

'So perhaps Lexi ran to the club for all the reasons Olivia has no doubt drilled into you. But whatever labels Olivia has decided to slap on Lexi, you can't be surprised she came to Ava's assistance. Or yours. She never gives up on the people she cares about.'

'Neither do you. But don't fool yourself.'

'I can't stand it, Finn!' she said. 'She'd come so far! None of this should ever have happened.' Rachael rubbed her fingers jerkily against her forehead. 'It must be the drugs. They're messing with her mind. I know she's still in there.'

'There's only so many times you can get in her way. She's already threatened you.'

'Did you hear what I said to her?'

'I wish you hadn't.'

Rachael's gaze fell. 'It would have been worth it if she'd just opened up. We were so close.'

'Olivia thinks—'

'I don't want to hear any more about what Olivia thinks. I'm sorry. I'm not denying her qualifications, but every person's actions, every situation, can be open to interpretation and there's an obvious ulterior motive behind hers.'

He frowned, puzzled. 'What ulterior motive could Olivia possibly have?'

Rachael's look was incredulous. 'You!'

'What?'

'If you're going to be deliberately obtuse can we please forget it and get back to work on Cronin?'

'I'm not being deliberately …' He breathed out rather than slap back. *Calm*, he thought. 'We're doing everything humanly possible. You've pulled in every member of staff you can wrangle.'

'It doesn't seem like enough. Did you tackle McCabe about your people-smuggling theory?'

'Didn't get a chance yesterday with all the Cass stuff. I'll try and fit it in today. And something else struck me last night. When we went to pick up Skink, there was an odd array of clothing on the line, seemed like a lot of people living in a small house. There was also some commotion in the house when we arrived. If we decide the club could be harbouring illegals, it might be worth checking that they're not there.'

'Have Olivia address it with McCabe; we've got enough to worry about.'

'I would have yesterday, but she spent most of the afternoon making sure Cass was looked after.'

'Why?'

'Because I asked her to. I thought she could help.'

'I'm sure she did.'

'She's a good person, Rach.'

'I'm sure she is.'

'You should get to know her.'

'I—'

'Let me guess, you're sure you will?'

Rachael's mouth twisted, but before she could answer, there was a knock on the open door.

'Rachael. There's something you need to see,' Linc said, his face grim.

'What is it?'

He opened his laptop and Cronin appeared onscreen. 'He's posted this on every social media platform.' He pressed play.

'Hello, everybody. My name is Arthur Cronin. Ten years ago, this happened to my family.' The horrifying video of Laura's and Mikey's last moments played through. 'Let me tell you a story—the story of how this came about.'

Cronin recounted it all, from the set-up, to the arrest, to the deal. He took his audience through the events of the day his family were stolen, the delay in looking for them and the cover-up by the team of police handling his case. He recounted it all as best he knew it.

Then Meera and Noah flashed onscreen, huddled together in the corner of a dark room.

'Justice is not always easy to look at, but it must be served. The police must know they are accountable. Especially those who make false promises. As I watched the last thirty seconds of my wife's and son's lives, now we will watch the last thirty seconds of theirs. But not yet, Lisa Cassidy, not yet. I will inform the media ten minutes before I make this grand gesture in the name of all who have been the victims of police injustice. So be ready.'

Finn was chilled to his core. 'There must be a way to trace that.'

'Can we?' Rachael asked Linc.

'I don't know, but you might want to get people on it.'

'Get Neutron back here. We need to talk to him.' She pressed her hands to her temples. 'Damn it, I need Lexi!'

CHAPTER FIFTY

I log on under the watchful eyes of everyone, except the login I enter is wrong. I swear under my breath, repeat my mistake.

'What's going on?' Cronin asks.

'It's like the whole system has been shut down.' I try something equally as useless. Fail again.

'Are they the credentials you used last time?' Nate asks, frowning at the screen.

'Of course they are!'

'Then how is that possible! You said we were ready!'

'I was! They know what we're trying to do! Neutron must have done something extreme. No external traffic is getting through. It's not going to work.'

'What about that backup plan? Cyber's program,' Nate reminds me.

'If I can't get through I can't access it!' I say. I swing my gaze around the room accusatorially. 'Did anyone mess with this? Touch it at all? Do anything that might have given anything away?'

'Who could?' Zander asks in genuine disbelief.

I make a frustrated sound and thump the keys. 'This can't be fucked up now!'

'It must have been Skink,' Zander says.

'That's not possible,' Nate says.

'More likely they're locking everything up after hours until they track us down,' I say.

'Okay, forget it,' Cronin says. 'We'll just blow them up.'

There's a round of objections.

'I think …' I say, turning in my chair, trying to look reluctant, '… I think I can still do this, but I'm going to need to get in there.'

'Into police headquarters?' Zander asks in disbelief.

'Preferably with Neutron onsite.'

'Not happening,' Cronin says with a dismissive wave.

'He doesn't need to know what we're after, why or where it's going. I just need him to let us in and someone to make sure he doesn't interfere while I'm working,' I tell him.

'Then what?' Cronin says, eyes narrowing with suspicion.

'I'll set the computer up to encrypt the information as it downloads and it can go straight through to the buyer.'

'How long will all this take?'

'From the time I get on the computer? A couple of hours, tops.'

I sense he's going to say no, but I know the club wants the money so I use that.

'Look, you're getting in there anyway, get me in too and I'll make the club a few million dollars richer.'

There's more rounds of chatter, this time of agreement and I sense Cronin weakening. I've decided the only chance I have to do anything about this situation is to get them to take me into HQ with Meera and Noah and somehow raise the alarm once we get there. Or use Neutron to if I can't. It's not much, but it's a chance.

'No,' Cronin says, and I think it's over. Then he says, 'The two jobs will remain completely separate. No crossover. You get yourself and Rocco in. You'll need to be out before six am. Then Cass's family can be on the prime-time morning news.'

'Rocco?'

'Insurance.'

Fuck. 'Okay …' I think about it some more. 'And I'll need Cass.'

'What?' Cronin snaps.

'If I ask Neutron to get me into HQ, he'll refuse. If we take him by force, we risk drawing attention to ourselves. Cass is the only person we have a hope of convincing to get Neutron there and us inside without being detected.'

'Why would she do it?'

'Because we have her wife and son.'

Cronin thinks about that. Then he smiles, his lips slowly stretching wide. 'You tell her they're safe if she cooperates.'

I'm not convinced. 'Really?'

'No. This is just what she told me. I cooperate, my family will be safe. Now you tell her the same thing. It's perfect. When she cooperates, when we get what we want, then she can watch her family die. As I watched mine.'

The entire room waits silently for my answer.

'Okay. Let's do it.'

'No more objections?' he asks, voice laden with suspicion.

'Cronin, I don't like it. At all. If I thought there was any chance of changing your mind, I would. But you're going to do this with or without me. We may as well get the millions and maybe … maybe once this is all over you can trust me again.'

More murmuring from the other members, nods and even a couple of cheers. Sick fucks.

'Okay. But Lexi? You will be in contact at all times. One wrong move—if you mute your mic, if communications go down, if you try and warn anyone—I'll have my cop blow the bomb immediately. Cops will come from everywhere. Understand? I don't think Rocco would take kindly to that.'

'Got it.'

'They'll need a spare,' Freddie says. 'One for each hostage and someone to take care of anything unexpected. Send Zander in with them.'

'I don't know. These two are close.'

'Brother. Trust me. Zander's the best fighter we've got. Something goes wrong, you want him in there. You've waited a long time for this.'

Cronin hugs Freddie, slapping him on the back. 'You are a true brother to me. Okay. We'll do that.'

Nerves are jumping in my stomach as I go back to my room. Involving Cass is crazy. There's no way to predict how she'll react. But she really is the only option I can think of. There's no chance she'll believe that, if she cooperates, Cronin will let her family go, but the lure of seeing them again might be enough. But how am I going to do anything with Rocco and Zander watching my every move? The uncomfortable answer is I can't do this without Zander. I have zero faith he'll choose to help me instead of the club, but just a little that I can raise my plan with him and he won't report it to Cronin. The biggest pull I have is Noah.

I know Zander's crashing here tonight so I go knock on the door of the room he's been using. I wonder if it still stinks.

He opens it. 'Well, this is a nice surprise,' he says. 'Joining me?'

I push into the room. Notice he's been cleaning his pistol. He scoops it up.

'You may as well keep that out.'

'Why?'

'Because after what I'm about to tell you, you're gonna have to make a decision, and if it doesn't go in my favour, I'd rather you shoot me than Cronin get hold of me.'

He sighs and waits. 'Go on, out with it.'

'I'm not going to let Cronin murder Meera and Noah.'

'You're kidding,' he tells me, wide-eyed. 'And let me guess, there's no computer problem.'

'Good guess.'

'You don't think Nate saw through that "closing down the whole of headquarters" bullshit?'

My stomach does a little jump. My explanation was a bit on the far-fetched side. 'Is he going to say anything?'

'Kept his mouth shut this long, hasn't he? But he's not gonna help, either. He won't completely betray the club.' He rubs a hand over his head in an agitated movement. 'I don't fuckin' know what to do.'

'You're gonna do the right thing,' I tell him.

He sends me a sideways glare. 'You're so sure.'

'Yeah.' I step forward and place my hands on his chest then look up into his eyes. 'Because I know you. You're the guy that carried

Mikey around on your shoulders and gave him aeroplane rides, who snuck him lollies and taught him to catch a ball and tickled him until he couldn't breathe. You're the guy that saved me from an arsehole when I thought I was grown up enough to be here and I wasn't, the guy that stepped in to help Caitlin. The one that looks after his dad and makes sure prospects don't beat Rocco at pool, and paedophiles don't harass kids he hasn't even met. You're a good guy, Zander. You're not going to let this happen.'

'I'll be betraying my president. Cronin.'

I slowly shake my head from side to side. 'Do you think the old Cronin would have blown up a child? Do you think he'd ever have led his club down that path? That man out there … that's not Cronin anymore. What's out there is nothing but a bitter old shell of a man who's let years of pent-up hatred twist his mind into something vile and evil. He thinks murdering people, even innocent people, will make everything right. What's going to happen on the other side of this when it doesn't? He'll never go back to being who he was. Look in his eyes. That part of him just isn't there anymore.'

'You're right,' Freddie says, opening the door and startling us both. 'But you might want to be a bit quieter. Not hard to eavesdrop from out there.' Then he says to Zander, 'You told her the plan?'

'Damn it, Dad! I was getting to it.'

'Plan?' I ask. 'All we need to do is sneak a message through—'

'You're not talking to anyone,' Zander snaps. 'You even say the word "cop" and I shut this down now. The download goes through, the club gets the money. All that shit goes ahead as planned. The only alteration …'

'Is what?'

'The bomb doesn't go off,' Freddie says.

I'm stunned that they've already thought this out, agreed to it. My brain is racing. 'Great but … how do we pull that off?'

'Nate might have done us one more small favour.' Freddie holds out a little black box about the size of a mobile phone with three stubby antennas poking from the top. 'Battery-operated jammer. You know how they work?'

'Yeah. They transmit the same frequencies as phones and the two signals collide and cancel each other out.'

'Right. Cronin's gonna have his cop close by making sure everything goes to plan. He's gonna be using a mobile to trigger the bomb. Whoever this arsehole is, he has to call that phone.'

'Got it. If the modified phone attached to the detonator can't receive the call, it can't convert the signal into the electrical current it needs to set off the detonator charge necessary to trigger the main explosive.'

'Huh?' Zander asks.

'As long as we can block the signal to the receiving phone, the bomb won't go off,' Freddie says. 'But these little phone jammers only have limited range. You're going to need to be within nine metres of that bomb.'

'Okay ...'

'Nine and a half and you go boom. Understand?'

It's two am and I haven't slept. How could I? I stand under the shower for several minutes trying to wash away the hangover-like dregs left from needing sleep but not being able to achieve it. When I give up on the idea, I get dressed. I can already hear voices in the bar so I go out there to see who's up.

I stop dead when I walk in the door.

Cronin, Zander, Nate, Woolly, Freddie and all four of Cronin's men are standing around watching Rocco strap explosives to Noah's tiny body. Meera is crying quietly between two of Cronin's men, eyes locked on Noah, her expression one of distraught devastation. She flicks her gaze from her child just long enough to silently plead with me, and I can't breathe for the hurt and desperation that hits me. One of Cronin's men looks at me, smiles. His eyes are dark and scary as hell. Creepy. A flicker of recognition skids through my mind, but it's lost in the horror of what I'm witnessing.

'What is it?' Noah asks, his baby face red from tears, but curious.

'It's a blast-off suit,' Rocco tells him in the gentlest voice I've ever heard him use. 'Like Superman.'

Noah frowns. 'I like Spider-Man. Why do I have to wear it?'

'Because you're the star of the show.'

'What does this do?'

'Hey, hey, little dude, don't touch it.'

'Why not?'

''Cause you'll ruin the surprise. Let's get this jacket on over the top so you're not tempted to play with it, okay?'

'Why is Mummy crying? I want to go home.'

When his wet little eyes hit mine, I'm done. I can't. I. Just. Can't. The sob escapes my lips as I push through the doors to the corridor. I breathe rapidly to try to control myself as my legs lose their strength and I slide down the wall, press my hands to my mouth.

When I hear the door open I assume it will be Zander, maybe Freddie. But it's Cronin. I can't help the look of utter repulsion I send him.

'The suit is just insurance in case we run into any trouble on the way. Once they get there, it will be taken off.'

'Oh, thank goodness you're blowing them up with a different bomb!' I spit.

He sighs heavily. 'You think I'm a monster. But you don't understand.'

'You're right. I have no fucking clue,' I snarl, getting to my feet. The anger has made me feel stronger. 'None. I *idolised* you! You *loved* Mikey. You *adored* him! How can you stand in there and watch while that sweet little boy's wrapped in C4? Cronin, *please.* This is not you.'

He looks past me down the corridor. Smiles sadly. 'It's no wonder Laura thought so much of you. You are alike in many ways. She is disappointed in me. She tells me that, don't you, my love?'

I look down the empty corridor and realise the full extent of his fucked-up mind. 'What—what is she saying?'

'What she's said all along. That I don't need to do this. That it won't make any difference.'

'She's right. It won't.'

His eyes return to mine. 'It will to me. The boy and his mother will be gone soon. You may stay away until they leave. I will have Rocco collect you when it's time.'

He walks back through the door and is gone.

No. I run to the computer lab. I can't take any more chances. I can't let this happen. The door is locked. I try it again anyway. Rattle the handle desperately.

'It's not going to open,' Zander tells me.

I kick it. What the fuck was all the kicking and punching good for if it can't help me now?

'Hey,' he says, wrapping his arms around me and pulling me back. 'You're making a racket. Cut it out. You want Cronin to ground you? Then how much use will you be?'

I shove him off and drag my fingers roughly through my hair. 'What if we can't—' My voice breaks.

'Lexi, calm the fuck down. We *can*.'

CHAPTER FIFTY-ONE

Tuesday, April 5

As we approach Cass's home I see a dark sedan parked out front.

'That's cops,' I warn. 'Don't stop, just cruise past. Zander, get down.' I slide beneath window level just in case. I've calmed myself, given myself a decent lecture and hope my head is where it needs to be to pull all this off.

Rocco drives past. 'You're right, I see 'em.'

'I should have thought of that.'

'So now what?' Zander asks.

'I guess we park in the next street over, see if we can get through the back way.'

'How do you know there's not more in the house?'

'I don't. But I doubt it. Just have to be careful.'

Rocco turns a corner, then another one. 'How many houses down was she?'

'Not sure, hold on.' I check my phone maps, work it out. 'Park near that big brown fence,' I tell him. Because of course, the home behind Cass's has the highest, most difficult-to-scale barrier in the street. I undo my seatbelt and open the car door.

Rocco follows suit. 'Watch the car,' he tells Zander. 'And turn on your comms. Be ready to move.'

It takes longer than it should to get us both into Cass's backyard. We crouch in the darkest back corner, only moving towards the house after watching and waiting for several minutes. When I get to the back door, I discover she has the best security door you can buy. I have a small moment of panic about getting in and whatever other security she has on the place when Rocco whispers, 'Window's open.' I look up and see one above us.

With much more lithe grace than I would have credited him with, Rocco scales the house, then lowers his arm and pulls me up. I refuse to be impressed, because what he does with his strength is strap bombs to babies.

Rocco removes the fly screen and the window slides open quietly until it's wide enough for us to step in.

'What are you guys doing!' Zander says in my ear.

'It took a while, okay? Shut up,' I say in barely a whisper, then freeze when I hear the rustle of blankets.

Fuck, we're in the bedroom. A light goes on and a red-faced, swollen-eyed Cass is sitting up, gun outstretched. Her face reflects her shock.

'Lexi?'

'If you pull that trigger,' Rocco says, 'you'll never see them again.'

I can see the indecision in her eyes. 'What are you doing here?' she asks. 'What do you want? Where's my family!'

'Shh! Is anyone else here?' I ask.

'No.'

'Sure?' Rocco presses. 'Because if you're lying, your wife and kid are dead.'

'Yes. Sure. Outside, but not in here.' She turns her gaze to me. 'You've got Noah and Meera?'

'If you want to see them again, you need to come with us now.'

A broken sob erupts from her throat. Lacking any sense of self-preservation, she drops the gun and scrambles out of the covers. She's wearing a t-shirt and cargos. I'm guessing she's fallen into bed in yesterday's clothes. I suppose she's not sleeping much, with her family under Cronin's control.

'I need you to do something for me,' I tell her before we go any further.

'Anything,' she says desperately. 'Please, whatever happens, I need to be with them.'

By the time Cass sneaks us into headquarters and up to cyber, Neutron is already at his desk. His expression turns wary as he sees us all pile in.

'Sit there,' Rocco orders Cass. When she's where he wants her, he secures her hands and feet to the chair.

'What are you doing? You said I could see them!'

'You will! Shut up.'

'Get me into the system,' I tell Neutron.

Neutron's face is clammy and he's staring at Rocco like he's gonna pass out. 'I—I—'

Rocco removes his gun from his jeans at his lower back and points it at Neutron's head. 'Do it now!' he orders.

'Okay! Okay.'

'Slowly, Neutron,' I warn him, watching him like a hawk and hoping he doesn't try and pull anything stupid. But with a few keystrokes, we're in. 'Right, move.'

He gets out of his chair with his hands up.

'Don't need this one anymore?' Rocco checks, his gun still on Neutron's head.

'I might!' I say quickly. 'If anyone figures out what's going on, they're going to call him to make sure it's legit. He'll need to take that call.'

Rocco grunts and points Neutron at another chair. 'Sit down.' When Neutron does as he's told, Rocco secures him as he did Cass.

I spend a moment acquainting myself with Neutron's computer then find what I'm looking for and get to work. 'Okay, it's underway,' I announce once I've got it under control. 'Now we wait.'

'How is everything going?' I hear over my earpiece.

'Perfect,' I tell Cronin. 'We were a bit late getting started, but we'll still be done in time.'

'Yeah, boss,' Rocco says. 'All going to plan.'

'In time for what?' Cass asks.

Rocco grins at her. 'You'll see.'

If possible, Cass's face loses even more colour. For several minutes, no one speaks as the download ticks on. Then Cass shifts, trying to drag her chair closer to me. Rocco puts a boot on it and glares at her.

'Lexi,' she says shakily. 'Tell me what's happening.'

'It'll be okay,' I tell her, but I can't make eye contact. Because what if it's not?

'You told me I could see them.'

'You will in a few minutes,' Rocco says. 'You'll get a really good look.'

'I want to talk to them.'

'That wasn't the deal.'

'Lexi,' Cass says to me. 'I'm sorry. I'm sorry I was so horrible to you. It wasn't about you. Those memories were painful. You brought them all back. I—' Her voice cuts off on a sob. 'I told myself I'd never do anything that wasn't proper procedure ever again, no matter who ordered what and I lived by that and then you showed up and you broke all the rules and were this big constant reminder of what I'd done and I couldn't bear it. I still have the heart. The little heart Mikey gave me. It's made out of clay. I loved that little boy too. I—'

'Shut up,' Rocco says with a bored sigh. I keep my eyes focused on the screen as my heart shatters for Cass.

She tries again after several more minutes tick over. 'Lexi, please. Meera is the kindest, most loving person you'll ever meet. And Noah … he's just a little boy. He turned four three weeks ago. He loves Spider-Man. Remember how Mikey loved—'

The sharp crack of Rocco's backhand to Cass's face tips her chair over. 'I said shut up!'

'Hey,' Zander says, carefully righting the chair and sitting Cass back up. 'That's enough. How can she watch with her eyes swollen shut?'

'He's going to kill them, isn't he? He's going to make me watch them die.' It's not much more than a pained whisper.

Rocco bends down to get in her face. 'Course not. If you cooperate, we'll make sure they're protected.'

She doesn't buy it. I see her mind click with his meaning almost as soon as the words are out. 'Where are they!' she screams. 'You said I could see them. I want to see them!'

'In a minute,' Rocco repeats.

Cass quickly works her way up to hysterical. Rocco's fists are tightly closed but he doesn't touch her again except to put a length of tape over her mouth.

More time passes. The only sound is Cass's noisy attempts to breathe through her nose while sobbing. I wonder what's going on elsewhere in the building. Whether Meera and Noah are in whatever place Cronin has seen fit to carry out his grand gesture and where that might be. Every now and then I catch Neutron staring at me, before he quickly averts his gaze. I feel bad, but keeping him alive is the best I can do right now.

Finally I get an alert. The download is complete. I see the slight tensing of Zander's body as he walks casually closer to Rocco.

'Okay, it's done,' I announce, nerves bouncing wildly in my stomach. 'Cronin, we're ready to move.' I have to assume he's still listening.

'Good,' Cronin says. 'I'll see you when you return. I will start my broadcast now.' I hear a faint click that I assume means he's closed his connection.

Zander has his arm around Rocco's throat before I can even turn around. Rocco thrashes, fights, but Zander's arm is locked tight and after a few seconds, the giant falls. Zander takes his gun and restrains him.

I pounce out of the way as Zander cuts through Neutron's ties. 'You need to find them,' I tell Neutron.

'Find who?'

'Cass's family. They're here somewhere! You have to hurry!'

He looks confused, staring at me with a muddled frown. 'You don't know where they are?'

'Neutron! Does it look like we're really working with that guy?' I flick an arm in Rocco's direction. 'Look on the security cameras and find Meera and Noah!'

His face clears as a light comes back into his eyes. 'Do you want me to call for help?'

'No! Cronin's got a cop onside and I don't know who or what they're monitoring. One hint something's off and they'll blow them early. Find them, Neutron!'

Cass is making desperate sounds behind the tape and Zander gently removes it.

'What's happening!' she demands. 'You're going to help them?'

'We're trying,' I mutter, my attention glued to all the screens of security footage Neutron's furious typing has somehow projected around the room. 'Zander, check the broadcast.'

I scan the security images, room after room, floor after floor. It seems to take forever. Too long. I hear a movement and realise Rocco's already waking up. On Zander's phone, Cronin is broadcasting another speech.

'I promised justice for my family. But everyone who has been wronged can take heart that even those who seem untouchable can be punished.'

'He's going to kill them,' Cass sobs.

'Got them!' Neutron exclaims. 'Ground floor. They've disabled the lift. Damn, I can't get it back online.'

Cass's breath catches at the image of Meera and Noah in the lift space. Meera is clutching Noah in her lap, a bomb is sitting at her feet. A display is paused on thirty seconds.

'I've got this,' Zander says, but I snatch the jammer from his hand.

'I need you on Rocco in case he tries anything.'

'I'll shoot the bastard.'

I grab his shirt and stare up at him hard. 'You're not killing anyone. Watch him, put him back to sleep if you have to. I need you here.'

Zander looks torn. Then nods. 'Remember, the signal blocker only works to a nine-metre range. You need to be close.'

'Got it. I'll hide the jammer behind the security screening desk. That's more than close enough. I'll be right back.'

He tosses me Rocco's gun. 'Just in case there's a problem.'

I catch it then I'm running for the lift that I know will open right next to theirs.

My heart is racing faster than my feet. The lift opens almost instantly—no one else has used it since we did, and I press G.

'Cronin's still talking,' Zander says in my earpiece. 'You've got time.'

The lift descends quickly. Four, three, two …

'Lexi, where are you?' Zander asks.

'Almost there. Why?'

The doors open and I step out, almost crashing into a startled Rachael.

'Because the cops just showed up!' Zander tells me, too late.

There are more police swarming in from everywhere. 'Fuckin' grab the bitch and get back up here!' Zander roars in my ear.

'Lexi! What are you doing here?' Rachael demands. I see her fingers wrap more closely around her weapon as she looks around for any other threats.

'Hurry up! Do it!' Zander says.

'Don't let them die!' I hear Cass yell. 'Please!'

Nine metres. If I go a floor up will I still be in range? Self-preservation and desperation pull me in two different directions. Meera and Noah are in the lift right beside mine.

The words, 'He's about to start the countdown!' come from somewhere in the room.

I'm not sure if it's a choice or the fact my legs have frozen but I let the lift doors close behind me. I take in a sea of faces in a heartbeat. I wonder why no one's moved then notice several sets of eyes resting on my gun. On Rachael's proximity.

'Put it down, Lexi!' Brighton orders, stepping into view. 'You're under arrest.'

'Lexi, take a hostage and move! Now!' Zander snaps again.

One of these people has to be the one working for Cronin. The one willing to press a button before Cronin is ready but only if it's absolutely necessary. No one's going to ruin Cronin's grand gesture unless they have to. I feel the press of the jammer against my lower back.

'Lexi,' Rachael says calmly, getting my eyes on hers. 'Give me the gun.'

'Just explain!' Neutron yells over the earpiece. 'You're in position. Tell them.'

I open my mouth to speak before I hear Rocco laughing. 'Congratulations, you idiots! You think Cronin's grand gesture is one woman and child? You think that's why he sent all the cops in here? All you've done is get yourself caught, bitch! The whole place is gonna go up. We need to get outta here!'

'What?'

'Lexi, give it to me,' Rachael orders.

Nine metres. He's about to start the countdown.

'She even spoke to the bastard and still didn't recognise him.' Rocco is laughing crazily. 'Stupid old fart was offended. Ron's a dickhead but she's a fucking idiot. We've got ten seconds after the first bomb goes off to be gone!'

Who the hell is Ron? Wait, he's one of Cronin's men. Which one?

'Thirty seconds!' I hear.

Rachael extends a hand for the gun. With no other choice, I grab her around the throat and put the gun to her head. 'Drop your gun!' I order.

'What are you doing?' she asks in a distressed squeak but does as I tell her.

I pull her back a step, putting her between me and everyone else. 'Keep still.'

My actions bring on shouting, chaos. Then a new order. One with way too many guns pointed at me.

Ron. My mind flicks to the man with creepy eyes Cronin had brought in. Creepy eyes … like the guy who'd done his best to ignore Rachael upstairs outside the meeting room. Cronin's thug. An air-conditioning tech. My eyes flick to the vents overhead and back again. Oh, fuck. *The whole place'll go up*. How many bombs are there?

Standing here is useless. I can stop the bomb intended for Meera and Noah but with more bombs in play, the only way to be sure none of them go off is to be in range of whatever cop has the detonator. But who is it? I keep behind Rachael as I scan the room. I have a gun to an inspector's head. If one of those cops can get a clear shot, I'm dead.

'Lexi, let me go. Right now!' Rachael snaps. She sounds more pissed than scared.

'I can't do that.'

'Lexi, don't move!' Cass begs.

'What are you on about?' Zander yells at Rocco.

Everyone's speaking at once. There's too much happening, too fast. I can't focus.

'No one shoot!' Finn shouts, stepping around Brighton and several tactical officers. 'Lexi, don't panic, okay? I'll get you out of this. But you need to let Rachael go and put the gun down slowly.'

'Don't do it!' Cass again. 'They won't listen! They'll overpower you and take you away. My family!'

'They're dead anyway!' Rocco yells, no longer amused. 'We need to get outta here. Get these fucking ties off me!'

Finn's eyes don't waver from mine as he lifts his hands to show he's unarmed and steps forward. 'I'll come over, you can swap me for Rachael and talk to me.'

'Finn, don't be stupid!' Brighton says.

'Twenty seconds!' I hear from Cass, a moment before it's echoed by an officer in the lobby.

'Who is it?' I whisper. 'I need to know who it is!'

'Who is who?' Rachael asks.

'Rocco, talk!' Zander orders.

'Stop!' I snap at Finn as he edges closer.

'You're not going to shoot me,' he says with quiet confidence.

'Don't bet your life on it,' I snarl. 'Get back!'

'Let Rachael go and everyone will back out, okay?' McCabe calls from somewhere behind Finn. 'We'll let you go.'

'Shut up!'

'Just give me the gun,' Finn continues calmly.

'I can't *do* that.' I tighten my hold on Rachael and point the gun out over her shoulder at Finn.

'Ten seconds!'

'Lexi … please,' Rachael begs. 'We have to get to Meera and Noah.'

'You can't.' My finger twitches on the trigger as Finn moves again. 'I said *stop*!' He's almost too close.

'I won't let you die over this.'

'Five!'

'McCabe!' Rocco screams. 'You need to stop McCabe from detonating the other bombs!'

'What?' My gaze flies back to McCabe and then I see it. His gun in one hand, a mobile phone in the other, held at his side, his finger hovering. He presses a button.

Nothing.

The air whooshes out of my lungs as the first bomb doesn't blow. But what about the others? McCabe takes his eyes off me in confusion as he backs towards the doors and checks his phone. The only way to keep him in range is to take him down. I aim the gun at McCabe but Finn blocks the shot. There's no time left and only one way to make him move.

I pull the trigger.

Finn drops like a stone.

'Finn!' Rachael cries out.

The whole room freezes as I aim again, this time at McCabe.

'Oof!'

Rachael elbows me hard in my side and my next shot goes high as she knocks the gun from my stunned grip. My nose explodes with pain as she throws her head back hard into my face and twists, slamming me against the lift doors. Hands are grabbing me from everywhere, forcing me down. I'm quickly cuffed and dragged to my feet. Rachael is bent over Finn, looking at me in shock, but all I see is McCabe backing for the doors, the mobile phone still clutched in his hand. He gives me a *what can you do?* kind of smile that has me kicking against my restraints.

'Federal Police!'

I hear the shouts as Lloyd's team finally swarm into the building.

'Justin!' I call desperately. 'It's McCabe! The phone's a detonator!'

Justin Matthews spins around. 'McCabe! Freeze!'

'What? Oh, bullshit!' McCabe laughs from the entryway. 'Don't be ridiculous. Get her out of here!'

'Show me your hands!' Matthews orders.

McCabe's face twists as, from the doorway, his eyes look to the floor above. He's going to do it. I have a split second to panic as his thumb moves on the phone.

Another shot echoes through the foyer.

The phone crashes to the floor as McCabe grabs at his arm. Blood pours from the wound Matthews has put there. 'Next one's lethal force!' he warns McCabe when he looks like he's going to pounce on the phone. Two more agents secure McCabe while another moves in and carefully picks up the phone.

'What is going on?' Rachael demands.

There are guns everywhere and no one seems to know where to point them, what's happening.

Matthews weaves his way across the room. 'Let her go!' he demands and my wrists are released.

'Is Finn all right?' I ask, desperately trying to get a look. When I do, he's leaning up on an elbow, grimacing and breathing heavily but very much alive.

'Yeah,' Matthews says and looks me over. 'Are you?'

'Honestly,' I admit as I press the fingers of one hand to my throbbing nose, 'I've been better.'

CHAPTER FIFTY-TWO

The computer lab was packed with club members, Cronin front and centre, staring in confusion at the screen. The bomb had done nothing. Why hadn't McCabe detonated it? The green light shone zero. That was his cue. Why were Meera and her son still alive? He looked at the teary faces of both, the terror of the woman, the wriggling panic of the little boy. For a moment he saw only Laura and Mikey and his heart softened, shamed over his actions. Then the vision of Laura holding Mikey close, the terrible knowledge in her eyes, the white flash of light. The aftermath. And his whole being raged, rejected the unfairness of it all.

'Why didn't it work?' he demanded.

'McCabe mustn't have gone through with it,' Nate said.

In a fit of fury, Cronin swiped the contents of the desk onto the floor: a keyboard, a mouse, a drive and a coffee cup all launched at speed. Smashing.

Nate opened another screen where a news station had interrupted regular viewing to cover the unfolding events. The headlines should have been reporting two explosions, one in the lift, followed by another large enough, Cronin had hoped, to take out most of the ground floor and everyone crammed in it. Instead the tagline scrolling across the screen told of a bomb plot foiled at police headquarters.

Devastation coursed through Cronin in burning, resentful, waves. All the time, money and meticulous planning that had gone into organising the near impossible. All Ron's clever work, all those years of dreaming about justice. All had come to nothing.

'There!' Nate said, and pointed to the screen.

Cronin saw McCabe, a bloody bandage around one arm, led out in handcuffs and put into the back of a police van. 'Stupid man! All he had to do was press a button!'

'There's Lexi!'

She was being escorted by several Federal Police into a black sedan.

'No cuffs,' Nate noted. 'But they're looking pretty serious.'

Now Rocco appeared, cuffed. Was put into the van with McCabe.

'What's he doing?' Nate said, as Zander and another man with red hair were shown just inside the doors, talking to police.

The shot changed again, to a reporter.

'Turn it up!' Cronin ordered.

'For those just joining us, we're here outside police headquarters where police have prevented a bombing attempt by Arthur Cronin. Inside it's believed two civilians are trapped in an elevator with explosives while police work frantically to free them. We can't confirm at this stage but there is some talk that there were potentially more explosives in the air-conditioning ducts of the building, though we're waiting on confirmation of that.'

'They're coming through the roof,' Nate said as back on his monitor, two heavily clad men in black tactical gear dropped gently to the floor. One attended to Meera and Noah while the other worked on the door.

'They're getting away!' Cronin growled. He could watch no more. To see them reunited with Lisa Cassidy would be too much. He pushed past the gathered members and burst out of the room, tearing at his hair and muttering obscenities on his way to his office.

'They outsmarted you, my darling,' Laura said gently. 'It can't be helped.'

'They betrayed me!' he roared. 'Zander! Lexi! No handcuffs for them. It must be them!'

'Your own mind betrayed you. Your hate. They were never going to murder that little boy and his mother. Not after what they went through with Mikey and me. They loved us. We were family.'

'I loved you! More than anyone else! I did this for you!'

'Cronin, are you all right?' Freddie asked at the door.

'Fuck off! Your son did this!' He grabbed his gun from the top drawer and pointed it at Freddie.

But it was Laura he saw standing there. Smiling. The gun wavered, dropped.

'Ah, guys?' someone called from the hallway. 'There's sirens incoming.'

Sirens. This was not how he would go down. They would not have the satisfaction. He grabbed a bag from under the desk and pushed past Freddie. He went upstairs, got in his ute and, with a line of police coming in off the road, took off towards the back of the property.

He drove over the end of the dirt road and bounced into the bush to where the trees dappled shade onto a carpet of ferns. This would do.

He unpacked the bag—two shotguns and a rifle—and emptied boxes of bullets onto the ground in order to load them. One last block of C4, timer attached, ready to go.

He waited for the police cars to follow him in, watched them stop short in a line, watched officers swarm out and take cover. He heard them order him to come out slowly with his hands up. He took Mikey's heart from his pocket and pressed his lips to its worn surface. Then he started firing.

He hit four men before taking two bullets, then a third. Knowing time was short, he started the timer. This one would blow the old-fashioned way: thirty seconds, no interference. He watched the seconds tick by, heard the snap and tread of approaching feet in the undergrowth. The world faded. Cronin smiled through his pain. Because there was Laura, Mikey in one arm, the other outstretched. Welcoming him home.

Three seconds after Arthur Cronin took Laura's hand, officers charged in and the world, once again, exploded.

CHAPTER FIFTY-THREE

'Lexi was working for us,' Patrick Lloyd told the room several hours after the events at police headquarters. 'I'm sorry we couldn't tell you.'

Finn sat at the table with his and McCabe's teams, nursing some powerfully aching ribs. He'd point blank refused to stay at the hospital once the X-rays had revealed a cracked rib and a lot of bruising because neither would kill him and he needed to hear this. But he had accepted some medication which had taken the edge off, even if it also made him light-headed and slightly sick.

'Why not?' Rachael fumed.

'To keep Lexi safe. We knew we had a dirty cop, we just didn't know who it was.'

'I can't believe McCabe was working for Oxacot,' Olivia said from beside him. She'd been fussing over him since he'd arrived. 'I never suspected anything. I thought he could have moved faster on the case at times, but nothing like this.'

'McCabe became involved after taking a bribe from the MC last year. He'd been experiencing financial difficulties and it was a significant amount of money. As the MC was already under investigation from organised crime, his job was to divert suspicion from the club's activities by pointing the investigation in the wrong direction. He pushed the drug agenda to keep everyone off track about the people smuggling and sabotaged the case in a multitude of ways we're still figuring out.'

'But perhaps you could start from the beginning for those of us trying to catch up?' Rachael snapped.

Lloyd laced his fingers together on the table. 'Six months ago we were contacted by ASIO. They had intercepted details that police headquarters was at risk of a potential cyber attack. They believed the threat to be linked to an attack that occurred on US soil two years back. Hackers along with bribed officials within the FBI obtained data stolen from key departments that included intel on organised crime. They believe it was used by an international smuggling operator to forge new business relationships and eliminate competition.'

'Let me guess, that international smuggling operator was Oxacot?' Finn said.

Lloyd nodded.

'For Oxacot's schemes to work, they need local assistance,' Matthews said. 'They recruit local crime families, outlaw motorcycle gangs and the like to handle the operations and establish contacts at the docks and in law enforcement to smooth their path. As in the US case, the intel pointed to one or more dirty cops within headquarters and, given what happened in the US, we had to assume they could be quite high-ranking. So, we had to hold our own, separate, investigation to the one we discovered was already being run by organised crime.'

'While spying on ours,' Rachael said.

'Later, yes. When you became involved in a joint operation with organised crime,' Matthews said. 'Hoping to catch out any cops on their payroll.'

'But back to the beginning,' Lloyd said. 'After receiving ASIO's intel, we put an agent on the docks to keep eyes and ears out for any gossip that we thought could potentially provide us with a lead. This agent was your victim, Haitao Chen.'

'You said he was a seafarer on shore leave from a shipping company,' Rachael said.

'That's the story we went with, yes. He had recently reported back with confirmation that Breen's MC was involved with Oxacot. He was trying to record evidence of this when he was killed. I'm sorry for all the cloak and dagger on that. His identity had to remain confidential. We didn't want to spook the MC or Oxacot.'

'I understand,' Rachael said stiffly.

'Chen had obtained his information through a gentleman by the name of Desmond Harris.'

'You're kidding.' Finn almost laughed, then sucked in a sharp breath at the pain that radiated around his chest.

'Chen had befriended Harris on the docks and figured out he was running deliveries for the MC. Harris had some decades-old outstanding warrants we offered to bury if he was able to assist with information on schedules and the like.'

'Desmond willingly gave that up?' Finn asked sceptically.

'It was that or a potential prison sentence.'

'But Desmond dumped Chen's body,' Rachael said.

Lloyd nodded. 'Harris contacted us when Chen was murdered. He explained what had happened and we told him to carry on the charade.'

Rachael's eyes widened. 'You authorised him to do what he did to a federal agent?'

'Harris got Chen's body out fast. He wanted to make sure he was in charge of it so we could recover his remains for his family, but for Harris's safety, the disposal had to look legit so he did what needed to be done. However, that nearly blew up in our faces when his loyalty was questioned. So, as you know, Dawny called Lexi for help, initially not realising she was police, which is of course, when homicide became involved.'

'Go on.'

'Once we had identified Chaos Reigns as being in Oxacot's pocket we needed to infiltrate the club in order to discover who they were working with in law enforcement and what their plan was. We had to figure out a way to not only prevent it, but to find something to pin on Oxacot that could bring the company down. That's where Lexi came in.'

'Yes?' Rachael said coldly.

Lloyd smiled wryly. 'She did say you'd be unimpressed by all this. You want the details?'

'Better late than never.'

He nodded, sighed. 'When we found out about Lexi's prior involvement with the MC, that combined with the computer skills Lexi possesses were huge red flags for us. I mean, she was almost too perfect for it. We investigated her thoroughly, established she wasn't on their payroll and decided she could be very handy to our operation.'

'So you got her fired?' Finn asked.

'Following some complaints lodged against her, we staged her dismissal, picked her up on her way back from headquarters and invited her in.'

'Only staged. Which is why her status was never updated in the system and she was able to continue to get in for so long,' Rachael said, putting it together.

'Correct.'

'And she agreed to all this.'

'She did. We sent Lexi in playing the disgruntled employee slash I hate the police card to see what she could find out. What she ended up doing was becoming pivotal in the club's deal with Oxacot then sabotaging it.'

'You dragged an inexperienced police officer into a multinational, multiagency operation and placed her in extreme danger!' Rachael snapped.

'She seemed more than capable.'

'You don't have the first clue about the issues she has. Like substance abuse for one.'

'Fair call. Though you might like to know she didn't take the MDMA. She concealed it in her hand and turned it over to us for analysis. She knew what she was getting into, Rachael, better than most. She handled it.'

'You wouldn't have known if she was handling it or not though, would you?'

'You're missing the bigger picture. Because of her skills and her background, she was the only one who could have pulled it off. To be a success, the operation needed evidence of Oxacot paying Breen for the stolen intel. The deal needed to go through. That meant we had to let Breen steal the information and sell it *before* Oxacot could be stopped. Of course, releasing all that sensitive information to a foreign criminal organisation was out of the question. So Lexi came up with the idea to send them a bogus sample as proof, with the rest of the download encrypted, on the agreement that once the money went through they'd send the decryption program. She raised it with Breen and he went for it.

'We had the best possible plan and that should have been it. Lexi was all set to download the information remotely, provide evidence it had been paid for and the job would have been complete. A done deal with no security risk to our data and the opportunity to shut down one of the big guns in international smuggling. But, of course, enter Cronin. With Gordon and Wallis dead and Cassidy on his radar, we needed to talk to Lexi to see if anyone in that club knew where he might be.'

'That's why you had us bring her in,' Rachael said. 'For a face-to-face catch-up.'

'Correct. She couldn't tell us anything more at that time about Cronin but with everything else running smoothly, we sent her back in to complete the operation.'

'What changed?' Finn asked.

'Lexi's priorities. Despite her instructions, when Detective Cassidy's family was taken, first and foremost, she was going to get that woman and child out alive.'

'That sounds about right,' Rachael said. 'So what did you do when your inexperienced, untrained asset suddenly went rogue?'

Lloyd spread his hands. 'There wasn't a lot we could do. She went against our instructions and offered Cronin the name of the man who arranged his family's murder in order to get him back on the scene for an arrest. That was the last we heard from her until today.'

'She could have been dead!' Finn grated.

'She wasn't. We now know Cronin and those in the club still loyal to him overthrew Breen. Cronin was returned as president and as the club was set on the money from the deal and it was all but done, Cronin went along with it in order to secure support from the club for his own plans.'

'Which were?'

'Initially he only gave away the plan to murder Meera and Noah at headquarters. He called it his grand gesture, not only to pay Cassidy back for her deceit, but to do it at the heart of police headquarters where the publicity would be huge. Lexi countered by contriving a problem hacking into headquarters following your discovery of one of her methods of entry.'

'One of?' Rachael asked.

'Yes. She had also reconfigured cyber's new security program to report to her rather than its admin so she could identify weaknesses in the system and exploit them.'

'Of course she had,' Rachael said.

'Knowing she needed to be onsite in order to stop the execution, Lexi convinced Cronin she'd have to download the data from headquarters. Zander and Fred West knew what she was doing and were onside. They helped develop the plan.'

'It obviously worked. Do we know why the bomb didn't go off?' Olivia asked.

'The timer on the explosives was bogus—a stunt to replicate the original crime. The actual detonation was to be done remotely through a mobile phone device, giving Cronin the opportunity to detonate early if something went wrong. The plan therefore was to download the data, then, during a small window after the download when Cronin moved off comms to begin his broadcast, to incapacitate Rocco, locate Meera and Noah and get close enough with a signal jammer to stop the explosion.'

'That's why she went down to the foyer,' Finn said.

'By which time Cronin had begun to exercise his real plan to lure as many police as possible into headquarters for his show. Cronin had told Lexi his dirty cop would be nearby with the detonator keeping an eye on everything, ready to blow the explosives when the time came. Or before, if necessary.'

'She had no safe way of alerting anyone to what was going on,' Linc said.

'What she did have was the comms with Zander, Rocco, Cassidy and Jim Hudson. While everyone downstairs was telling her to put her weapon down, Rocco was going to pieces upstairs, blabbing

Cronin's real plan in order to convince them to let him go and get out of the building before it blew. Her position prevented the first bomb going off but knowing there were more bombs, Lexi needed to take down McCabe so he didn't move out of range of her jammer and detonate the others.'

'And then I nearly ruined everything by subduing her,' Rachael said.

'You couldn't have known. And that was quite the feat, by the way. You managed to tackle Lexi and somehow stay between her and a room full of armed officers at all times. You were protecting her.'

Rachael sighed. 'Habit.'

'And you.' Lloyd's eyes swung to Finn. 'I know you're in a world of pain but if she'd been on the level you could have had your head blown off.'

'Lexi's not a killer. We both know that,' Finn said.

'She's a killer cop. She'd make an exceptional agent. I wouldn't mind having her on our team.'

'That would be up to her,' Rachael said. 'When can we see her?'

'Ah ... she headed home to get some rest. She mentioned calling into headquarters tomorrow.'

'Thanks.'

'Oh, and Rachael? I'm recommending her for a CV. She put her life at serious risk and saved the lives of dozens of police as well as two innocent civilians.'

The Cross of Valour, Finn thought. The highest honour. It was only awarded for acts of conspicuous courage in circumstances of extreme peril.

Rachael smiled. 'She's earned it.'

CHAPTER FIFTY-FOUR

Wednesday, April 6

Whispers and quiet shuffling wake me early and I get off the lounge to see what's going on. The smell of baking has me instantly salivating. When did I last eat?

Dawny and Desmond are talking in the kitchen and Dawny's things are by the door.

'What are you doing?' I ask sleepily.

'House hunting!' Dawny says excitedly. 'Those lovely police Desmond dealt with have torn up those warrants so Desmond's a free man! We need a place to stay. Something bigger with a nicer sized bedroom. No offence. This one has done the job in the short term. I'm sure you'll be very cosy in it. I bought you a present. A new bed frame,' she says, which explains the box beside the door. I saw it last night, didn't query it. 'Couldn't get the exact same one, so I found a rather nice alternative with a bookshelf. Can never do too much reading, that's what I say. And there's some new sheets in that bag there. I'm rather fond of the ones I've been using so I thought I'd take them with us. You don't mind, do you?'

'Hell, no. Why do I have a new bed frame?'

'Small accident, never mind.'

'You broke my bed?'

'If you insist, we'll chip in for a new mattress. Nothing wrong with that one though, I promise you. You won't be catching anything off us.'

'Good to know. Where are you staying until you find this house?'

'Oh, here and there, got a few loose ends to tidy up so trouble doesn't go finding us again. We'll be in touch shortly. Now, I know you don't like emotional farewells, so we'll just head off. I've left a couple of pies in the oven. Never could work out which was your favourite, so there's a lemon meringue and an apple. You should take them out in ten minutes to cool. Ta-ta!'

'Lexi,' Desmond says with a polite nod.

'Bye—guys,' I tell the back of the door. As usual when Dawny leaves, the vacuum of the silence is overwhelming.

I check my phone and have several messages from Caitlin, updating me on what's going on. She's been questioned, she's not in trouble, but she's having issues getting out of the station as a minor without a guardian. I message her back and tell her to stay put, I'm on my way. Then I call Bailee, take the pies out of the oven and tidy myself up.

'Where are we?' Caitlin asks when I pull into my carpark an hour later.

'Home.'

'Your place?'

I get out. 'Our place. For now, anyway.'

'What?' She gets out and looks up at the building.

'You promised you'd talk to my sister, remember? She works for the Department of Communities and Justice. I asked if she could help and she's going to. She's on her way to see you now. You need to do some paperwork with her but she's leapt ahead and got you an interview with an independent high school operated by Youth Off The Streets. Assuming all goes well, you can start pretty much straight away. As for accommodation, it could take some time to get everything sorted. So until then, I'm keeping an eye on you.'

'Serious?'

'This is not charity. You're going to school. You're going to apply for a part-time job. You're gonna help around the apartment. You're going to work your arse off. You're not going to drink alcohol, smoke cigarettes or do MDMA. Do you understand? I'm not a sociable person. There'll be times you're going to wish you were still on the streets but you—'

Caitlin throws her arms around me.

'Okay. You need to know from the outset, I don't hug.'

'Tough shit.'

I let her hang off me for a few seconds then shrug her off. 'Okay, enough. Here she is.'

Bailee pulls in beside us and I introduce them.

'Thanks, Lexi,' Bailee says with a smile for Caitlin. 'I'll drop her around when we're done.'

I hope to hell I know what I'm doing.

I go back upstairs and look around. My new apartment. Just me. Heaven. I may as well enjoy it while I can. I stick my head in the bedroom and see one end of the bed is on the floor. The frame has split. I don't think about how that's possible; I just don't need that sort of imagery behind my eyelids. The mattress has been propped against the wall. I'm going to have to take this bed apart to get it out and—fuck—put together the other one. I don't have a spare for Caitlin, so I'm going to have to do it today in order to give her the lounge.

I wonder how she is with a screwdriver.

I sigh and open my laptop to go online, hoping I can get a bed for the spare room delivered today and if anyone does assembly. The best I can get is Monday.

Because it's all too hard, I flop on the lounge and stare out the window. Enjoy the silence.

I remember I'd told Lloyd I'd call in at headquarters today. That had just been a ruse so I could avoid going back late yesterday after debriefing. My stomach instantly churns as I think about walking in there and facing everyone, and my mind goes back to holding the gun at Rachael's head. Shooting Finn. Fuck.

I shot Finn. I suppose, following the events of the last couple of weeks, he's just damn lucky I aimed for the vest. I bet he's got some decent bruising.

I wonder how he and Rachael feel about everything now they know the truth. And by everything, I mean me. I still haven't decided how I feel about them. It's not that I blame them for treating me like a criminal—I've been playing one. But the real me still went through that shit they threw at me.

I huff, annoyed with myself. I'm being a sook again. I smell the pies and decide I may as well become an emotional eater, too. The apple pie has cooled the most so, embracing my new identity, I take a giant feel-sorry-for-myself slice and sit back down to enjoy it.

I've only had a few bites when I hear the bike engine throbbing into the driveway. This should be interesting. I get up, look out and see Zander staring up at me with that same expression he'd worn when I'd bugged him to death about Cass. He's gonna be pissed about the cop thing. I'm gonna have to go down and face the consequences.

'You were working with the cops the whole fucking time?' he spits at me by way of greeting when I arrive in the driveway.

'Yeah. Most of it. With one lot or other.'

'No wonder you wouldn't let me beat the shit out of that Finn guy.'

'I didn't let you beat the shit out of that Finn guy because he's my friend! And so are you. I didn't want him hurt and I didn't want you locked up!'

'I guess that's why you told the cops I'd been working with you the whole time.'

I grin. 'You were. You just didn't know it at the start.'

'Way to be manipulated.'

'Way to avoid a prison sentence.'

He tips his head in acknowledgement. 'Though I'm not sure if this intensive whatever …'

'Corrections order.'

'Yeah, is going to be better or worse. You should see all the conditions and the shit I have to do.'

'It's a custodial sentence! You're lucky to be serving it in the community. It's the best they were going to do for you, considering.'

'Considering what?'

'Considering just about everyone else is going to be doing various amounts of time inside. How did your dad and Nate go?'

'Looks like Dad'll be getting a community corrections order, Nate's going to do a deal for three years.'

'Ouch.'

'Could have been twelve. Most are looking at between four and eight years 'cause of the people smuggling. Club's gone to shit again.'

'What are you going to do?'

'Dunno yet. Rodger said he'd give me a job training MMA. He has a studio in Wyong. Or maybe I'll just get on my bike and,' he makes a swooping gesture with his hand, 'ride off into the sunset.'

I screw up my face. 'Unfortunately, that would be breaching your ICO. Sorry.'

He nods in resignation. 'Then I guess I'll see you at the studio. No less than three times a week or I'll send Rodger around to drag you in by the nostrils.'

'We'll see,' I say firmly. But I might just take him up on that.

'Someone else wants to see you.'

I look around and see Finn walking stiffly up the driveway. He stops when he spots us.

The churning in my stomach starts back up again. 'Ah … I should talk to him I suppose.'

'Give him hell.' Zander kisses me lightly on the lips. 'Take care, babe. I'll see you soon.' The bike thrums to life and, with a salute for Finn that has an equal chance of being mocking or peacemaking in nature, he roars off down the street and out of sight.

Finn. I'm not sure what to expect so I stand where I am and wait for him to walk over. When he does, neither of us seems to know what to say. It's awkward. Everything has shifted.

This is ridiculous. I box up all the difficult shit spinning around in my head and put it away. He did his job, I did mine. Simple. The sooner we get over this crap, the better.

'Okay,' I finally say. 'I can't—'

'We need to talk about all this.'

'—stand out here in the driveway all day.'

'Then would you walk with me?'

Walk with him in that state? 'I don't think so.'

'I understand.' He looks disappointed, like somehow this is all his fault and I'm holding it against him.

'I don't think you do. Watching you walk is painful. Besides, I have to put a bed frame together and I have no idea what I'm doing.'

'Didn't we just get you one of those?'

'Dawny … you know what? Don't ask. Just follow me.' I grimace for him. 'Take your time.'

Once in the lift, I ask, 'How's Cass and her family?'

He smiles. 'They're going to be okay. Cass is taking some time off and after some rest and counselling I think they're planning on heading off to India for a couple of weeks. Cass wants to make sure they all see you before they go. They want to thank you.'

'Not necessary,' I say. 'But I'm glad they're doing all right.' I let him into the apartment and point to the box. 'So that's it. I'm not sure what to expect, Dawny picked it. The other one is still in the bedroom.' I walk in and show him the broken frame. 'It's wrecked.'

'Lexi.'

The tone suggests he's about to get all deep and meaningful and I don't want to. I don't want the awkward to come back.

'I can't see you crawling around on the floor but maybe you could at least tell me what to do?'

'Lexi.'

'I know my name, Finn. I think I still have your screwdrivers and stuff …'

'Lexi!' he says again, this time in amused frustration. He turns me around so I can't run away to find those screwdrivers. 'I should have had more faith in you. I was … too busy feeling sorry for myself to see it.'

Fuck. Don't want to analyse that. 'Okay. Screwdrivers?'

'And …' he prompts.

'Ah, look, about the whole shooting you thing. Missing the ceramic armour was tempting. So you're welcome.'

My relief when he laughs is crazy. I *hate* this emotional shit.

'I'm sorry,' he says sincerely.

I shift on the spot. 'Yeah, all right. Me too. Can we just be over it now?'

'Fine by me,' he says, obviously sharing my relief. 'Go get those screwdrivers.'

CHAPTER FIFTY-FIVE

'So this Caitlin person is living with you?' Finn asks. We're sitting in Rachael's office waiting for her to appear. Finn convinced me to come in and see her, and it was slow going getting in here. Everyone we walked past in headquarters wanted to say hi and congratulate me. It was weird. And Rachael's a no-show.

'Just temporarily while Bailee gets her sorted.'

'I thought you would have been keen to get your own space back.'

'It's oddly quiet after Dawny. Besides, I want to help her.'

'Let me guess, she reminds you of you?'

'I didn't realise I had options until I was twenty-eight. It would be nice if she got there sooner. Bailee's organising housing and school and Zander's coach has a studio with a little shop attached. He's going to give her some part-time work.'

'So are you two a thing or what?'

'Are Zander's coach and I a thing?'

He pulls a face. 'You and Zander.'

'No!' I object in a way that leaves him in no doubt that he's being completely ridiculous.

'Oh. I thought you were. It looked like it.'

'Oh. Right. Nah, he acts like that with all the girls. Easier just to go with it.'

'Is it?' he asks. 'That's interesting.'

'Is it?' I reply in the same tone. 'Thinking of trying that on with a certain blonde organised crime detective?' I tease.

But something in his expression tells me he already has.

'Oh, I see,' I tack on coolly. Then in an attempt to shift the conversation while I process that, I say, 'You said the two of you found out where Breen was stashing the people he was smuggling in?'

'Skink's house,' he says but I know he's trying to work out my reaction to him and Brighton.

'I can't believe they were able to keep that people-smuggling shit from me.' I should be happy for him, but *Olivia Brighton*? Why does it have to be *her*?

'You seemed to have enough going on in there to worry about.'

'Being *conflicted* aside,' I mutter, and see him flinch. I gather he doesn't know about the complaint letter Brighton added to Cass's in an attempt to get me fired.

'Are you … cross … about Olivia and me?' he asks, his gaze probing.

I tell my face not to give anything away. I'm not sure it listens. 'So you're like a thing now or what?'

'What? No. I mean, nothing official. But I like her, Lex. So … we'll see.'

'Whatever makes you happy,' I say, and barrel on. 'Rachael knew I was coming in, right?'

'Yeah, she …' he checks his watch, 'should be here any second.'

'Good. I've already spent way too much time hanging around places being bored lately.'

'Oh, I'm boring?' he protests. 'What do you want to do?' A wicked gleam enters his eyes. 'What about … Lexi, baby, dance for me!' he says in a pretty good mimic of Breen.

'The last guy who called me "Lexi baby" died miserably. Don't tempt fate.'

'So, what other hidden talents have you got?'

'Seriously?' I say, not really in the mood. 'How about you first?'

He presses a hand to his chest. 'I'm pretty banged up. I got shot recently.'

'Nasty.'

'But I reckon I could match some of those fancy moves of yours.'

I can't help the laugh. 'Oh, yeah? Well, that's bound to entertain me. Off you go. Let's see it.'

He takes a few ridiculously uncoordinated steps, almost trips, winces and sits stiffly back down. 'Ta-da!'

'Nailed it.'

It's his turn to laugh. 'Okay, smartarse, you'll have to show me how it's done one day.'

'Oh, I could teach you, but only until you break a bone or too much furniture.'

'So just a short lesson then.'

'Five minutes, tops,' I agree. I catch a movement in the doorway and look up to see Rachael standing there.

'I'll, um, leave you guys to it,' Finn says.

I watch him retreat, glad we're back on our regular footing. But now I have Rachael to deal with.

'Thanks for coming in,' she says after a moment.

'Sure,' I reply.

She walks around her desk to sit down and places a booklet in front of her before looking me over. 'How are you. Recovered?'

'I'm fine. Glad it's over.'

She takes a deep breath, gathers herself together. 'Well, you were right. I regret it. I don't even know what to say.'

'Yeah, Finn and I went through that yesterday. It sucks. Best just to move on.'

'I wasn't sure you'd even talk to me.'

I have a speech ready in my head and I hope it's enough to get this over with. 'The way I look at it, you were willing to hurt my feelings to save me from spending half of the rest of my life behind bars at a time when I was clearly under the influence of drugs, alcohol and a very nasty criminal.'

Her face loses some of its tension. 'That was the motivation, yes.'

'I won't say thank you because, man, I could have happily committed a homicide with my bare hands and done some very nasty things to your remains. But I appreciate you didn't want to give up on me. Also, my nose is still sore and you bruised my already bruised ribs. I've learnt some cool fighting moves lately. You'd better not try that again.'

Finally I get a proper smile. 'You were very convincing. Has Lloyd asked you to work for him yet?'

'There is something pretty cool about the "agent" title. It's like every spy movie ever. I could be a Bond girl.'

'If that's what you want.' But she doesn't look happy about it.

'Nah. I'm all good thanks. I just got a new apartment and … I have friends here.'

'Family,' Rachael corrects me softly.

'So I guess I'll be going back to general duties and …'

The booklet Rachael brought in is spun around and slid across the desk to me. 'This is what held me up this morning.'

'What is it?'

'Your enrolment form for the Advanced Diploma of Police Investigation you're going to have to complete before you can do your Detective Designation Course.'

'Okay, thanks, but what's the rush? I haven't done nearly enough time in general duties to complete the detective's course yet.'

'Actually … you're officially accepted into the course as soon as that diploma's done. When an officer is pivotal in closing three major cases and becomes the recipient of a Cross of Valour, there's room to manoeuvre on such things.'

'A what?' I ask, genuinely shocked. 'I don't deserve an award! I held a gun to your head and shot Finn!'

'You put your own life in extreme peril to save dozens of police and civilian lives. Cronin's men had set several explosive devices in the air-conditioning vents, which would have brought down the first floor and killed everyone underneath—and that's on top of the risk you took infiltrating Chaos Reigns to take down Oxacot. You might not think you're deserving of recognition, but everyone else begs to differ. The award is yours, though you'll have to wait a while to officially receive it at our yearly awards ceremony. Congratulations.'

'Ah, thanks,' I mutter, embarrassed. 'But all I really want is a chance to hunt down Vaughn.'

'Which you're going to get. I'll be putting together a task force on Vaughn over the coming days. You're on it. I'll provide more details shortly but right now, you need to go home and prepare yourself for another big case.'

I take that in. 'He's coming back?'

Rachael nods grimly. 'For you.'

ACKNOWLEDGEMENTS

The Lexi Winter series is proving to be the most rewarding and most difficult series I have written to date, and I'm loving every moment of it. I'm overwhelmed by the support Lexi continues to receive from readers and reviewers—thank you—and I am incredibly grateful to each and every person who helps me bring her stories to life.

My special thanks to …

Jo Mackay and the entire team at HQ/HarperCollins, for the stunning covers, rigorous editing and fabulous marketing, as well as all the support along the way.

Kylie Mason, for the amazing job you do on the manuscripts.

Cecelia Ramsdale, for the incredible work you do on the audiobooks.

Clare Forster and Benjamin Paz for your tireless work and belief in my stories.

Tea Cooper, Charlie Smith and Paula Beavan for your fabulous critiquing.

Kate Jackson and Sergeant Danny Jackson, you both are priceless!

Steve Apps, retired Inspector, QLD Police, for continuing to share your vast knowledge and experience.

Bel Jensen, you're amazing. Thanks for your help with all those tricky questions.

Dr Christine Wade for your quick and valuable assistance with those medical questions.

Peter, for all that IT knowledge!

Of course, to my family, without whose support I could never get these books written.

And once again to the readers and reviewers who support my stories in so many different ways. You are so very much appreciated! Thank you.

PRAISE FOR SARAH BARRIE'S LEXI WINTER BOOKS

'Phenomenal. Lexi Winter is the gritty hero I didn't know I needed … I'm now desperate for more.'

—Bestselling Australian author Nicola Moriarty

'Dark, gritty and filled with unexpected twists and turns, *Retribution* is brilliant and picks up to a relentless pace in the second half. Don't start reading this before bed … there's no way you'll be able to put it down.'

—*Better Reading*

'Barrie has produced an impressive and fast-paced crime thriller with *Retribution*. Following complex protagonists across several compelling investigations, this is an awesome read that is guaranteed to keep readers on their toes.'

—*Canberra Weekly*

'This quick paced thriller stuns with many heart-stopping moments of danger, violence and destruction. Intense, fast moving and consuming, I was completely on edge while reading *Retribution*.'

—*Mrs B's Book Reviews*

'Dark, propulsive … relentless and filled with unexpected twists and turns.'

—*The Australian* on *Retribution*

'Sarah Barrie at her nail-biting, heart-stopping best in this riveting novel of a flawed, gutsy heroine who emerges from a dark past to prey on the predators.'

—Bestselling Australian author Tea Cooper on *Unforgiven*

'A gritty, twisty journey of suspense. Recommended.'

—*Canberra Weekly* on *Unforgiven*

'If you like a read that keeps you on the edge of your seat, this addictive, suspenseful thriller is for you.'

—*Woman's Day* on *Unforgiven*

'There is drama and suspense aplenty in this gritty tale.'

—*Sunday Telegraph* on *Unforgiven*